BASTARDS FROM THE BUSH
CHRONICLE 2

Meadehampstead Book Publishing

Copyright © Shaun Clements 2017.

ISBN: 978-0-6-482265-7-4 Paperback
ISBN: 978-0-6482265-8-1 Kindle

MP

**MEADEHAMPSTEAD
PUBLISHING**

BASTARDS
FROM THE BUSH

CHRONICLE 2

JOSEF SCHULTZ

CONTENTS

SYNOPSIS CHRONICLE 1

The narrator, Josef Schultz, a coloured man born in Namibia, is working for a drilling company in the notorious gold mining town of Kalgoorlie, Western Australia. By sheer coincidence – and much to Schultz' delight – he and some of his workmates are told that they are being sent to Namibia, as local drilling work in the outback is becoming scarce due to Aboriginal land claims. These men are representative of blue collar workers that can be found in any town or city in Australia, whereby they voice their fears, homophobia, racial bigotry, male chauvinism, and suspicion of authorities in an open and unabashed manner.

As they prepare the equipment for shipping to Africa, Schultz gives a background to himself and his workmates, plus the political incorrectness of many of the local goldfielders. Being a half-caste, he has had first-hand experience of the difficulties of being a dark-skinned orphan in Western Australia during the era when Aboriginal children were being stolen from their parents.

Two drill crews are assembled to go with Schultz to Africa. Josef and his two drill offsiders Jeff Panizza and Nick Lovadina; Dave Wheeler and his offsiders Steve Spence and Bob Reynolds. A mechanic, Ernie, is going with them in order to keep the drilling rig in good order.

'BASTER'

Old Kobus Van Wyk reckoned that my mother, Anna Barends, was one of the most beautiful women in Basterland. Her romance with my father, Christian Witbooi, was smiled on by all the elders or ouderlings of Great Namaqualand. Apparently there were no great men in those days; since neither a 'raad' nor a commando had been officially formulated. There had only been talk of setting up a commando, what with the South West heading towards very uncertain independence. No doubt the Ovambo would win government because of their far greater numbers. Nevertheless, the Ovambo were just trespassers from the north. Who would be the better rulers – them or the Boers?

Yes, the pairing of Anna Barends and Christian Witbooi was smiled on by all those who would be called on to be great men. Anna's family had come from respected Griqua and Koranna stock, while Christian was the great nephew of the most revered Nama leader of them all. Hendrik Witbooi! Christian had taken up with the cause that was struggling against the Boers and their Apartheid regime. He had spent most of his adult life in jail. In those days – just like in the days of the early Oorlam trekkers – there was no prejudice amongst the blacks and the coloureds. They had one common enemy in the white supremacists. Christian had been seen with great freedom activists such as Andimba Toivo y Toivo and some dubious ones such as Sam Nujoma. There were no ill feelings amongst the Baster, the Nama, the Herero, the Ovambo, or even the Damara for that matter. Would things remain the same if the Ovambo took power?

Things were really stuffed up when my mother took off with Wolfgang Schultz, a German more than twice her age. While all the blokes around the place were fairly pissed off, the women in Rehoboth could understand where Anna was coming from. Schultz was white, therefore – being white – he had a lot more to offer than any ordinary Baster joker. Especially Christian Witbooi; seeing that he was in jail most of the time. Being a freedom fighter amongst the men folk may have been good for kudos and all that; however it didn't put much tucker on the table. Whites in general had more money and they had nice houses and motorcars.

According to Kobus my father caught up with my mother after she went off with Wolfgang. They came to an agreement that they would each take one of their twin sons, Jonker and Kido. My stepfather to be didn't much like my brother Jonker because apparently he was the more belligerent of the two of us. And that was at the early age of two! So, as it turned out, I went with my mother and Wolfgang to Perth, Western Australia, and Jonker had to stay behind in Rehoboth. My real father was murdered by the South African police not long after that.

As for my mother? Soon after we arrived in Western Australia, Wolfgang – who was my legal stepfather by then – got a job as a diesel fitter in a nickel mine at a place called Kambalda in Western Australia. The whole situation went pear-shaped after that once my mother met quite a few affluent, younger, white men. They, in turn, hung around our place like a dirty smell. Then, just dumping me with my stepfather, she ran off to the eastern states with a young Aussie scumbag who introduced her to drugs. She died in a Salvation Army hostel for women after taking an overdose of heroin in Parramatta. Wolfgang was crying his eyes out when he told me what happened.

CHAPTER 1

THE DARK CONTINENT! NAMIBIA
– ARSE END OF THE WORLD!

Johannesburg Airport was chock-full of people of all races and descriptions when we at last worked out how to get to the transit area. Although I hadn't slept a wink, a hangover was gradually sneaking in and my guts felt queasy from my not eating on the plane. With our entire party guzzling away, the plane had run out of beer half way across the Indian Ocean, so we hopped into some red South African wine instead. The others looked pretty shot up, bar Nick, who appeared to have an acute fascination in all that was happening around us. It was five-forty in the morning and outside the airport terminal it was still dark.

"Hey, there's a bar of some sort over there," Jeff announced. "Looks like it's open. You coming?"

Although the idea of consuming any more alcohol made bile burn in my throat, Wheeler reckoned a cleansing ale would have therapeutic benefits to offer him. His offsiders had gone off to explore the departure area after a warning from him not to get lost. I was pleased with the bar. Not only could you get grog, there was a place around the corner where you could get coffee and breakfast and things.

The airport let us know in no uncertain terms that we had arrived in Africa. Nearly all the airport staff were either black or coloured and there were blackfellas in the shithouses mopping away and emptying the rubbish bins. Everyone seemed to be tipping them after they took

1

a piss or used the bog, or even if they just washed their hands and face. I took part in that ritual after taking a slash and handed one black bloke an Aussie twenty cent piece.

He pointed to the coin and asked me something in some dialect that I found out later was Afrikaans. When I told him I only spoke English, he then spoke the same language quite fluently. "What is this?"

"Australian money."

"I cannot cash coins. Only notes. You got rand?"

"Tough shit!" I told him and walked off highly miffed that the first tip I had ever handed out in my life could be received so flippantly. He had pressed another point on me, though; there was a need to purchase some appropriate currency.

I rounded up Nick, Dave and the others and we went to a Volkskas bank counter. Our Aussie one hundred dollar notes bought heaps more South African rand. When I pointed out that we were travelling to Namibia, the bank clerk reckoned that wasn't a problem as the South African currency was legal tender in that country and was of the same value one-to-one as the Namibian dollar. Namibian dollars, however, weren't welcome in South Africa. I was becoming an expert on the Dark Continent already!

After an hour or so and three coffees my guts settled down enough for me to take a beer. The others were well and truly stuck into it by then. They had discovered a Namibian beer, Windhoek Lager, and it was pretty good stuff.

By the time our plane left for Windhoek at eleven-thirty that same morning, we were all quite smashed. A stewardess came round with the drinks trolley and I noticed that our party was the only one asking for alcohol. They only had South African beer, Castle Lager; still it went down the same way as the Namibian brew.

As the SAA Airbus heaved itself into the sky, it slowly leaned westward, giving us a panoramic view of Johannesburg. Despite the smog the most fascinating features were the tailings dams and mullock dumps from the Witwatersrand gold mines. They literally formed square-shaped mountains; some positioned even in the suburbs of the city. There looked as if there was one slimes dam right next door to the city centre itself! Of course we had plenty of similar dams and dumps in Kalgoorlie, but they were mostly away from human habitation, bar the massive mullock dumps from the Super Pit. Seeing the huge Witwatersrand workings dotted all the way out to the horizon on both sides of the plane, it was possible to only slightly imagine the enormity of what had taken place since gold had first been discovered on the 'Ridge of White Waters' in 1886. There must have been hundreds of millions of tons of rock taken from those mines! The South African gold mining game dwarfed Kalgoorlie's operations *totally*.

Half way through the flight the co-pilot announced that we were flying past Gaberones, the capital of Botswana. The ground down below looked dehydrated; tiny dots of thorn trees and bushes surrounded by ochre and brown dirt devoid of grass or any surface water. The roads and farm fence lines could be seen stretching for miles. The whole of Botswana seemed to be divided into huge paddocks; some almost stripped bare of vegetation from overgrazing, others not in such poor shape; making the whole vista appear like some gigantic chessboard. Now and then there were massive cracks in the board when dried-out riverbeds meandered across the countryside; in places slightly shaded in by trees and scrub.

The Airbus started its descent. Namibia looked hardly different to Botswana, perhaps even more parched. More hills, though, that jutted out haphazardly; stark and black in their surroundings of lighter coloured sand. There didn't seem to be a blade of grass anywhere!

Jeff was leaning over so that he, too, could see out the window. "Arsehole of the fuckin' world! It looks the same as the Pilbara, 'cept the bloody Pilbara's more like an oasis."

I was also a little disappointed. We had both read up on Namibia from a book Dave Wheeler had bought from a news agency back in Perth. The book informed us that Namibia was an arid country sandwiched between the Kalahari and Namib deserts; on the other hand it had been full of pictures of running rivers; lions, antelopes and elephants at waterholes; green grass and wildflowers in their millions. All bullshit! The glossy photos in the book were a total antithesis to the drab olive and khaki that confronted us.

We had a shithouse landing! The plane jerked, bucked and veered all over the runway just before its wheels touched the tarmac. Even then I wasn't sure if the pilot had the bloody thing under control. When things settled down a voice came over the intercom: "Sorry ladies and gentlemen, a dust devil blew across the runway as we were touching down... Welcome to Namibia."

An Omen?

The air outside the plane was stifling! The Windhoek International Airport terminal was one huge, corrugated iron shed with ineffectual air-conditioning. The six of us stuck together as we approached an immigration booth. Dave, being the so-called boss of things, was left to do the talking. When he denied that we were tourists and that we intended to work in the country; that was when the shit started. The immigration official, a redoubtable looking, black woman with a whole bunch of braids hanging off the back of her head demanded that we produce our 'wheck peemeets'. We all got our work permits out and gave them to Wheeler to pass on to her; meanwhile she had thoroughly searched both her nostrils with her right index finger, and her eyes bulged out when she found a piece of snot on the end of it. She looked quite tidy in her immaculate, white blouse and three gold bars on her epaulettes; red, green and blue Namibian coat of arms on one sleeve, but her unashamed nose picking exercise and vacant look let her down rather considerably. One at a time she studied the work permit forms minutely, then, after flicking through every page of our Aussie passports, she asked Wheeler if we *were* in fact Australians. He readily admitted our having come from down under, yet she still wasn't satisfied with our work permits or other documentation. So much so she went and fetched another official; a black bloke with four gold bars on his shoulders.

He, too, seemed mystified by our paperwork, even after making doubly certain that our faces resembled those on the photos in our passports. He handled the work permits as if they were toxic. What was more, it became obvious that he didn't even know what the various forms meant.

Another black joker joined the party and he only had one gold bar. His English was pretty good and he seemed to know more about what was going on than the three and four gold bars did. The black woman started another search of her left nostril – thankfully finding nothing sinister – and the other bloke with the four gold bars sauntered off. By that time we found ourselves alone in the customs and immigration hall. The one gold bar wanted to know more about us: "And what kind of work will you be doing here, sah?"

"We'll be drilling," Dave informed him.

"Eh?"

"We'll be looking for minerals. Gold, copper and stuff like that."

The official was intrigued. "Ah yes! And where in Namibia shall you be working?"

Wheeler was taken off guard by that one. "I don't know for certain. We're working for some mining company over here."

"I see! Where did you get these permits?"

"Our boss got 'em in Windhoek when he was last here."

"I see," the official nodded gravely that time. "And where are you staying in Namibia?"

Dave was equally ignorant about that, too. "I'm not sure. The company over here's organised things. Here," he handed a business card to the bloke, "this's the name of the company's representative."

That seemed to do the trick. He stamped all our passports, and then stopped me as I went to go past him. "You are *really* an Australian? I am sure I have seen you sometime before."

"Yeah, mate – a naturalised citizen. I was born here in Namibia, though."

His face lit up. "Where?"

"Rehoboth."

"Ah, Rehoboth! And how long have you been away from Namibia?"

"About thirty-two years."

"Aiee, but that is a long time! So you are coming home now?"

"I reckon so."

"Welcome! Welcome!"

"Good on ya, mate!"

Then the customs people ambushed us and there was an army of the bastards. We had bottles of duty free grog and cartons of smokes stashed everywhere. "How much alcohol do you have?" one of the black customs jokers asked.

"How much are we allowed?" Dave asked him back.

That confused the bloke, causing him to change the subject, "Do you have any firearms or ammunition? Any drugs?"

"No, mate, they don't let us have 'em in Australia."

Still they wanted our suitcases opened. Having prodded their fingers through all our clothes and gear, they were satisfied that we could leave.

Out in the almost deserted reception area stood a Neanderthal waving a piece of cardboard with 'W.M Growford Drilling CO' emblazoned on it. A white bloke; heavyset but muscular; short and stocky with red hair and ginger beard. He had a huge forehead that formed an upside down ledge over his ape-like eyes. Seeing the sign he was waving around to all and sundry, we had no choice but to approach him with our baggage trolleys.

"Are you the Australian drillers?" the cave man wanted to know.

"Yeah, mate – I'm Dave Wheeler."

"Hermanus – Cornelius – Kotzé. How do you do?" After Dave introduced all of us and we had shaken his hand, "I thought you might have missed your blerrie plane in Joburg! What took you so blerrie long in there?"

As we made our way out to the car park Wheeler explained how it needed three different immigration people; a one, three and four gold bar official to process our entry documentation.

BASTARDS FROM THE BUSH

Kotzé had an explanation for our treatment: "Ja, welcome to Africa! Once the kaffirs take over you get wholesale corruption and nepotism. The kaffir with the one stripe probably was the only one who has had any training. More than likely the other ones have got relations in SWAPO. Goes on in every department. That is why the place is falling to blerrie pieces."

"What do you mean by SWAPO?" Jeff asked.

"South – West – African – Peoples – Organisation. SWAPO is the political party in power. Just a blerrie bunch of baboons, criminals and terrorists."

We were led to a Land Rover station wagon that had a two-wheeled trailer hitched to its rear. As soon as we had loaded our cases and gear up on the vehicle's roof rack and in the trailer, Kotzé steered in the direction of Windhoek.

Bloody hell but he turned out to be a real yapper, and he had old Dave held completely captive in the front seat! First off, we found out that he was the client company's contract geologist in charge of the drilling. Also, he was an avid Land Rover enthusiast and believed that those vehicles were the best four-wheel drives that had ever been made by man. That was in spite of the fact that the British had stuffed up everything in Africa. Then we heard how – after the white South African government had left the country in pristine condition – Namibia was going to the dogs because the blacks had taken over. Even the kaffirs had found independence disappointing. You couldn't eat freedom and it didn't necessarily give you employment, new cars and houses like the whites had always had. Then we heard there was a large German population residing in the country; mostly ex-Nazis, drunks or arrogant bastards in general. Yet they kept the place together. Furthermore, Namibia produced the best beer in Africa, and excellent South African wines and brandy were readily available. It hadn't rained properly for years, and, as a result of the drought, the city of Windhoek was due to run out of water at any moment. Regardless of that, no water restrictions had been imposed since the kaffirs wouldn't know how to impose them in the first place. It was still possible to get good food, clothing and kitchen appliances in the shops and most of the cuisine was either Boer or German. The kaffirs lived mostly on mielie-pap or maize meal and could only afford meat once a week, despite their new-found freedom. Four main black tribes inhabited the place; the Nama, the Damara, the Herero and the Ovambo. He mentioned other tribes with weird names, then, of course, the San or Bushmen who chose to live in the Kalahari Desert. Apparently they were probably very similar to our aborigines. Huge opportunities existed in the mining and exploration fields since the country had been the domain of the major South African mining companies that had recently pulled out and had only been looking for elephant sized mineral deposits in the first place. Namibia had one of the highest occurrences of AIDS in the whole of Africa. Finally, Kotzé was born in Oranjemund, but had a South African passport; he was also the son of a supervisor on the diamond mines, who was such a cretin because he never stole any diamonds. His old man had passed away not long back.

The outskirts of Windhoek looked clean and modern as we entered the suburb of Klein Windhoek. We never got to see the city centre immediately, as the Land Rover was turned to the right onto an avenue named after Nelson Mandela. A couple of hundred metres after that we pulled up in front of a steel gate that served as an entry to a high wall that was gaily festooned with rolls of razor wire. Kotzé produced a red, plastic gizmo and pointed it at the gate. The gate rolled open, revealing a substantial, two storey house. Once the vehicle and trailer were through, the gate rolled shut behind us.

"Your quarters, gentlemen. I have fully stocked up the house with food and provisions, and there are plenty of towels and bed linen," Kotzé was very proud of himself.

The house was a beauty! Even by Perth standards it was a mansion. It had eight bedrooms in all, a sauna, a Jacuzzi; a balcony that completely encircled the upstairs part, and an egg-shaped swimming pool in the middle of the back lawn. From the upper floor we could see for a fair way to the east; the city proper being blocked out by hills. Most of Windhoek was situated on hills made up of flaky, green, micaceous schist, and rock fairly jutted out of everywhere. Where there weren't thorn trees the gardens bloomed with Jacarandas, bougainvillaea, date palms, cacti and the odd aloe and cypress. Otherwise the place looked bloody boring to the eyes: In fact it really looked quite barren! The only real greenery around the place was surrounding the public cemetery. From the balcony we could see into one of our next door neighbour's yard which surrounded a mansion similar to ours. There was no garden there at all; only sand and a half-dead cactus. There was also a swimming pool; still it was only about a third full of water that was dark-green and slimy from neglect. Kotzé reckoned the black bloke who lived there was a big chief in the Namibian police force, and he hadn't paid either his electricity or water bills for months, so both services had been cut off. His spouse and kids, who were often left on their own for months at a time on account of the good police officer being shacked up with a mistress elsewhere, had to rely on a rain water tank and candles. God knew what they used for cooking?

We were quite overwhelmed when Kotzé introduced us to our two housemaids, for the thought of having servants was totally foreign to us! One was Wilhelmina, a Nama, and the other was Hesta, who was a Damara. I don't know who were more shy and giggly, them or us Aussies? They had been engaged to do the cooking, keep the house clean and to wash our clothes. There was also a gardener coming around every Tuesday and Friday.

"Hey, Jeff, you'd better not go leaving skid marks in your underdaks," Nick opined.

Very much to our great glee, Jeff went as red as a beetroot, though I didn't think the maids had any idea of what Nick was talking about. It was four pm; knock-off time for them and both girls needed money for their taxi fares back to the township of Katutura.

"Time for an ale!" Wheeler was adamant. "Flamin' hell – it's ten o'clock at night back in Kal'! We're falling behind you bastards – we're fuckin' falling way behind! Jeff! Nick! Locate some fuckin' lager!"

Kotzé showed that he had a kind side to him; not only did he go with Nick and Jeff to buy half a dozen crates of beer, he also volunteered to take us to his favourite pub, the Zum Wirt. When we arrived at that establishment the downstairs bar was crammed full of Germans, Austrians, Swiss and all sorts; none speaking English. The room was scarcely ten metres by seven metres. Luck smiled on us, as there was a table alongside one wall that some people vacated, thus allowing the seven of us seats. Tafel Lager seemed the most popular ale amongst the mob, so we decided to give it a shot. As we quaffed away it soon became noticeable that we were the main attraction. Blokes were glancing over their shoulders and muttering to each other. Nick introduced himself with a thundering, hollow belch that embarrassed all of those around the room and Kotzé as well. They tried to ignore us from then on. For the first time ever I wasn't the only coloured drinker in the bar, as a couple of coloured blokes and a coloured sheila were sitting at the table adjacent to ours. The barmaids and waitresses, all coloureds, were friendly, flirtatious – just great! Something deep inside warmed me to them immediately. I could almost sense a mutual reciprocation coming from them, for they smiled appreciatively when I thanked them for their services and gave them the odd tip or two. It didn't take long to discover that the Germans and Austrians or whatever were fairly ignorant bastards. When served, they didn't even bother to look up, and once they received their change they counted it every time; looking as if they hoped they had been ripped off. There was a total absence of blacks, although we had seen hundreds back at the Windhoek Airport and out on the streets.

Dave had a pen and some paper on the table and he was working out some sums with Kotzé. Suddenly his face lit up and he called across the table to me, "Christ, Joe, have you worked out how much we're paying for grog over here?"

I shrugged and shook my head at him.

"These five hundred mil' ales are costing only a buck twenty Aussie. Smokes are about two bucks a packet. Seriously, you can get a feed for less than three bucks!" He had calculated that one Aussie dollar was buying nearly five bucks Namibian!

"We'll have to drink more," Jeff was certain. "This stuff's only four percent alcohol. Not like Emu Export. What're the cops like when it comes to drunken driving?" he asked Kotzé.

"You would need to be blerrie unlucky. They seldom hassle the whites. It is the blacks they generally go after."

Kotzé had to go home to his missus, so we decided to investigate the city's main street, Independence Avenue, for more possible watering holes. We passed a large multi-storied hotel, the Kalahari Sands, which was also a casino, but decided not to go in because it looked too upmarket and expensive. A few blocks farther on we came across the Hotel Thüringer Hof that sported a bar called the Wurlitzer. Before we entered the bar that was facing out onto Independence Avenue, we gave way to a skinny, bearded bloke who was singing in German or whatever at the top of his lungs. He was totally rat-arsed and actually fell flat on his face in the main street, then immediately following that he was very nearly run over by a black taxi driver. He finished his crossing of the street on his hands and knees, and then at long last he reached a car park. Taking almost an eternity, he struggled to his feet and unlocked the door of an ancient Volkswagen Golf. He started the car, which he then drove off without putting the headlights on. Having driven through a red traffic light, he roared down Independence Avenue, crashing the vehicle's gears all the way.

"Christ, the fuckin' cop shop's just over there!" Dave was incredulous. "Those cops out the front must've seen him!"

It was truly amazing! The Hotel Thüringer Hof was at the corner of an intersection that had traffic lights. Opposite the front of the hotel was the car park, and then diagonally across from it was a cop shop that looked as if it was the city's main one. There were some cops standing outside the place, and what looked like a couple of patrol cars were parked nearby. The cops had obviously seen the German's antics, but had treated them as an innocent, everyday occurrence!

We found the Wurlitzer Bar to be excellent. It had been so named because it boasted a huge Wurlitzer jukebox. There was a bar running down most of the room, and a myriad of tables and chairs were scattered everywhere. The place also had a bistro set up for meals and stuff. Unlike the Zum Wirt, the clientele was a fairly equal mixture of blacks, coloureds and whites, then, except for one black barman, the waitresses and bistro staff consisted of mainly coloured girls. Naturally we ordered beer immediately and after a short time we absorbed almost by osmosis a fairly decent German bloke by the name of Konnie. He was quite a fountain of information. He had been a wireless officer in the German merchant navy, then had settled in Namibia back in the '70s and had become an electrical contractor, builder and general Jack-of-all-trades. Where Kotzé had generally run the country down to the ground, Konnie assured Jeff and I that Namibia had some very good points going for it. He reckoned that most of the Germans, Swiss and Austrians were only there since they wouldn't be able to survive financially in their mother countries.

He went on to add, "You will come across many white people in this country who cannot accept that the blacks have taken over government. You will never find them saying anything positive about the country, therefore you can quite easily get the wrong impression. There is some building and development going on here in Windhoek, though not as much as before. Admittedly a lot of German aid money is involved, but there are a lot of private investors moving in from South Africa and elsewhere... The government is also stable since the Ovambo have taken power, and they are by far the largest tribe in Namibia. They are an affable and friendly people and they generally let you go about your business undisturbed. So far I have came across only a small amount of corruption amongst the new government departments that I have personally had to deal with, nonetheless – like in all African countries – corruption is gradually taking over everywhere. Mind you, there was far more of it under the Boer regime. Then again, there was also a border war being fought and just about all of the locals benefited by the huge sums of money that the South African government was pouring in... Are you staying here long?"

I shrugged. "Six months. Maybe more."

"Then why not enjoy yourself? No one here will bother you and there is plenty this country has to offer. They make beer better here than they do in Germany."

"Talkin' about beer – it's your shout – you bastard!" Jeff informed me, so I ordered another round.

Konnie was intrigued by the way we Aussies insulted each other; especially when we referred to each other as being bastards, and then there was our foul language and the way Jeff, Nick and most of our number belched freely. Belching, he claimed, was considered a very bad habit in his childhood hometown.

"You call each other bastards? We have a lot of bastards over here," Konnie informed us. "But these people do not consider the term derogatory at all. We have many coloureds here who proudly refer to themselves as Bastards, Bastas, Baster, Bastaards or Basteurs. It all means the same. We have the Rehoboth Baster for instance."

"I was born in Rehoboth," I told him.

"So that makes you a genuine bastard!" Jeff insisted delightedly.

Unlike with Jeff, the fact that I was born in Rehoboth captivated Konnie. "Then how come you are with these Australians?"

"My stepfather and mother emigrated to Australia."

He nodded in understanding. "It is amazing how many coloureds have made their way over there. I know several people who drink in this hotel who have relations in Australia – Germans and coloureds. When the South Africans took over the country from the Germans, it did not take them long to introduce their Apartheid laws. Despite Hitler's efforts during the Great War, in many cases we Germans are not as racially prejudiced as other white colonials, for there have been many mixed relationships. Also with the Austrians and the Swiss.

JOSEF SCHULTZ

During Apartheid it was a contravention against the South African morality laws to have mixed-race relationships, so many people had to leave the country. As you can see by the coloured population around us, there have been a great many multiracial interrelationships, and, in spite of their laws, the Boers themselves contributed themselves in no small way."

Wheeler and I decided to call it a day, for we knew the boss was bound to be seriously pissed off with Dave not having contacted him when we first arrived in the country. It was way too late to call him by then. The rest of the jokers reckoned they had more howling at the moon to take care of. There was no real hassle with their plans, as there wasn't much for them to do until the rig arrived in Walvis Bay. We waved down a taxi driver who insisted he could take passengers to most places around the city, including the black townships, but Klein Windhoek was out of his way; nevertheless a blue Namibian ten dollar note convinced him otherwise. His driving nearly made me shit myself and there was no way his vehicle was roadworthy! I could hear screeching sounds as bare brake callipers ground away at tortured, worn-out brake discs; the right-hand wheel wobbled as if it was about to desert the vehicle at any second and the indicator lights were dead. On the dashboard there was a tarnished Saint Christopher statue, and I could have sworn I had seen the old bloke lower Jesus to the ground in order to make a run for it!

Claiming that he was the boss cocky while Ernie wasn't around, Dave insisted on having the house's main bedroom that had its own bathroom, so I grabbed the next biggest one. We had a last beer out on the balcony, considering the night was beautiful and warm, and then I was out to the world.

CHAPTER 2

JEFF GIVES SOME POOFTERS A KNUCKLE SANDWICH!

"Fire! Fire! Oh fuck – fire! Cops! Wake up – you bastards!"

I was wrenched awake and ran down the stairs in sheer panic!

"Fire! This's the Kalgoorlie Fire Brigade! Call an ambulance! Come on – wake up!"

The boys had returned and Dave was really pissed off, "Keep it down, you fuckin' dickheads! You'll wake the whole bloody neighbourhood! Fucksakes – give it away!"

"Hey, don't fuckin' swear in front of sheilas!" Nick reprimanded him.

They had brought back about half a dozen women of every shape, size and hue. As I was only in my jocks, I raced back to my room to put some jeans on. I heard banging and crashing from where Spence was trying to find some glasses. I examined the sheilas more closely. They mostly resembled dogs, bar one tall, skinny coloured. All of them no more sober than the blokes.

"You should've seen this place we ended up at," Jeff told me. "What was it called, Nick?"

"Casa Blanca!"

"Yeah, that's it. It was full of lezzies and fuckin' poofters. Weren't there long when..."

"Jeff gave a couple of shirt lifters a slapping," Bob Reynolds cut in.

15

"Bloody oath, I did!" Jeff agreed. "This one bastard come up to me and wanted to sell his arse for fifty bucks. When I told him to piss off, his mate comes up and offers the same deal, so I gave 'em both a knuckle sandwich."

"The cops pitched up in seconds flat!" Steve Spence added.

"That's all we friggin' need!" Dave glowered at Jeff. "We've been in the place for less than twelve hours and we've got strife with the cops."

"Nah, it wasn't like that," Nick assured him. "The cops asked us if we were okay, and they carted the pillow-biters out."

"Yeah, and where'd the Sheilas come from?" Dave demanded.

Nick grinned. "The Casa Blanca. Picked 'em up easy as piss! Fuck me, when the locals found out we were Aussies, every fucker wanted to know us. They treated us like fuckin' royalty, cobber!"

It was time for me to go back to bed. It was three in the morning and I felt that if I had drunk any more beer, it would have poured out of my ears. Luckily the upstairs part of the house fairly smothered the sounds of the festivities below, and the noise had become just a dull roar.

I woke up to someone calling, "Is anyone home?" It was Kotzé. I glanced at my watch; it was a quarter past eight in the morning. There was no sign of my Aussie associates when I went downstairs.

Kotzé reckoned he was prepared to kill for a black coffee, so I told him that he would have just as good a chance of finding some as me. While searching the kitchen cupboards, he surveyed a war zone of empty beer bottles, glasses, ashtrays and various items of men and women's clothing.

"You people have an orgy last night?" he suggested as he ladled percolator coffee into a filter.

"It looks like someone has," I nodded. "Me, I flaked out before the others."

His eyes bugged out when a plump, black woman came down the stairs wearing nothing but polka dot panties; her melon-like tits swaying from side to side. "Cigarette?" she croaked.

16

BASTARDS FROM THE BUSH

I gave her two smokes. After getting me to light one for her, she waddled back upstairs. Kotzé handed me a cup of coffee and I searched the cupboards for sugar.

"It is a good thing we do not still have Apartheid," he warned me. "Otherwise you might have had the police swarming all over the place."

I wasn't really happy having the bloke there. "Yeah, shows you how bloody pathetic the Boers were. Do you reckon Apartheid was a good thing?"

"It started before I was..."

The phone rang. It was the boss! "Where the fuck was Dave?" I was asked.

It looked like Wheeler had soldiered on with the others when I had gone to bed, for he looked like death warmed up when I handed him the phone. A fairly decent argument ensued with him telling all kinds of bullshit about the phone not working, and he was protesting all kinds of innocence. I saw Kotzé carefully listening in on the conversation; taking mental notes, the slippery bastard!

"What's up?" I asked Dave once he had put the phone down.

"Fuckin' dickhead! What difference would it've made if I'd called him earlier? He's like a fuckin' kid sometimes... Ernie's pitching up from Cape Town tomorrow evening. How come the old prick's in Cape Town? He reckoned the rig's arriving in Walvis Bay on Monday." He looked at his watch. "It's Friday, so we haven't got long to go. Bloody can't wait to get back drilling, mate... Those sheilas still here?"

I shrugged. "One is, anyway, she come down with next to fuck all on. I'm like you, mate, it'll be good to get back drilling. This sitting around drinking piss's gunna kill us."

I carried out a survey of the various bedrooms in order to get the others up on deck. Jeff was screwing a black sheila about a fifth of his size, dog fashion. It was a hilarious sight; reminiscent of a dog trying to fuck a cricket ball. There was the stink of old sex; the room smelled like the hold of a Japanese tuna boat. My mind jumped to the thought of AIDS and I almost sighed with relief when I spotted a couple of empty condom wrappers lying on the floor. He glanced over his shoulder and saw me standing in the doorway, but he kept on pumping away regardless; the ash from the cigarette in his mouth dropping like snowflakes onto her back.

Nick was sound asleep, wedged between two sheilas, both coloured, and Spence and Reynolds were cuddled up to black women, including the one with the polka dot panties, so it looked as if Jeff was wrong about them being poofters. The best looking sheila was using Dave's ensuite shower. I locked the bathroom door behind me and dropped the hard word on her, but she wouldn't have a bar of it. The thought of offering her money for a shag crossed my mind, but she looked so pathetic that I started feeling sorry for her. I was rained on by insults when I tried to prod the others out of bed and get things going.

"Steve and Nick, get rid of the birds," Dave ordered. "Hermanus," he turned to Kotzé. "Where can we get some hire vehicles? We'll need a couple?"

Kotzé reckoned he knew where the best vehicle hire outfit was and agreed to take Nick and Steve there; however he looked highly pissed off when Wheeler asked him if he could drop the sheilas off in town. He argued that they should blerrie walk; nevertheless both Dave and I talked him into it. Jeff was too hung over to be of any use.

"I don't know about you, but that Boer bastard gets on my tits," Dave told me when we were alone with Jeff. "I don't know why, but I can't hack the prick."

"You want to watch him," I cautioned. "He was all ears when you tried bullshitting the boss."

"He's the contract geo'," Jeff reminded me. "He gives Dave any crap and we can make his life a misery."

"Hey, Dave," I altered the conversation, "you should've seen Jeff here rooting this black sheila. A real Wild West bull rider he was. Fair rode her into the ground!"

"Fuckin' near killed me, too!" Jeff admitted.

"Your missus'll fuckin' kill you when I tell her," Dave assured him. "If AIDS doesn't get to you first."

Jeff wasn't too bothered. "This friggin' hangover's gunna fuckin' kill me long before anything else does... Guess what, you jokers?"

"What's that?" Dave and I asked almost in unison.

Jeff looked all knowing. "You know all those plaits and things these black sheilas have in their hair?"

"Yeah?" Dave humoured him.

"They're fuckin' made of plastic! Seriously, they've got these plastic hair pieces that they kind of stitch into their hair and plait afterwards."

"Is that a fact, Jeff?" Wheeler looked him up and down with disdain. "I really needed to know that the black women over here have got plastic hair. Thanks for the info, mate, I'll make sure I write it down somewhere. Seriously, Jeff, I can sleep soundly at nights – all my earthly torments have disappeared – the world's in safe hands 'cause there's sheilas going around with flamin' plastic hair!"

It was pretty clear that Dave had further glass in his liver when Spence, Reynolds and Nick came back with Kotzé and two white Land Rover Defender station wagons. He waited for Kotzé, who was busily admiring the vehicles, to get within earshot, "Where'd you get these fuckin' heaps of shit? Couldn't you get any Land Cruisers?"

"It was all they had," Nick complained. "Beats fuckin' walking."

Dave still wasn't comforted. "You can shove 'em up your arse – sideways!"

CHAPTER 3

WE SEE A WART HOG! JEFF SEES LIONS UNDER EVERY BUSH! THE MIGHTY NAMIB DESERT!

We picked Ernie up at the airport, and then the next morning we headed for Walvis Bay. First off, we searched for a place that sold iceboxes or eskies, so that we could take a few cold beers for the journey. It was bloody hot that day, and Wheeler warned us about the danger of dehydration setting in. We had a quite a convoy; Kotzé driving alone up front in his Land Rover; Nick driving with Dave, Ernie, Jeff and me in one; followed by Spence and Reynolds driving the third.

"Get out and push the bitch, Jeff," Ernie instructed as our vehicle had trouble with the first set of hills that surrounded Windhoek.

Jeff wasn't having that, "Push the bastard yourself, ya fuckin' mutant!"

"What the fuck's that?" Nick bellowed; pointing out in front of the vehicle as a strange animal sauntered across the road.

Dave knew his wildlife. "It's a wart hog."

"We aren't back in Oz now, you know," I told Nick. "You won't see any roos over here."

"Reckon we'll see some lions?" Jeff queried no one in particular.

"Friggin' bound to," Dave jeered. "Herds of fuckin' elephants, too."

The sarcasm was lost on Jeff and he was all eyes on our surroundings. What was more; he was convinced that he had caught glimpses of several lions and leopards hiding amongst the incessant thorn trees that bordered both sides of the road. The countryside was fenced off

20

on either side of us; the land was parched, and whatever few blades of grass – that did exist – were burned to a khaki colour. Every now and then we saw desperately thin cattle on the side of the road being herded by black blokes using sticks with red bits of cloth on the end of them. We arrived at a place called Okahandja, and as we were cruising through the place we saw two incredible black women! They had kind of upside-down tricorn hats made out of colourful material, then the beautifully patterned dresses they wore reached all the way to the ground; the skirt parts puffed out like crinolines. They seemed to glide along like a couple of Doctor Who Daleks. When I asked Kotzé later on about them, he told me that they were Herero women. Apparently they had copied their mode of dress from the early German women settlers. He also claimed that they wore about eleven petticoats in order to puff their dresses out, which must have been bloody hot in that Namibian sun!

We headed straight west from Okahandja as our journey took us in the direction of the Atlantic Ocean. Kotzé pulled up our convoy at a place called Karibib in order that we could refuel the vehicles. He pointed to the long rows of high hills that formed east-west, parallel ridges on either side of the town and informed Wheeler that some of the drilling targets existed there. We then went through a place called Usakos where Dave insisted that we should top up the eskies with beer and ice. It was a bonzer idea, for we were due to cross the Namib Desert before reaching the sea and didn't want to break down without adequate supplies of ale to sustain us. The farther west we travelled the more arid it became; the thorn trees became scarcer and at last disappeared altogether, being replaced by weird looking succulents and stunted bushes. Those in turn gave way to stark, black and grey, jagged rock formations and gypsum flats totally devoid of any sort of vegetation. We saw a sign: 'KEEP OUR DESERT CLEAN."

"This's what I call real deserty-desert," Ernie assured Jeff.

"It's like a fuckin' moonscape," Jeff differed with him.

To me the Namib Desert was awesome! It wasn't at all like the deserts I had seen back in Aussie or in books where sand dunes were everywhere.

When we got out of the vehicle to take a slash and investigate things more fully, I found the ground to be as hard as concrete! Jeff had hit the nail on the head; it was like being on the moon or some other planet. I looked closely at a narrow ridge of rocks, and, to my surprise, they were covered by yellow, green, orange and red lichens; all in Day-Glo colours! Those lichens, Kotzé informed me – plus a variety of beetles, snakes, lizards and chameleons – survived only because the moisture of the Atlantic fogs and mists travelled so far inland. Though we couldn't see it immediately, the Namib Desert was alive with all types of activities!

The desert seemed to go on for an eternity, then just over a stony crest popped up the seaside town of Swakopmund. The desert virtually stopped at the fences of the first houses we passed; there was no buffer – just desert – just houses, and we saw a whole heap of sand dunes lining the coast to the south. Regardless of its barren surroundings and the date palms planted everywhere, Swakopmund, due to some of its Gothic architecture, looked in places as if it had come straight out of a European travel brochure. Some of the buildings had 1901; 1905; 1907 etched in concrete over their front doorways. We didn't stop in Swakopmund, but went straight south across a long bridge that headed towards Walvis Bay.

As we travelled south Namibia categorically displayed that it was indeed a land of contrasts. To our left was a sheer wall of golden white sand dunes towering hundreds of feet high; on our right was the steel grey Atlantic Ocean smashing against the rocks and surging with huge tentacles of dark green and brown sea kelp. While the dunes shimmered from the heat, the wind coming off the sea was almost uncomfortably cold. Out on the western horizon we saw several vessels obviously searching for fish; after that, almost on the beach itself, we saw a settlement of luxury houses practically surrounded by miniature sandstorms. It was a queer place to build a holiday village.

When we eventually reached Walvis Bay I was slightly disappointed with the place. Except for when you went south around the extremity of the natural inlet, it was an absolute dump. Rows and rows of square, featureless houses with what looked to be painted, canvas roofs to protect them from the ever-present sea salt. Pelicans and other water fowl roosted on everything and there was bird shit everywhere. Lion and Castle beer advertising signs were rusting on shops and buildings all over the place; a legacy from when the enclave had once been ruled by South Africa. To the east there was only sand, sand and more sand that had a restless, wandering nature about it; first trundling across the main road to the east, then, as if changing its mind, it wafted back to the west again. There was a grader scraping little dunes of lazy sand off the road.

Ernie wanted to take a recce of the port facilities in order to try and find out where the rig would be unloaded. It was also his job to organise a suitable working area where we could reassemble everything. When we arrived at the port gates we were confronted by two black security men; one casually displaying that he had an AK-47 assault rifle in his possession. Ernie had a letter from some outfit within the complex; although when he queried the guards about them, neither man seemed able nor willing to help him. No, they didn't have any communication system from their barrier to the port buildings. No, they didn't know anything about the people Ernie wanted to see. No, they weren't about to assist us in any manner whatsoever.

"For fuck's sake, Ernie!" Dave lost his patience. "Let's book into a hotel and make some phone calls from there?"

"People around here always as mutant as this?" Jeff asked Kotzé about the security blokes.

"Ja, they normally are. The kaffirs, that is. Lateral thinking is an anathema to them. Getting a kaffir to make a decision is like trying to find a black virgin above the age of seven. They do not want to attract any attention from their superiors – they just want you to go away and leave them to their nose-picking and armpit-scratching. That is what they are expert at. That and breeding. I hear the Walvis Bay population has grown by twenty-one percent in the last six months. It means that the black Namibians can multiply faster than a Jumbo jet can fly."

We booked into the Sea Lion Hotel, but by that time all the business offices including the port had closed for the day. Once we had deposited all our gear in our various rooms, we assembled at the hotel's bar to brood over our situation. The manageress, a fairly attractive, blonde, middle-aged German, looked fairly happy with so much custom coming through the door in one go, especially during the off-season, and she gave us each a shot glass of *Apfelschnapps* to go with our Tafel Lagers for free! Soon after she left our group in the capable hands of a friendly black barkeeper who claimed that he was an Ovambo.

Ernie was getting panicky and most probably he was having second thoughts about being our El Supremo in Namibia. "The bloody rig's supposed to be arriving tomorrow," he told all of us. "They'll probably dump everything on the docks and piss off. We'll need a fuckin' crane and all sorts of gear."

"Hey, Jeff, would you tell the manageress to get fucked if she asked to sit on your face?" Nick wanted to know.

"Fuckin' oath – I wouldn't! That's where I'd love to have a ten-inch tongue..."

"And be able to breathe through your ears?" I completed one of his favourite sayings.

"Bloody oath, cobber!"

"Let's see that letter," Wheeler held his hand out to Ernie.

"Do you reckon she's married?" Nick asked me.

"I didn't notice if she had any wedding rings on."

"It looks pretty straightforward to me, Ernie," Dave waved the letter around. "You've got this outfit here, Du Preez and Seun. They've gotta workshop in the port, so they'll probably have mobile cranes and welding gear."

"Hey, Hermanus, are you a Japie?" Steve Spence enquired of Kotzé.

Kotzé appeared not to hear him.

"What the fuck you on about?" Bob Reynolds wanted to know.

Steve had been talking to the barman who had informed him that white South Africans weren't only known as Boers – he pronounced it *Boorers* – but Japies as well. The word Japie sounded more like *'yarpee'.*

CHAPTER 4

KNIFE FIGHT AT THE BLUE MERMAID HOTEL!
NICK KICKS SPENCE IN THE BALLS!
AIDS CRAWLING UP THE WALLS!

After we had dinner at the Sea Lion Hotel we decided to celebrate the imminent arrival of the rig by going in search of some wine, women and possibly song. All with the exception of Ernie, who insisted he wanted an early night; the poor, old bastard. Kotzé came up to scratch when it came to picking a venue, for he recalled an establishment from his younger days called the Blue Mermaid Hotel. It was an absolute dive; nevertheless it harboured certain imponderables that set fire to our imaginations. The place looked as if it doubled as some sort of a brothel; accommodation upstairs and a fairly rank, smoke-stained bar below. The beer was top rate, even if the other people in the bar looked as if they had escaped from some bizarre horror movie! There were a couple of Russian sailors off one of the fishing trawlers; both pissed as newts. Then there was a black bloke and a German arguing and looking as if they were ready to kill each other at any second. Behind the bar there was a fat Japie with about forty double chins and a gut that hung down farther than Jeff's. In addition to that we found half a dozen or so sheilas hanging around the place, all coloured, and they really captured our attention the most. They had to be the roughest, most motley bunch of dogs that any one of us could have come across in our total years put together! One woman had a bandage wrapped

25

round her head and there was a huge bloodstain that almost covered her forehead! Another one had an empty eye socket; the rest looked skinny and as if they hadn't had a wash, combed their hair, or had a change of clothes since they had reached puberty. They all looked fairly happy with our arrival!

After we had had a couple of beers Wheeler nodded over his shoulder at the woman with the missing orb and he turned to Jeff. "She's the one for you, my old son."

"Fuckin' bullshit!" Jeff was instantly electrified. "I wouldn't touch her even with your dick."

"And why not?" Dave grinned. "She's been keeping an eye out for you all evening."

Nick nearly choked on his beer and bubbles dribbled out of his nostrils. "My fuckin' oath, Jeff!" he gasped with laughter. "It's a good way not to get AIDS. Fuck her in the eye socket – it'll be tighter than her pussy."

"You fuckin' sick arseholes," was all Jeff had to say.

By that time a couple of the sheilas had befriended Reynolds and Spence, and probably to kill off any inhibitions the two blokes might have had lurking deep within their souls, they produced some marijuana and the two offsiders were soon coughing and wheezing from the stuff. Nick insisted on having some and a skinny sheila was soon bobbing up and down on his knee. All in all our surroundings became fairly cheerful as the smell of the weed's smoke filled the room. Even Kotzé let his hair down and I could see that he was more than interested in one of the coloured women. Jeff must have been in a good mood, too, for he went over to the black bloke and the German and told them that if they didn't stop shouting and arguing he would bang their heads together. The German immediately got to his feet and took a swing at him, but Jeff dropped him like a stone with a cracking head butt. That in turn caused the two Russians to yell something in their mother tongue, and it was apparent that they agreed wholeheartedly with what had transpired.

"Can you chuck the blerrie fool out?" the Japie barkeep asked Jeff. "The blerrie bugger has been causing problems all evening."

Jeff grabbed the unconscious German by the back of his neck and belt and hurled him out on to the pavement. One of the coloured whores quickly ran out and searched the man's pockets, and when she returned the bartender demanded half of what she had found. He reckoned that the German owed him a fortune on the slate. The black bloke who had been arguing with the German slumped to the floor unconscious from the grog.

Wheeler pointed over at Reynolds, Spence and the two Sheilas who had come up with the marijuana. "What if the cops come?" he asked the Japie. "Won't they bust the place?"

"Agh no, man! My brother is a policeman. No one bothers me here. You can do whatever you like, as long as you pay for it."

"What about. . ? Oh – Christ!" Dave was stopped dead in his tracks by the sheila with the bandage around her head. She left no doubt that she rather fancied him, and there was no way in the world that she had any intention of allowing him to knockback such a generously offered opportunity.

"What've you got that I haven't?" Jeff was thrilled at his discomfort.

"Come on, Dave," Nick howled, "buy the fair damsel a drink. Where are your fuckin' manners?"

Wheeler pushed a twenty dollar Namibian note into the woman's hand and motioned to her to lay her charm's at Jeff's front door, but one of the sheilas that was with Spence and Reynolds went up to her and demanded the money.

The crap flew in all directions after that! The women with the bandage refused to hand over the browny-coloured note, so the other one hit her with a beer bottle that was still half full! Right on the forehead – right in the middle of the bloodstain! The bottle bust, splashing froth everywhere and there was blood dripping down from the bandage. The recipient just shook her head and lammed right into the one who had hit her. The fight became really dinkum because they both produced knives and started slashing at each other!

"Hadn't you better stop 'em?" Dave asked the barkeep nervously, while Nick offered to take a bet on which woman would get disembowelled first.

"No way, man!" the Japie was adamant. "I could get stabbed!"

It looked as if the sheila with the bandage was gone for all money, as her eyes were full of blood and it was obvious she couldn't see her opponent properly. The other combatant looked as if she was ready to gut the poor soul when suddenly the woman with the missing eye brought a chair crashing down on her head! We were soon to discover that the one-eyed woman was the sister of the one with the bandage, so we had two unconscious forms lying out in the street and the two siblings split Dave's money fifty-fifty once they had received the right amount of change from the barman. Bob Reynolds was fairly pissed off, as it was his companion who had been dropped like a blind mullet.

It was easy to see that Nick was overjoyed with everything that had transpired. "Fuck me dead, you'd have to pay to see all this if we were back home! Jeff! Things are getting too quiet! Fuckin' organise things, ya big, fat bastard!"

"I'll fuckin' organise *you*!" Jeff warned. He turned to the Boer barkeep. "Give us another beer, mate."

By that time the sheila that Kotzé was interested in, was all over the Japie geo' like a rash. He was also pissed out of his brain and he was grinning like he had won the lottery.

Then, to cap everything off, Nick moved in on Spence's new friend and Steve wasn't going to have a bar of it. They started shaping up to each other, which Dave and I thought was rather strange, for we agreed that the woman looked old enough to be either of their mothers and twice as ugly. It wasn't a good fight, though, inasmuch as Nick managed to kick Spence in the balls and his adversary wasn't much good after that. Wheeler and I were also quite mystified by Nick's activities, since it wasn't like him to deviate too far from the rules of Lord Queensbury. Besides, he wasn't even interested in the woman he had got into the scrap over. Perhaps he was only trying to impress her?

He then went to stomp on Spence's head, but Jeff intervened. "That's enough," he insisted. "Fuckin' give it away!"

Kotzé and Reynolds stayed behind while the rest of us went to take Spence back to the hotel. On the way past Nick kicked the German in the head, instantly causing Dave to take umbrage: "Don't, you'll fuckin kill the bastard! You've done enough damage to Steve already."

"Yeah," Jeff supported him, "I told you to give it away, ya fuckin' mutant!"

Nick was too full of himself to take that. "And you're gunna make me, are ya – ya big, fat arsehole?"

I felt obliged to step in, as the last thing we needed was a brawl in the main street of Walvis Bay. "Nick, if you don't seriously pull your head in, you'll be up against *both me and Jeff.*"

"I could have both of you, if I was in the mood," he shot back at me, then he found an aluminium Coke can that he kicked all the way back to the Sea Lion Hotel.

At breakfast the following morning it was fairly simple to detect that Kotzé was both hung over and embarrassed. Jeff offered nothing to comfort him, "I thought you fuckin' Boers didn't like darkies? Bloody take a smell of you – you stink like a sardine can that's been left out in the sun for a week! What's your missus gunna say if you go home with a dose of the clap?"

Reynolds also looked horribly sick, so I also decided to have a poke at him, "Hope you used protection? That place would've had AIDS crawling up the wallpaper. How you feeling – you could be dead in a couple of weeks?"

Spence came limping into the dining room. He was bow-legged like a buckjump rider and he winced as he sat down at the table. He acknowledged to Dave that his balls had grown easily four times their normal size!

"What the fuck happened to you?" Ernie asked him. When the little prick found out what had transpired, he decided to give us all a lecture: "I'm not fuckin' having this!" he was adamant. "The holiday's over, you bastards. Christ, what sort of an example are you setting here in Namibia? I'm not having you blokes getting around making us look like a bunch of dickheads. Any more of..."

"Ah – get fucked – Ernie," Wheeler was bored with the little man and we all agreed.

CHAPTER 5

THE RIG ARRIVES!

Du Preez and Seun looked as if they could be really useful to our cause. When Ernie called them, a bloke reckoned he was coming straight round to the hotel to see him. Sure enough, a blue BMW pitched up and out climbed a massive, beer-gutted bloke with a balding head, black beard, and such tight-fitting mini shorts his testicles looked as if they were in the process of bursting free at any second! "How is it?" he asked Ernie. "Koos Du Preez."

After introducing himself and shaking hands with all and sundry, he and Kotzé got into a fairly prolonged discussion in Afrikaans that fairly pissed us Aussies off because we couldn't understand a word being said. Both could speak English, so it showed what ignorant bastards Japies were.

There was a real fuss when the ship came in. Unknown to us someone from Du Preez and Seun had phoned all the newspapers and other media, telling them that a monumental happening was due to occur in Walvis Bay! Not only were we surrounded by a dozen or so reporters and their cameramen, plus a battery of TV people; a couple of flash Mercedes Benzes arrived and disgorged what appeared to be pretty high up government officials. That seemed to attract an army of cops as if by magic; all armed with pistols, AK-47s and a variety of other automatic weapons. We had such a crowd on the dockside there was no room to off-load the drill truck and support vehicles. Fortunately sanity prevailed and the cops cordoned off an area.

Making it clear that he intended to hog the limelight, Kotzé did all the talking: "I am the geologist in charge of this operation," he wanted the whole country to know as the cameras whirred. "I have always tried to promote the untapped mineral wealth of Namibia. Here is an opportunity for employment and exports..."

"How many people shall be employed?" some government official in a flash suit and sunglasses butted in; clearly wanting to participate in some of the free publicity. "We in the government have left no stone unturned to find long-term employment possibilities for the people of Walvis Bay. The white South African supremacists let this town wither and die once they learned it was being returned to the rightful hands of the Namibian people. Our government for many years have known that there is oil out there," he pointed in the direction of the Atlantic.

The bloke obviously didn't have a clue about what was happening, and had thought that it was an offshore oil rig that was being unloaded. It was an uncomfortable Kotzé who had to explain to him that the rig was of the onshore variety, and, once it had been reassembled, the thing was travelling inland miles from Walvis Bay. Also, in the first stages of everything, mostly Aussies might be doing all the toiling.

Another government official, a massive, fearsome looking, black sheila; her head sporting a complicated network of intricate, plastic plaits, tried to conceal the previous official's gaffe by asking very cleverly: "How much gold will you be digging out in the next six months, and what shall it be worth in Namibian dollar terms?" She also told Kotzé that she had heard that there were many gold 'deepots' all over Namibia simply waiting to be dug out; also copper deepots and stainless steel deepots.

The Japie geo' assured her that he certainly agreed that she could be right; however that was what the drilling rig was for – to test the deposits for their economic viability, and that viability could only be gauged once intensive feasibility studies had been carried out. What was more, he had adequate capabilities – trained into him by many years of hard-earned experience – to take care of all those imponderables.

Following that comprehensive mineralogical and metallurgic analysis was needed to be carried out in order to design the most efficient plant and extraction systems. Then, of course, everything was inextricably hinged to world metal prices and transport costs etceteras. He soon lost her undivided attention for she started giggling and waving and blowing kisses into the Namibian Broadcasting Corporation's TV camera. Possibly for the benefit of her mum and dad, or maybe friends who had a chance of seeing her on the telly?

After a while the reporters, camera operators, TV people and government jokers became bored with things and we were left to organise getting everything to Du Preez and Seun's workshop.

"How did I do?" Kotzé asked Dave.

"Do what?"

"How do you think I looked on the TV?"

Wheeler could be quite hurtful sometimes when he hadn't had his first beer for the day: "Up to shit, mate! You made a real fuckin' dickhead out yourself."

"Hear, hear!" Jeff agreed.

Du Preez and Seun's establishment was everything we could have hoped for. Not only could they supply suitable transport and lifting gear to get the various bits and pieces of the rig to their workshop, the building also had an overhead crane, welding gear, lathes and all the necessary tools to do the job. They had excellent Swiss, German and Japie fitters who were about to make Ernie's life a breeze.

CHAPTER 6

JEFF'S GOT CRABS! PURPLE OINTMENT!

After we had transported all the gear to Du Preez and Seun's workshop we returned to the Sea Lion Hotel for a sundowner. Kotzé was probably still embarrassed by his previous evening's activities, for he reckoned he was going to give the grog a spell and that he had an old mate in Walvis Bay that he wanted to look up. The German manageress was serving, so we were on our best behaviour. Ernie was much more relaxed and he insisted on paying for the first shout. Jeff was next to me in black shorts and a blue singlet, and Dave was on the other side of me. I couldn't help noticing that Jeff had an itchy crutch! Every now and then he snuck his hand below the bar and gave himself a good scratch. Subsequently, out of the corner of my eye, I noticed a tiny, tick-like creature on his arm that was obviously sucking his blood. Not one creature, but several! I had seen those things before on another offsider back in Western Australia. Body crabs! *What joy of absolute – bloody – joys!*

"You gotta pen?" I whispered to Wheeler, and he handed me a biro. I wrote on a beer coaster advertising Holsten Bier: "JEFF'S GOT CRABS!!!" With Jeff's eyes glued on the manageress' gorgeous thighs, I pushed the coaster over to Dave.

Wheeler's eyebrows lifted. "I see!" He handed the coaster on to Steve Spence. Spence handed the coaster on to Bob Reynolds and Bob passed it to Ernie.

"Oh really?" the little mechanic's face lit up.

BASTARDS FROM THE BUSH

Nick ended up with the coaster and he burst out laughing. "Dear – oh – dear!" was his only comment.

Somehow all the clandestine activity must have caught Jeff's attention, and then he saw that we were all staring at him. "What you looking at, ya bunch of mutants?" he sneered.

"Nothing, Jeff," Wheeler assured him. "We've just noticed the tide's gone out."

"What're you talking about?" Jeff was baffled. "You can't see the sea from there."

"Nein, the tide only goes out this morning," the manageress proved that she was familiar with the Atlantic's habits at Walvis Bay. Right at that moment the Ovambo barman came to relieve her.

Jeff obviously reckoned it was all right to return to his usual animal self once the manageress had left the room. "What you fuckin' talkin' about, Dave?"

"Nothing really," Dave replied. "Just that the tide's out and the crabs are on the rocks."

We all burst out laughing and Nick tossed the coaster to Jeff. The big, fat bastard saw what was written on it and his face went scarlet. "Who's the fuckin' dickhead that wrote this?" When a wall of silence met him, he told no one in particular, "I haven't got crabs. Unlike you, ya dirty bastards!"

"Bullshit – you haven't!" I told him. "Look there – they're fuckin' crawling all up your arm! You've been scratching your balls all day!"

He examined his arms and scratched the crabs off. There was the stark look of fear in his eyes. "You'd better go and check your balls," Dave advised him. "If you've got 'em on your arms, there'll be millions suckin' on your crutch."

Jeff went out to the Gents shithouse and he came back a very troubled man. He turned to Wheeler for comfort. "What should I do?"

Dave looked at his watch. "The chemist shops are most likely closed by now. Don't worry, they aren't too hard to get rid of. You can get special ointment that knocks 'em off."

35

"There's another way, Jeff!" Nick was all excited.

"What's that?" Jeff asked.

Nick pointed at the rows of spirit bottles behind the bar. "Get a bottle of rum or whisky or something. Something nice and powerful. Then you gotta go down and sit on the beach. When you..."

"Fuck you and your bullshit!" Jeff wasn't amused. "Be fuckin' serious, I'm not..."

"Hang on – let me finish," Nick interrupted him back. "I *am* being serious. When you get to the beach you pour some rum into the sand and make a paste. You just smother your balls with the paste."

That seemed to make some kind of logic to Jeff. "And will that knock 'em off? Does it make 'em suffocate or something?"

"Nah!" Nick shook his head. "They get pissed on the rum, then they stone each other to death with the sand."

Jeff called us every filthy name his warped imagination could muster, while we shrieked with laughter. The Ovambo bartender was fairly nervous that he was about to kill someone.

When things settled down I decided to work Jeff's case a bit, "Feel your temples – are they sore?"

He touched the sides of his forehead. "No. Why?"

"I remember when I was kid over here. Just before I left with my folks for Aussie, an uncle of mine went bonkers 'cause he caught crabs. They poisoned his blood. I can't remember..."

"Fuckin' crap!" he cut me off.

"He isn't kidding, Jeff," Ernie quickly stepped in. "Before we left Perth I went to see the Tropical Diseases Hospital. The boss sent me 'cause he wanted me to check on what jabs and vaccinations we'd need. The doc' there warned me about the body crabs you get over here in Namibia. Like Joe said, some can stuff your brain, whilst others can spread rabies."

Nick and Steve burst out laughing at that, but Dave waved them to silence. "Ernie's not bullshitting, Jeff, but it depends on the woman you got 'em off. She was one of the black sheilas back in Windhoek – not so?"

"Yeah," Jeff agreed. "I certainly didn't get 'em off my missus."

"How do you know, Jeff?" I demanded.

"Fuckin' boong!" he shot back. If looks could kill, I would have haemorrhaged to death!

Wheeler made sure that the barkeep's attention was elsewhere. "I'm not kidding, Jeff," he continued. "That sheila was more than likely an Ovambo. They come from right up north on the border with Angola. Up there they've got stacks of rabies 'cause the Ovambo's favourite tucker's dog meat. Not only that, the Ovambo have tribal relations who live in Angola and Zaire. You've heard about that Ebola virus in Zaire. That's what stuffs up your brain."

That really frightened Jeff. He had most certainly heard of the Ebola virus one night on the TV back in Kal', for he came into the yard the next morning and accused everyone, including the boss, of having it. It was his pet subject for days. "I'm gunna go to the hospital," he announced.

"Bloody hell, I wouldn't go to a hospital in Africa!" I added my bit. "You'll get fuckin' AIDS! They'll go sticking dirty needles into you. Millions of people over here have got friggin' AIDS."

Dave felt sorry for him. "We're only pulling your leg, Jeff. You've only had 'em for less than a week. The crabs over here are the same as the crabs back in Aussie. They're a pain-in-the-arse, but, like I said, you can get cream that soon gets rid of 'em... Hey, bartender – another round of beers, cobber!"

Nick wasn't happy to release the topic, though. "You might've been kidding, Dave, but what you and Ernie said makes a lotta sense. Same as what you said about AIDS, Joe. You take that Ebola virus and AIDS... Dave, you reckoned that sheila Jeff knocked off could've come from up near Angola? I read in the NAMIBIAN newspaper that stacks of blackfellas are coming into the country from Angola 'cause of the civil war and bullshit up there. Now, if those blackfellas really have got some rellies who come from Zaire – where that Ebola virus is – Jeff could be really stuffed!"

"Ah – get fucked!" Jeff told him. "What would you know, ya fuckin' mutant?"

"No, *I am* being serious, Jeff," Nick was all wide-eyed innocence. "You think about it. You also think about it, too, Dave. Some blackfella up in Zaire fucks a chimpanzee or a monkey or something, and he picks up the virus. He then goes and fucks some Angolan sheila, who also gets the virus from him. She then goes into Namibia and some Namibian bloke knocks her off and also gets the virus. So what happens if the sheila Jeff knocked off was also fucked by the Namibian bloke who rooted the Angolan sheila?"

"Fuck me dead – this's getting complicated," Dave shook his head.

"Jeff was using a franger," I told Nick.

"Doesn't matter," Nick assured me. "Jeff's got crabs – right?"

"True," I agreed.

"Okay, now crabs drink your blood. If they're anything like mossies, they'll squirt stuff out of their guts before they start suckin' up your blood. AIDS lives in blood, so those crabs could be carrying both Ebola and AIDS. Rabies, too, if Dave's right about the Ovambos eating dogs. We'd better lock our doors when we go to crash 'cause if Jeff starts foaming at the mouth – he *might* fuckin' bite someone!"

Nick's theory must have had a lasting impact, for when it came to hitting the fart-sack, we all locked our doors and Jeff borrowed some Dettol from Ernie and poured a fair bit over his crutch and around his arse. He was up all night after that because the antiseptic burned the crap out of him! He scrubbed his balls with both hot and cold water; still he ended up with blisters on the most tender places possible, and the crabs were still hanging in there!

It was hilarious when Wheeler and I accompanied him to the chemist the following morning, as only two women were on the premises. A fat Boer and quite an attractive coloured girl. We left Jeff to do the talking, but he couldn't quite bring himself to say that he had crabs. What didn't help matters was that the two women hardly spoke a word of English. I went out to the vehicle and enlisted Kotzé's help and the Japie geo' rattled out something in Afrikaans that had both women blushing

38

and giggling with embarrassment. Jeff's face was a deep purple like the ointment he was given!

The same ointment looked like it had done some good, as we didn't see Jeff scratching his balls more than usual after that. Nick was the source of some further humour a couple of days later. It was during breakfast at the Sea Lion Hotel and we had the dining room to ourselves. The kitchen staff had lined up some tables so that the seven of us could be seated together, and he was sat opposite Jeff.

With his eyes almost bulging through the thick lenses of his glasses, Nick pointed his fork at Jeff, "You munched on her pussy, Jeff – you dirty – rotten – bastard!"

Jeff was caught totally off guard by that, "What the fuck you on about, ya fuckin' mutant?"

Nick leaned closer to him over the table, and then he nudged Steve Spence who was sitting on his right. "You've got crabs up your fuckin' nose! You must've chomped on that Ovambo sheila's snatch back in Windhoek!"

Steve took a closer look at Jeff and appeared to be of the same opinion: "Fuck me dead, Jeff! How could you – you fuckin' dirty – bloodthirsty – cannibal?"

Jeff quickly reamed out both his nostrils, but could find nothing sinister on his fingertip. "You get fucked, Nick, before I seriously mullet you," he warned. "Fuckin' same with you, Spence!"

"You won't dig 'em out like that," Wheeler decided to join in, "'cause after a while the fuckin' crabs really get their heads buried in deep. If you really did have a munch on that sheila's pussy – and you've got crabs up your nose – that could be really friggin' dangerous! Your nasal passages connect with your brain."

It was later on that day when we found out that Jeff certainly wasn't taking any chances, for there was a slight tinge of purple in both his nostrils. Nick was delighted by that, for he had been bullshitting him all the time!

CHAPTER 7

A SHAG FOR A BOTTLE OF WINE!
RACIST BOER BASTARD!
A CURE FOR AIDS! FEMALE CIRCUMCISION!

Realising that it would take a week or more to get the rig ready, Dave and I decided to do something constructive by getting Kotzé to show us the ground where the first part of the drilling program was to be carried out. Our two Land Cruisers hadn't suffered unduly from their three-week voyage, so we were mobile under our own company's steam once more. As it turned out the first gold-copper prospect wasn't far from Rehoboth, at a place adjacent to a defunct copper mine called Klein Aub. When we arrived in Rehoboth Kotzé recommended that we should stay the night at the government-run Rehoboth Spa, as there was no other accommodation available close to the project, bar possibly a couple of much more expensive game farms.

When we finally reached the prospect all sorts of strife broke loose. "You call this a fuckin' grid line?" Dave poured scorn all over the Boer geo'. "If you think I'm gunna take a rig through all this crap, you can get fucked!"

He had a point, for all Kotzé had in regard to drill sites were lines of six-inch steel pegs with aluminium tags wired to them. No clearing had been done; just thorn trees and bushes. Furthermore, the terrain was up and down and all over the place. There was no way we could move a 40-ton rig from site to site without wrecking something.

"It is not my concern," Kotzé was indignant. "All I have to do is show you where to start drilling and when you have drilled deep enough. What you do with the drilling rig is your blerrie business."

"Like fuck it is!" I joined in the conversation. "It's up to the client to clear the sites and level the ground. You'd better get your finger out, or the fuckin' rig's not coming out here."

"I shall have to ring up the company," Kotzé warned. "They will not like this one blerrie bit."

"And they can get fucked, too," Dave wasn't worried. "You should've read the contract, or can't you fuckin' read?"

We headed back to Rehoboth feeling quite good at having abused the Japie. The town probably wasn't one that a person would write home about, or be that proud of being conceived in. I saw the Saint Mary's Catholic hospital I was born in, the church, and the town hall that was named after some previous Baster kaptein by the name of Hermanus Van Wyk. The streets and thoroughfares were mostly loose gravel and sand, and dust wafted over the houses and shops whenever a vehicle went past. One of the most popular forms of transport amongst the Rehobothers were donkey carts; some powered by a single, emaciated animal; others pulled by two or three.

It was getting dark and Wheeler suggested we should get some beer to take back to the bungalow at the spa. Kotzé reckoned that we could get grog twenty-four hours a day in Rehoboth, as there were almost as many liquor outlets or '*drankwinkels*' in that town as could be found in the rest of the country put together. The one we pulled up in front of literally had a halo of drunks around it. People of all ages; adults and children, females and males. Some totally unconscious on the dusty ground outside the store; others inside the place; sitting on the floor or flaked out altogether. Jokers begging for money or to buy them booze surrounded us. There was even one old bag with no teeth, who offered us a bonk for one solitary bottle of Grenada wine! What I found depressing was that they were mostly coloureds like me; clothes in tatters, bodies stinking and dirty. I was pleased to get the hell away from there.

41

JOSEF SCHULTZ

The spa was an oasis amongst the dusty, sandy streets, humanity and the millions of dogs. They had an Olympic sized swimming pool, plus a fairly luxurious indoor spa pool; both fed from underground hot springs. Not wanting to get into the rigmarole of buying food and cooking in our bungalow, we decided to find a place to eat out, and Kotzé recommended we should try a resort that was on the banks of the Oanob Dam, which was about four or five miles from the centre of Rehoboth.

It was a pretty good idea. The resort was done out in huge thatch and camel thorn rondavels, and there was a nifty bar built of roughly-hewn, varnished timber which had a wagon wheel with bottles of spirits on it that the barman swung round to whichever bottle he required. Like in the outback of Western Australia, there was a late, golden red sunset that was fast fading in the peacock blue sky, but still allowing us to just see the dammed-up water below us. A cool breeze blew over the water and the ice-cold draught beer tasted like nectar. The waiter-cum-barman-cum-manager, a coloured, was ecstatic at our arrival and reckoned we could have a choice of chicken peri peri Portuguese-style, or curried lamb. Dave and I reckoned the curried lamb was just the shot, though Kotzé – being a real whinging bastard – reckoned he fancied neither, and that the lamb was probably some goat that had died of some disease or of old age. He asked if there was any steak, and when our host apologised most profusely that there was none, Dave and I heaped ridicule on the Japie and told him to make up his bloody mind; the lamb or the chicken? He most reluctantly settled for the chicken, but then told the waiter to have it well cooked because he didn't want food poisoning.

"You need to keep an eye on these guys over here when it comes to having your blerrie food handled," Kotzé informed us that loudly that everyone around our table could hear. "They wipe their bums with their hand and then they pick up your food. They have no idea what the word 'hygiene' means. It is all right for them, as they have got cast-iron constitutions." He then pointed out to the last of what we could see of the dam water. "The previous white government built this dam. The same with the roads, the bridges and the railways. I doubt if you shall see many more projects like these happening from now on, especially without foreign aid. Under white rule South Africa and South West Africa – as we knew Namibia then – suffered years of sanctions and built all these without a cent in handouts. You get the kaffirs taking over and they cannot achieve anything without overseas donations or soft loans. It has happened all over Africa and not one black country has made a success of things."

Wheeler had to disagree with that and his vast general knowledge came to the surface, "What about Botswana? That country's got more overseas financial reserves than any other country in the world. South Africa, even under you Boer bastards, never achieved that – even when you didn't have sanctions."

That didn't hassle Kotzé too much. "But who has created all their infrastructure? Botswana has some of the richest diamond pipes and base metal deposits in the world, but who blerrie found them – the blacks? No way, it was the whites. It was the whites like De Beers who invested the exploration dollars and developed the diamond mines. It was companies like Anglo American who found the base metals. When we come to the kaffir, all he knows is how to graze his goats, sheep and cattle and how to make children. The whites have done everything else for him. The hospitals, the inoculations for their cattle, the fertilisers and chemicals for their agriculture."

"Okay, so how did the whites achieve anything over here?" Dave's voice was all scorn. "It was only 'cause you had thousands upon thousands of black labourers who you paid sweet stuff all. You paid 'em a pittance to what you paid the average Boer arsehole, so without 'em you wouldn't have achieved a fraction of what other white-governed countries have."

"Ja, that could be so, but what do we have now? We have higher salaries for the blacks these days, but the money is going down the drain as a result of their incompetence. Especially with the inherent nepotism that goes on in Africa. It is costing five times as much to get five times as little done. When you . ."

"Perhaps if you'd given 'em a little bit of education and training?" Dave butted in. "With your Apartheid laws it didn't even enter your minds – did it?"

"That is also correct, though can you educate and train them? I have seen kaffirs given Doctorates and Masters' degrees at universities in Helsinki, Stockholm and Eastern Germany, and they have still come back knowing nothing. We used to call them *darkie* diplomas. They can learn things parrot-fashion, but can they apply their new-found learning? Can they think laterally? Name me one instance where a black has contributed to science or invented something? What about silicon chips, aeroplanes, or a humble steam engine? What about aspirins, X-RAY machines, or any kind of mechanical device? They went for centuries without the use of a wheel... Tell me, when have they ever been able to write down a historical account of themselves? It was only because they have learned from the whites that they have started taking notice of their past. Besides, you Australians are a pious, hypocritical bunch of people."

"Oh yeah?" Dave was all ears.

Kotzé leaned back in his chair grinning, and then he leaned forward and pointed a finger at Wheeler. "You and the other Australian do-gooders have so much to say about us Boers, but what about your aborigines? You also segregated them by dumping them on reserves that are some of the most inhospitable places on earth."

"At least we put 'em somewhere," Dave countered. "You wouldn't let the blacks settle anywhere. You just moved 'em on with your army, cops and bulldozers. You shifted 'em around from pillar to post and your actions were all contrived at having a handy labour force wherever it was most convenient to you. That way you could have workers on tap for the lowest wages possible."

The Boer was still looking much chuffed with himself. "Okay," he agreed. "We pushed the kaffirs around and denied them the vote. We denigrated them and refused to give them decent education. Our police murdered them in the police cells and we paid them little or nothing. But you Australians – you told the aboriginal people that they were not fit to be the parents of their children. You not only insulted them, you actually stole their children from them! Thousands of children stolen off their parents and forced into homes where you Christian, white do-gooders claimed you had a much better upbringing to offer them. What you had there is tantamount to racial genocide, the way you ripped a culture apart. We Boers can read newspapers, too, you know. All the evil of your ex-convict ancestors is coming home to roost, not so? How will you compensate those black families for that atrocity? Shall you be giving them some rights to their land, or are you going to pay them millions to make up for all the misery? We may have mistreated the kaffirs, still at least we refrained from robbing them of their children."

That hit Dave right between the eyes! He tried his best to recover, "Yeah, but that was in the past."

"Ja, I was expecting you to say that," the Japie knew he had kicked a goal. "You are also poking a finger at our past. South Africa and Namibia have been granted independence, and now the kaffirs are grabbing everything, regardless of the consequences. We tried to take their country off them and now the Asians are trying to take your country off of you. When they do succeed, how would you like them to steal your children? They might think you are also unfit as parents, what with your methyl amphetamine, homosexuality and pornography? So what are your feelings about that? We Boers also read books and international magazines. Take for instance the wonderful New Zealanders who live across the Tasman Sea from you good people. What about all the British and Maltese children that were sent over to New Zealand in order to find a better life? I read in an article how scores of these children had been molested and raped by good and loving New Zealand foster parents who lined up at the wharves to pick them out. It must have been like a meat market – I will take that little girl there – I prefer boys, so give me that little fellow there... Also, when it comes to real decadence, what about the gay and lesbian Mardi Gras' you people cherish so much in Perth and Sydney? You have virtually thousands of men and women who publicly advertise their perversion and the moral decline of your country. I understand that Sydney bears the rather dubious title of being the 'Homo Capital of the world'? A label that those who fought at Gallipoli must surely be proud of? To we humble Boers that sort of behaviour constitutes downright filth. Not only our Bible, but every Christian Bible warns everyone against such putrid human behaviour. Your society is obviously sinking into an abyss, yet you feel you are so superior to us... Let us take a look in our own back yards, gentlemen, before we start criticising others? Let us not have the pot calling the kettle black, and let us not have those people living in glass houses throwing stones? When it comes to amicable race relations, let us not forget your noble Tasmanian ancestors who formed a human chain across the island in order to displace the entire Tasmanian aboriginal population. We Boers may be condemned for our brutal Apartheid regime, but at least we did not attempt to destroy entire tribes. We fought wars against the Zulu, Xhosa and various other Bantu tribes, yet there are still millions left today. Too many, in fact. No, I suggest that you take a much closer look..."

He fell silent when the waiter brought our meals. A wine list was put in front of me and I handed it to the Boer. He in turn ordered a bottle of South African pinotage that wasn't half bad.

"And, gentlemen, let us see what benefits the kaffirs have received with their new-found independence?" Kotzé continued his diatribe. "Look at what the wonderful, Christian Americans donated to them? Pornography and filth on the television and in magazines. Hustler, Playboy and Penthouse magazines and suchlike were banned in both this country and South Africa because we were nervous about blacks seeing naked white women. I am sure that might sound very puerile to you, nevertheless let us examine all this fine American culture? What have they given the blacks – sex, violence, filthy language, homosexuality, drugs and same-sex marriages. All these wonderful things that you Australians have injected into your own culture long ago as you followed the Americans like so many sheep. The way I see it, at least a third of the American TV programs promote lesbianism and homosexuality, and these same programs attract some of the highest ratings with the audiences. It is the same with Australian television, too, not so?"

Wheeler's reply took me completely by surprise, "Well, at least we agree on one thing, mate, the world's being taken over by fuckin' poofters and lesbians."

"Ja, it seems to be so," Kotzé looked pleased to have found some common ground. "Now God is starting to interfere at long last."

Dave didn't seem so sure with that one, "How do you mean?"

"AIDS!" the Japie was triumphant. "It is killing people by the thousands, and it is God's way of wiping out this sordid nonsense. We are seeing..."

"Hang on a sec'," Dave cut him off, "there's a helluva lot of innocent kids and people getting caught up with AIDS. You can't..."

"Ja, but look at the prime movers of this disease," the Boer interrupted him back. "The homosexuals, prostitutes and perverts – the initial carriers of the virus. Innocent people have been tragically caught up via blood transfusions and so on, and countless unborn children – I agree – but this AIDS is the product of societies that have sunk into oblivion. I read in some scientific journal that AIDS amongst the San Francisco homosexuals was traced back to Haiti. White homos were travelling on junkets there, where these good American men could get sex with young Haitian black boys. I suppose it is the same with those Australian and New Zealand pederasts that go to Thailand and the Philippines to seek out young Asian boys? I have heard the Australian diplomatic services are full of paedophiles. Do you not see – AIDS is a plague that was born out of perversion?"

"You're oversimplifying things," Dave argued.

"Ja, I agree again – of course I am, so let us examine the fundamentals of all this. AIDS is the product of promiscuity and perversion. In white countries like America you have outright perversion, for we see on American television that homosexuality, lesbianism and sheer and utter filth is promoted. It is not only promoted by television, but also by Hollywood. You take for instance that Australian actor who was in that homo cowboy film. It is getting that way that I need to turn off the television whenever my young son comes into the lounge room. We are being literally bombarded by American filth at all times of the day or night. Look at all that garbage that is being dispensed by the good Yankees during their lunchtime shows. That Jerry Springer show for example. Utter garbage filled with total losers who do not seem to have the slightest vestige of pride or morality."

"Yeah, but what did you Boers have during Apartheid?" Wheeler jabbed back. "You people had such strict censorship laws, you wouldn't've had a clue of what crap your government was getting up to. They kept you in the bloody dark like mushrooms."

"Ja, you are right. During the Apartheid Era we had almost total censorship of our television programs and newspapers. Admittedly it was one way of keeping both the black and whites in the dark, but look at what that television censorship protected the whites and our children from... The kaffirs as well... The sexual filth and perversion, plus the foul language and the total degradation that comes with so-called modern society that the Americans and you Australians seem to keep so close to your hearts... Now – as I was saying – this AIDS business is the direct product of perversion and promiscuity. In Africa, amongst the blacks, there is the promiscuity. The kaffir in general has no moral principles whatsoever, and he will mate with anything, whether it is human or animal. Seriously now, I have recently read in a South African newspaper that some female race horses were raped by some black stable boys... Okay, so the principal prime movers of AIDS are persons who have no moral standards whatsoever. The blacks prove this beyond all doubt, nevertheless I see how some are dutifully and deliberately carrying out God's work other than by their rampant sexual activities."

"And how's that?" Wheeler seemed intrigued.

"It is quite straightforward, really. AIDS is cutting down the kaffirs at every level. Government ministers, so-called black entrepreneurs and the humble bush types are dying like so many flies. AIDS is certainly not discriminating, while on the other hand the disease is being assisted in the most able fashion by the black governments themselves. You take for instance how the blacks in government in South Africa – the ANC – are claiming that AIDS is not the direct consequence of the HIV virus. What is more, the ANC government is refusing to give the blacks free anti-retroviral medicines that can hinder the passage of HIV from mother to child. This is all propounding the slaughter, gentlemen. I believe that there is some cold, solid, logical reasoning behind the ANC's thinking. South Africa has almost fifty percent unemployment, despite their new-found independence. Good old Nelson may have captivated the hearts of all and sundry around the world, but his so-called magic has not created any outstanding employment opportunities for the teeming thousands of unemployed. The average black is no better off. We do know…"

"What the fuck's that gotta do with AIDS?" Dave insisted.

"Okay, please let me explain. The concept of independence is simply great for those in government, plus their favourites. These blacks shall make billions out of independence through robbery and deceit, just like our corrupt white politicians did during Apartheid. But the fifty percent unemployed are a bit of a hassle to all this new-found freedom and fun, are they not? From this sector comes the crime and disillusionment, and this in turn can only be followed by rioting and civil unrest. We have the perfect formula for future civil war and gallons of bloodshed like we have had in Angola, Liberia, Zaire, Mozambique and countless other black-governed countries on this continent. Such civil war can knock these government thieves and criminals off their lucrative perches… So, what do we have, gentlemen?"

"You were gunna tell us," Dave reminded him. "You're only going around in circles talkin' shit."

"I am not, and you should see this in the near future. The ANC government is deliberately enhancing the spread of AIDS. Instead of handing out anti-retroviral drugs, we have the Health Minister – the Right Honourable Manto Tshabalala-Msimang – insisting that garlic, lemons and a certain species of African potato can cure HIV. So which tree has she just climbed down from? In her government they have a united front against any logical solutions to the pandemic, so I believe the ANC is deliberately facilitating the spread of AIDS in the hope that the unemployed will literally die out."

"What a load of fuckin' crap!" Dave was all derision.

"Is that so?" Kotzé stared at him in mock despair. "It is an age-old, African solution to an African problem. If there are people in the way – kill them, starve them, or destroy them with famine and disease. It has been their method for centuries. Look at Rwanda, Dafur in the Sudan, and take for example the millions of people that have been slaughtered in Angola, Zaire and Sierra Leone. And I mean *millions*, gentlemen, and only in the last few years. The ANC government has millions of unemployed, so why not kill them? Killing millions of people with AIDS is quite subtle when you come to think of it. It would cause far less shock and horror than the methods employed by the kaffirs in Sierra Leone where they cut off limbs, enslaved and raped children, plus burned people alive in their mud huts. Perhaps we should admire the ANC government for their forward vision, as it is very unusual for a kaffir to take the future into consideration? They have come across an ideal solution for a problem that must come to haunt them some time in the near future... The trouble is that the tragedy is more far-reaching in countries such as South Africa, Namibia and most countries south of the Sahara. The skilled blacks are earning much more reasonable salaries, and that is fair enough. Those people with some genuine talent are getting ahead, but it is the same people who are getting the worst hit. With more money they can afford to be promiscuous. The men have no trouble in seducing the women from poorer families with their new-found wealth and affluent possessions, thus AIDS is penetrating the more important echelons of black society. It is the worthwhile blacks that are being struck down and there is no one ready to take their place, so the business and technical sectors are suffering... To summarise, gentlemen, we are going to end up with a terrible hiatus – the skilled kaffirs are being wiped out by AIDS, and corruption and nepotism are burying the opportunities that should be coming the way of the younger generation. You wait and see – the speed with which chaos will arrive in places such as Namibia and South Africa can only be tenfold when their governments – like the government of Zimbabwe – decide not to bother with concealing their incompetence and daylight robbery... Then, Gentlemen, there is another thing."

"And what's that?" I spoke up for Dave, who looked as if he had had a gutsful.

The Boer filled up our wine glasses. "We have certain tribal doctors both here and in South Africa, who – like our good minister Madame Tshabalala-Msimang – also believe that they have a cure for AIDS. By doctors I mean witchdoctors, of course. Most kaffirs in Africa still believe in their magical powers. All the same, these good doctors have come up with a remarkable prescription for the cure of HIV or AIDS. When I say remarkable, *it is* when you consider it involves raping babies and two-year-old infants. The younger the..."

"Ah – bullshit!" I told him. "Now you're really..."

"No, Joe, it's fair dinkum," Wheeler stopped me. "Some black bastards over here reckon you can cure AIDS if you have sex with a virgin. The newspapers over here are full of it."

"Ja!" Kotzé looked overjoyed, "And the younger the better! Virgins amongst the black women are as scarce as rocking horse manure, therefore the blacks take the extra precaution of raping infants. Even two month old babies! Every second day the police are coming across infants that have been ravaged by kaffirs. If you do not find that sufficiently debased, infants and children over here are considered excellent components for the manufacture of medicine with our good kaffir doctors. They make what they call *'muti'* out of them. I hear that a child's liver, heart or kidney is excellent for virility or a cure for the common cold. That a slice of an infant's brain is very good for raising one's IQ. Then, of course, there is the infant blood for health tonics and power potions... And that, gentlemen, is not bringing to your attention female circumcision."

"Female circumcision?" I looked at both Dave and Kotzé. "I didn't know women were circumcised? I thought it was only blokes?"

The Boer geo' just laughed. "That may be in Australia, but on this continent it is endemic. That is our wonderful kaffir for you. You go to places like Kenya and..."

"He's kidding?" I sought assurance from Wheeler.

"No, cobber, you get some tribes that cut out their women's clitorises so that they don't get any pleasure out of a shag."

"That's fuckin' sick!" I told him. "What a bunch of bloody queer bastards!"

While Dave looked rather forlorn, Kotzé was beaming. "Ja, I could not describe it better myself. In many places in Africa female mutilation is rife. As I was about to say – you go to Kenya for instance. Female circumcision is common practice amongst the tribes there, and you are getting the kaffir men chasing after Ugandan women since their own women are too dull in bed. Do you see the farce in all this? They cut out their own women's clitorises, and then they seek sexual pleasure from women who *have not* been mutilated? Now, David, you tell me what that says about our gracious kaffir? He forces his own tribal women to have their clitorises cut out, and then he pursues other tribal women because he finds them more sexually satisfying"

Wheeler pushed his plate to one side and lit a smoke. "You're making it sound. . ?"

The conversation was cancelled abruptly when a coloured bloke, possibly in his late twenties, came up to our table. He started jabbering away at me in Afrikaans.

"I only speak English," I told him, putting my hands up in mock surrender. That really seemed to piss the bloke right off!

Kotzé stepped in, "He says he knows you and your name is Jonker Witbooi. He wants to know what you are doing back in Rehoboth and why you are talking to Boers?"

"Tell him he must be mistaken."

The Japie rattled off something in Afrikaans that made the coloured joker even more agitated. He then reverted to fairly good English and told me I was fockin' – he pronounced 'fuck' – 'fock' – stupid for being back in Rehoboth and that I was about to be caught. By whom he didn't mention.

"Join us for a beer?" Dave suggested to him, but he was having none of it. He went over and joined another table-load of coloureds and they all sat there drinking grog and scowling at me.

"They've friggin' got their wires crossed," I told my companions, feeling it wouldn't be a bad idea banging some of their coloured heads together.

CHAPTER 8

YANKS MAKE DICKHEADS OUT OF THEMSELVES! ROBERT MUGABE IDENTICAL TO RWANDAN GORILLA!

Wheeler's cursing and muttering in the kitchen of our bungalow woke me: "You bloody useless cunts! You fuckin – dickheaded – sick bastards!"

"What you on about!" I asked.

"The fuckin' dirty – fuckin' Yanks!" He held up a *DAILY MAIL & GUARDIAN* newspaper. "Take a look at this. The flamin' Yanks've been torturing the Iraqis and they've been fuckin' sprung!"

He wasn't kidding! The first picture I saw was of some poor joker with a hood over his head with kind of robes on. He was standing on a box with wires attached to his hands and neck. Apparently, if he fell off the box, he would have been electrocuted!

"Look at that fuckin' – dirty – poxy slut!" he pointed at a photo of some female soldier with a smoke in her mouth pointing her finger at an Iraqi bloke's naked crutch. "Typical Yank trash!"

The newspaper article covering the Americans' treatment of Iraqis at the infamous Abu Ghraib prison had a great deal more that troubled him. There was another photo of the same female soldier holding on to a leash that was around another Iraqi's neck as the poor bastard was lying on the floor. There was a further female soldier grinning like an idiot and bending over a corpse. There were blood, bodies and shit everywhere!

BASTARDS FROM THE BUSH

The photos could only be described as disgusting, and they adequately fuelled Wheeler's total dislike for Americans. "This's the fuckin' god almighty Yank for you. And they reckon they're gunna export democracy and fuckin' human rights to the Middle East? As usual, they've fucked things up, same as they did in Viet Nam. You want something fucked up and the friggin' Yanks'll fuck it up. Seriously, what a *stupid* bunch of dickheaded arseholes? What sort of credibility do they reckon this's given the coalition forces now? And we've got Aussie diggers over there? Look at the way they're using women to humiliate those Iraqi men? No wonder the bloody Trade Centre got blown away? When you see this, it's obvious that we're looking at a sick, perverted society, and you had that fuckin' Boer bastard carrying on about the blacks last night? What difference is there between the Yanks and the African blackfellas?"

I decided to pour petrol on his fire, "What do you reckon old Johnny Howard thinks about all this?"

"Johnny – fuckin' – Howard? He's got his head buried so far up the Yanks' arses, you can only just see the heels of his boots. We may need the Yanks to keep the slopes' out, but do we have to be degraded by the bastards? I bloody tell you, Joe, if..."

We were disturbed by the Japie geo' surfacing. "Ah, so you bought the paper? I was not aware that they sold this one in Rehoboth. The Baster mostly read the Afrikaans papers... Aiee – yi – yi – look at this! What the blerrie hell have the Americans been up to?"

Wheeler pounced, "Yeah, and you reckon the blacks are bad?"

"This is sickening," Kotzé's huge forehead compressed. "These Americans have played right into the Arab terrorists' hands. This makes fantastic propaganda for that Osama Bin Laden, so now you shall have thousands wanting to join his cause. Look at these American women soldiers here. This can only destroy any goodwill they might have had with the Iraqis. I wonder what the rest of the coalition soldiers think? What kind of officers have the American military got? You are right, David, the Americans are behaving no better than our kaffirs over here."

JOSEF SCHULTZ

The Boer found another picture in the newspaper that captured his attention. It was a photo of Zimbabwe's president, Robert Mugabe. He asked no one in particular, "Who was that guy that said there was a gap amongst gorillas, monkeys and humans? There was a place in Australia named after him?"

"Darwin?" Wheeler suggested.

"Ja, that is the guy. Darwin was his name. I tell you – he was wrong, man."

"How come?" I asked.

The Japie looked at both Dave and I and shook his head sadly. "It is easy, man. Darwin said there was some kind of gap between gorillas and humans. A missing gap."

"Missing link, you mean?" Dave corrected him.

"Ja, that is it – missing link!"

By that time I was fairly interested. "So? Fuckin' get on with it."

He nodded. "This Darwin fellow was wrong, as he said there was some kind of a missing link. You look at Mugabe's picture here, man. There is no missing link. Mugabe has more ape in him than human. Just look at his face from his nose downwards and the size of his forehead. Look at the shape of his skull and his eyes. Look at his upper lip. How can there be a missing link when you find creatures like Mugabe right in the middle? You see the same animals in the jungles around here and elsewhere throughout Africa. You take for instance the gorillas in Rwanda. I've seen several kaffirs very similar to them. Mugabe's head is an almost exact replica of that of a Rwandan gorilla... No seriously, man, you had that Professor Leakey in Kenya, plus scientists in Ethiopia, looking at skeletons that are thousands of years old. They keep saying that they have found the bones of the first human. All they need to do is go to Zimbabwe and study Mugabe. They will find an ape who wears clothes. The man's grandfather was a Rwandan gorilla."

I had a closer look at the photo. Robert Mugabe most certainly resembled a gorilla that I had seen back in the Perth Zoo.

BASTARDS FROM THE BUSH

"Have you seen what this idiot has done?" the Boer continued his vilification of Zimbabwe's president. "He and his thieving scum have stolen the farms off the whites and now we have famine and millions are starving. Those kaffirs took over the farms and all the machinery that was in perfect working condition. If there is one thing you can really trust about a kaffir is that he breaks or totally wrecks anything you put in his hands. Zimbabwe used to export thousands of tons of cereals. It used to be called the 'bread basket' of southern Africa, but now they have a shortfall of hundreds of thousands of tons and half the population are starving."

"And it's got fuck-all to do with the drought they're having up there?" Dave poked at him.

"Ja, of course the drought is causing untold hardship. I had an uncle who was farming in Zimbabwe for many years, but he is dead now. Even in the worst droughts the country could at least feed its own people. Now Zimbabwe has to import grain, but the Mugabe government has bankrupted the country and the aid organisations have had to step in. It simply goes to show you what happens when you give a country to kaffirs to run. Look what it says here – they do not even have the seeds to plant. Even if the farmers can get a crop out of the ground, do they need to give it away for free? With seventy percent unemployment, therefore a similar amount living below the poverty line – plus six hundred percent inflation – who can afford to purchase what the farmers *do* produce? In the old days before the whites came along, if a kaffir or his village ran out of food, he had no hesitation when it came to raiding the village closest to him. And I am not mentioning that he would most probably kill his neighbour and rape his neighbour's wife and daughters in order to keep things interesting. The way Mugabe and his thugs in government are carrying on, it only highlights the fact that the whites have had zero influence on the kaffirs after all these years."

"Stop talking a load of shit," Wheeler told him. "The whites exploited the blacks in the past and they're flamin' exploiting the poor bastards as we speak."

That appeared to astound the Boer. "What on earth are you talking about? Nearly every kaffir country south of the Sahara would have gone down the plughole if it were not for the assistance and aid being donated by white-governed countries, or possibly people such as the Chinese and Japanese."

"Bullshit!" Dave was resolute. He had had about four breakfast beers and was really starting to loosen up. "Take the fuckin' Yanks and the EEC with their fuckin' agricultural subsidies. There wouldn't be a farmer on this continent that could compete with those. What're the bloody Yanks and the European Community really doing for the people over here? Okay, so they're putting in the odd bit of cash here and there, plus food aid and so on, but their trade practises are crippling the economies of most African countries. Furthermore, they're plundering Africa's natural resources for a pittance of what they could be worth. There are no secondary industries being created in Africa 'cause the Europeans and the Yanks've kept 'em all for themselves. It's just sheer, bloody-minded, white greed. Admittedly you've got poverty and misery over here 'cause some black bastards are running the place, but you've got people such as the Yanks and the EEC manipulating everything to their advantage. They're giving in one hand and then taking back double with the other. You tell me where the blacks are getting any sort of a level playing field when it comes to trade and commerce."

"Ja, okay, so does that mean that the kaffirs are totally blameless? If you want secondary industries, you need people to put in the investment monies required, and most of that money has to come from overseas because most black countries are bankrupt. Who could possibly want to invest in Africa if a coup or civil war can destroy your assets in the twinkling of an eye? Are you trying to say that the kaffirs are totally innocent of their corrupt and murdering ways? Do you exonerate their tribalism, civil wars and all the bloodshed? Do you condone their..."

"Go and get fucked!" Dave had grown tired of his constant yapping.

CHAPTER 9

THIEVES IN THE WINDHOEK MANSION! NICK TRIES TO SHAG ONE OF THE SERVANT GIRLS!

Wheeler and I decided to head for Windhoek so that he could phone Ernie to see how the rig was going. Kotzé followed us in his Land Rover. There was no sign of the maids at the Windhoek mansion, although the refrigerator had been emptied of all the beer we had left there, and our entire supplies of coffee, tea, sugar and non-perishable food had disappeared. There was no evidence that the house had been broken into or anything.

The Boer was fairly spewing about it. "This is blerrie typical! If you do not lock everything away, the blerrie kaffirs steal it."

I had noticed that there was a lock on the refrigerator door; a phenomenon I had never encountered back in Aussie. "Is that why they have locks on the fridges?" I asked him

"Ja, we need to have locks on everything. Also, just because the house is empty, they go sneaking back to the township to breed more kids. I am going to sack them right away."

"What for?" Dave scoffed. "The house's tidy and they've only taken a bit of coffee and some tea. Back in Oz most employers supply their workers with coffee and tea."

Kotzé wasn't placated. "You were away only a couple of days and I purchased enough provisions to supply ten men for a month. They have blerrie looted the place. I had better check all the sheets, towels and blankets. I suggest you check what clothing you and the others left behind. Check on how many odd socks you have. When you chuck out an odd sock, those kaffir bitches will end up with a full pair back at their house. There is massive unemployment in this country, and those bitches were delighted that I had hired them because – *believe me* – I had hundreds of applicants. So then what happens? I give them work and they turn round and steal everything they can lay their hands on. With all you people being away there was very little for them to do, still they cannot resist stealing from you. I tell you, man, it is inherent in the kaffirs' genes."

The Japie proved to be a prophet; when I checked through my gear I indeed had three odd socks. A shirt, a pair of underdaks and a leather belt were also missing. I probably wouldn't have noticed if he hadn't of told me to check my cases, and I was little pissed off about it.

Wheeler managed to get through to Ernie at Du Preez and Seun's workshop. The little mechanic had few problems in life, for the rig was coming along just fine. It appeared that Steve Spence had recovered from the kick in the nuts Nick gave him, as he had managed to get a shag from the blonde manageress of the Sea Lion Hotel. Apparently the blokes had been barred from the Blue Mermaid Hotel, since Jeff – in his wisdom – pissed all over the floor in the bar and gave the fat Japie proprietor a hefty backhand for complaining about it! Typical Jeffry Panizza-style methodology that I had seen utilised in countless outback pubs in West Aussie. As it turned out the proprietor *did* actually have a brother in the Namibian police force, and that individual warned Jeff and the others never to put a foot in his brother's establishment again. Nick, Steve Spence and the others didn't object too much about being forbidden the dubious charms of the Blue Mermaid, and they reckoned that Jeff giving the proprietor a good smack across the mouth was an excellent ploy when it came to promoting cordial Australian public relations in the seaside town of Walvis Bay.

Wheeler suggested that Jeff's obnoxious behaviour was the product of his jealousy about Spence shagging the manageress. There was some logic to his assumption, as the thought of having a tumble with her in the cot was an enticing one. It clearly showed that Jeff didn't require Dave's or my assistance when it came to making his way through everyday life. In fact Dave went on to tell me that he was reassured that the plane trip to Namibia obviously hadn't had any real effect on Jeff's behavioural patterns whatsoever, and such constants in our troubled world had an excellent effect on morale. Some time had elapsed since Jeff had assaulted a publican, therefore the planet was keeping the same distance from the sun and all in the universe was just fine!

As far as the maids went, the Japie geo' went ahead and tramped them. There wasn't much Dave or I could do about it since the boss back in Kalgoorlie went along with his decision. Kotzé had very little trouble replacing them, as hundreds of women of all descriptions arrived at the house, eager for employment at half the expense that it had cost previously; thus adequately displaying the fact that Namibia undeniably had a chronic unemployment problem.

Nick wanted to have his filthy way with one of the new employees; gone was his shyness when it came to being introduced to domestics. Although the girl seemed quite keen to accommodate him, the Japie geo' forbade such a lurid proposition, and a fair argument broke out over who was in charge of the servants; our drilling outfit or our client's company?

CHAPTER 10

JEFF TANGLES WITH A BOER!

Ernie finally got the rig reassembled and we had it, the support truck and everything parked outside the front of our house in Klein Windhoek. That in itself caused quite a stir considering there was a huge Boer who lived across Nelson Mandela Avenue from us, and he objected to having such paraphernalia cluttering up 'his' street. His spouse, a lean, mangy looking bitch with a moustache, agreed with him wholeheartedly. Most unfortunately for them, they met Jeff first, and on hearing their complaints, he told the Boer to get fucked and for his fucking missus to do likewise!

The Boer was probably quite justifiably infuriated and was rolling up his sleeves when Nick, Kotzé and I pitched up on the scene, and then there was a fairly in-depth conversation in Afrikaans between Kotzé and the Boer who was busy shaking his fist at Jeff.

"Speak English – ya fuckin' mutants!" Jeff insisted. He really loved calling people 'mutants' and that didn't help the situation in any meaningful way.

That upset Kotzé as much as it did the Boer and his wife. "I have had enough of your foul language, bad manners and arrogance. Either apologise, or these people shall call the police. They have a legitimate complaint, as this is no place to leave all this machinery."

"Apologise – be stuffed – Jeff!" Wheeler had come along by then and had picked up on what was going on. He pointed to the Boer and said to Kotzé, "He's the one who's the fuckin' arrogant bastard. The friggin' gear's on our side of the road and isn't blocking his way or anything. He doesn't own the fuckin' road." He turned to the Boer and his wife. "Haven't you got anything better to do with your time 'cept coming over here with all your bullshit? Now – piss-off!"

The Boer looked as if he was about to have a go at Dave, although when Nick and I edged closer, he changed his mind. He didn't let things go at that because about ten minutes later a cop car arrived; it must have been just round the corner. It pulled up in front of the Boer's house and two black cops got out and stood at his gate. They weren't game to go into his yard, all the same, for there were two massive Rottweilers that had obviously been trained to hate darkies of any description; howling and barking their total dislike for those guardians of the law. Then at last the Boer and his missus came to the gate and there was a bit of a confab before they followed the cops across the street in our mob's direction.

"What do you want now?" Dave tried to look very frustrated.

One of the police blokes, who looked as if he was really unhappy about being caught up in an argument among whites, opened the dialogue for their party, "And, *Meneers*, what is happening with you?"

Wheeler, as usual, was the first to speak, "We've just brought this gear from Walvis Bay. It's been here less than one hour and we'll be shifting it to Rehoboth in about one hour's time. Can you please tell that to this Japie idiot?"

I noticed a flicker of amusement in the black cop's eyes; still he kept his face like a statue. "And where are you from?"

"Australia."

"Australia?" The cop pronounced it 'Orstraalie'. "I see! So you are moving all this soon?"

"Yeah."

The cop then turned to me. "I have seen you somewhere before. Where do you come from? Are you working for these Orstraalians?"

"Not for them, but with them, cobber. I'm also from Australia."

He shook his head. "I do not think so. You come from around here. Where is your passport?"

"Here," I undid the button of my top pocket and removed my passport. I opened it at the relevant page so that he could see my photo in it.

"Ah, but I see that you were born in Namibia?"

"Many years ago. I've lived in Australia ever since."

"Can you give me any further proof of that?"

I pointed to the Aussies around me. "Ask them?"

That seemed to satisfy the man. "Very well, I can see no problem."

"But these people swore at us," the Boer's wife tried to keep things going, the dopey dog.

The cop nodded. "Please, Meestah," he beseeched Dave, "we Namibians are a peaceful people, so please do not use bad words with others."

It all ended there, bar the Boer couple wandering off; muttering how law and order had completely broken down in Namibia, and Jeff having a last poke at Kotzé: "What did you want me to apologise for? Where's your fuckin' guts?"

Kotzé had no answer for him. As it turned out he had had quite a shit of a day. When Ernie turned up with the rig and heard what Dave had to say about the drill sites, he got stuck into the Japie right away. "Read the friggin' thing!" he shook some papers under Kotzé's nose. "The contract states quite clearly that the client's responsible for putting in adequate fuckin' drill roads."

That was where Kotzé proved beyond all doubt what a stubborn, stupid drongo he could be. Not only did he refuse to read the wad of papers that the little mechanic held out to him, he also insisted on phoning the client's company headquarters in Vancouver, Canada. The managing director of that company reckoned he hadn't seen such a contract, either, so he then phoned the boss back in Kalgoorlie and claimed that he didn't have anything to do with drilling condition contracts, but left that in the hands of the company's geologists or consulting geologists. Our employer then phoned Ernie and stated point-blank that he had a copy of the same contract right in front of him, signed by some bastard by the name of 'Kootzee', and that the contract covered the site requirements in black and white. Ernie then told the boss that he had the so-called 'Kootzee' right in front of him, and the arsehole had refused to read a copy of the contract he had. The boss then called Vancouver and he and the company's managing director both agreed that this 'Kootzee' must be an unadulterated dickhead. The managing director then phoned the Boer geo' directly and threatened to tramp him there and then for being a 'damned fool'. To add to the Japie's woes, Ernie claimed that once we had reached Rehoboth we would be all set to drill, so he had better get his finger out and arrange a bulldozer or something for the sites, as the rig would be on stand-down rates of five thousand Australian bucks a day. That equated to being about nineteen thousand Namibian dollars, which shook the poor Boer bastard even further!

CHAPTER 11

TENTS & PIT LATRINES!

A couple of hours later we were booked into the Rehoboth Spa with the rig and the other vehicles tucked safely behind that establishment's eight foot high, cyclone fence. Having moved such massive gear through the town we attracted a fair amount of curiosity from the townsfolk and we were almost immediately inundated by requests for employment by a myriad of black and coloured jokers. To our amazement we discovered that we could hire a cook, someone to do our laundry, or a labourer for less than five bucks Aussie a day. There was no way that we could knock an opportunity like that back, and there was bloody near a riot when it came to picking out some workers. In the end we put all their names on bits of paper and drew four out of a driller's hard hat, so we got a fair mix of them: An Ovambo, a Nama and two Rehoboth Baster. We then told our new recruits that they should come back in a couple of day's time with a swag, knives, forks, spoons and plates, and they were over the moon when they heard that the tucker was being supplied for free. Ernie was also pleased, for we were abiding by what the boss had promised the Namibian Home Affairs Department; we were hiring locals and we would be training them to do at least something or other.

Kotzé was anti everything we did. "You should have told me that you might be putting people on the payroll. These Rehoboth Baster will rob you out of house and home. They steal anything which is not bolted down or cast in concrete."

Ernie changed the subject, "The contract says the client has to supply the accommodation. We can't go driving backwards and forwards from here to the site every day. It's too bloody far."

"There will be some tents available," Kotzé informed him.

"Tents?" Jeff was incredulous. "We're not sleeping in fuckin' tents! You Japies uncivilised or something? We gave up using tents in Aussie fuckin' years ago."

The Boer geo' agreed with him on that, yet reckoned he had scoured Windhoek for caravans and had come up with not a solitary one that was for hire. Nor could he rent one of those chemical shithouses, so we would need to use pit latrines with quick lime.

We went back to the Oanob Dam resort for dinner and it was much lighter when we got there that time. The manager-waiter-bartender etceteras was overjoyed to see Dave and I, especially since we had brought five extra clients. Kotzé had gone home to Windhoek for the night. As it turned out one of the coloured blokes, whom we had agreed to employ, came by; he had been fishing on the dam wall. We invited him to join us and he spoke pretty good English. His name was Wilfred and he kept staring in my direction, and looking as if he wanted to ask me something.

Finally I had a go at him, "What's up with you, mate? Yeah – I am a coloured, and yeah – I was born in Rehoboth at the Catholic hospital, but I've been living in Australia for years."

He didn't look all that convinced, though he went along with things as if he might have believed me. When Dave told him we were drilling near the old Klein Aub Mine he reckoned his uncle had a farm not far from there and that the drought was taking a shocking toll on all the farmers around Rehoboth. Many of the farmers, when the grazing had run out even on the sides of the main roads, had had to sell their cattle and sheep to the South Africans for rock-bottom prices and were left with only their goats which had turned the countryside into a desert.

Wilfred gave us a fair insight into the local politics of the Rehoboth Baster. Some many decades before, he wasn't absolutely sure when, apparently the German, Emperor Kaiser Wilhelm I, signed some kind of a deal with a Baster kaptein, and had given the Baster their own reserve of land or '*gebeid*' where the people enjoyed a certain amount of autonomy. Only the Baster had authority to live there, to own farms there, and to use the special town lands laid out to the south of Rehoboth. Now the place was being invaded by all comers; especially the Ovambo who had set up a squatter's camp on the outskirts of the town, and it was their goats that had overgrazed the town lands. The modern Baster still had a kaptein, who had led the people in a peaceful revolt against this invasion; however the new government, made up of mostly Ovambo, had sent heavily armed soldiers to the town and the current Baster kaptein had been forced from his house that overlooked Rehoboth. He had had to live from then on right inside the town; on the flat part with the other common people.

He probably had more to tell that evening, but he almost fell apart with panic when the coloured bloke, who had challenged me the previous time I was at the resort, pitched up on the scene and sat with some other coloureds at another table not far from ours. The little bloke hastily excused himself and was gone like a shot, leaving our party under the hostile eyes of the coloured and his cronies.

I looked around at Nick, Jeff and the others and thought of mounting a challenge of my own, but Dave could read my thoughts. "Calm down, Joe," he warned. "Those jokers'll have thousands of mates around the place and we'll get fuckin' massacred. Like you said the other night, they've more than likely got their flamin' wires crossed and are mistaking you for someone else. I'm fucked if I can see why, though, you've gotta be one of the ugliest bastards God ever put breath into."

CHAPTER 12

NICK & JEFF THREATEN TO SHAG ERNIE!

At long last we had the drill rig on site and there was a real hive of activity going on as we set up camp. We had twenty thousand metres of drilling to do, so we would be staying there for a fair stretch. Kotzé had brought a white field assistant with him, plus a couple of coloured sample monkeys from Windhoek. He immediately started to piss us off with his camp regulations and whatever. First off, he had grudgingly agreed to supply our labourers with a tent, but then he insisted that all the non-whites should set up their camp well out of sight from the whites' accommodations. Also, that the non-whites must have their own shithouse and that they would look after the shithouse being used by the whites. If that wasn't enough, the non-whites should be strictly rationed when it came to their tucker, as they were blerrie lucky to be getting it for free and there was every likelihood that they were capable of eating us out of house and home if given the slightest opportunity. The latter was bullshit, for we drillers had all agreed to pick up the cost of our labourers' tucker. It was only going to cost a couple of bucks Aussie per labourer per day. The field assistant, Hennie Van der Merwe, an emaciated sort of a Boer prick who wore no socks with his shoes, was all in agreement with his boss. There was no way he was sleeping next to kaffirs or coloureds.

It was noticeable that Wheeler had acquired a dislike to Boers of all descriptions, and he wasn't backward when it came to advertising it:

"And who the fuck do you reckon you are?" he asked the skinny Boer. "Where I come from, mate, field assistants are fuck all. What makes you think I want to sleep anywhere near you? Our labourers can sleep wherever they fuckin' feel like it."

Our tents weren't bad. They were of the round 'Bell' variety and could easily accommodate three camp beds with plenty of room to spare. The portions of the tents that reached the ground could be tied up; thus allowing any breeze that came along to cool things down. Two of the tents had to be shared by drill crews, so I had to put up with Jeff and Nick in mine. Dave had to do likewise with his offsiders. Kotzé shared another tent with his field assistant, while Ernie had insisted on having one to himself; the pompous, little poofter. Nick tried to make out that he was convinced that the reason the little mechanic wanted to sleep alone was so that he could wank himself all night without anybody hearing him. For some reason Ernie took offence to such a slur and reckoned that Nick was to be in charge of keeping the camp free of rubbish, so Nick told him that he could do something to himself that was physically and biologically impossible, and several times at that!

The shithouses were dug about a hundred metres from the camp in opposite directions. It appeared that the non-whites didn't want to shit next to the whites, either, and they were quite happy having their camp some considerable distance away. We even had separate showers; canvas buckets with shower roses hanging from a branch of a thorn tree.

When Ernie had packed all his gear into his tent, someone raised the point that it was the first time that he had *ever* had to stay the night in a drilling camp. Notwithstanding the fact that he had spent many years fixing drilling rigs in the field, he had always managed to sneak back to town, or to some outback pub or comfy motel room. The little bloke couldn't do that while we were in Namibia since – after all – he was in charge of everything.

Jeff and Nick fronted up to his tent and claimed they were about to fuck him there and then! Jeff reckoned it was a sacred initiation rite amongst drillers; like crossing the equator on a ship or something.

BASTARDS FROM THE BUSH

It was exactly the same kind of chat that I had heard back in the outback in Western Australia whenever a new drilling camp had been set up. We had some blokes, mostly with wives and kids, claiming that their work mates had all of a sudden become very sexy, and that they were going to fuck them whether granted the authority or not. And then we had the intended victims promising that they would be fucking the would-be rapists first. In addition we had some blokes swearing that they hadn't lost their virginity and that they wouldn't be getting fucked under any circumstances. Generally it was the clients' geologists who received the most attention on account of the fact that most of them believed drillers to be feral creatures with no particular sexual preferences whatsoever. Considered to be educated and people with some refinement, they were targeted in that manner by us lower species. All in all it was more or less harmless banter.

When Ernie looked over at Wheeler and me for comfort, we both took Jeff and Nick's side and I told him that he had a chance of escaping any serious pain if he didn't struggle too much. Dave also promised that Jeff was an old campaigner when it came to carrying out such rituals and was bound to be gentle with him. He also assured the little mechanic that Jeff would most likely be employing a condom. On the other hand Nick confessed that he preferred rough, savage sex, and generally refused his victims the use of Vaseline; therefore recommended that Ernie should bite his pillow if the pain became too unbearable. He then went on to reiterate his dislike for condoms, and declared that his sperm was so powerful that it could even put an old fossil such as Ernie up the duff!

The poor, little bastard appeared most relieved when he found out he was having his legged pulled. Meanwhile Kotzé declared that he had never come across anyone so barbaric and uncouth as Australians. Bob Reynolds told the Boer to watch himself or he could personally arrange to make him pregnant. Jeff agreed one hundred percent that Bob was just the man for the job, plus he expressed his bewilderment that he hadn't made Steve Spence pregnant some years before. Steve took offence to Jeff's musings and there was bloody near a blue; nevertheless Dave and I weren't about to be having any brawls on our first evening under Namibia's stars, regardless of Jeff's evil intentions. It was damned good to be getting back to some yakka. With the rig about to be working once more, we drillers in our entirety felt that life had returned to some kind of normalcy.

CHAPTER 13

FIRST METRE DRILLED IN NAMIBIA!
WOUNDED LEOPARD!

Dave tossed a coin to see which crew was taking the first week's night shift. The result of the toss dictated that I was to take it. It didn't bother me, for I preferred working at night as there were less people around to bother you. As the drilling was just starting off, both crews went along to see the first drill hole collared. When the Schramm's compressor was started up and the hammer started thumping away at the schist rock, it was like music to my ears. Dust flew out of the sample cyclone into a clear, plastic sample bag and Dave – being the driller in charge – had drilled our first metre in Namibia!

It was absolute dream drilling, for the rock came all the way to the surface, unlike many areas in Western Australia where you had to drill through metre upon metre of puggy clay that tended – if you weren't careful – to block the hammer bit. The schist wasn't hard, either, so he was punching down a six-metre rod in seven minutes flat, causing a whole variety of problems for Kotzé and his crew. We had about forty sample bags lined up in rows of ten by the time the sampling crew had split and numbered half a dozen samples. It was terrific watching the Boer and his field assistant running around like chooks with their heads cut off. Splitting forty kilogram samples was bloody hard work and it became obvious that those two hadn't done much manual toil in their lives before. It reminded me and my crew of the episode with the poofter, Peter Jermyn, back in West Aussie.

73

An hour or so went by and the Japie geo' had had enough and he went up to Dave who was standing by the controls.

"Looks like you've got a serious problem, cobber," Wheeler agreed, cutting the rig back to an idle. "Contract says we only have to put a metre sample in those bags and then line 'em up in rows of ten. The sample's all yours once we've done that, my old son. We've got sheilas back in Aussie who can work faster than you bastards. In this kind of drilling we're gunna be getting four hundred metres a day – piece of piss – and we're gunna be working two shifts. I suggest you get your finger out." Having said that, he revved up the compressor again and more rods disappeared down the hole.

Not only did Kotzé encounter problems with the sample splitting; he also had to try and examine the rock chips in the drill cuttings, so that he would be able to tell the driller when the holes were deep enough. In order to do that he had to sieve out cuttings from each sample bag and then wash them in a bucket of water. He asked if he could use some of our labourers to help out, but we told him to get stuffed.

There was a complete balls up for a few days. The rig went on stand-down rates once more and he went back to Windhoek to phone his client company's managing director to get permission to hire another half-dozen labourers and to purchase an additional riffle splitter. Not a single such gadget could be found in the whole of Namibia, so one had to be ordered from Johannesburg. By the time we got going again there was quite a community camped out on the prospect.

Our labourers turned out to be bloody good value. The Ovambo, Philemon, was not a bad cook, while the Nama, Klaus, kept our tents tidy and our work clothes clean. Wilfred and the other coloured guy, Herman, became more than useful around the rig. In fact they reminded me of when I first started out drilling. They were desperately eager to learn about everything that was going on around the place. They cleaned air filters, greased nipples and kept all the various diesel tanks topped to the brim. They both preferred working on my shift, probably because I, too, was a coloured, and Dave went fairly crook about it. Nick and Jeff scorned him down, but what the hell; labour was dirt cheap, so Wheeler hired two more Baster from a farm that wasn't that far away from the site. As Wilfred and Herman learned more about the job, such as being able to handle the heavy drill rods in tandem with the cable winch, Jeff and Nick started taking life easy; the bludging pricks. I trespassed on their new-found leisure by making them take turns on the rig controls.

We were averaging at least seven hundred and fifty metres every twenty-four hours when things came to another sudden halt! It was a classic drilling situation to be found anywhere. Though Kotzé and his small army of sample monkeys weren't doing too bad a job on the sample splitting, the laboratory that was receiving the sample splits was falling way behind. To compound the problem further, the splits had to be sent all the way to a Cape Town laboratory, as there was no commercial lab in Namibia that could do fire assaying for gold, bar one small outfit that no one in the Namibian exploration game seemed to trust. The Boer geo' needed assay results so that he could work out where to put further drill holes.

Consequently the rig was parked, leaving us drillers with time on our hands. Several things came to mind. Firstly, that we should send our labourer's back to town on no pay. That was Kotzé's idea; however Wheeler and I objected to that since the cost of their wages was minuscule when it came to the money that was being blown in all directions by the client company. We got our way on that one. Secondly, it was suggested by Ernie that we should go on to the site at Karibib and start drilling there, but the client company was having some legal strife with a German prospector who actually owned the prospects both at Klein Aub and Karibib. Apparently the company only had an option to purchase the prospects and they would only be paying the full purchase price if the drilling results proved satisfactory. It was a real stuff up.

With idle drillers there was bound to be some comedy. Jeff desperately wanted to believe that Namibia was still full of dangerous animals, even though most had been shot to near extinction in the area we were working in. Dave and I decided to arrange something special for him. The first step we took was to get Wilfred to pass the word round that one of the farmers neighbouring the drill site had seen a huge leopard heading in our direction. More than that, the farmer had shot and slightly wounded the feline bastard, so it would certainly be in a very bad mood! That almost had Jeff in goose bumps and the rumour was made even more authentic when some of the labourers also believed the story and started shitting themselves. They became most anxious about leaving our vicinity in extreme haste, as to them it was obvious that wounded leopards should definitely be avoided. We had to calm them down in secret. After that we had to go to a town called Kalkrand that was roughly sixty miles south of Rehoboth. That was where Herman's folks lived. Herman's old man had this nifty gadget made out of a huge gourd, and somehow – by pulling a jagged stick backwards and forwards through an orifice in the gourd – we could make a snarling noise that he swore blind sounded exactly like a ferocious, very pissed off, wounded leopard.

Following that an elaborate plan took shape. It was a Friday night, so everybody, bar Jeff, Wheeler and I, were heading to Rehoboth for shopping and a drink or two. Nick, Steve and Bob Reynolds reckoned they wanted to see if they could get onto some Rehoboth snatch, while Jeff had sworn off all Namibian females, what with him having had the crabs. He, Dave and I were staying behind to guard the camp and all the gear. We had no vehicle, except the drill and support trucks, yet didn't see that causing too many problems, as it would only be for a few hours. What Jeff didn't know was that everyone had been told to leave their vehicles parked out of earshot, and they were going to sneak back to the camp and keep a suitable distance in order to observe the goings ons.

It was a beautiful, starry, Namibian night. Dave, Jeff and I were sitting back in our camp chairs; bottles of Tafel Lager at our fingertips, plus a beautiful fire of 2000 year old camel thorn wood burning close to our work boots. It was bloody amazing how cold it got on that drill site at night. Herman reckoned it was because we weren't too far from either the Kalahari or Namib deserts, and that the Atlantic wind had no trouble in reaching us, although we were 150 miles inland!

Jeff was recounting a fight he had had with six abos outside the Criterion Hotel back in Kalgoorlie when he was suddenly interrupted by a bloodcurdling snarl coming from out in the darkness. "What the fuck was that?" he yelped.

"What was what?" Wheeler sounded all nonchalant.

Another snarl ripped up the silence. "Did you hear that?" Jeff was out of his seat and staring in all directions.

That was my cue. Trying to sound as shit-frightened as possible, I howled, "It must be that fuckin' leopard the farmer saw!"

In no more than two seconds flat Jeff was in the cab of the support truck, and, in order to keep the charade alive, Dave and I followed him a second after. That vehicle had driven too many thousands of miles on terribly corrugated roads, therefore its windows refused to wind all the way to the top. Jeff had a jack lever at the ready, fully prepared to kill anything that might dare to stick its head through the window on his side. A couple more horrendous noises pierced the night, like someone sawing through a hollow log, but that time the source was even nearer to the camp.

"What the fuck we gunna do?" Jeff begged to know.

"Hey, Jeff!" Wheeler called out.

"What?"

"If he tries to get in your side, put your arm down his throat – grab his arsehole with one finger – then pull him inside out!"

I was nearly crook from trying to stop laughing. Jeff wasn't mollified at all. "Be fuckin' serious, you bastards! Those friggin' leopards are bad news. It gets in and we'll be history. Have you seen the claws on the fuckers?"

There was another snarl to our left, then another one to our right. It was Dave's turn to call out in alarm, "Hang on a sec' – what the fuck was that?" I was really starting to admire his play acting, then I quickly realised he was being fair dinkum!

"What's the problem?" I asked.

"Herman can't be in two places at one time, so there's something else out there." As if to prove his point, we could hear the sounds of people running away and screaming with fear. Again a snarl broke out on each side of the truck.

"What the fuck's Herman got to do with things?" Jeff was getting a little panicky.

Wheeler had become equally nervous and tried to explain: "Herman's got this gadget that makes leopard noises, and we organised things to scare you. But you heard the others taking off, so there must be at least two *real* leopards somewhere out there."

"What about the farmer seeing one?" Jeff reminded him.

"That was all bullshit," Dave confessed. "Oh, shit!" He was interrupted by even more roars.

I picked up on what he was getting at. "You don't reckon Herman attracted some dinkum leopards with that gourd thing of his?"

"He must've done," Wheeler agreed. "Christ, I hope the others have gone to get a gun of some sort."

"Where the fuck they gunna get a gun?" Jeff scorned him. "Unless they go to the cop shop in Rehoboth?"

"There'll be plenty of guns there all right," I agreed with him. "Besides, the farmers around here are bound to have guns as well. I think I remember Wilfred saying his uncle had a .308. That'd be plenty to blow the arse off a leopard. He doesn't live far from here."

We were in an awful bind. We couldn't start the truck, for the keys had been left in my tent. Jeff tried crossing the ignition wires, but there was a bright blue, electrical flash and everything was stuffed up altogether. We smoked the last three smokes I had in my top pocket, for the others had left their cigarettes by their camp chairs. No one was game to leave the dubious safety of the cab to fetch some more, even though we had cartons of them in our tents. The growling and roaring didn't stop, either!

After about a couple of hours of that Jeff was really getting impatient. The moon was in its last quarter and the last tiny sliver of it disappeared over the horizon, leaving everything in total darkness. The leopard snarls had abated for a while; yet no one dared to move.

"Where the fuck's everybody?" Jeff disturbed the silence. "They'd better not fuckin' leave us here much longer. I'm dying to take a piss."

"Why don't you go and take a look?" I challenged.

"Fuck you, Jack!" came his immediate reply. "*You* go and take a look. Being a fuckin' nigger – not even a leopard'll spot you in the dark, unless you smile."

CHAPTER 14

JEFF DECKS KOTZÉ! THE COURT CASE!
I REMEMBER THAT I HAVE A TWIN BROTHER!

Dawn revealed all, for Nick, Spence, Reynolds, Ernie and all the labourers soon surrounded us. They were fairly pissing themselves with glee. As it turned out Wilfred had obtained another leopard-roarer in Rehoboth, so the joke was also on Dave and me. All the sounds of people screaming and running in fear had been his idea; the clever, little, Baster bastard!

"Ha, ha, ha!" Kotzé was really delighted with all the events that had transpired, and he was eager to prove to all that he had learned at least one Aussie term by insisting on calling Jeff a 'blerrie dickhead'! Then, of course, Jeff had to give him a smack in the chops! It was a bloody good one, too, for the Japie fell flat on his back; blood flowing freely out of his mouth and nose; slowly congealing in his moustache and beard. Ernie, Dave and I went straight into damage control. Jeff had done the absolute unthinkable! Crapping all over, or abusing a client's geo' verbally was one thing; nevertheless thumping one was very definitely outlawed. So, if we didn't move fast, Jeff would be travelling home on the very next plane with no job to go to after that. The first thing that crossed my mind was to bullshit our way out of it by saying it was Kotzé who had thrown the first punch, as it was a matter of his and his field assistant's word against ours, but the labourers had seen what had happened and we couldn't involve them; even though they seemed most satisfied at seeing the Boer being knocked arse over tit. Wheeler and I, followed closely by Ernie, helped the Japie get to a camp chair. Nick fetched a bowl of water and some ice cubes from one of the eskies. We fairly kowtowed on our hands and knees to that bastard, yet he – knowing exactly what kind of strife Jeff was in – was hell bent on getting as much out of the situation as possible. His first threat was that he intended to lay assault charges with the cops in Rehoboth. After that he was determined that he was going to phone the client company's managing director, who in turn would call our employer demanding that Jeff be sacked.

After we had cleaned up the blood and had cooled him down a bit, I could see in his pig-like eyes that he had some sort of strategy on board, and it didn't take long to decipher what was going on in his head. Strangely enough, he had changed his mind and didn't really want Jeff to get the tramp; still he insisted that since we had time on our hands we should hold a court hearing to decide on Jeff's punishment. Although the whole thing sounded fairly corny, we drillers had no choice but to go along with him, as we didn't want to see Jeff having to go. As things turned out Ernie went as Jeff's defence councillor; Kotzé went as prosecutor and Hennie Van der Merwe – Kotzé's field assistant – went as the judge. The rest of us, drillers and labourers, were to be called up as witnesses. The little mechanic immediately objected to Van der Merwe being the judge and wanted a jury, since Kotzé was Van der Merwe's boss and the skinny Japie was bound to be biased if he wanted to keep his job. However Kotzé, who insisted that all the witnesses would be biased against him – yet alone a jury made up of the same people – overruled that. He was wrong there, for he had hired more labourers than we had, so they would also be wanting to keep their jobs.

I wasn't sure if we had got the correct legal procedure arse about or whatever, but the defence was given the go ahead to start everything. The way Ernie carried on, it wasn't hard to believe that he had always wanted to be a lawyer. "Your honour," he said to the judge while pointing his finger at Jeff, "here we've got an individual who's mentally unfit to stand before you, and therefore I must call for a mistrial."

Kotzé jumped up from his camp chair. "I object, your worship, the defence has no expert witnesses to verify my learned colleague's suppositions."

"Is it?" Van der Merwe just stared at him.

"Ja, your worship," the Japie geo' was quite clear about that. "The defence needs to produce expert witnesses to comment on the defendant's mental suitability to stand trial."

The judge turned to Ernie. "And what do you have to say to that?"

Ernie pointed at Nick. "I do have an expert witness, your honour. Doctor Lovadina has known and treated my client's illness for the past fifteen years."

Nick had to go and sit in a camp chair that was designated to the role of being the witness box. That really got everyone interested in the whole farce, plus a far bit of grog had been consumed by one and all.

"Doctor Lovadina," the little mechanic started out, "you are a psychiatrist, are you not?"

"If you say so?"

"Of course I bloody say so! ... And how long have you known Mr Jeffry Panizza?"

"Like you said, sir – fifteen years".

Ernie looked very happy with the 'sir' bit. "And is it true, doctor, that Mr Panizza has the mentality of a two year old?"

"Hey, you get fucked!" Jeff butted in; causing all those in the gallery who understood English to burst out laughing.

Like Ernie, Van der Merwe was well into the swim of things by then. "Hey – you – yourself!" he pointed a finger at Jeff. "You blerrie keep quiet, or I will hold you in contempt of my court. You are in enough trouble as it is." He had obviously seen a law program or two on the telly.

"I apologise for my client," Ernie tried to soothe the situation. He turned to Nick once more. "And is it also true, doctor, that my client resorts to the actions of a two year old, like throwing tantrums and deliberately soiling his trousers when he can't get his own way?"

We had to wait some time for Nick to stop laughing. "Yeah, it's true. He craps his pants at the drop of a hat. Especially if he can't have his own way."

Ernie also found that answer satisfactory. "I see... Now tell me, doctor, is it also true that the only treatment for my client's problem is to pump hot, soapy water up his anus via a hosepipe, and doesn't *that* make my client feel humiliated?"

If his question didn't have the gallery pissing ourselves laughing, Nick's answer had us in fits, "No, sir, in fact he quite likes it!"

"Order! Order!" Van der Merwe yelled while banging on an upturned steel bucket with Kotzé's geology pick.

Things calmed down a fraction following a brief recession during which cold beer was handed out to all and sundry.

"Doctor Lovadina," Ernie continued with his defence, "I'm rather perplexed. How on earth can anyone possibly derive any enjoyment out of having soapy water squirted up one's anus?"

"It's probably because he's kinky?" Nick suggested. "He's always smiling when he gets it."

"Order! Order, or I shall have you all thrown out!" The judge battled to keep us in line.

Dave was also called as an expert witness to testify on Jeff's behalf. "Doctor Wheeler," Ernie addressed him, "you are a physician expert in prescribing treatment for the mentally insane. Is that not true?"

"Correct, sir, I've had twenty-five years of experience dealing with the criminally insane."

The little mechanic frowned at all those before him as he mentally constructed his next question. "Well then, Doctor Wheeler, why was the hosepipe up the anus necessary?"

Dave was quick as bullet. "It's all to do with the patient's brain size, sir. With Mr Panizza here we're dealing with a brain slightly larger than a bee's testicle. When you're..."

"You can get fucked, too!" Jeff cut him off.

Van der Merwe beat the shit out his bucket with the geo' pick. "Control yourselves – all of you! I refuse to tolerate this kind of behaviour in my court. You," he pointed again at Jeff, "I give you this last warning – any more outbursts from you and I will have the bailiffs take you to the cells."

"What fuckin' cells?" the defendant demanded.

It required more beer to silence the court. Ernie continued to question Dave, "Doctor Wheeler, please carry on from where you left off."

"As I was saying, sir, we're talking about brain size. We indeed have a tragedy here because Mr Panizza hasn't always had this rather pathetic mental condition. When he was approximately two years old – this's clearly demonstrated by his moronic behaviour – his earwax turned putrid, thus damaging the very few brain cells he once possessed. Then, of course, his mother tried to drown him an hour after he was born. Normally the procedure would be to insert the hosepipe in one ear, but unfortunately Mr Panizza's brain was so small that I felt the risk was too great. I feared that his brain would've been washed out of his other ear... Thus the rectal insertion."

Ernie sipped at his beer, waiting for the laughter to die down. Even the judge had tears running down his cheeks. Once a modicum of quiet returned, he carried on, "Doctor Wheeler, you've heard Doctor Lovadina's testimony. As you know from your years of practice, he's one of the world's most prominent psychiatrists. How do *you* explain Mr Panizza's penchant for having a hosepipe inserted in his anus?"

"Yeah, I hold Doctor Lovadina in the highest professional regard," Dave assured him. "We've worked together with innumerable patients and have spent many intense sessions discussing Mr Panizza's illness. On each and every occasion – and employing a great deal of thought – we've arrived at the conclusion that Mr Panizza's a very sick pervert who prefers other obese men sexually than he does members of the opposite sex. This's clearly borne out by..."

BASTARDS FROM THE BUSH

He had to dodge an empty beer bottle that Jeff had thrown at his head. When things settled down again Ernie called several witnesses to the stand, including me, who all swore blind that we had always believed Jeff to be insane, and on no occasion whatsoever had we ever seen him lay a finger on Kotzé. Steve Spence went even further by swearing that he had seen the Japie geo' being bashed in the face by a masked man in a jockstrap, who was driving a donkey cart. The donkeys pulling the cart, three in number, had green flames shooting out of their nostrils and black smoke billowing out of their arses!

Ernie was required to sum up for the defence. He was a little pissed by then. "Your honour and members of the jury, let me..."

"There ain't no fuckin' jury," Jeff reminded him. "Just a judge who knows fuck all, anyway." Van der Merwe, who was also as pissed as a fart, forgot to reprimand him.

The little mechanic battled on, "Your honour, there's clearly no case to be answered to here in this court. I'm sure, by the outstanding professional witnesses' testimonies that have been brought before you, that I've proved beyond all reasonable doubt that Mr Panizza can't be held responsible for his actions... What do we have here, your honour? I shall tell you. We have a very sick pervert amongst us, your honour. You've heard Doctor Wheeler's testimony. Here we have a demented creature that prefers obese men to women. You've heard Doctor Lovadina's testimony. My client, the poor pathetic dickhead, enjoys having a hosepipe inserted up his arse – I mean anus... Also, your honour, there's some doubt as to whether a crime really did actually take place. The witnesses I have called up, everyone a well respected member of the community, all categorically deny that Mr Panizza visited any violence on Mr Kotzé. Your honour, you heard Mr Spence swear that he had seen Mr Kotzé struck in the face by a masked man in a jockstrap driving a donkey cart. You heard his horrific description of the demonic donkeys... Your honour, I'm not saying that my client should go unpunished. Such a low life needs to be punished, but I beg..."

"Hey – whose friggin' side *are* you on?" Jeff interrupted him.

"You shuddup!" Ernie hurled back at him. "I'm the one who's fuckin' defending you. You keep butting in, and you'll be in real strife!" He faced the judge once more. "Before I was so rudely interrupted by my client, I was begging your honour to show mercy to this low life. Punish him, as I know you must, even so I appeal to your most generous nature to show leniency. That's all, your honour".

It was Kotzé's turn to say something and fortunately, since the beer had also got to him, he didn't have too much to say. "Your worship," he began with. "It is not customary for me to do so, but I must congratulate the defence for at least getting half of their facts right. You will also please note, your worship, that I said only *half*. The expert witnesses called up by the defence have painted a picture of a perverted imbecile who has no hesitation in fouling his trousers at the slightest whim. A specimen who prefers the doubtful charms of members of his own sex. Worse than that, an intellectual midget of the..."

"He wants another smack in the..." Jeff tried to butt in.

"Shut your face!" Ernie yelled at him.

The Japie geo' continued: "That, your worship," he pointed at the defendant, "clearly demonstrates the dangerous, impulsive disposition of the character you see before you. He has threatened violence on me again... Nonetheless, is not this immature behaviour some ingenious disguise? Do you not sense the dark chill of evil present in this court, your worship? Here we have a creature whose mind is so twisted by perversion, yet it is clear that all his actions are certainly premeditated. He knows at all times exactly what he is doing. Look at the spell he has cast on those simpletons called up by the defence. Not the good doctors, but the everyday citizens that have come to testify before you. You have heard their perjury submitted as a dire consequence of his diabolical influence. Let us remain with the logic of reality, as it is impossible for green flames or black smoke to emanate from any orifice of a donkey. Science has proved such phenomena are an impossibility. Furthermore, the Rehoboth police cannot allow anyone to drive a donkey cart clad only in an athletic support. Not only would it impinge on decent citizens' sensibilities, there is the safety factor involved. Please consider the multitude of thorns that abound in our beautiful country?"

He took a huge slug from his beer bottle, then he looked over at Jeff, "Let all of us here consider the uncivilised, savage actions of the defendant. Anyone with the slightest iota of intelligence would adjudge the defendant's violence as being accompanied with malice and aforethought. So surely, your worship, the brutality of this beast has been denied by false witnesses. Look here," he pushed his face close to Van der Merwe's. "You can see my swollen upper lip and the blood that still lays congealed in my left nostril. Even the defence admits this barbarian should be punished, yet they plead for leniency... I recommend, your worship, death by lethal injection, hanging – or at least have the Rehoboth police confiscate the hosepipe."

Kotzé had to wander off to have a good chunder from all the beer he had consumed. We were all fairly horribly done up by then; nevertheless we all reckoned he wasn't such a bad bloke for not getting Jeff tramped. Furthermore, the court case had done a good job on breaking up the monotony.

Much better than that, Ernie, for some insane reason, decided that he was enthusiastic about giving Jeff a slapping! He challenged Jeff to a blue and skipped around him; shaping up like a professional boxer.

"Ah – get fucked – you scrawny wart!" Jeff pushed him away.

"You reckon you're bloody clever, don't ya?" the little mechanic kept at him; getting ready to throw a punch. "Let's see how really fuckin' good you are? Come on and try'n have a poke at me, ya big, fat, arsehole. Come on..."

Jeff pushed him away again. "Fuck-off, Ernie, before I fuckin' mullet you!"

"For fucksakes!" Wheeler got between them. "Ernie, give it away before Jeff flamin' kills you. Jeff – back off! Christ, look at the pair of you! What do you reckon the labourers are thinking? You're carrying on like a pair of dickheads."

Dave and Ernie worked out a punishment that turned out to be priceless to Kotzé, though a fate worse than death for Jeff. For the next week he would have to serve the Boer geo' his meals and call him 'sir'; furthermore he had to open the Japie's beer bottles for him. I noticed that Boer kept his mouth shut from then on.

Wilfred was also pretty done up from the grog, so I felt it a good time to ask him a few questions about the coloured bloke at the Oanob resort. "That coloured guy at the Oanob bar? Why were you so shit-scared of him? What's he got against me?"

The little Baster quickly looked about for the possibility of escaping my attention, but I had his arm held firmly in one hand. "There is something very strange going on, boss. You are just like someone else who used to live in Rehoboth. With that cut on your throat, you must be him, yet you have also been in Australia for a long time. It is impossible that you are not the same people... Do you have a *broer*?"

"What's a *broo -er*?"

"A brother?"

That rocked me. "Yeah, I'm supposed to have a brother. I haven't seen him since I was about two years old. I can't remember a thing about him. He stayed with my real father when my mother and stepfather went to Australia."

"He must have been a twin?"

"Yeah, he was. Do you know him? Is it possible to get in contact with him?"

A flicker of fear blinked in his eyes. "No, I know nothing about him."

He tried to pull away, but I held him on to him. "Listen, Wilfred," I tried to calm him, "there's no way I'll tell anyone that you've spoken to me. But this guy could be my '*broo-er*' and you can't blame me for wanting to know more about him?"

"It is very dangerous to talk about him. The authorities are trying to catch him and there are a lot of people who are doing their best to stop them. Please, boss, do not make me say more. I can get into very big trouble."

"That coloured at Oanob – is he try'n to catch my brother?"

"No, boss."

"Should I speak to him?"

That really panicked the little bloke. "No, man, he will blerrie kill me, boss! Stay away from him – he is very dangerous."

"Who can I speak to, then?"

"We can go and see my uncle."

CHAPTER 15

BASTER FARMER JAKOBUS VAN WYK!

Getting a Land Cruiser for him and me to go and see his uncle caused a few problems because Dave, Ernie and the others wanted to know what I needed a vehicle for. Not wanting to disclose that I might have had a brother who could be in strife with the authorities, I told them that Wilfred had an uncle who possibly knew of some distant cousin of mine, and I was going to find out if I still had any relations in the Rehoboth area. Jeff and Nick wanted to come along; however I told them that Wilfred's uncle had a pathological hatred for all white men. Especially those of Italian descent. Jeff was prepared to let things go at that, but Nick accused me of going queer and that I was hunting Wilfred's bum. He also hurriedly released that topic when I accused him of being jealous and suggested that he should steer his affections in the direction of Jeff.

The first thing that hit me when I arrived at Wilfred's uncle's farmhouse was the stink of cattle shit! Although there wasn't a cow to be seen anywhere, there was a yard almost adjoining the house that contained a mound of the stuff; dark brown and steaming in the hot sun. Millions of flies with metallic green arses literally made the air vibrate as they swarmed around us when we alighted from the Toyota. Some mangy, mongrel dogs came hurtling out of the driveway, and though they appeared quite keen on seeing Wilfred, they left me with no doubt that they fancied tearing off one my calf muscles. An elderly, chubby, coloured woman with grey hair and a faded blue dress came out to see what the commotion was about. She adopted the same attitude as the dogs; she was happy that Wilfred was there, then she didn't bother disguising the fact that she wished I was not.

"Kobus!" she called in the direction of the house. "Kobus!"

An old coloured bloke came out on to the veranda of the house. He totally ignored my companion and berated me in Afrikaans. Wilfred interrupted him hurriedly in the same language and the old man's eyes bugged out with obvious disbelief.

The old man spoke in English after that, "It is impossible! Why are you lying?" he asked me.

I instantly took offence to his accusation. "What am I bloody lying about? What the hell's going on?"

He shook his head. "We knew about there being two Witbooi brothers – twins – born to Christian Witbooi, but it is impossible that the other brother could have had his throat cut also."

"My throat wasn't actually cut on purpose," I tried to clear matters. "It was from an accident when I was a kid. I went through a window and the glass cut me."

He was obviously Wilfred's uncle, and he fired an additional salvo of questions at his nephew in Afrikaans, and the answers came back at him equally as fast. Even more questions were asked, and even more answers were given.

"Can you speak in English?" I demanded. "I'm not interested in hanging around being insulted in Afrikaans."

"You had better come inside," the old man decided.

I was led into a smoke stained, but spotlessly clean kitchen. We sat around an ancient pine dining table that had been bleached white from years of scrubbing. In the open hearth the old woman was stirring something in a three-legged kaffir pot that was steaming over a pile of blood red embers. The old girl lifted the pot to one side and made room for a smoke blackened kettle, and all the time the old bloke stared at me, shaking his head. I soon found out that he was

JOSEF SCHULTZ

Jakobus Van Wyk and his wife's name was Sophia. They were third-generation Rehoboth Baster whose ancestors had originated from the Fraserburg district of the Cape Colony, and direct descendants of Hermanus Van Wyk, an esteemed Baster kaptein who had settled at Rehoboth back in 1870. It was the same Hermanus Van Wyk who the Rehoboth community hall had been named after.

I wasn't interested in them; it was my look-alike or possibly my long-forgotten brother whom I had come to find out about, and why everybody was so shit-frightened when it came to talking about him. "Can we clear this up once and for all?" I asked the old man. "Wilfred here reckons there's someone getting around here that looks identical to me, and he's in some kind of trouble. I'm supposed to have a twin brother over here. He's obviously..."

"What is his name?" the old bloke interjected.

I shook my head. "I don't know. We were split up when I was a tacker. He stayed behind with my father when my mother and stepfather emigrated to Australia. For some reason or other my mum and stepfather refused to talk about him, and I never heard 'em mention his name."

"That is impossible!" old Jakobus scorned me. "How could you not know the name of *your own* brother?"

That pissed me right off. "For Christ's sake, why should I lie? I've lived in Australia all my life and have only been in this godforsaken country for just under a month. Come out to our camp and I can introduce you to people who've known me for years. If it *is* my brother we're talking about, I'd like to catch up with him. He's the only relation I know of."

"I cannot say anything more," he tried to end the topic.

"Ah, come on, what's the matter with..."

The old lady interrupted me when she placed chipped enamel mugs of tea on the pine table. She then produced a tin of condensed milk that reminded me of my childhood; when I was kid at the orphanage I loved the stuff so much I would have been prepared to kill a couple of Catholic nuns for it.

"Was your mother's name Anna?" the old girl wanted to know.

"Yeah!" I eagerly agreed.

"And did she marry a German called Wolfgang Schultz?"

"Yeah, she did!"

"What name was your mother born with? Her maiden name, I mean?"

That had me pondering for a while. "I think it was Barends... Yeah, I'm sure it was Barends."

She turned to her spouse. "What do you think, Kobus? He could be Jonker's brother?"

He drained his tea in one gulp and shrugged his shoulders. "I cannot say anything until I discuss this with the *raad*."

"Who's this '*raad*'?" I queried. "What're you talking about?"

My questions quickly made him uncomfortable. "It is nothing – an Afrikaans word that means nothing."

I had had enough of all the bullshit by then, so I stood up to leave. "Come on, Wilfred, I'm getting out of here. I've had as much crap as I can stand for one day."

When we reached the outside yard Wilfred's aunt came hurrying out. "Wait! Take some figs with you for the people at your camp. I have some fresh ones and some dry ones. In spite of the drought we have had a good crop this year. There are also some fresh eggs that I collected this morning."

It was hard to refuse the old dear. One couldn't help liking her, what with her missing front teeth and whatever. Sure enough, in the yard there was a huge tree laden with gigantic, purple figs. She handed over a plastic bag of both fresh and dried ones. In a plastic ice cream container she gave Wilfred a dozen or more brown, speckled eggs.

The old man came out of the house and walked up to me. "Please, my son, I do not know what is going on. Perhaps you are trying to deceive me? Perhaps I am seeing a miracle? I dare not do anything until I have spoken to others. It is simply too dangerous. Please believe me, if the need arises that we should talk again, I shall tell Wilfred."

JOSEF SCHULTZ

We headed back to camp. Wilfred, his mouth full of dried figs, was shaking his head and he muttered a word that sounded like '*yussess*' over and over again.

"What you on about?" I looked over at him.

"It is real strange, boss. My uncle is scared of nothing, but he was unsure how to take you. He still believes you are Jonker Witbooi, who could be your brother. You cannot blame him, as Jonker has green eyes exactly like yours, and he has a cut on his throat just like yours."

"And do you know this Jonker Witbooi?"

He clammed up real tight after that.

CHAPTER 16

BLACK MAMBA! DAVE GETS A SHAG!

We arrived back to discover that the camp was in total confusion. There were people walking around everywhere with sticks, shovels and lengths of hydraulic hose. There was quite a fair bit of jabbering going on, and it was abundantly clear that a good deal of grog had been consumed since Wilfred and I had been away.

"What gives?" I asked Nick. "Why's everyone so interested in our tent?"

"Fuckin' snake, mate! Jeff saw a bloody snake go in there!"

"He's probably got the DTs?" I suggested. "First he sees lions under every thorn bush – then we get leopards – now we've got snakes in our tent."

He was all serious. "I reckon he's dinkum, cobber. Bloody near shit himself. He reckoned it was about ten foot long, and Herman thinks it could be a black mamba. Apparently, if one of 'em bites you, you can kiss your fuckin' arse goodbye. They're deadly poisonous, mate!"

It was apparent that those locals amongst our number had a very profound respect for what might have been a black mamba, judging by the distance they kept from my tent. Ernie was sneaking up to it on tiptoe, a shovel held above his head at the ready, while Kotzé reckoned a shotgun was far more appropriate.

"Go on, Ernie, kill the bastard!" Jeff shouted encouragement, also from a judicious distance. "Should've fuckin' seen it, Joe – it was half a mile long!"

"Come on, Ernie!" Nick was also barracking at the top of voice. "I left my smokes in there."

"Behind you, Ernie!" Dave yelled at the top of his lungs, causing the little mechanic to drop the shovel and run for his life, amidst yells of derision and people calling into question his fortitude.

"Smart man!" Hennie Van der Merwe complimented the bloke's hasty withdrawal. "If that is a blerrie mamba in there. Especially a black mamba – and it bites him – you may have to start digging his grave. Those snakes have been known to chase people, and they can move along the ground faster than a race horse, man. By the time you got him to Rehoboth he would be dead, unless you had a helicopter. Besides, they probably do not have the proper anti-venom there... That is *if* Jeffry saw a snake at all?"

"Too right," I agreed. "I wouldn't be surprised if he's try'n to get his own back on that leopard caper we pulled. "Hey, Dave!" I went over to join him and Ernie. "You reckon Jeff really saw a snake, or is he just bullshitting?"

"I reckon he's dinkum," Wheeler told me. "You should've seen him come out of your tent. He was like greased fuckin' lightning!"

"The only way to flush him out is to use smoke," Kotzé was adamant. "No animals – reptiles, fowls or mammals – like smoke."

"Bonzer idea!" Ernie was all for it.

I wasn't. Especially the way he, Nick, Jeff and Kotzé went about things. First off they attempted to work out which way the wind was blowing, and that was mad, what with the wind blowing in all directions the way it was. They settled on the theory, since it was late afternoon, that the wind had a habit of coming from the coast or at least a south-westerly. Then they chiselled out the top of a twenty litre oil drum that they filled with a mixture of sump oil and diesel. Using a piece of oily rag as a fuse, they set fire to the drum and a couple of seconds went by and they had one almighty inferno on their hands! Not only that, a fair dinkum gust of wind – that was actually coming from the east – happened along and blew the flames all over the tent!

BASTARDS FROM THE BUSH

In no time flat the tent was ablaze. Snake or no snake, my suitcase and swag were in that tent and fortunately both were beside the doorway. A spot that, considering I was the driller, I had grabbed for myself when we first set the tent up. I saved everything except for my steel toe capped rig boots, which crapped me right off, as I had had them handmade during a trip to Hong Kong. Nick and Jeff lost everything; clothes, travel documents, swags; the absolute works!

"We're gunna have to cut back on the piss," I told Ernie and Wheeler. "We carry on like this, and someone'll get hurt. Where the fuck are we gunna sleep tonight?"

"Fuck me bloody dead!" Jeff surveyed the black, smoking circle that had once been our accommodations.

Nick was poking through the ashes with part of the tent pole; his bed and belongings just embers. "I can't see any sign of the snake, Jeff, you cunt! I didn't see it friggin' leave. If you were bullshitting – I'll," he poked the length of pole at Jeff, "ram this up your arse!"

"Bigger men than you have tried smaller things," Jeff sneered back at him. "Our fuckin' passports are in amongst that lot. Now we'll never get back to Aussie. Let's see if that piss you put in the esky's cold?"

Nick and I shared Ernie's tent until we found a replacement back in Windhoek. I had salvaged my swag and camp bed, so I was comfortable enough, while Nick slept on a groundsheet with only a blanket. Jeff slept in the cab of the support truck where no leopards or snakes could attack him.

The whole set up was becoming a farce. We couldn't drill on account of the slackness of the assay laboratory, so all we could do was hang around the camp. The rig was on stand-down rates a further time; still the boss back in Kalgoorlie was getting manic because there was three times as much in it if we were getting the metres. That meant us drillers dipping out sadly, for there was no production bonus for us, either. Ernie found out from the boss that the client company's head geologist was absolutely livid with Kotzé, for he should have made better arrangements for the sample analysis.

JOSEF SCHULTZ

All in all we became shrouded in with a sense of unease, what with the rig being idle. We kept the labourers on at half pay and Jeff, Dave, Ernie and I hung around the camp, where we drank beer and read a selection of Hustlers, Playboys and other stink books that we had brought with us from Kalgoorlie. Some coloured girls came over from what was left of the mining settlement at the Klein Aub copper mine, and surprisingly enough it was only Dave who eventually shagged one of them. That time his dick worked one hundred percent and he was a changed man. Furthermore, the girl he coupled with was really quite attractive and had him quite smitten with her. Her name was Magda, and much to my amazement she made out that Wheeler was the man of her dreams It was all pretty corny, really; Dave was introduced to the folks; mum, dad, brothers, sisters and cousins, and they welcomed him like some long-lost son on the times he went to see her. Even though he was more than double Magda's age! I noticed that he was buying most of the tucker, smokes, beer and brandy on those visits. Apparently the vast majority of her relations were both unemployed and broke, and had to rely on a bit of rustling and poaching to get by on, plus the odd hand out from other relations lucky enough to have jobs in Windhoek or places elsewhere. As was to be expected, Kotzé didn't like the idea of a white bloke hanging around with a coloured. By taking on a coloured, one would have to take on the relatives; aunts, uncles, cousins; in effect all the multitude of hangers-ons. Like a flock of Kalahari vultures they would all come swooping down to pick his carcass clean, and, for once in his life, it looked as if the Boer really had a handle on the truth.

CHAPTER 17

ORGIES IN WINDHOEK! THE WALLABIES PLAY THE SPRINGBOKS! CONFINED TO CAMP!

Nick, Steve Spence and Bob Reynolds preferred spending their idle hours in Windhoek, where they sure indulged in all sorts of frenetic activities. Obtaining copious amounts of pussy in Namibia's capital was as easy as drinking piss according to Nick; German, Boer, Swiss and that belonging to just about every indigenous tribe that the country had to offer. He claimed that being seen with single Aussie blokes was considered a fairly prestigious pastime amongst the local birdlife. In fact they had had marriage proposals from at least a dozen or so Boer sheilas; all seeking to obtain Australian citizenship in order that they could escape the black regimes both in Namibia and South Africa. Despite Jeff's run in with the body crabs, the offsiders feasted themselves on coloured, Herero, Damara, Ovambo and Nama maidens with total, insatiable abandon! With the mansion in Klein Windhoek at their disposal they were like Roman emperors, while some of their drunken orgies attracted notoriety, jealousy, or downright disgust from the local Windhoekers. Some repairs had to be done on the mansion as a result of Nick and Bob Reynolds having to evict an unruly Polish reveller. Rather than using any of the numerous doors available to them, they actually discharged the Pole through one of the lounge room windows! If that wasn't irresponsible enough, Nick had a competition to see how many sheilas he could pack in with him in the spa bath. According to Steve Spence, there were thirty bodies stacked in the bath before the floor in the upstairs bathroom started to cave in, and there was bloody near a holocaust! Naturally the landlord cut up rough, so the boss docked Nick's, Bob's and Steve's wages to cover the damages.

"You fuckers had better be using frangers," Dave warned our lusty workmates. "You've been told countless times that Africa's crawling with fuckin' AIDS. They reckon that there's forty percent AIDS in Namibia, so every second woman you fuck'll have it." That had Steve and Bob in a bit of a cold sweat because they admitted that on a couple of occasions they had been too drunk to bother about condoms.

"You're dead men walking," I tried to comfort them. I asked Steve, "If you die before we get home, can I have that computer and gear you've got back in Kal'?"

"You can kiss Jeff's arse!" he told me.

Then, as destiny desired, there was a rugby test match on one of the Super Sport TV channels; the opposing sides being the Australian Wallabies and the South African Springboks. The match was being held in Cape Town in South Africa.

The Casa Blanca night club and bar that the blokes had visited on their first night in Namibia was showing the game on a big screen, so Nick, Bob and Steve had seats in the front row. Although Namibia had suffered dreadfully under South Africa's mandate with its ludicrous Apartheid laws, it appeared that most Namibians – black, white or a mixture of both – were dead keen to see the 'Bokkes' win.

Steve Spence reckoned that the whole afternoon had started rather awkwardly; right at the beginning of the test match. When the national anthems were sung; Australia – with the Wallabies being the visitors – had its anthem sung first and most of the mob at the Casa Blanca had kept their silence more or less as a sign of respect to the establishment's Aussie component.

However: when the Afrikaans verses of South Africa's national anthem were sung:

BASTARDS FROM THE BUSH

'Ringing out from our blue heavens
From our deep seas breaking round.
Over everlasting mountains
Where the echoing crags resound.'

Bob Reynolds started to belch and he was joined by both Steve and Nick. It was another of Steve's crazy ideas that they had been practising on for days; each being able to cover a verse. Being typical drillers they knew how to compress air in their throats in order to manufacture belches on demand. A delighted onlooker stated that they had given out a guttural but fairly accurate interpretation of the Boers' most sacred mantra "Die Stem", topped off with a resounding, choking fart from Nick. Talk about good Australian public relations!

Then, as fate preferred, the Springboks won by a couple of points, and some of the Casa Blanca's punters thought it might be useful to pour shit on the Aussies. As it turned out, it was a half dozen or so Boer bastards from the Republic of South Africa.

Nick didn't want to put up with their disrespectful comments at all. First he claimed that since the rugby match had been played at Newlands, that was in Cape Town, South Africa, the entire integrity of the game was in doubt since the Boers and Japies would have rigged it. Secondly, as Australia was leading the world in cricket, rugby, hockey and most other sports, Australians were the master race, and that all Boers and Japies had to be lesser beings, poofters or wankers.

Things turned really nasty when one of the Boers mentioned the perversions harboured by some of Australia's military. He had heard on the SABC news that six Australian soldiers in a Townsville military barracks had killed four kittens. One kitten had been dragged behind a motor bike, and then had been run over by the back wheel of a four-wheel drive. The other three kittens had been doused with petrol and had been set alight. If that wasn't enough, another Boer had heard how an Australian SAS soldier had been arrested for planning to kick his girlfriend in the guts in order to abort her baby.

JOSEF SCHULTZ

We Aussies in Namibia had heard the same news bulletins emanating out of Australia and were equally disgusted; nevertheless Nick – having no credible defence against such accusations – resorted to one of his age-old methods of retaliation. He became repulsive. He told the Boers that that their women resembled wombats and dingoes he had shot back in Australia, and that all by himself he was perfectly capable of sodomising all the Boers' and Japies' wives, mothers, aunts and sisters for the princely sum of one South African ten cent piece that was worth one fifth of the value of an Aussie ten cent coin. If that wasn't insulting enough, he went on to declare that all Boer women preferred Aussie blokes to Boer blokes because all the world's Boers were a pack of arseholes.

That was bound to make the Boers take umbrage, and it did. In addition to that, Nick was really lucky that Steve and Bob could handle themselves when it came to the art of bare-knuckle brawling. The distressed proprietor of the Casa Blanca later reported that three hundred glasses had been broken. Seven tables had been smashed beyond repair, along with nine chairs that he had just recently purchased. At least a dozen of the establishment's front windows had been broken, while the door to the Ladies shithouse had been ripped off its hinges and all the cisterns in the Gents shithouse had been wrenched from their mountings. Or at least that was what was on the list that the cops read out in the magistrate's court the following day. It was also mentioned that two of the Boers had been hospitalised; one with a broken nose, ankle and jaw; the other with three broken ribs and a broken arm. Unbeknownst to the Aussies and the Boers; during the fracas the Casa Blanca's Ovambo chef had raped one of the kitchen hands; a young Damara boy of sixteen; though the responsibility for that caper wasn't laid at the door of the combatants.

Much to Ernie's mortification and despair he had to organise a lawyer to represent the offsiders. It was a sheer fluke that he managed to hire a black lawyer, a massive Ovambo with a goatee beard, who was big mates with the magistrate; who in turn was also an Ovambo that came from the same village in northern Namibia.

BASTARDS FROM THE BUSH

There was a dream outcome to everything when some local currency changed hands discreetly. The police investigation had managed to ascertain from the majority of the Casa Blanca's patrons, mostly coloureds and blacks, that the Boers had started the whole situation. The Aussies had been good losers and had been more than happy to shout the bar free drinks since the Wallabies had lost. It had been totally unnecessary for the Boers to be so rude to the Aussies which, of course, they were.

The Boers' lawyer tried to argue that the Aussies started the affair by insulting the Afrikaans portion of the South African national anthem by deliberately belching, but the Ovambo magistrate, who had spent a couple of years being beaten and tortured by members of the ex-white South African Defence Force for being a member of SWAPO, chose to ignore him.

After summing up all the damning evidence against the Boers and Japies, the Ovambo magistrate fined them two thousand Namibian dollars each, plus a further seventeen thousand dollars for the damages caused by the melee. We found out later that the Ovambo chef was let off scot free because the kitchen hand withdrew his complaint. It came to light that the Damara was a thorough poofter himself; still he preferred that people sought his authorization before helping themselves to his arse. Despite the excellent conclusion to everything Ernie insisted that Nick and the others would be confined to our drilling camp until more work was available.

For some days after Jeff was going around with a look of profound regret on his face. Why hadn't Nick and Spence and them invited him along to the Casa Blanca? Like with most races other than Italians and Aussies, he had acquired a dislike for Boers, and he was saddened on account of the fact that he hadn't taken part in the brawl. The backhand he had given the proprietor of the Blue Mermaid Hotel and the smack in the mouth to Kotzé had scarcely been enough to sustain him, especially when he heard that some of the Boers' bones had been broken following the rugby. To overcome that feeling of deep loss he went in search of Spence, and accused the Tasmanian of fathering both of his sister's kids. Spence in turn was particularly fond of his two nieces, so readily put up his fists. Perhaps it was from the successes he had so recently enjoyed at the Casa Blanca?

Ernie was as quick as lightening on that occasion and he ordered Jeff to drive into Rehoboth for more beer, as our camp supplies were running low. Such a mission must have appealed to the big, fat bastard, so further bloodshed was averted.

CHAPTER 18

BASHING COMING MY WAY!
BASTARD APARTHEID REGIME!

Wilfred and his uncle drove up in a red Datsun bakkie, (they called vehicles with trays on them 'bakkies' in Namibia) and the old man was pretty friendly to me. So much so he invited me over to dinner. I agreed only on the condition that I was the one supplying the refreshments, and it soon became clear that brandy was the Baster in general's favourite drop. I purchased two bottles of Namaqua Brandy and one of Grenada wine for old Sophia from the Klein Aub liquor store, plus I rifled a dozen or so bottles of Tafel Lager for me from the camp's supplies.

Just like the grog shops back in Rehoboth, the Klein Aub *drankwinkel* was by far the most favoured institution in that settlement. It was like as if it was a Mecca where pilgrims came to pray. Similar to the rest of the hamlet's buildings it was fairly run down without a drop of fresh paint anywhere. When the mine was working there may have been some prosperity; however there was nothing left to sustain the people who had taken over some of the old mine buildings and compounds. It reminded me of mining towns in Western Australia; when the gold or nickel or whatever ran out; what once could have been a thriving community just up and died. The whole of Klein Aub was hopelessly depressing; you could almost smell the despair of unemployment and poverty. The people, a mixture of coloureds and blacks, resembled scarecrows; small kids with snotty noses, their parents and elder brothers and sisters with eyes shrunken from too many hard times and alcohol. Like zombies they studied me in my good clothes, and there was a look of sheer bewilderment when I handed over a red one hundred Namibian dollar note to a pregnant, very light-skinned coloured girl with no teeth who was serving at the counter. She had the features of someone who had been attractive once, but her hair was matted and her legs, arms and body had gone to fat. There were scabs all over her legs. She couldn't have been more than twenty-five or twenty-six, but she held herself like a sixty year old. The store stank of brandy-poisoned chunder, marijuana smoke and ruin. Even the mongrel dogs looked like a pack of derelicts; as if they hadn't had a proper feed since they had left their mother's dehydrated tit. All obviously too cowardly or stuffed to take a bark at me. Like their owners, they looked as if they had simply given up on life or anything exciting; same as the donkeys harnessed to their carts in the blazing sun; their owners too slack to find shade for them. Only one ancient, wrinkled joker demonstrated any capability of animation. He insisted on showing me an old medal he had pinned onto a filthy jacket that was no more than rags, and then he held out his hand obviously wanting money. Wilfred gently steered him to one side, all the while talking softly in Afrikaans. He pressed something into the ancient's hand and was rewarded by the slightest hint of a spark in the old man's eyes of the fires that once might have burned brighter in days long gone.

"That old man is over a hundred years old," Wilfred told me as his uncle steered the bakkie away from Klein Aub.

"He looks older than that?" I suggested.

"Ja, he was at Sam Khubis in 1915 when the Germans tried to kill all the Baster because they refused to fight against the Boers and the British," he added.

"Sam Khubis is a short way from here," Old Jakobus joined in. "Wilfred, you must take Josef and show him Sam Khubis one day."

106

BASTARDS FROM THE BUSH

When we arrived at the farmhouse the dogs challenged us again and they were still pretty keen to let me know that they still fancied *at least* a taste of me. What made the hair stand up on the back of my neck in sympathy with theirs was the fact that the coloured bloke, who had been so hostile to me at the Oanob resort, was standing on the veranda. He had two other jokers with him who didn't look too fond of me, either. They came towards me, and I really resented not having either Jeff or Nick with me. Sensing that a bashing could be coming my way, I quickly looked around for a weapon, and as I was carrying the two bottles of brandy, I thought of smashing them to together to use their broken necks as a deterrent. Then old Jakobus probably sensed what was on my mind, for he soon took the middle ground between the three coloureds and me, and he was jabbering away in Afrikaans while they looked me up and down as if I was dog shit. They kept pointing at my eyes and my throat; all the time firing questions at the old man who seemed flat out being able to explain. It was as if he didn't believe a word he was saying, either!

Finally Wilfred got his two bob's worth in and he introduced me to the coloured I had previously met at the Oanob Dam, "Carl, this is Josef Schultz, my boss. Josef – this is Carl Zes." Zes grudgingly took my hand as if it had a scorpion in it.

I was introduced to the other two, Petrus Klaase and Fritz Manasse. There was another debate in Afrikaans with fingers being pointed at me by all parties. Even old Sophia joined in, and though I couldn't understand a word she was saying, I had a feeling she was on my side.

I was asked to show my passport, but I jacked up on that one. "Stuff you!" I told them. "I've had a gutsful of showing my passport to everyone."

That started another debate which pissed off Sophia. She challenged them in Afrikaans and mentioned the word 'raad' again, and then she threw her hands up in what looked to be disgust and disappeared through the front door of the house. That in turn seemed to act as a sort of signal to Zes, Klaase and Manasse, for they left the veranda, climbed into a light-blue Mazda bakkie, and drove off with Jakobus yelling instructions after them.

"Bring those bottles in, Josef," Sophia called out. When I did so and placed them on the pine table, she was also curious to know, "How do you spell your name?"

"J-o-s-e-f."

"Your mother give you that name?"

"No, I'm pretty certain it was my stepfather."

She poured a healthy slug of Grenada wine into a thick, clear glass. Having taken a sip, she looked at me knowingly, then murmured, "If you are who you say you are, your father used to call you Cupido or Kido after your great-great-uncle or great-great-grandfather? I have never been able to work out which."

"That is enough!" old Jakobus scolded her. "Go and see if the hens have laid more eggs, you prattling woman."

She in turn ordered her nephew, "Wilfie, do your favourite auntie a favour and check the hens."

"I told you to go!" her husband bellowed that time, the cranky, old, chauvinistic bastard.

"Ja – *Meneer*," she said in a real scornful voice. "Ja – *Ou Baas*. I shall go this minute. Shall I be allowed to come back inside if they have not laid any?"

That made the old bloke do his block altogether. He grabbed a log of firewood from the cooking hearth and just missed her face when he swung it at her. Like – if he had connected – she would have had her nose smashed or her jaw broken! I looked over at Wilfred to make sure I wasn't imagining things, and by the look in his eyes he was equally startled. Fortunately the old girl made it to the door without spilling any blood, and then old Jakobus filled a glass tumbler to the brim with brandy. He drank it all down, and then filled it to the top again. Smiling, he held the glass towards me, "*Baie Dankie!*" He certainly didn't look like a man who had practically tried to bludgeon his wife to death with a piece of firewood!

"Cheers!" I held a bottle of beer against his glass.

"Pay no attention to that old woman," he instructed me. "She talks too much. I might have to thrash her one of these days."

I tried humouring him, "That's if she doesn't thrash you first?"

It seemed to work, for both Wilfred and he almost pissed themselves laughing. "You are most probably right," the old man agreed. He then stared at his glass, his eyes instantly shutting out any amusement he may have felt. "But she talks too much all the same. I am serious – one day I will need to cut her tongue out." He drank more brandy as he concentrated on what he was about to say next. "Josef, you need to talk to some people in Rehoboth..."

"What for?" I queried him. "I don't need to talk to anybody. It's people that should be talking to me. I've had enough of this bullshit. What about the way those three arseholes on the veranda looked at me as if I was a piece of shit? You can all get fucked as far as I'm concerned..."

"Please wait," Wilfred cut in, clearly nervous that I had sworn at his uncle. "Do not talk like that to Uncle Kobus. When you learn what is going on, you would never think of speaking like that to him again. Please listen, it is very important."

"Ja, it *is* very important," the old man nodded vehemently; his hand was shaking as he poured more brandy into his glass. "No one dares to talk like that to me... Like I told you when you visited the last time – we may be witnessing a miracle. I can say no more, other than that you must speak to people in Rehoboth. If you do not, they shall speak to you if you continue to stay in this country much longer."

"Who are these people?" I asked.

"I do not know yet. Carl Zes will let me know, and then I can arrange things with Wilfred to pass the word on. Please, I am not trying to insult you. It is very – very important."

When the old lady returned she had collected a few more bags of figs for drying and mentioned that a couple of the older hens had a chance of having their heads chopped off if they didn't start laying eggs pronto. She carried on as if her husband's violence towards her had been a figment of my imagination. I soon learned that the Van Wyks, especially Sophia, had gone to a great deal of trouble in preparing for my visit. I also discovered that offal was considered by the Baster to be the very finest tucker; even more than fillet or rump steak, for she had asked a neighbouring farmer's wife to put aside two ox hearts that she had stuffed with minced lamb's liver and homemade bacon. Those she baked with sweet potatoes and parsnips that she had grown in the farm's vegetable garden, then, boiling in the kaffir pot, she had mielie-pap bubbling and swelling away. The kitchen was awash with the fragrance of her spices; sticks of cinnamon that she broke up and put in with mashed pumpkin; cloves of garlic and fresh sprigs of coriander that she added with red chilli peppers to the meat. For dessert she had stewed figs with condensed milk. The plates we ate from may have been chipped and cracked; the knives, forks and spoons may not have come from a matched set, but the tucker was absolutely top rate!

Old Jakobus gave me a rough idea of his age when he recounted how he had been a stretcher-bearer in the South African Union's defence forces in North Africa during the Second World War. He had signed up with the South African Army in Stellenbosch when his job at grape picking had run out. The only thing that seemed to have stuck most steadfastly in his memory was how his mates, who had been killed by Rommel's Africa Corps, weren't allowed to be buried next to white South African soldiers. Even amongst the death and destruction of the Second Great War, Apartheid had been alive and healthy, even though the National Government hadn't yet been voted into power. He had been involved in the heavy fighting around Sidi Rezegh where a number of black and coloured stretcher-bearers had been killed and buried with whites in a common grave. Apparently, not long after, the South African Army Headquarters ordered that the bodies be disinterred, and they were placed in separate black and white gravesites.

In the trenches at the front lines many black soldiers or auxiliaries earned the respect of their white comrades and earned high praise for their fearlessness when saving wounded soldiers under the most hazardous conditions; nonetheless these cordial relationships among the whites, coloureds and blacks didn't always reach back to the home front in South Africa. Jakobus pointed out one example; in 1943 a dance was arranged in Pietermaritzburg's City Hall by the Mayor, a Mrs Russell, for the Coloured Welfare League. This was gatecrashed by white soldiers, leaving two whites and one coloured civilian hurt. The South African military brass was all pissed off with the City Council that they claimed shouldn't have allowed the use of the hall for coloureds. Old Jakobus' younger brother Manfred had been there and he had been responsible for '*dondering*' one of the whites, but had escaped any attention on account of the fracas.

When the Germans at long last capitulated in Europe in May 1945, 20,000 blacks and coloureds joined a 'People's Day of Victory' march that took place in the streets of Johannesburg, and it was organised by the Council of non-European Trade Unions, the ANC and the Communist Party. Completely contrary to this new-found spirit of peace and togetherness, the white government announced the cash and clothing allowances for discharged servicemen. Five pounds in cash and twenty-five pounds in clothing for the whites, and three pounds cash and fifteen shillings clothing for the coloureds. For the blacks it was two pounds cash and a two pound khaki suit.

When he received his war service payout, Jakobus purchased an old, treadle operated sewing machine and headed back to South West Africa, as Namibia was known then. He had a vision of setting up his own tailoring or clothes recycling business; nevertheless an incident occurred that totally shattered any kind feelings he may have had for the Boers. His precious sewing machine was on the roof of a bus that was transporting him back to Rehoboth. When it arrived at the border of South Africa and the South West, there was a police roadblock guarding the bridge across the Orange River that separated the two countries. As the South West was under South African mandate, there was no reason to have customs or emigration requirements, yet the

Boer cops insisted on searching the bus and its passengers; all coloureds or blacks. Two of those cops climbed onto the roof of the vehicle, and they carried out their search by hurling the passengers' luggage and goods onto the concrete bridge below, thus smashing the sewing machine beyond repair. There was absolutely nothing that Jakobus or his fellow travellers could do about the wanton destruction of their possessions, for criticising the Boer authorities most often led to a beating or a stint in jail. He just had to carry on up to Rehoboth with all his army service money blown in those few short seconds.

Arriving home penniless, he had no choice but to work for Boer or German farmers who paid him the princely sum of ten shillings a month, which changed to four rand a month in 1961 when decimal currency was introduced in South Africa and the South West. On many occasions his almost non-existent wages turned out to be exactly that – nonexistent. If he was working as a shepherd for some of these farmers, and should a jackal or a lynx kill a lamb or a goat kid, he was docked several months pay in compensation. That was despite the fact that in some cases the farmers, who were often broke themselves, had no adequate facilities for their flocks to be protected properly. It was no better than slave labour.

His luck changed dramatically when his brother Manfred managed to get him a job at Alexander Bay in South Africa on one of the De Beers alluvial diamond mines, as both he and his brother managed to knock-off diamonds on the odd occasion that they sold to a Portuguese grocer in the black township in Alexander Bay. It must have been quite a lucrative pastime since Manfred eventually set himself up as a building contractor, and Jakobus managed to save enough money to purchase his two thousand hectare farm in the Rehoboth *Gebeid*. Luck further smiled on him when he made an offer on the land and buildings, for the previous owner had been fatally gored by a bull, and his widow had no chance of coping without sons and a drought that was similar to the one that Namibia was currently enduring. Things had become so dire for the widow that he managed to purchase the land and buildings for a solitary rand per hectare. Regardless of that, old Sophie assured me that farming in the Rehoboth *Gebeid* was a very touch and go affair and she and her husband were battling to make ends meet.

She wasn't kidding there, for when I surveyed my surroundings the Van Wyks had little to show for the thirty odd years that they had lived on that farm. Their dwelling exhibited a total lack of worthwhile maintenance, and the outbuildings and fences were in disrepair and had mostly fallen over. What livestock I did see were horribly emaciated, and the only object of vibrancy about the place was the burgeoning fig tree weighed down by all its fruit. That and the shiny, red Datsun bakkie that seemed totally out of place in such desolate surroundings.

If there was one thing that had flourished on that farm, it was the Van Wyks' hatred for the Boers. Both had witnessed the Apartheid regime from start to finish, and their abhorrence hadn't diminished a speck even though Namibia had been independent for well over a decade. That almost fanatical loathing was also held against the SWAPO government, whom they claimed was no better than that of the previous Boer one. According to them the Ovambo, who made up the majority of the members in parliament, were looting the country, and slowly but surely Namibia was going down the drain. The schools were running out of text books; the hospitals out of medicines; their taxes were going through the roof and there was nothing to show for them. Unemployment was reaching catastrophic proportions amongst the rural Baster.

CHAPTER 19

STEVE AND BOB PRANG INTO A SHOP!

There was never a dull moment to be had in Namibia by the look of things! It was about two-thirty in the morning when old Kobus dropped Wilfred and I off. There was an earnest debate in progress outside Wheeler's tent. He, Jeff, and Nick seemed real pleased to see me. Kotzé and Van der Merwe were nowhere around and the labourers were huddled in a group about fifty yards away, talking quietly amongst themselves.

"Why's everybody up?" I asked Dave. "It seems every time I turn my back on you bastards, there's something going on? Don't tell me Jeff's fuckin' decked both Kotzé and Van der Merwe this time? Where's Ernie and the others?"

"That flamin' Spence!" Dave blurted out.

"Yeah, the fuckin' mutant!" Jeff added.

"Steve's had a prang!" Nick added further. "Fuckin' drove into an old building!"

"Bob's got serious head injuries and he could kark it," Wheeler's voice sounded almost hysterical. "Steve's in a pretty bad way, too."

"When did this happen? Was he pissed? Where are they? What the fuck are you all doing here?" I fired at them in quick succession. "Somebody should be with 'em. Christ, we can't..."

"Ernie's with 'em in Windhoek," Jeff butted in.

"And how did they get there?"

"This outfit called Medi-Rescue came in. They landed their plane on the friggin' road!" he was all overwhelmed. "They don't stuff around those bastards! They've taken Steve and 'em to the Medi-Centre. It's a hospital of some sort. Ernie told us to come back to camp and that he would handle things. Reckoned he was gunna call the boss... That fuckin' Steve!"

Wheeler explained all. Steve and Bob had taken a Land Cruiser into Rehoboth. Their journey didn't end there, for they decided to visit the Aris Hotel that was approximately eighteen or so miles out of Windhoek on the Rehoboth road. They had made it safely back to Rehoboth after getting a gutsful of grog at the Aris pub, but about halfway between Rehoboth and Klein Aub Steve couldn't take a corner that led into the tiny settlement of Kobos. The vehicle left the road and crashed head-on into an abandoned shop; the bricks and concrete of the building stopping the Toyota dead in its tracks! Neither of them, like most Namibian drivers, were wearing seat belts, so Steve mangled himself against the steering wheel, while Bob Reynolds flew through the windscreen and smashed his head into the front wall of the building. For some peculiar reason I felt like cracking a funny: What was the point of ram-raiding an empty shop? But, judging by the demeanour of those around me, a joke of that nature had every probability of going down like a lead balloon. Nonetheless, some of the Baster who lived at Kobos heard the crash and went to investigate, although none had a vehicle to go for help. Fortunately two bakkies came from the direction of Klein Aub and the drivers recognised our company vehicle. One bakkie went racing off to Rehoboth to organise the emergency services; the other drove back to our camp. By the time Dave and the other Aussies arrived at the scene of the accident, a light plane decked out as a Flying Doctor set up had taken off from the Eros airstrip; a small airfield situated right within Windhoek itself. In about twenty minutes flat the plane had landed on the Rehoboth-Klein Aub road and the pilot and a paramedic jumped out with bandages and drips and things. There was just enough room to take Ernie when they took off again. Wheeler reckoned Bob's head was really caved-in, and Steve was screaming his lungs out; bright, foamy blood pouring out of his mouth. What added to the tragedy of things was that if they had been wearing seat belts, the outcome could have been *very different*. No wonder the Aussie cops back home had come down so heavy on people who didn't wear them. The Namibian authorities were either too fucking slack or too stupid to enforce such a law, thus making it compulsory to wear seat belts. Either way, it didn't cost anyone bugger all to wear a seat belt, except for maybe pregnant women or whatever.

Nick tried to inject some sunshine into all the gloom, "Well, Dave, at least it looks like old Steve and Bob don't have to worry about those sheilas they fucked without a franger back in Windhoek?"

Wheeler ignored him and handed out bottles of Tafel Lager as we pulled camp chairs around a fire burning in front of my new tent. "This trip's turning out to be a fuckin' nightmare," he told everyone once he had lit a smoke and made himself comfortable. "I've had a shithouse feeling about all this ever since the plane's wheels first touched the runway when we arrived..."

"Like when the plane hit that willy-willy?" I interrupted him. "Thought the pilot had lost it. A kind of omen, you reckon?"

"You might as well fuckin' call it that," he agreed. "Just about everything that can stuff up – has stuffed up. We've hardly drilled – your friggin' tent burned down – Jeff decked Kotzé – and now Steve and Bob could've karked it for all we know. Next thing the fuckin' boss's gunna be over here, and he isn't gunna be too bloody charmed."

"At least you've got your dick working properly?" Nick suggested kindly.

"Yeah," I agreed. "How are you getting on with Magda? Her folks still bummin' off you?"

Dave seemed pleased that the discussion had wandered elsewhere, "She's okay, I tell you. I'm thinking of pushing through the divorce with my missus and taking Magda back to Aussie with me."

"You're fuckin' kidding!" Jeff was aghast. "You're cunt-struck – you are!"

It took more than a comment like that to get Wheeler going. "No, I'm fair dinkum. You give me half the pay I'm getting and I could give her a ten times better life back in Kal'. There's plenty of blokes my age who're bringing in Filipina women."

"Yeah, and look what a fuck up that is," Nick scorned. "Those old bastards bringing those noggies in are just pulling themselves. Soon as the bitches marry the suckers and get Australian citizenship, they piss off with some younger bloody noggie bloke, then they start breeding like fuck and you start getting noggie kids all over the fuckin' place. Same as the fuckin' chogies."

"He could be right," I told Dave. "How old's Magda?"

"About eighteen."

"Now you're *really* pulling yourself," Nick sneered. "How old are you – nearly fifty? She'll piss off with the first young joker she comes across."

"Maybe not, if he knocks a couple of kids out of her," I tried to stick up for Wheeler. "Taking on a sheila with kids could be a different proposition. I'd be careful there, though," I turned to Dave. "Kotzé was telling me that the coloureds here aren't like the abos. You can get a throwback. A kid that's as black as the ace of spades."

"Yeah, and you're a fuckin' coloured," Jeff reminded me. "And you're from around here. What's to stop you having a reject or whatever? Would you marry one of your own kind?"

I didn't know if Jeff was looking for a bunch of fives or not, but I decided to have a go back at him. "Marry? Me? You've gotta be joking, mate. Unlike you and Dave, I'm not into this love business – I'm more into lust. I'm too fuckin' smart and there's too many pebbles on the beach. I can see where Dave's coming from, though, our coloured women over here would piss all over your white Aussie women. Your sheilas are the ones with the balls in the outfit. Not only do they wear the daks, they like to have you by the nuts with their teeth. Look at your missus – she's got you by the short and curlies. Call Dave cunt-struck, he's no..."

"Fuckin' give it away, you blokes," Wheeler stopped me. "We've had enough bullshit for one night, without you two dickheads getting stuck into each other. There's been enough blood 'n guts."

"You reckon the boss'll come over?" Nick also seemed eager to break the tension between Jeff and me. Strange that, for he loved watching a good brawl. Perhaps the car prang had taken him aback a bit?

"My bloody oath, he will!" Dave picked up Nick's olive branch. "Specially after tonight. Did you see old Ernie? The poor bastard nearly cracked up altogether."

"Serve's the fucker right," Jeff told him. "He wants to be boss, he should be able to handle things that come his way. I bet it's the first time the little prick's had any authority in his life. He's fuckin' really up himself telling us blokes what to do."

"And Bob, he was pretty stuffed?" I asked Wheeler.

"No kidding, cobber, his head was all squashed in. Like when you bring a spoon down on a boiled egg. He still had a pulse, but he looked like a stunned mullet. He'll be flamin' lucky if he pulls through. Steve wasn't much better. Christ, but he fuckin' screamed! Just like a sheila screaming. I don't reckon he's gunna make it, either."

Later on I went to bed with several things to ponder on. As I lay there in the dark the consequences of the accident really came back to roost. Especially when I remembered how I had asked Steve if I could have his computer and gear back in Kalgoorlie if he died in Namibia.

I hadn't had much to do with Spence and Reynolds before we came to Africa, therefore I didn't really know either of them all that well. Strangely their faces seemed blurred in my memory, even though we had been in Africa for some considerable time. The thought that either could die at any moment sent shivers down my spine. Spence had been too drunk to drive. I had driven a vehicle hundreds of times under the same circumstances, so had Dave, Jeff, Nick or most drillers and offsiders I had come across. The fact that we would be having breakfast in the morning without Spence and Reynolds being present was a truly troubling one.

BASTARDS FROM THE BUSH

My mind wandered on to Dave's infatuation with Magda and what Jeff and Nick had had to say. Especially what Nick had mentioned about Filipina women. I believed that being a half-caste I was perhaps luckier in some ways than Jeff and Nick. I had been to Bali with them on several occasions, and in most cases we had made our way though Jakarta to get there. While Nick and Jeff voiced their disgust of Indonesians and Asians in general, especially after the Bali bombings, I couldn't find the slightest reason to dislike them at all. The women, that was, as I found the Indonesian men to be scrawny, sleazy, untrustworthy looking types. As a matter of fact, not having a satisfactory female companion whatsoever, I found most Asian women quite enchanting. Their colour certainly didn't upset me and I found their doe-like eyes rather sensual.

I remembered Kev' Growford's words back in Wingellina when it came to other Aussies' loathing for Asians. "People who harbour hatred for other races are just carrying an unnecessary millstone around their necks, mate. What I mean is – if you insist on going around hating the Asians or other races – you have to carry one helluva extra burden that just bends and buckles your mind. People should have better things to do with themselves than carrying around a load of illogical hate."

"Yeah, but the place's being overrun with chogies," I reminded him. "Ten years ago in Kalgoorlie we only saw a couple of 'em. Now they're fuckin' everywhere. They're taking all the jobs."

"Bullshit! Have they taken your job?"

"Not yet, they haven't. I hear they'll work for fuck-all, so it's only a matter of time."

"When's the last time you ever spoke to a chogie?"

I searched for an answer. "About a week back. There was a chogie sheila who served me at the deli in Coles. The place's crawling with fuckin' Asians."

"You ever fucked an Asian?"

"Not even with your dick, mate." I had lied to him because once when I was in Perth I had called up an escort agency that specialised in Asian women. I had shagged Indian whores before and had found them delightful and much the same colour as me. They were more or less no different to white hookers, and they seemed less troubled by my own skin colour. My reason for hiring an Asian prostitute was to overcome some doubts that Nick and Jeff had sown in my brain. Nick had told me that Asian women's pussy hairs were dead straight, while Jeff reckoned their pissflaps went sideways instead of up and down; thus matching their eyes. The particular girl that came to my room indeed had rather sparse, dead straight pubic hair, though her fanny certainly didn't go sideways.

Not long after I tried out a Filipina hooker in one of Kalgoorlie's brothels. She had a beautiful face, excellent legs and body, plus a perfectly normal pussy. What was more, she showed me a catalogue magazine of Filipina girls who wanted to marry Aussie blokes. I suddenly realised what some of the old bastards in Kalgoorlie could see in them. Legions of young, beautiful Filipina women who were prepared to marry old, decrepit Aussie bastards in order to escape the poverty in the Philippines!

The thought of acquiring a mail order bride was an enticing one. Basically I had everything I wanted in my house and the other possessions I had accumulated so far, yet there was one huge, black hole in my existence; the lack of a female companion to share my life with me. The reason why I didn't follow up on Filipina brides was that I was fearful that I would earn the disgust or dislike of my workmates; especially my employer, Wally Growford..

Dave's thoughts of taking Magda back to Kalgoorlie and marrying her – regardless of the feelings of those around him – gave me a great deal of comfort. If he could ignore the feelings of our workmates, then so could I. Perhaps I could find a beautiful Baster sheila and take her back? If not, maybe a Filipina sheila? I could even go over to the Philippines to make sure I didn't get a fat or ugly one? Those enticing thoughts pushed out the dark ones about Bob and Steve's prang.

CHAPTER 20

BOB KARKS IT! MOFFIES –
BOER NAME FOR POOFTERS!

Ernie arrived back in camp shortly before dark the next day. Not only had he brought extra food supplies and a couple of dozen crates of beer; he had the oil on Steve and Bob. Bob died before the plane reached the Eros Airport and Steve was immediately flown to some hospital in Cape Town, what with no facility in Namibia being able to handle his kind of horrific injuries.

It was easy to see that the little mechanic was pretty shaken up. He drank beer after beer, chain-smoked, and his eyes exhibited the nightmares galloping through his head. As he got drunker he kept on saying over and over again: "I fuckin' shouldn't've let 'em go. Christ, that bloody Steve was always driving too fast. I should've stopped 'em. They were friggin' pissed even before they left here. This's my responsibility. I should've taken the vehicle keys. I should've bloody stopped 'em..."

"Fucksakes – shut the fuck up, Ernie!" Jeff could take no more of his whining. "They were grown men. Did Bob ever regain consciousness? Do you reckon Steve'll come good?"

"Steve was just as fucked," Ernie's voice was barely a murmur. "His ribs penetrated his lungs and his bloody neck was broken. This German doctor reckoned he'd be a fuckin' wheelchair case if he lives, and he's got about a ten percent chance of pulling through."

"And you reckon the boss's on his way?" Dave wanted to know.

"He reckoned he'd be on the next plane. He said we have to stay in fuckin' camp till he arrives. Kotzé's gunna pick him up at the airport and bring him out here. Mean time we've gotta stay put. No bloody heading into town – nothing."

"What fuckin' difference is that gunna make?" Nick argued. "We aren't all dickheads like Steve and Bob. What's the boss gunna achieve by coming over here? It isn't our fault we're not fuckin' drilling, and he should've bloody organised things a lot better. We don't need him pouring shit all over us."

The camp with its surrounding thorn trees, dust devils and blazing heat became almost like a prison while we waited for something to happen. What with all the previous days of inactivity before the accident, boredom was slowly killing us. We had read the Playboys and Hustlers from cover to cover and had long grown tired of debating on which woman in the magazines had the best legs, tits, face or snatch. They no longer gave us erections, as our imaginations had all been played out.

Except for Nick. I definitely heard him wanking himself one night in our tent! It was about one in the morning, so he probably reckoned Jeff and I were out to it. It was something to break the monotony: "Hey, Nick, you were pulling your pud last night!" I challenged him in front of the others whilst partaking of my Wheaties for breakfast. "I hope you weren't wanking over Jeff's missus?"

I got the required result. "Nick – you dirty bastard!" Wheeler scolded. "Hey, Joe, did he change hands at all?"

"Leave my missus out it, ya boong arsehole!" Jeff wasn't too charmed.

If Nick was about to be humiliated, he sure set out to disappoint me. He claimed that he hadn't been satisfied with only pulling himself just the once; however had embarked on a masturbation marathon that lasted till the sun came up. Then, in order to further revolt all those present, he declared that he had come so many times in his sleeping bag and wanted to know if he could borrow mine so that he didn't have to wade around in so much porridge.

As a matter of fact the women in the magazines, who had given some pleasure when we had first thumbed through the pages, became the targets of ridicule once we had grown bored with them. "Ah – fuck – take a look at this, you bastards!" Dave was all disgust.

I did as I was told and he was pointing at a blonde who was crouched over some bloke's cock; her arse in the air and giving a clear view of what her fanny looked like from behind. "So what?" I demanded.

"Do we have to stare up her flamin' arsehole? She's half a day away from getting piles. Look at the fuckin' brown halo around her ring piece. Her arsehole looks like a blown-out truck tyre!"

Van der Merwe came along to see the object of Dave's derision. He pointed at the blonde's rectum. "That is for the moffies."

"What's a fuckin' moffie?" Nick had also joined the crowd.

"Moffies? Moffies are what we call homos. You know – short for hermaphrodite?"

That delighted Nick. "Hey – Jeff!"

"What do ya want, ya fuckin' mutant?"

"You're a fuckin' moffie!"

That opened up a debate on male homosexuals who were referred to as being pillow-biters, chocolate-lips, arse-bandits, dung-punchers, shirt-lifters and chutney-punchers. Not to mention the more mundane labels such as gays, faggots and poofters. Naturally Jeff had to accuse Van der Merwe and Kotzé of both being chutney-punchers. Not only since all Boers had to be poofters, but also because all Boer women were the exact replicas of arseholes. After what happened to the Japie geo', neither Boer was game to mount a retaliatory campaign against him. Then again, and using Wheeler's fancy words, Jeff *was* rather expert at testing the furthest extremities of a person's sensibilities!

"Fancy pulling your dick out of some joker's arse and finding a big knob of shit stuck on the end of it?" Nick suggested to Dave.

"That's why I'd never fuck you, Nick," Wheeler assured him. "You're too full of shit!"

That had us all laughing like jackals. Nick tried to defend himself, "I've got a nicer arse than Jeff's. It's got me fucked why you keep sniffin' around his."

"You get fucked – ya moffie!" Jeff obviously liked the new word we had learned that day.

CHAPTER 21

I KILL AN OSTRICH! OLD MAN EMU!

An ostrich came visiting that afternoon, causing some considerable interest. The dopey bastard wandered right into the camp and was instantly surrounded by the remains of both drilling crews, Ernie and the labourers. One black labourer, who was probably a Damara, just missed its head with a rock.

Nick's love of animals immediately came to the fore, "Don't – you dirty, black bastard! Don't try'n hurt it!"

I was at a loss as to why we had the bird surrounded. It was becoming very nervous and dashed in all directions, only to be cut off by one of us in the circle.

"Watch out, these bastards can give you one helluva boot!" Wheeler showed off his knowledge of the species.

"It is a male! They are very good to eat," Herman also knew about those lanky birds.

"I'll friggin' eat *you*, Herman!" Nick was appalled.

"It must belong to one of the farmers nearby," Wilfred told us.

Then disaster struck! The ostrich finally had had enough of all the harassment and it made a determined effort to get away, but put one foot in the steel bucket that Van der Merwe had used to hammer the geo' pick on during Kotzé's court case. The bird fell heavily to the ground; got up again, but fell as a result of its leg being broken.

"Ah – fuck! Its fuckin' leg's broken!" Nick yelled in horror. It was a pathetic sight, for the bird was down on the ground and spinning itself round and round with its good leg.

"Kill the fuckin' thing!" Ernie shouted. "Put it out of its misery!"

"Can't we save it?" Nick desperately asked Herman.

"No, boss, its leg is very badly broken."

That was true; the ostrich's leg had a bone sticking right out and it was poking out even more every time it moved. I ran to the support truck and grabbed the heavy, stainless steel jack handle that Jeff had selected to defend himself against the imaginary leopard. I took aim at the bird's head, but its long neck was ducking and weaving all over the place. In the end I grabbed the jack handle with both hands and swung it at its neck with all my might. It took about three hits in the neck, and then one direct on the head before the bird at last lay still.

"Bloody hell!" Nick was visibly upset. "Oh, for Christ's sake! Are you sure it's fuckin' dead?"

Despite the fact that the ostrich's neck was broken in a couple of places, Herman cut its head off to make sure it was indeed devoid of life. Our Ovambo cook arrived on the scene with a big kitchen knife, but Nick stopped him, "Leave the bastard alone!"

"It's dead, Nick," I assured him. "Let the labourers have it for tucker."

There was a melee as willing blacks and coloureds gathered round the carcass. In no time at all they had the creature skinned and they divided up the meat. A fairly sad thing happened some time later, though, for a lighter coloured female ostrich came close to our tents, obviously looking for its mate that was by then only a pile of skin and feathers. Herman gathered those last remains and insisted that the hide and feathers would fetch good money back in Kalkrand if he used enough salt to preserve them.

In order to try and cheer Nick up, I reminded him of the emu episode in Capricorn, Western Australia.

"Yeah, you dickheaded mutants!" Jeff also recalled what I was talking about.

And what a saga that was! Jeff, Nick and I had been drilling in the iron ore country in the Pilbara, and were moving the rig from one contract to another. Drilling iron ore was tough on both men and machinery and it was right in the middle of summer. I might have been darker than both of my workmates, but that Pilbara sun had burnt us as dark brown as the iron ore ridges we had been drilling. We headed for the roadhouse at Capricorn, and the tiny settlement's pub and motel setup was like a beautiful mirage in all that heat. We parked the rig and the support vehicles in the shade of some peppercorn trees, and then we checked into the motel. Just as we were taking our bags into our rooms an emu came sauntering up to us; by all appearances dead keen to become the best of mates. We found out in the pub that the bird was a pet of the publican's missus and was always on the lookout for free handouts. Apparently its favourite tucker was fried chips.

After having spent some weeks sweating our guts out in all that iron and prickly spinifex grass, naturally putting away a few gallons of beer was a top priority. Jeff had a thirst almost double Nick's and mine, and it was barely dark when he was as pissed as a pickled mullet. He barely managed to put away a steak sandwich and chips before heading off to the fart-sack.

Nick and I weren't that far behind him, and as we were leaving the pub's restaurant I noticed that Nick had wrapped up all his chips in a paper serviette. "What you up to, Nick, you gunna have a midnight feast or something?"

"Nah, mate, where's that fuckin' emu?"

I found that typical of Nick; he had saved his chips for the friendly bird. How nice of him I thought? I couldn't have been more wrong!

"What do you reckon, Joe? Let's see if we can con the emu into following me into Jeff's room? Once we get him in, I'll lock the door and we'll see what Jeff has to say about it in the morning?"

It seemed a bonzer idea at the time. We had no trouble locating the emu, and, being a trusting kind of creature and a fried chips addict, it eagerly followed Nick into Jeff's room. It was when Nick shut the door behind it that all kinds of strife broke loose! For starters, it was obvious that the bird had never been locked up in a motel room before, so it went dashing all round the place, squirting out a trail of inky black, liquid shit as it went along! It must have tried to jump over Jeff's bed and gave its occupant a good boot in the back, for Jeff woke up roaring his lungs out. From my own personal knowledge of such an animal, emus seemed to communicate by making hollow but quite loud bonking noises in their throats.

What with all the banging, crashing, bonking and shouting, it didn't take long for a small crowd to be assembled outside Jeff's motel room. By that time the emu had kicked Jeff a couple more times before making its final bid for freedom.

Neither the publican, his missus or Jeff were the least bit thrilled, and the emu's owner reckoned she was going to call the cops. Her spouse backed her up one hundred percent on that one because there was literally bird shit and feathers everywhere! The refrigerator in the room had been knocked over, and all the coffee cups and saucers and things had been smashed to smithereens. There were huge holes and dents up and down the door from where the terrified bird had tried to kick its way out.

Nick and I had made it to our rooms with only seconds to spare, and we too, came out and surveyed the scene with both horror and disgust.

Jeff was just standing there in his jocks, eyes wide with fury, and we could see welts on his shoulders and back where the emu's pointy toes had gashed into him.

Trust Nick to try and make the whole situation worse! "Fuck me dead, Jeff, the Pilbara sheilas may be as ugly as a hatful of arseholes, but try'n to fuck an emu's going way over the top – you horribly sick fuck!"

Strangely enough that seemed to mellow the publican and his missus, for the sight of Jeff clad only in his jocks chasing Nick south down the Great Northern Highway was a hilarious one! That's what was good about outback folk; at least they had a sense of humour. A couple of hundred bucks changed hands for the mess that was made in the room, and peace returned to the Pilbara once more. From then on in the iron ore country Jeff was given the nickname 'Old Man Emu'.

CHAPTER 22

BOSS IS SERIOUSLY PISSED OFF!
STEVE ALSO KARKS IT!
WE HAVE A WAKE FOR STEVE & BOB!
GHOSTS IN THE SHITHOUSES!

Our employer arrived in a real poncey Mitsubishi Pajero with all kinds of colourful stripes along the sides of it. Kotzé had followed him in his Land Rover and had brought Van der Merwe with him. I could see by the boss' face that he was really going to hand out some shit! "What the fuck's been going on?" he asked us as we assembled round him.

"What do you mean – what the fuck's been going on?" Jeff asked him back.

"What do I mean by what the fuck's been going on?" the boss was incredulous. "First you're having piss ups and orgies back at the house in Windhoek and wrecking the fuckin' place, and then you end up in fuckin' court for blueing. If you're not bloody doing that, you're burning fuckin' tents to the ground. You fuckin' knocked the geo' here arse-over-tit, then a company vehicle gets written off – killing Bob!"

Ernie was keeping as far as possible in the background, so, as always, Dave was the first to have something to say. He pointed an accusing finger at Kotzé. "You've obviously been listening to this dickhead, and like a fuckin' sheila – he's been telling stories out of school. We came here to fuckin' drill, not sit on our fuckin' arses! When the flamin' rig was going we were getting three hundred metres a day on each shift.

130

Take a look at the rig – it's in bloody mint condition. Take a look at all the gear... The tent was an accident, and if we want to fuck sheilas over here, it's none of your fuckin' business. You can get fucked for mine!"

"Right – you're tramped," the boss wasn't having that. "Pack up your gear and Ernie can run you back to town." He then vented his spleen on his mechanic: "Fuckin' hell, Ernie! I really trusted you. I really thought you could handle things over here?"

"Who's gunna drill on Dave's shift, now that you've tramped him?" Jeff inquired.

"You can, Jeff," the boss replied.

Jeff wasn't too thrilled with that idea. "Up your fuckin' arse! Dave's done fuck all wrong. You tramp him and you might as well tramp me. You aren't using me to have a go at Dave. No fuckin' way!"

"You can fuckin' tramp me, too!" Nick wasn't about to be left out of things. "We've done fuck all wrong. We can pay for the tent and stuff out of our wages, and we've settled things with Kotzé. If he carries on about Jeff decking him, I'll really mangle the fuckin' bastard! As for Steve and Bob, they've taken vehicles out millions of times."

"How's Steve?" Ernie cut in.

"The bastard's gunna die," the boss told him. "I stopped off in Cape Town. The doctors can't do anything for him... Christ, Dave – they were your offsiders – you useless cunt! Why the fuck didn't you make...?"

"Who the fuck do you reckon you're talking to?" Wheeler interrupted him. "Who you calling a cunt? I don't have to be spoken to like that by you. Who the fuck do you think you are? What happened to Steve and Bob – happened. Okay, so they *were* my offsiders, I couldn't be keeping tabs on 'em twenty-four hours a day. You've given me the tramp, now shut the fuck up!"

The boss was taken aback by Dave's tirade. "But you shouldn't've let Steve drive if he was pissed. What do you reckon, Joe?"

I just shrugged. I wasn't thinking of buying into the argument on anyone's side. Although I agreed with Dave, Jeff and Nick: We hadn't done anything wrong, but I certainly wasn't looking to be sacked. Being dark-skinned back in Aussie, I wasn't about to tarnish my reputation of never having been given the tramp by a drilling company.

"Fucksakes, give us a beer!" the boss demanded; suddenly popping the tension like a balloon. We all grabbed camp chairs and formed a circle in order to discuss things. The labourers kept a curious distance from us, and it was clear to see that they were dead keen for things to be resolved, so that they could get back on to full pay.

"What gives with the lab?" Wheeler asked Kotzé.

"Agh, they have done about two thirds of the samples, but the results have been rather disappointing. The rock structure must be more complicated than I first thought. I need to have some ground magnetometer work carried out, so that I can work out what is happening."

"And how long's that gunna take?" the boss asked him. "The bloody rig's been idle for too long and a fuckin' bloke's gunna go broke at this rate. I haven't even covered the expenses of getting the bastard over here."

"A geophysics crew should be arriving first thing tomorrow morning. If I can get the results plotted up the day after, which they say I will be able to do, we should be able to start drilling again the day after that."

"Not a fuckin' second sooner," our employer was adamant.

He didn't hang around for much longer. First he had to see some government officials from the Home Affairs Department in regard to Bob Reynolds' death, and to make arrangements for Bob's body to be flown back to Aussie. After that he had to collect all Bob's and Steve's gear that had been left in the Klein Windhoek house. When he reached Cape Town to see how Steve was going, Steve had also karked it, so there was further form filling for the boss to do in South Africa before heading back to Kalgoorlie. The South African Airways flight that flew him to Perth also had Steve's coffin on board. During his short spell in Cape Town he organised another laboratory to work in tandem with the one that Kotzé was using, in order to push the samples through faster. We heard later from Ernie that the newspapers back in West Aussie were full of stories about Steve and Bob's deaths in 'Darkest Africa'.

Out at the camp we drillers organised a wake for the two dead offsiders. There was plenty of beer put away that day and we had a barbecue. Dave, Jeff and I had our first taste of ostrich that the cook expertly grilled over some thorn embers. Nick didn't want a bar of it. Kotzé got stuck into the beer with us and he most likely made a dickhead out of himself in front of the geophysics crew, for he was totally rat shit when they reported to him at the end of their job. Van der Merwe passed out long before anyone else and he was lying on his back on the ground; his shirt sodden with puke and Jeff using his gaping mouth as an ashtray.

The next day we still had nothing to occupy us, as the Japie geo' had to plot up all the magnetometer readings. That was further hindered by the fact that he had a cracking hangover.

To add to our discomfort we had just had an outbreak of food poisoning in the camp. Not really serious stuff, just diarrhoea and vomiting amongst us Aussies. The cook, not ever having had much to do with freezers, had let some mince go off, so we had to charge backwards and forth to the pit latrines. It went on for a couple of days and nights. Night time was the worst for me, as the latrines were a fair way from the camp and shrouded in darkness. I kept getting the feeling, when I was squatting over one of the pits that the ghosts of Steve Spence and Bob Reynolds might be looking over my shoulder. I had had that ludicrous feeling ever since they had both been killed, so generally tried to answer the call during the daytime, but with my crook guts I had no choice in the matter. Then I noticed that whenever I used the latrines at night, Nick was never far behind me. I wasn't imagining things – whenever I went for a shit – he would be in one of the other cubicles grunting and groaning away. I didn't know if it was one of his antics or not, so I decided to have a go at him, "You queer or something, Nick?"

"No, cobber – why?"

"How come whenever I go for a shit, you follow me? Especially at night time? You craving my arse or something?"

"Fuck no, mate! I'm just shit-frightened of the spooks."

"What the fuck you on about?"

"Steve and Bob. Whenever I go for a crap, I'm shit-scared Steve and Bob are gunna grab me!"

I was pleased to have a kindred spirit. "You – too?"

"Yeah, mate, the fuckin' shithouses give me the willies when it's dark."

"For fuck's sake, don't tell the others, otherwise they'll scorn the fuck out of us."

"Too bloody right, mate!"

Old Jakobus arrived at about lunchtime the following day and he invited me to talk with someone in Rehoboth. Wilfred and I had to go in the old man's bakkie because Ernie wouldn't even think of letting another company vehicle out of his sight.

CHAPTER 23

OUMA WITBOOI! MY TWIN BROTHER IS SOMEWHERE IN NAMIBIA! KRYSTAL!

Like most of Namibia, Rehoboth was also a place of contrasts. When you first entered the town along the main road from the Windhoek side; to the right there were affluent, modern houses with BMWs, Audis, Mercedes and brightly coloured four-wheel drives parked in front of them. To the left of the road the town, proper, was made up of less salubrious dwellings; some quite comfortable looking with nice gardens; others half-finished, and some absolute hovels made of corrugated iron, pieces of plastic sheeting and cardboard. Somewhere in the middle of the affluent area and the not so affluent area stood the town's municipal buildings, schools, shops, the church and the Catholic hospital. Along the main highway there was the odd donkey or horse; horribly worn out from hunger; searching for the tiniest shred of sustenance.

The house old Jakobus headed for was a mixture of brick and mortar, with corrugated iron renovations, and there was a concrete pad where the walls of an additional room hadn't been started on. The walls in the lounge room-cum-bedroom-cum-kitchen amply displayed that the roof leaked, for I could see weird, surrealistic patterns where water had trickled freely over the smoke-stained paint. Like Sophia Van Wyk's house, the smell of burnt firewood had permeated everything, yet the place was as clean and cosy as possible under the circumstances. In pride of place on the mantelpiece that hung over the cooking hearth there was a whole collection of Christian religious icons; crucifixes, pictures of Holy Mary carrying Jesus; Saint Michael saving some kid from the devil with a huge sword in one hand – the whole box and dice. All dusty and blackened by smoke.

Also, as if in pride of place, there was a little mongrel dog sitting on one of the lounge chairs. Some Rhodesian Ridgeback must have got down on its knees to root the dog's tiny whippet mother, or the other way round, for the only asset the animal had to be proud of was a ridge running down its back. One massive ridge; tiny body, tiny legs, tiny head; tiny everything, bar the ridge. A ridge with legs!

Sitting on one of the other faded, green, velvet lounge chairs was a more formidable sight altogether! There was a very old woman sitting there. As old as, or even more ancient than the codger who had shown me his medal back at the Klein Aub grog shop. She was fairly chubby in her floral skirt and stained, pink blouse. All her skin – face, neck, arms, backs of her hands and ankles – was shrivelled liked a coffee coloured raisin. Coffee with lots of milk added. Her eyes were a funny, light grey colour, making it hard to choose whether she was either a European or a coloured. All her front teeth except for her canines had gone missing, which gave a rather ferocious look about her.

Not only did she giggle her delight at seeing me, she spoke English better than I did! "You aren't Jonker! You must be his twin brother. Oh – Lord save us! That scar on your neck's not quite the same as his, though."

"You can go now, Wilfred," Jakobus ordered his nephew. "Wait in the bakkie, or go and get yourself a cool drink at the petrol garage. Do not go far, for we should not be here for too long."

Wilfred looked quickly over at the old lady. It was clear he wanted to listen in on things. "Agh – *Ouma*?" he pleaded.

"Off you go, Wilfred," the old lady wasn't having him hanging around. When he left, she turned to me. "Sit down, boy – sit down. You must be Kido? I was wondering if we would ever see you again."

"His name is Josef," Jakobus cut in. "At least that is the name that his stepfather, *Meneer* Schultz, gave him. Anna must have agreed to it also."

"Agh – no, man, we've always known of the boy as Kido! There's no reason to change now. Tell me," she came back to me, "what's happened to your mother and Mr. Schultz? Incidentally, I'm your great aunt on your father's side. Possibly great-great aunt. My name's Elsabeth, and I'm also a Witbooi. Like you and your brother, Jonker, I'm related to Hendrik Witbooi – *Kaptein van die Witbooi-Hottentotte*!" She claimed the latter with undisguised pride. "My goodness, your mother and Mr. Schultz must have left over thirty years ago. Tell me all about Australia."

Having instantly taken a liking to the old dear, great-great aunt or not, I tried to give her as accurate a picture as possible of what had happened from when I had arrived in Aussie up to me sitting there before her. She cluck-clucked at the news of my mother's drug overdose and claimed that drugs were wiping out the Baster Nation. "Drugs and alcohol!" she exclaimed. "Every second day we have a death as a result of those devilish poisons. It isn't just *dagga* weed, either – they're getting much more dangerous things from South Africa. Things were much better under the Boers, for at least their police had some control over these things. The police now – even our Baster constables – are simply hopeless. For all I know, they're probably involved. Wait till..."

"Come now, Elsabeth," Jakobus calmed her down. "Nothing can be worse than living under the Boers. Their cops were twice as corrupt. Any corruption involved with the police today was well and truly handed down by the white regime in Pretoria. They made excellent teachers."

"What rubbish!" the old girl argued. "We're in a far worse purgatory under SWAPO. We've gone from the frying pan into the fire. There's no... ."

Jakobus turned to me. "You should have seen the old days, Josef. If the cops ever stopped you, you never dared to smile – you never dared to speak – you dared not to do anything. You had to stand there looking down at the ground because if you were brave enough to look them in the eye, you could be punched, kicked or arrested. They looked for any excuse to hit you. Then you had to grovel, Josef – yes *Meneer* – no *Meneer*. As far as they were concerned, they were gods, and if you were black or coloured you were a criminal and someone to be beaten and humiliated. They always worked in pairs and you could be picked out at random. One standing behind you, emptying your pockets and stealing any money you might have, and the other one standing in front. You never knew where the first blow would strike you – in the solar plexus or the kidneys. They were trained to inflict terror and no passerby, black or white, would dare interfere. They treated our women in exactly the same way. If you attracted the attention of the cops, you seldom walked away without shedding a drop of blood or two. No, I tell you, son, there was nothing..."

A woman in her early twenties wearing a smart, blue, bank teller's uniform interrupted him. In had walked the most incredible creature I had ever seen in my *entire* life! I immediately got to my feet and felt a dork, and then I sat down and felt an even bigger one. In seconds my thoughts started whirling around in my head. She smiled at everyone, then at me, and I could see that my whole demeanour was making those around me embarrassed. Not old Elsabeth, though, for I saw a quick, calculating gleam flash in her eyes.

"Krystal – this is Josef Schultz. We used to know him as Kido Witbooi."

I jumped up again to shake her hand and she smiled when she held hers out. She didn't say anything, probably since she didn't have anything to say, and I just stood there like a mute mullet. Her delightfully soft hand gripped mine quite firmly, sending electric shocks through my body.

Finally the old lady introduced some sanity into my numbed brain and I let go of her hand, "Make some coffee, Krystal. Be careful now, I've had a great deal of trouble getting that coffee stain out of your other work blouse." Krystal placed a blue, imitation leather handbag on the couch beside Jakobus and she set about doing what the ancient old biddy had told her to.

"What was I saying now?" Elsabeth wanted someone to remind her.

"Enough politics," Jakobus quickly interjected. "So you definitely think that Josef is Jonker's brother? You are absolutely certain?"

"Of course I am, you old fool! Look at his eyes, for goodness sake. Where have you seen another Baster's eyes like that? Anna's twin boys were identical."

"Are you Jonker's brother?" Krystal had joined us again and was sitting next to Jakobus, who was noticeably pissed off from being called an old fool by Elsabeth. Her eyes stared wide with interest and I nearly swooned at the attention she was giving me.

I felt like a cracked gramophone record playing when I answered her, "I could be. My stepfather told me I had a twin brother, but neither he nor my mother talked about him. They never mentioned his name, so this's all news to me, too. My real father wasn't mentioned all that much, either."

Elsabeth told Krystal all about my mother and stepfather and I got a kick out of the fact that the much younger woman seemed interested in my past. It gave me a chance to examine her out of the corner of my eye. She had the most incredible legs that she held in the most ladylike way as she sat on the couch. She had slender hips, body and shoulders, and breasts that hardly protruded from her white uniform blouse. Her fingers were long and slender, and to my relief she wore no rings of any sort. In fact the only jewellery she wore was a very thin, gold chain around her neck that dangled a tiny crucifix. Her teeth were perfect, complimenting a beautiful aquiline face. Her dark eyes danced when she smiled and her jet-black hair was straight and captured in a very practical ponytail. Her skin was roughly the same shade as mine; light brown, like a very well tanned European. When she walked over to take the kettle off the coals I soon became aware that she may have been a fraction taller than my six foot. She held herself and walked like an aristocrat; like a fabulous model out on a boardwalk; like a long-legged thoroughbred racehorse being led into the winner's circle. She lit up that upside-down house and I felt appalled that she had to put up with just being in such a place.

I felt I had to talk to her, "Do you know this Jonker Witbooi, Krystal?"

"Ja, everybody..." She quickly looked to the old man and woman, her beautiful face and eyes looking totally confused. "At least I have..."

"We aren't here to talk about Jonker," Elsabeth butted in. "We're here to talk about *you*, Kido."

I had an immediate rush of blood to the head, "My name's Josef – not Kido. If this Jonker's my brother – why the hell all the secrecy?" I was immediately ashamed of my outburst because I could see that I had upset them. I felt especially bad in front of Krystal and desperately tried to make amends, "Look – I'm really sorry. If I've got a brother somewhere around here, I'd like to catch up with him. That's all – I apologise if you think I've been rude."

"It's all right," the old woman sighed. "We can understand how you must feel. But please trust me – you shall meet up with him very soon."

"Is he in some kind of trouble?" I asked her.

"He's in politics against the government. Anyone who opposes SWAPO needs to be very careful. You'll find out everything in good time."

As old Jakobus was driving Wilfred and I back to Klein Aub the words I had sneered at Jeff came back to haunt me. Love? Lust? Thinking of Krystal made my guts swim! Did she know Jonker Witbooi? Was she his girlfriend? Like the old lady, was she related to me some how? What the hell was her surname?

I tried to put myself out of my misery by asking Wilfred, "What's Krystal's surname? Is she a Witbooi?"

Amusement leapt into the little Baster's eyes. "Krystal's surname? Let me see now, I think..."

BASTARDS FROM THE BUSH

"It is Diergaardt," the old man stopped the crap. "She comes from one of the great Baster families like we Van Wyks. Rehoboth's kaptein is a Diergaardt." He pronounced the name Diergaardt similar to 'deerhart'.

CHAPTER 24

I PICK A BLUE WITH JEFF!

The boss had told Ernie to make do with local labour, for he wasn't willing to send any more Aussies over. Nick went over to Dave's shift and they had Herman with them, while Jeff and I took on Wilfred full time. As our new offsiders were doing as competent a job as Steve and Bob had ever done, we had a huge row over what they should be paid. For starters, Bob and Steve had each been getting twenty-five times as much as the two Baster put together. Ernie, obviously trying to suckarse the boss by keeping costs down, suggested that we should triple their pays at most; still Kotzé was absolutely horrified when Jeff suggested they should get Aussie rates in Namibian dollars. That would have amounted to more than two thousand Nam' dollars a shift, and then there was extra money to be had from the metres-drilled bonus. Van der Merwe – a white man – was only getting two hundred Nam' dollars a day. In the end Ernie agreed to pay Wilfred and Herman the same as Van der Merwe was getting. That killed two excellent birds with one stone; Herman and Wilfred nearly swooned over their pay hikes; the Boer field assistant was all poxed off since coloureds were getting the same amount of brass as he was. I threatened both the newly-affluent Baster with a slow and hideous death if they let on to the other labourers what they were getting, for I was sure we didn't want to set any new pay precedents in Basterland.

We drilled another couple of thousand metres before Kotzé pulled the rig up again. The assay results had totally confused the Japie.

Everybody was pissed off, bar me. Twenty-four hours a day my thoughts were full of Krystal. When I was standing at the Schramm's controls I longed for her to be nearby, so she could see how casually I handled such magnificent gear. I was the driller; king of all around me; no ordinary Baster. Thoughts of her made me want to push far more metres than Dave. Me – a coloured – earning far more than a white man!

I got so carried away with that idea that I nearly bogged the rods when the hammer penetrated a fault in the rock and groundwater started pissing out everywhere. With so much water pouring into the bottom of the drill hole, I hadn't given the compressor enough time to blow the rock cuttings out, so the rods jammed.

Being a world class driller, Jeff could see that coming a mile off. "What the fuck you doing – ya fuckin' mutant? We're gunna need foam to clean the bastard out!"

Nevertheless, that was the kind of person I had become. The powerful detergent we used to make the foam with was up to scratch and we soon had the rods turning freely again. Coming from Baster farming families both Herman and Wilfred were delighted with that sudden source of potable, subterranean water, and Wilfred couldn't wait to tell his uncle. Such knowledge could only be worth money to the old man. What with the drill hole being vertical; it was only a matter of finding some sort of a pumping device to tap that new-found treasure.

The thoughts of romance had me in such a good mood I decided to start a blue with Jeff. The last time we had come to blows was at the Whitehouse Hotel in the outback gold mining town of Leonora, but the cops, Nick, and a couple of dump truck drivers working in an open-pit nearby, stopped things just as Jeff was starting to get the upper hand. He had got the better of me by hitting me over the head with a pool cue; otherwise I was doing rather nicely before I got my brains rattled. With no pool cues being within easy reach of the drill site, I wasn't content to let such an opportunity go by; not on that fine day, anyway. Besides, I had a long-handled shovel hidden in front of the back wheels of the drill truck.

"When you gunna to take a shower?" I asked him casually. "I know we've only got cold water to wash with, but fair fuckin' go, cobber."

"What the fuck you talkin' about?" I had aroused his curiosity.

"About you – you friggin' stink! You shit yourself or something?"

Jeff was particularly mindful of his personal hygiene: I had seen him sometimes take five showers a day when it was hot weather, so I had really struck a raw nerve.

He sniffed under his armpits; checked the soles of his work boots to see if he had stepped on anything nasty, then, "It isn't me. I can't smell anything."

"Bullshit!" I scorned. "You're just used to your own fuckin' stink. You stink like a Kalahari vulture's crutch – ya dirty, fat bastard. You'll have me dry reaching at this rate. It's no fuckin' joke – you stinking piece of shit. Get the fuck out of my nose!"

He went up to Wilfred. "Can you smell anything?"

"No, boss!"

"He wouldn't say so, even if he could," I insisted. "I know what – you bloody fell into one of the pit latrines. You're such a fat bastard, you caved the side in and fell in the shit. Chrissake, go and have a shower – ya dirty, fat bastard – before I chunder! I reckon you haven't had shower since we've been on site. Those shower buckets are okay, so get some soap on you before I smack you in the mouth and kick your fuckin' stinkin' arse!"

He stared at me in disbelief. "What the fuck you on about?"

"Jeff," I tried to sound all worn-out, "you stink of rotten kippers. Like a wart hog's jockstrap. Haven't you had a shower since you knocked off that sheila back in Windhoek? Remember – the one who gave you crabs?"

"I had a shower when I got up this morning. It's probably your breath – ya fuckin' boong arsehole!"

144

BASTARDS FROM THE BUSH

I took a swing at him, but missed his face and grazed his ear. I threw two more punches that hit the target that time and his upper lip was pulped. Being very mindful of the fact that he could finish me off with one of his mega-punches, I quickly moved in to kick him in the groin; however he sidestepped and barely missed me with a head butt. I pushed him away and we both shaped up for a good blue. The last I had seen of Wilfred was a streak of lightning heading for the camp. My love for Krystal most probably had addled my brains, for Jeff landed a real beauty in my guts, then he knocked me backwards off my feet with an uppercut. He went to stomp on my head, but I rolled away and jumped to my feet. He was really on the ball on that occasion. Instead of losing his temper and going apeshit – which was his normal caper – he kept his guard up and I was hard-pressed at dodging his fists. Fortunately he was hitting me on the shoulders and the top of my head because I didn't want any burst lips or cut eyebrows. I had plans of seeing Krystal again. By constantly circling him I soon had him tiring, and just as I was about to take the initiative, a vehicle's horn tooted behind me and he landed an absolute pearler on my jaw as I looked round to see what was happening.

"Jeffry!" a voice shouted out as he booted me in the guts.

Not far away two vehicles had come to a halt. One was Kotzé's Land Rover and the other was a Land Cruiser station wagon. Out of the Toyota climbed two black individuals who looked a bit fearful of coming any closer. The Boer stood between them and us. "What the blerrie hell is going on?" he wanted to know. "This is the Senior Mines Inspector," he indicated to one of the blacks, "and here is the Permanent Secretary for Mines."

Jeff and I shook hands with the two officials once we had wiped the blood off our knuckles on the back of our overalls. We must have looked a sight, what with Jeff's bloody mouth and me covered in dust from being knocked to the ground.

The rig's hydraulic motor and compressor were still idling away contentedly, so I revved up both engines and had the hammer thudding away like a jackhammer. We put a new rod on as if nothing had happened and the sample monkeys went about their work splitting the samples. I had totally forgotten about them since I had decided to stir things up with Jeff. The one black bloke who had been introduced as being the mines inspector was trying to get his mobile phone to work; a bloody vain endeavour since we were miles out in the bush, while Kotzé was busy walking around the rig with the permanent secretary. Without saying anything more to us, they climbed back into their vehicles and headed in the direction of the camp.

"I would've fuckin' had you if those jokers hadn't pitched up," Jeff assured me.

"Ah, crap – you were dead on your feet! You need to get a lot more fit – ya big, fat bastard."

CHAPTER 25

I GO IN SEARCH OF ROMANCE! HENDRIK WITBOOI – ONE OF NAMIBIA'S GREATEST SONS!

I always felt quite coy when I quizzed Wilfred about Krystal: "How old's Krystal?"

"Twenty-two – maybe twenty-three. You like Krystal, boss?"

"She's okay. Where does she live?"

"With old Auntie Elsabeth. She has been living with her since I was born."

"Where does she work?"

"In a bank."

"I know that. Which bank?"

"One in Independence Avenue. She travels in and out every day with my Uncle Manfred. Why so many questions, boss? You must like her?"

"Yeah, I do. I like her a lot. Better than most women I've ever met. I more than like her."

My embarrassed frankness seemed to trouble him. "I see."

That had me worried. "Does she have a boyfriend? She could be married even – couldn't she? A beautiful woman like that must've swarms of men chasing after her? Every day she must come across jokers wanting to go out with her?"

"Agh no, man! She has no boyfriends and she is not married. Auntie Elsabeth keeps chasing everyone away. When she comes back from Windhoek she goes nowhere except for church with all the old women in town. She never leaves Auntie Elsabeth."

That made me feel a lot better, yet I still had a theory to test. "Are you sure she isn't Jonker Witbooi's girl?"

No matter how much I prodded him – even threatening to give him the tramp – I couldn't get him to come up with a word about my supposed brother.

With all the confusion of the dud assay results that he had received from the Klein Aub prospect, Kotzé was instructed by the client company to take the rig to Karibib, so things could be sorted out later. Apparently some agreement had been reached with the German prospector; therefore the Karabib prospect was available for drilling. I had a grand master plan to pull off before I left the Rehoboth area. It involved visiting old Elsabeth's ramshackle dwelling just before Krystal got back from work. It definitely didn't involve Wilfred and old Jakobus being there.

I had a run in with Ernie. He had hired a Datsun one tonner utility to go in the place of the written-off Toyota Land Cruiser. It was dark-green with metallic silver stripes down the side. The Baster and Japies seemed to love stripes on four-by-fours, and the vehicle was almost brand-new, having done only about three thousand kilometres. I wanted the vehicle and Ernie was still a bit shell-shocked about letting us leave the camp on private business.

With my heart set on obtaining romance, I soon lost patience with the little dickhead, "I'm taking either the Land Cruiser or the Datsun. You make up your mind which, but I'm gunna take one of 'em. You can tramp me if you like, but I'm going. You can spare one vehicle."

He could be a real whinging bastard at times, "You heard what the boss said about taking vehicles off the job. You saw what happened to Bob and Steve. Never mind you getting the tramp – I'll also get fuckin' tramped if I let you. Christ, we can't afford anything else to happen. The road into Rehoboth's getting more and more stuffed every day. It needs a friggin' grader on it."

"Look – fuck you – Ernie! One – I'm not pissed like Steve was. Two

– I should be back before ten. Three – I've driven millions of miles on worse roads in the outback. A fuckin' sight more than you. I can assure you, I won't even have one bloody beer."

"For fucksakes – give him the Datsun keys, Ernie," Wheeler joined in. "I can't stand the two of you whining and sobbing and carrying on. If he goes out there and kills himself, it's just fate, mate. How do you like that?" he grinned broadly. "Fate – mate?"

Being a spiteful sort of a ponce, Ernie only let me take the plain, white Land Cruiser. Nick wanted to know where I was going, but I told him to mind his own business and that I was taking no bastard with me. He announced to all those around him that I was bored with wanking and was bent on hunting up some Baster snatch. Wilfred looked at me as if he could read my mind. He caught my eye as I was starting the vehicle and he only shook his head and smiled.

It didn't take long to reach Kobos. There had obviously been a stuff up with the towing outfit that Ernie had organised to remove the wrecked Toyota, for what was left of it was still in the tiny, roadside hamlet. The wheels had vanished, alongside the gearbox, steering wheel, differentials, radio and seats. Because the front of the vehicle's body was wrapped around the engine, it was still there; although the clutch cylinder, power braking system and air cleaner were also missing. The ute was a windowless shell; even the door and window handles had been taken. I looked inside where the driver's seat had been, searching for Steve's blood, and there was none bar a black tarry patch that had congealed on the steel floor of the vehicle. More or less expecting to see a whole halo of gore on the front wall of the building, where Bob's head had collided with it, I saw not one drop. A coloured and his spouse came promenading past in a donkey cart and I had to laugh when I saw that the cart had a Land Cruiser differential, rims and tyres. It was certainly a flashy chariot!

Driving to Rehoboth was a breeze, yet trying to locate Elsabeth's house was a far different matter. The time before, with old Jakobus driving, I hadn't taken much notice of where we were going. With the majority of Rehoboth's streets being unsealed, I managed to create a dust cloud that must have gone into every house in that town, then – after irritating the shit out of ninety percent of the dog population – I decided to try and get some directions. I pulled up at the Total roadhouse on the main road and asked a coloured yobbo about where I could find Elsabeth Witbooi's house. He didn't know where to start helping me, as there were millions of Witboois in Rehoboth. Millions could be found in Windhoek as well. In fact Namibia's Deputy Prime Minister was a Witbooi. When I told him I was looking for a very old lady who was living with a younger woman, Krystal Diergaardt, he couldn't help there, either, for countless Diergaardts could be seen scattered throughout not only Rehoboth, but in Windhoek, Mariental, Keetmanshoop and even Kalkrand. He reckoned that the Witboois and Diergaardts came from some of the most prominent Baster families around; like the Swartboois, the Detlingers, the Van Wyks, the Izaaks and the Christians.

I had attracted a bit of a crowd by then; kids looking for money; blokes wanting a lift south to Keetmanshoop or north to Windhoek; a few mangy Baster dogs that looked as if they were on powerful depressants. Just when I thought of giving it away, a coloured bloke in a well-fitting, grey suit got out of a lamp red BMW and came over. It was Carl Zes! He gave out some sharp instructions in Afrikaans and he and I were soon standing alone.

"How is it?" he asked. Shit, but the bloke's attitude had changed! His smile displayed more gold than what we had found on the Klein Aub prospect. "What is the problem?"

"I'm try'n to find Mrs Elsabeth Witbooi's house."

His eyes narrowed and the gold vanished. "It is Miss Witbooi – she is not married. What do you want to see her for?"

My hackles rose. "For starters – it's none of your business. I was round at her house the other day with Jakobus and Wilfred Van Wyk."

"With Jakobus?" He frowned as he pondered on that one, then he shrugged. "I will show you. Follow my car."

BASTARDS FROM THE BUSH

I followed his BMW only to learn that the house was just around the corner and I had gone past it at least a dozen times. He pointed his arm out the car window at the house and didn't bother stopping. When I pulled up in front I took mental bearings of where the church bell tower and other prominent landmarks were, so that I could easily find the place again. I was running pretty late and was certain Krystal would be back in the house by then. I was feeling ridiculously shy, and while I plucked up the courage to approach the front door, I surveyed the garden and houses on either side. The house I was visiting had no garden; only one date palm that was thriving; some dead pot plants encircled by old car tyres on each side of the front door, plus sand, dead weeds and dust. There was a bit of a chook enclosure against one cyclone wire fence, though the chooks had long since gone. The neighbours' houses were quite lush in comparison; more but smaller date palms; patches of dried-out lawn, hibiscus bushes, jacaranda trees and irises.

"Hi, Josef! Come inside!" Krystal was standing there at the door, making my heart thud. She was even lovelier than the memories I had stored up from the previous visit.

"I'm just admiring the garden," I said stupidly.

"What garden?" she laughed. "We need a man around the place. Are you any good with a spade? Wilfred tells me you are a hard worker, and also that you are very good to work for."

Those words had me in raptures and I mentally took note of all the good things I could do for Wilfred. I followed her into the house like an obedient zombie.

Old Elsabeth looked as if she hadn't moved from the lounge chair she was sitting in since my last visit. The dog, too; its ridge all standing up in mute hostility as I entered the multipurpose room. The ancient old dear looked exactly the same; identical clothes, the stains on her blouse; everything precisely the same. Identical, bar the fact that she was wearing a pair of tortoiseshell, horn-rimmed spectacles that magnified her grey eyes about ten times over. She had a whole lot of note pads and pieces of paper on a table in front of her, plus some pencils, crayons and a ballpoint.

"I was wondering when you'd be back," she informed in a voice that didn't give a hint of whether I was welcome or not. "Krystal, make coffee. Kido, you sit down. You may smoke only if you give me a cigarette."

I was delighted to give her a smoke and even gave her the remainder of the packet, as I had a spare full one in my top pocket with my passport. I lit her cigarette for her and she had a paroxysm of coughing that brought tears to her eyes.

"Really, *Ouma,* you should not be smoking," Krystal scolded, making me feel guilty at being so generous with my smokes.

Elsabeth recovered enough to say, "Nonsense, my dear. I've been taking tobacco for eighty years and it still hasn't killed me... Now, Kido, to what do we owe this pleasure?"

"I want to know more about my family," I blurted out. "I didn't want to talk too much in front of Jakobus Van Wyk. I've lived without knowing about my family for so long. You know old Kobus, you can't get a thing out of him."

"I see. I'm afraid it isn't the right time or place to talk about your brother Jonker – it's up to other people to tell you about him... How can I help you?"

"My real father? I know nothing about him. What happened to him? Where'd he come from? Where's he now?"

Krystal interrupted us when she placed enamel mugs of coffee where we could reach them. It was a black, sugarless brew, but I wasn't about to complain. Coming from her, it had to be nectar from the gods.

The old woman took a gulp of the scalding coffee as if her mouth was made of asbestos, then she peered with those huge, magnified eyes at me. "The only way to understand your family is by knowing their past. Your father is no longer with us. The Boers killed him. On the eleventh of December – yours and Jonker's birthday – 1962. That was three years to the day after eleven people were killed when the residents of the old location protested against being forcibly moved to the Katutura Township. Exactly four years after your birth. You would've been in Australia by then... Your father, Christian Witbooi, was so like his great Uncle Hendrik. Different men can be like different dogs. Some dogs – when you chain them up – lie peacefully, hoping someone might let them go. Others fight and pull, even if they end up breaking their necks. Your father was of the latter variety – he couldn't stand to be shackled by his fellow man, be they Boer, coloured or black. He spent most of his time in jail both here in the South West and South Africa..."

"The country is called Namibia now," Krystal reminded her.

"South West Africa – Namibia – it's still the same country," the old woman disagreed. "Except that our people's problems are becoming far worse... As I was saying, Kido, your father was always in trouble with the whites. Exactly like his great uncle. He never married again when your mother left. He was too heartbroken. In fact, he wasn't married to your mother, but they lived as man and wife."

"How did the Boers kill him?" I asked.

"They beat him to death, and then made out that he had accidentally hit his head against a wall. Just like with Steve Biko in South Africa, the Boer police *murdered* your father. He was one of the principals who organised most of the protests in those days. Coloureds, Ovambo, Damara and Herero alike admired him. There was no tribal differentiation then, as they had a common enemy – the Boers. Being an intelligent, articulate man, he was always a thorn in their side, so they brutally murdered him... I was personally there to witness the massacre in the old location. The Boers had made up their minds that the only method to get their way was to kill some innocent people. Our people – the coloureds, Herero, Nama and Ovambo – had always carried out our protests in a peaceful manner. We even had a protest where only the women from the location marched. At first it was started in order to have one of our Advisory Board members, Fritz Gariseb, released from custody, however some of the women had ulterior motives. You see – in the old location – a good many women earned their sole incomes by making *tombo*. This was a home-brewed beer that was actually quite nourishing. It certainly didn't contain as much alcohol as the white-manufactured beer. Anyhow, these women were very angry because the Windhoek Municipality had outlawed this practice and sought instead to force the commercially produced beers of the major breweries onto the people via a municipal beer hall that was located within easy reach of all the inhabitants... There were, though, some women like myself who were marching for far more profound reasons. South West Africa was a mandate country where the Boers had no right to force their filthy Apartheid laws on our people. They wanted to move the blacks and coloureds in order to segregate us from the white areas of Windhoek, for we were too close for their liking. The biggest farce was that the new location of Katutura – meaning 'We have no permanent abode' – wasn't ready to receive the thousands of people who lived in the old location. Hardly any of the new houses had been built, yet alone sanitation facilities, schools or other amenities. Furthermore, it was much farther for the people to travel backwards and forwards to work. On the minute incomes being paid to blacks and coloureds, bus fares would have been a great hardship to them."

"So what happened?" I asked.

"To cut a long story short – on the evening of the tenth of December 1959, quite a few of the people gathered in a peaceful crowd around the municipal beer hall. The Windhoek Council under Mayor Snyman had made up their mind that they wanted bloodshed. They knew, whereas our people didn't. It was the terrible noise of the shooting that appalled the people at first. We couldn't believe that the Boers would actually start killing us! The house that I was visiting was scarcely fifty metres away and bullets tore through the zinc sheeting of the roof! Everywhere there was screaming. Like moths to a flame we ran out in to our front yards. I saw a woman setting fire to the mayor's car and then she was shot repeatedly. In the light of the flames I could see two armoured cars, and by that time it seemed as if hundreds of people had guns and all were shooting as fast as possible in all directions. It went on for an eternity. Bullets came very near to us, so we ran indoors and lay on the floor with our hands covering our heads. Mercifully the shooting ceased, although the screaming continued for much longer... It was the embarrassment and guilt of the Boers that prompted them to kill your father. They were ashamed and needed a scapegoat, so – being typical Boers – they took it out on him because he had been one of the instigators of the protests and he was arrested. It took three years of torture, humiliation and abuse to finally kill him. I know this, for a black constable of the Windhoek Municipal Police Force witnessed their actions... Even the Boers couldn't have predicted the folly of their murdering ways. Your father was a sobering influence on the more radical elements of our people. His demise gave people like Sam Nujoma a totally free rein. At that time Nujoma was the organiser of the Ovamboland People's Organisation, which later became the South West African People's Organisation or SWAPO. The past, the present and future shall decide the ramifications of that. You mark my words."

The old lady finished her coffee, then continued, "You need to go back in history to understand a man like your father and we people of your blood kin. In all our Namibian roots there's Nama blood of some description. There's a Nama myth of origin that states there were once five brothers, each of whom became the patriarch of a Nama tribe or clan. The eldest was the ancestor of the 'Red Nation'. Another brother was the founder of the *Bondelswarts*, which literally means the 'people of the black bundle'. One brother was the ancestor of the *Veldschoendragers*, so named on account of the type of sandals they wore. Then there were the Fransman Hottentots and the Swartbois. Another clan was also present at the time, the *Groot Doden* or 'Great Dead'. The latter are not part of the same myth, but they claimed to be offshoots of the 'Red Nation'.' Also we have the *Karaloan* or *Tseib's* people, who also claimed to have come from the Red Nation."

"Most of our people also have blood ties to the Cape, don't they?"

Krystal, who looked as if she had heard that history lesson countless times before, interjected.

"True, but there's Nama or Khoisan blood in plenty of our people. Early historical records describe the Nama as being a warlike and scattered people, who didn't lay claim to any specific territories. An entirely self-sufficient, pastoral, nomadic people who mainly inhabited the area between the Orange River that forms our border with South Africa and the upper reaches of the Fish River. As there was a lot more grazing for their cattle in those days – unlike now since the Boer and German farmers have overgrazed the south – the different Nama identities lived fairly peacefully together. They more or less lived in a checkerboard fashion – the equal owners of the entire territory known as 'Great Namaqualand'. Don't mistake this for Namakwaland or 'Little Namaqualand' in South Africa, Kido, as they're two completely different regions, though the people who inhabit them have blood ties that go back for centuries. The main source of this common blood comes from the *Oorlam Afrikaners*, to whom we're also related. The origin of the word '*Oorlam*' has never been clarified. The words '*Oorlami*' or '*Oorlamshe-Hottentten*' are first thought of having come from the Eastern Cape. It's also been suggested that the word comes from the Malay word for 'white lamb' or 'barren ewe', but that sounds ridiculous. Personally, I believe it comes from '*Orang lama*', which means 'a person of experience', thus *Oorlams* are 'experienced people.' This opinion can be substantiated by the fact that many of their number were fine tradesmen – carpenters, wheelwrights, gunsmiths, builders and blacksmiths... More coffee, Krystal. I'm getting hungry, too. What's for dinner? Is there enough for Kido?"

I latched on to what I thought was a brilliant idea. "Why don't we eat out? There's a very nice place at the Oanob Dam. It's run by some very nice Baster people."

I was to soon learn that Elsabeth only ever left the house to go to church on Sunday mornings. Besides that, she never ventured any farther than from her lounge chair to the kettle and shithouse during the day, or from the lounge chair to her bed at night. Her dog did no more. The old girl even got quite huffy when I asked her and Krystal out, for to her eating out was a sinful waste of money. I asked if I could find some takeaway food from the Total roadhouse, but that was no more welcome than my first suggestion. Krystal assured me that there was plenty for me to eat, and when I volunteered to go down to a liquor shop to purchase some wine, I found that they were teetotallers; what with coffee being their only sin; except, of course, Elsabeth's odd smoke or two.

The meal was a pretty weird affair, comprised of mostly pigs' tails, some cabbage and macaroni. The pig tails were fairly different; the skin tasted just like ordinary bacon rind; there was a thin sliver of fatty, gristly meat, then digits of bone. There was bugger all eating in the tails, so I was quite happy when Krystal offered me seconds of cabbage and macaroni; both being quite plain what with no gravy of any kind or salt and pepper.

Despite Krystal's smart bank uniform there was an aura of abject poverty about the place. I hadn't seen inside the other rooms of the house; yet, if the living room was anything to go by, certainly no money had been spent on the dwelling for some considerable time. Beside the threadbare lounge suite, there was a tattered reed mat on the floor, and, instead of curtains, sheets of newspaper had been stuck to the windows for privacy. A forlorn bundle of thorny sticks was all the firewood they had. Like Sophia Van Wyk's house there was no electricity; therefore no refrigerator. When it was almost too dark to see, Krystal lit a solitary paraffin lamp that belched black smoke and soot up to the ceiling, scarcely illuminating anything bar the gold bits on the religious icons above the mantelpiece. I thought of lighting a smoke, but the atmosphere in the room forbade it.

The old Lady yawned and I became nervous that she might want to hit the fart-sack or something, for I wanted to spend as much time with Krystal as possible. "You were talking about our ancestors," I tried to keep her going. "So where did they come from?"

That really had her focused once more. "Mostly from near the Cape, like Krystal said. It was long before even the nineteenth century when they first started to trek. Everyone's heard of the 'Great Trek' carried out by the Boers, but there were a great many treks going on by others that have been forgotten by history altogether. With the advent of the Industrial Revolution in England during the second half of the eighteenth century, a huge amount of change affected all the people in the Cape Colony. As the Boers moved farther and farther inland, many of the African people became dispossessed and lost their cattle, property and lands. Regardless of the so-called romance of the 'Great Trek' in the whites' history books, the Boers could only be classified as murderers, thieves, rapists and cattle rustlers. There certainly wasn't anything romantic or noble about them. While a Bible could be found in every voortrekker's wagon, they were nothing but thieves, murderers and rapists. The most disaffected people were the Khoisan or Khoi Khoi. They'd been living in the Cape and its surrounds many-many years before the whites or the Bantu such as the Zulu had ever come near South Africa. With their land, property and stock stolen from them, a good many of the Khoisan people were subjected to terrible violence and they became both servants and slaves. With the arrival of the Boers many of their communities disintegrated – some choosing to serve their white masters – others opting to resist by forming commandos and trekking northward. This whole new frontier, from the Cape Colony north to the Orange River, was in a state of total upheaval. With the collision of white against black came violence, rape and sexual interrelationships between both races, thus creating a mishmash of offspring or bastards. Into this cauldron of humanity came slaves from India, Malaya, Madagascar, Ceylon and Afghanistan, for many of these people also escaped their masters and bondage to take part in the great movement outwards. I believe your father had some Afghan blood in him from your grandmother's side, thus yours and Jonker's beautiful green eyes..."

She stopped to light another of the smokes I had given her, and then carried on, "Probably the first of these commando communities to travel north of the Orange River into southern Namibia were the Afrikaners. These men are the founding fathers of one of the most important Namibian families today. Several clans followed them. There were the Gobabis people and the Berseba people, who have had towns named after them. Then, more importantly to you, Kido, the Witbooi people arrived under Cupido Witbooi, and they settled at Gibeon..."

"More coffee?" Krystal asked, and I was pleased that the old lady wanted some. Although her droning on was starting to grate, it gave me the opportunity to take some mental photographs of Krystal. Photographs to tide me over when I went to Karibib. I encouraged Elsabeth to tell me more.

"Yes well, the first great leader was Jonker Afrikaner. He was the third son of Jager Afrikaner. He was recruited by the Nama Red ..."

There was a strong smell of urine that permeated the room. The old lady had pissed herself, probably from drinking too much coffee or whatever. I tried very hard to make out that I hadn't noticed anything and wondered if Krystal would do something. She also ignored what had happened, and, in fact, got up to adjust the flame of the paraffin lamp.

The old girl obviously wasn't too put out, either, for she continued what must have been to her a holy scripture. Almost like the Jews and Moses. "The reason I am boring you with all this is ..."

"No – please – you're certainly aren't boring me," I assured her.

"Good! I need to give you a background to the troubles that face our people today. There's always been conflict of one kind or another in this country... Where was I now? Ah yes! Now we come to the most important family of all as far as we're concerned – the Witbooi. At the beginning of the nineteenth century Cupido or Kido Witbooi and his family were living in Pella just south of the Orange River in South Africa. While Cupido and other trekkers had moved to escape the overbearing Boers and other Cape settlers, they weren't the only ones who were trekking northward, for the Griqua and Koranna also emerged in that time in the history of southern Africa. You must remember these names – the Koranna and Griqua – for if you ever decided to stay in Namibia, you'll grow to realise the significance of how these people may influence our future here... Now – returning to Cupido or Kido Witbooi – the man your father named you after. In the 1820s he set out with his followers from Pella and first went to Griqualand that was then slightly north of the juncture of the Orange and Vaal Rivers. A land inhabited firstly by the Tswana people. You had invasions going on all over southern Africa – the whites invading the Khoisan – our people invading Namaland – the Griqua invading the Tswana. There were three levels of power – at the top the whites with their military genius and superior weaponry – the coloured Griqua and our people who knew how to use firearms – then the poor blacks such as the Khoisan and the Tswanas at the bottom of the ladder militarily. From there Cupido spent the next two decades moving around the very south of Namaland in the vicinity of the Orange River, and contact was made with the Rhenish missionaries in the 1850s. Then when..."

She looked like nodding off, so I tried to get her to focus, "And my Great uncle?"

"Ah – yes!" she brightened visibly. "Let me now tell you a bit about the greatest Witbooi of all. Hendrik! He was born in 1830 at Pella, the son of Moses Witbooi, who in turn was the son of Cupido Witbooi and a mother whom history has totally forgotten her name. His Nama name was Nanseb Gabemab and his Herero name Korota. He was the third son, and by 1884 was the eldest surviving. The first one had fallen before 1880 and the second, Izaak, fell in the Herero campaign of 1880. There was a fourth younger brother, Salomo, who was later on Hendrik's council. Hendrik was married to Katharina, whom over twenty years bore him at least twelve children. The first one was born in 1858 and the last around 1879. Katharina died in 1897... Hendrik was a very religious man and he and his eldest son made the church one of their prime occupations. Baptised with his wife in 1868, he became a church elder or *ouderling* in 1875… I have jumped the gun altogether here. I must be leading you round in circles. First let me remind you that most of our people intermarried with the Nama and even some Herero. Thus we all have a certain amount of Nama blood in all of us. The difference between the Nama and those who trekked to Namibia became almost non-existent, so that's why we don't resent the title 'Baster' or 'Bastard'. Especially if you take into consideration the huge collection of races that have jointly contributed to our genes…"

She paused a while deep in thought. " Let me see now – in the next few years, from about July 1880 to round about 1890, Namaland was about to go under a great deal of change because Jan Jonker Afrikaner was killed in 1889 by the Witbooi. During that time Hendrik led three raids against the European trading station at Otjimbingwe in retaliation against Herero misdeeds. He must have been quite a politician, requiring sheer genius when it came to sorting out all the troubles and tribulations of Namaland, while at all times there were the Herero and newly arrived Germans to take into consideration. He had unrivalled dominion over vast territories. In order to counter the threat posed by the Germans, he firmly established himself at Hoornkrans that was a fully fortified and centralised stronghold, while the none-combatants or *werft* – old men, women and children – remained at Gibeon. His following, what with all the people living in Hoornkrans and Gibeon, would have amounted to many thousands. Having emerged as the recognised ruler of Namaland, he then conducted an unmerciful war against the Herero and launched several raids during which he drove off thousands of their cattle and other livestock. This war ceased by the end of 1892 once Hendrik had negotiated for peace. He had seen this conflict being less damaging than what German colonialism could do. The Rehoboth Baster acted as mediators and handled the correspondence between Maharero and the Witbooi and they actually hosted the peace conference. When

Hendrik demanded three thousand cattle in compensation and Maharero refused to pay, the Rehobothers – who were sick of being the meat in the sandwich – offered to fulfil the Witboois' demands. This's where Kaptein Hermanus Van Wyk – Jakobus' great uncle – was such a distinguished man. He tried wherever he could to keep his Baster out of the conflicts since he realised that prosperity could only come with peace. Although several attempts were made to reach an accord, the feelings of hostility ran too deep with the Herero. Samuel Maharero, old Chief Maharero's son, refused to go to Rehoboth in order to conclude a peace agreement with Hendrik. Also by then the Herero had signed a 'Protection Treaty' with the Germans... All the while Hendrik had tried in vain to unite the various Namaland kapteins against the Germans. In his letters he pleaded with them not to sign these 'Protection Treaties', for he had this peculiar insight into what German imperialism meant. He pleaded with Hermanus Van Wyk of the Rehoboth Baster, Willem Christian of the *Bondelswarts*, Didrik Izaak of the Berseba polity, Zacharias Zeraua of the Otjimbingwe Herero, and Paul Frederiks of the Bethanie community. He pleaded with them to realise what the Germans' ambitions for the country were, yet his far-seeing appeal to unite against the European intruders fell on deaf ears. Finally, in April of 1893, the Germans declared open warfare on the Witbooi."

CHAPTER 26

MURDERING GERMAN BASTARDS! SAM KHUBIS!

Elsabeth searched through her bits of paper, and then triumphantly held up a crumpled document. "It didn't take long for the Germans to prove themselves to be both murderers and cowards. Major Von Francois – Kurt – Carl – Bruno – Von Francois – attacked Hoornkrans on the twelfth of April 1893 and I have here," she shook the document, "a copy of the statement of what happened written by Klein Hendrik Witbooi – Kaptein Hendrik Witbooi's son. Here – read it," she passed the papers to me.

STATEMENT OF KLEIN HENDRIK WITBOOI *(Son of Kaptein Hendrik Witbooi)* **AND KEISTER KEISTER** *(Onder-Kaptein of the Witbooi tribe).*

After the new German troops arrived at Windhoek, our Onder-kaptein Samuel Izaak who was at the time staying there, was told by Kaptein Von Francois that he, Samuel, must go to his people and tell the headmen of the Witbooi nation to talk with Kaptein Hendrik Witbooi about making a treaty with the Germans. Kaptein Von Francois also said that a letter to Hendrik Witbooi would follow on the subject.

When Hendrik Witbooi heard the message, he said that the great men must come together and consult with him and with each other as to the answer to be given to the letter when it came. They said, let us first wait and see what the letter says, so that we may make an answer when it comes. The Kaptein said, yes, that is best.

Instead of the letter coming, the soldiers followed Samuel, and early in the morning before sunrise the firing woke us. Hendrik Witbooi said to the people around him: Who can it be firing on us? I have made peace with the Damara (Herero): what is it? We did not know who it was, but Kaptein Witbooi told all his men to leave the settlement as soon as possible.

After all the men had left the German soldiers rushed into the settlement. Then we saw it was the Germans. The women and children where left in the settlement, and the soldiers began to shoot at them. They shot little children, children at the breast; children on their mothers' backs were shot through by the same bullet that killed the mother.

The women saw that the attacking party were white men, and stood still as they thought that their lives were safe and that though they might be taken away for slaves, they would not be killed. So we all thought. We thought the men would be killed, not the women. Some of the women ran away with the men, but most remained when they saw that white people were coming in, thinking they would be safe.

The women and children they shot in the houses, the wounded as well as the dead, they did not bring them out, but burned the houses over them. We know for certain that at least three women, a mother and two daughters, all wounded, were burned alive in the houses. This was seen by some old women who were not killed and were too crippled to be taken away prisoner with the other survivors. The Germans stayed in the place till the following day. On the day of the attack the Germans captured a church elder (ouderling) who was too old and infirm to run away, and who had hidden himself in some rocks. They tied him up and took him to their wagons, and shot him the next morning with three bullets.

Some of the women and children, part of whom were wounded, the Germans left behind; the rest, a large number, they took away to Windhoek. They took more than they left. Two of the women left behind died of their wounds. Our total loss on the place was eight old men, two young boys and 78 women and children. Of the two young boys one was Kaptein Hendrik

BASTARDS FROM THE BUSH

Witbooi's youngest son, about twelve years old, who was paralysed on one side. The other, Keister Keister's nephew, was about ten years old.

When the Germans attacked the place, three of our men ran into the church and fired on the soldiers. A soldier called on them to surrender, and our Magistrate, who was one of the three, said No! and shot the soldier dead. The three then escaped after firing several shots. We did not fire first. The Germans fired before coming into the place, our men did not fire until the Germans were inside. Those three men were the only men who fired at all. The Women told us that two Germans were buried on the place and three taken away wounded in the wagons.

We lost one buck wagon of the Kaptein's, two horses, several foals, cows and calves that were shot down, and some cows they took away and some sheep and goats. We lost all our saddles, about 50 or 60 destroyed or taken away; one good gun and some old ones, and some loose powder and a few cartridges. We had no idea that war was coming, so our cartridges were in our boxes and our bandoleers were empty. We only got away with our guns.

Signed: Klein Hendrik Witbooi.
Keister Keister – His Mark.
John Cleverly, resident Magistrate.

Witnesses: Henry W. Simpson.
Charles John Clay.

"Do you see the magistrate John Cleverly's name on the bottom of both those statements?" the old woman asked.

"Yeah?"

"He was an Englishman who was serving at Walvis Bay at the time. Walvis Bay belonged to the British in those days. Both my parents worked for him. My mother was a maid and my father a clerk. That's how I learned to speak such good English – he was a stickler at having us use the language correctly."

"Is that a fact?" I asked, trying to sound really interested. "So what

165

actually happened to Hendrik Witbooi? Did the Germans finally bump him off?"

"Of course, they did! They had to. Hendrik wasn't always fighting against the Germans. That murdering Von Francois – would you believe they have a statue of the devil standing outside the Windhoek City Council building? He was replaced by *Landeshauptmann* Theodore – Gotthilf – Leutwein in March 1894, who arrived in the country on the thirty-first of December 1893. Because of his murderous bungling, Von Francois had fallen out of favour with the Government in Germany and Hendrik concluded a peace treaty with Leutwein on the fifteenth of December 1894. Before this very little mattered to the Germans, but to subdue the rebellious Witbooi, for without doing so they never could have established a protectorate. Within weeks of his arrival Leutwein set up a series of small fortifications and outposts throughout the central and southern areas of the country. In one campaign he forced the Khauas and Fransman's, or Simon Koper's people, to surrender, then, while waiting for an extra two hundred and fifty troops to come from Germany, he tricked Hendrik into a two month truce. When he was finally ready to make his move, Leutwein engaged Hendrik in a number of skirmishes that have since been named the '*Naukluft Battles*'. Here – this's a German account of the last battle before Hendrik eventually capitulated.

THE BATTLE IN THE NAUKLUFT
Ludwig Von Estorff

The Naukluft, the refuge of the Witbooi our enemy, is a rugged massif that was under observation from our posts stationed to the south, north and east, while the main force being three under-strength companies of 60 – 80 men each and accompanied by two field guns of the type C/73 – was to seek out and attack the enemy in the mountains. Our attack was ordered on cancellation of the truce on 27 August 1894. The enemy's main force was located in a gorge that opens into the plain on the eastern side of the range. This gorge is the actual Naukluft, to which the entire range owes its name.

BASTARDS FROM THE BUSH

Even before daybreak on 27 August, 1 Company advanced into the Naukluft under my command, followed by two guns. 3 company was to support the main attack by climbing onto the plateau and then moving parallel to the gorge. Conditions, however, proved so difficult on the rugged flank of the mountain that the company was forced to abandon this approach and return to the gorge, where it now followed 1 Company. With active artillery support, the latter had succeeded in driving the enemy from several positions in a rapid advance, but certain sections of the enemy had regrouped behind the company and represented a threat to the artillery. 3 Company brought relief in this precarious situation, and the day ended with the withdrawal of the enemy.

The attack by the weak 2 Company, which was to penetrate via a gorge called Uhunis from the north, proved to be less successful. Enemy positions had been reconnoitred in the path of its advance, too. When the company reached the peak of an outcrop before daybreak, they found themselves surrounded by the enemy on all sides. The men, crowded together, came under such heavy fire from the invisible Hottentot marksmen that the company barely succeeded in holding the position, suffering heavy losses. In the dark of the night the company returned to the water with its wounded; the enemy also abandoned the area and joined the retreat of the main force into the inner redoubts of the massif.

During the next few days, 1 and 3 Companies pursued the enemy. They were led by Lieutenant Von Perbandt, as I had been wounded and could not continue. The troops followed the tracks left by the Hottentot's livestock; more often than not, however, it was extremely difficult to discern these tracks on the rocky ground. For this reason the enemy could be pursued only during the day, whereas one would usually benefit by marching at night. The sun burned down from a cloudless sky, while the temperature dropped to several degrees below zero during the night, which meant that the men were hardly able to recover in their bivouacs since no fires could be lit. Coats and blankets had been left behind on account of the shortage of pack animals. The small store of provisions they had with them also soon ran out. Horses could be led over the sharp sliding stones and rocks only with the greatest difficulty; most of them lost their shoes, some fell to their deaths. The field guns could not be brought forward, nevertheless the troops succeeded on one occasion in catching up with the enemy and driving them back after a brief exchange of fire, but on 2 September the advance guard walked into a Hottentot ambush and all its men – 1officer, 5 men were shot down at virtually point-blank range.

Making allowance for these adverse conditions, the pursuing section prepared for battle. This was to take place at a waterhole called Gurus, which the enemy had occupied. His positions were protected by deep gorges, and all attempts to outflank them met with flanking movements. The exchange of fire between the two sides lasted 36 hours; eventually it was the greater perseverance of the troops which won the day. The enemy withdrew. Again the pursuit continued, without provisions whatsoever for the last few days. Finally, on September 5, the troops reached the edge of the mountain range, but the enemy had run into a stopper group on the plain and was thrown back into the mountains, past the pursuing force.

The troops were exhausted, clothing and shoes in tatters; casualties had reduced their already thin ranks, and only four officers were fit for service. 2 Company, too, had come to the end of its powers; after the adverse encounter at Uhunis they had attempted to reach the west side of the mountain in order to wait for the enemy there, but they had found no water, lost the greater part of their horses on account of exhaustion, and succeeded only after arduous marches through the mountains in joining up with the pursuit party on the southern side of the massif.

The enemy had retreated into the mountains; although the werft (i.e the non-combatants) had dispersed when they exited the mountains onto the desert plain, and they had reassembled very quickly. The enemy had suffered only minor losses, his warriors had endured marches, clashes and deprivations without succumbing to exhaustion, and the mounted warriors had also suffered little in regards to their equipment or morale. It proved that the Hottentot were far superior to us when it came to marching, enduring deprivation, and knowledge and ability to use the terrain, i.e their agility. It was only in weaponry, courage, perseverance and discipline that the troops surpassed the enemy.

BASTARDS FROM THE BUSH

"You see!" old Elsabeth crowed, "Even the rank and file officers respected the Witbooi when it came to battle.'

"So how was Hendrik Witbooi killed?" I asked.

They old girl shook her head. "First let me tell you what he got up to following Naukluft... Like I told you, Hendrik concluded a treaty shortly after the battle. The Germans were also pleased to take a breather, what with the exhausting fighting. Especially having lost seventeen dead and having twenty-four wounded. The treaty stipulated that the Witbooi accept the paramountcy of the German empire and Hendrik retained twenty thousand square kilometres of territory, although a German garrison was installed at Gibeon. The Witbooi weren't disarmed, and – as a matter of fact – they sent small contingents of warriors to help the Germans subdue other African rebellions. Hendrik assisted in eight campaigns altogether. First against the Khauas where eight warriors were supplied along with negotiators and interpreters. Then seventy warriors were sent to help fight against the Mbanderu. After that a hundred and four men were sent against the Afrikaners. He arrived too late to support the Germans against the Swartbooi, but many of his men died from malaria. In 1901 he fought against the Grootfontein Baster, then a few years later against the Bondelswarts. Subsequent to that he sent eighty to a hundred men to fight against the Herero... Many historians and some of our people today feel that Hendrik's cooperation with the Germans was an act of betrayal. In some cases I have to agree. All the same, some of these accusations tend to be anachronistic, as everyone likes to hear about stories of African resistance to colonialism. Unlike some of the black criminals we have in SWAPO today, Hendrik was a man of integrity and stuck to his side of any agreements. Despite some of the white expats here that try to make out that he was devious, he rigorously kept his word and gave plenty of notice when he wanted to terminate an existing agreement. Politically he worked long and hard to be a guardian of his people. Then in 1904 all social and political relationships fell into upheaval with the advent of the drawn-out colonial war that lasted for approximately five years and ended with the Germans as victors. The days of diplomacy garnished with military force that Leutwein had adopted were soon over when the Germans sent in swine like General Von Trotha and his murderous *Schutztruppen*. He replaced Leutwein and was the German commanding officer in the Herero War... No – Von Trotha didn't want to just conquer the Herero – he tried to have every last man, woman and child slaughtered! Just like Hitler tried to do to the Jews. Those he didn't brutally kill, he drove into what is now Botswana. My word – when it comes to the mighty *Deutsche Sudwest Afrika* – the Germans certainly have nothing to be proud of... As for Hendrik, he had never been able to fully submit to the Germans. In October 1904, ten months after the Herero had fought to save their lands, property and livestock, Great Namaqualand – led by Hendrik Witbooi – surged up in war against the German imperialists. Namaland was at long last united under a man who was in his eighties. Only the Bethanie and Berseba people, plus the Africans of Keetmanshoop didn't join this army, which consisted of almost two thousand warriors. Although there hasn't been an in-depth historical account of the war, it was estimated that over two hundred military encounters took place, until Hendrik was eventually killed on the battlefield on the twenty-ninth of October 1905. I have here an account of the circumstances that led to his death."

She passed me a last sheet of wrinkled paper.

SKIRMISH AT VAALGRAS.

On 29 October the old Kaptein, pressed by his men, made another attack on one of the wagons of 3 Battery in the proximity of Vaalgras. Lieutenant Stage, who was stationed at Vaalgras with a half-strength 3 Battery, charged to the scene with the fifty or more men at his disposal immediately upon receiving news of the attack. The Hottentots took flight even before the Germans arrived, but the German officer energetically pursued on horseback and closed up on the fleeing Hottentots after a ride of some two hours. He attacked immediately, flanking them to the left and right; instead of making a stand, however, the enemy always fell back before the cavalry could get within the appropriate range. Following some hours of fighting, the horses were exhausted and the lieutenant had to end the engagement. Five dead Hottentots, one wounded, plus the greater part of the stolen livestock and provisions, one rifle and some horses were abandoned by the enemy. The German casualties came to one dead and one wounded.

This last skirmish," Elsabeth added," had a far more reaching affect than the writer of that incident could have anticipated, for it represented the wounding of Hendrik Witbooi. He was shot in the upper thigh, however was lifted into his saddle by his faithful followers, and so managed to escape. A short time after he bled to death, and according to Isaak Witbooi, who was probably his son, Hendrik died with the following words – 'It is over. I am done for. Now my children have peace'."

"People keep mentioning a place called Sam Khubis?" I wanted the old bag to believe that I gave a shit about Namibia's history. "What happened there?"

That caused her eyes to light up. "I'm glad you asked that." She quickly shuffled her papers. "Here it is! A historical account of what happened. Perhaps this will give you an idea of German treachery?"

SAM KHUBIS

Every year on the 8th of May, the battle of Sam Khubis is remembered. This historical battle took place on 8 May 1915, when the German colonial army attacked the Baster people who had fled to their last stronghold of Sam Khubis. The fear of total annihilation by a better equipped German army created a strong sense of common destiny.

The battle turned into a miraculous survival, which is celebrated every year to remind the Baster people of the threats faced, and that which can be overcome by Baster unity.

In 1885, the Kaptein, Hermanus Van Wyk, of the Rehoboth Baster signed a Treaty of Protection and Friendship with the German government. This international treaty arranged the rights and duties of the Rehoboth polity vis-à-vis the German colonial power. This treaty continued to be operational until 1914 when World War One changed the political landscape.

The Baster refused to take up arms against South African and British troops that were threatening to invade German controlled South West Africa. They also refused to guard captured South African soldiers and did not agree to patrol outside the territory of Rehoboth.

The escalation of events started on13 April 1915 when the German authorities demanded from the Baster Council that the armed Baster troops should go to Otjiwarango to guard South African Prisoners of War. If these demands were not to be met, all weapons in possession of the Rehoboth Baster had to be handed in to the German army. The Germans gave the Baster Council a three day deadline.

However the following day the Germans secretly 'disarmed' Baster soldiers in Sandputs. Several of the Baster soldiers tried to escape in which one was killed and another one escaped to tell the Baster Council of the events. In the mean time the Germans were also 'disarming' the Baster in Rehoboth. In the following days, several armed skirmishes occurred leaving a number of Baster and German soldiers dead.

These events lead to the cancellation of the 1885 Treaty by the German authorities who declared it null and void as of 22 April 1915. Consequently, the Germans sent many soldiers to Rehoboth, while in the mean time Baster families were fleeing to the Sam Khubis area, which was considered a militarily defendable position.

In the early morning of 8 May 1915, the Germans attacked the Baster stronghold of Sam Khubis, where a large part of the population had found refuge. The fighting lasted until the evening. The Baster feared that the superior weapons of the German army would mean a total defeat and possible annihilation the next day. However, the Germans withdrew from the fight the next day, leaving a relieved and hopeful Baster people behind.

The German withdrawal was caused by the South African army that was on the march and conquered the territory of South West Africa, including Rehoboth, to mark a new chapter in the struggle for self-determination of Rehoboth and the Baster people.

Before I left to go back to the camp, Elsabeth asked if I had any Namibian banknotes. I passed over a green fifty and she pointed to a pugnacious looking, old gent in a large, white hat. "His face is on all the Namibian currency notes. I don't know who thought of this, but the gesture's an accurate and justified one. If any man in this country ever fought for or cherished his peoples' independence, it was Hendrik Witbooi. Who knows – his inspiration may be of immeasurable assistance to our people in times to come?"

Somehow she forgot to return the fifty buck note. That didn't bother me a scrap, as my mind was filled with thoughts of Krystal and the fact that I was directly related to one of Namibia's most noble sons. Being blood kin of someone such as Hendrik Witbooi completely drove out any complexes I might have had about my coloured skin, and I was proud of being a Rehoboth-born Baster. I thought of passing on this new-found wisdom to my Aussie workmates, but then decided not to, as I didn't want arseholes such as Jeff and Nick to come up with any smart-arsed comments.

When I got back to the Klein Aub prospect I tracked down Wilfred. "As you've probably guessed," I told him, "I've been in to town to see old Miss Witbooi."

"Ja, boss – the *Ouma* or Krystal?"

"Both of 'em."

"Is it, boss?"

"Tell me. Krystal's working at a bank, right? She must be getting a fairly decent wage there, so how come they're so broke? You won't believe it, but we had a feed of pigs' tails."

"Ja, boss, I can easily believe it. There is nothing unusual about eating pig tails in Rehoboth and every Baster has eaten them at one time or other. You soon grow to like them, especially when you are hungry... Krystal gives all her money to the church, boss. She has the bank make out the cheque straight to the predikant."

"What the hell do they live on, then?"

"Some people in the community give donations to *Ouma* Witbooi. She is paid to be a historian. When she dies in another hundred year's time, Krystal will take over from her. You have heard the old lady, she knows all about our history. It is very important that we do not become forgotten about. Especially nowadays with the Ovambo taking over everything. We have a very honourable history, boss."

"We sure do, Wilfred," I agreed with him. I returned to my pet theory, "Are you sure Krystal's not Jonker Witbooi's woman?"

"Real sure, man. Krystal is nobody's woman."

"Do you reckon I could win some points with her if I went to church with her on Sundays?"

That really lifted his eyebrows. "Church? I really do not know, boss. That could be taking things too far. Do you normally go to church on Sundays? I did not see you go anywhere last Sunday."

"I haven't been to church since I was a kid." I quickly dropped the subject, as the thought of entering any Catholic establishment made me feel distinctly bilious.

CHAPTER 27

JEFF MAKES A DICKHEAD OUT OF ME! DRINKING COMPETITION AT THE HOTEL STRÖBLEHOF!

Although the access road and drill ramps on the Karibib prospect weren't bad, it was bloody tricky driving the rig and support truck to the first drill hole's marker. The terrain was that mountainous even a Himalayan goat would have given it a wide berth! Our lofty perch was on top of a huge marble ridge from where we could see for miles in all directions. We drew straws to see who would take the rig the last fifty metres; right to the edge of a precipice. Ernie drew the shortest straw; still he refused to go the whole way. I couldn't really blame him, as backing a top-heavy rig over a badly cut track and a two hundred metre drop waiting for the brakes to fail had my blood running icy cold in my balls as well.

"How's about you take the bitch the rest of the way?" I suggested to Jeff.

"You get fucked!" came his curt reply. "I've got a missus and kids to go back to. Ernie drew the shortest straw, so make him fuckin' drive the cunt."

"Your missus would've taken off by now," I assured him. "I heard the boss say he was gunna pay her a visit when he got back. You know how she likes that Merc' he's got. Better than your crappy fuckin' Holden Kingswood."

"What the fuck's Ernie doing?" he was looking over my shoulder.

As I turned to see what he was talking about, I was lifted up in a bear hug and next thing I was hanging half over the cliff face, the blood rushing to my head! There was absolutely nothing I could do, as he was kneeling on the back of my legs and my arms were waving in space. Suddenly my white hard hat came loose and I saw it slowly float through the air, then it bounced like a ping pong ball on the rocks hundreds of feet below. "For Christ's sake, Jeff!" was all that came to mind, for I was fair shitting myself.

"I keep telling you to leave my missus out of it," he snarled. "I've had a serious gutsful of you and your fuckin' big mouth. You don't know when to give it away – do ya – ya fuckin' smartarse? The reason why you can't get a decent woman's 'cause you're a fuckin' boong bastard. You've been a real cunt ever since I joined up with my missus. You jealous or something, you queer bastard? Just 'cause I don't drink in the pubs anymore after knock off time, you and the rest of 'em think I'm cunt-struck. I love that woman, so bloody lay off, or I'll…"

"For fuck's sake, Jeff!" it was Dave's voice breaking up the most emotional speech I had ever heard Jeff give. "You hold onto him, or you'll kill the bastard. He isn't fuckin' worth it, Jeff."

"Let the fucker drop," Nick's voice piped in. "See if he bounces?"

"Hey – no! Hang on! What the fuck?" Ernie came along and his voice was shrill. "Pull him back! Come on, Jeff! Please!"

As my heartbeat started hammering in my ears I was stupidly calculating that the little mechanic wasn't such a bad bloke after all. As for Wheeler and Nick, they could get stuffed as far as I was concerned. Furthermore, I was praying that if Jeff really did love his missus, he wouldn't want to be chucked into a Namibian slammer for murder. Or would Nick, Dave and the others cover for him? What about Wilfred – would he have the guts to tell the truth?

"Grab a leg each," Jeff shouted to the others. "The way I've got him, I can't get him back."

Nick and Wheeler grabbed one of my legs each and took up the slack while he got off me. Unceremoniously they hauled me back; peeling back my shirt and scratching my guts on the hard, silicified limestone. By the time they had me on safer ground they were pissing themselves laughing; therefore I didn't bother thanking them. I was too busy thinking of a way of retaliating against Jeff. For some peculiar reason I felt I had lost face in front of Wilfred and Herman; two of my fellow Baster. It was really strange because for years I had struggled to be accepted by the whites, what with my darker skin, back in Aussie. Suddenly it didn't seem too important to be able to prove myself to the whites; on the other hand I felt it was far more necessary to be a big deal in front of the coloureds and blacks. Somewhere in the new equation Krystal had to feature, as I didn't want word to make its way back to her via the Baster that Jeff had made a dickhead out of me.

Backing the rig to the cliff face still presented a problem. Nick volunteered to drive the truck; nevertheless no one trusted the brakes. Although the drilling gear itself was in mint condition, the old Ford eight wheeler truck it was mounted on was old enough to vote, and its owner had always scrimped when it came to brake maintenance and things. Besides, Western Australia was fairly flat and didn't have all that many cliff faces to offer, except on the odd occasion that we had had to drill on the edge of a man-made open-pit. When we did that, there had always been special safety barriers or bunds put up to stop anything going over the side.

Dave certainly didn't help things when he mentioned that our trip to Namibia was jinxed, so what could stuff-up – would stuff-up! If the rig went over the precipice, that would be curtains to everything.

"You back it back, Nick, and we can get some rocks to chock the wheels," Ernie suggested. "We'll get the hydraulics going and someone can be ready to lower the back rams. That'll bloody stop the bitch."

That became the plan; Nick would drive; Ernie and Dave would be on standby with rocks; I, keeping well to one side, would work the hydraulic ram levers. As it happened providence amply demonstrated that we were only half jinxed. The rig came back and the brakes weren't up to scratch. The wheels easily rolled over the puny little rocks Dave and Ernie had selected, so I had the rams down in a flash and the left one was snapped like a carrot, causing hydraulic oil to piss everywhere. The right ram held on long enough for Nick to have the truck in a forward gear and he quickly switched off the motor. The rig never went over the cliff! We found ourselves about one metre short of Kotzé's drill marker, but there was no way in the world that we were moving back one inch further. The trouble was that we couldn't jack the back of the rig level, what with the busted ram, so that meant Ernie having to go into Windhoek to find someone to repair it. When he came back he reckoned we would have to wait a couple of days for it to get fixed.

There we were with time on our hands once again. Fortunately our camp was only nine or slightly more miles from the town of Karibib, so we went in to study the town's pub life and fauna. First off, we tried the Hotel Ströblehof and it wasn't that bad. There was a small bar there that soon filled up with Boer and German farmers whose only topic was how the drought was kicking the guts out of them. Jeff and Nick got into a beer skulling competition and the barman, a black bloke – seeing a bonanza in trade sitting there right on the premises – encouraged them to make use of a massive glass made in the same shape as a boot. Naturally, being a couple of real show-off bastards, they readily took up the offer. In no time flat they had sunk a couple of boots each, and then they challenged the locals to do better. A couple of Boers and one German made suckers of themselves by wanting to do exactly that. They in turn sunk a couple of boots, though their belches weren't as loud as Nick's and Jeff's. Dave produced some hundred dollar Namibian bills and it was on for young and old to bet on who could drink the most before chundering. He, Ernie and I immediately put our money on Jeff, for we had seen him in action before heaps of times and knew the capacity of his huge gut. The two Boers looked pretty miffed that all the locals were backing the German. Nick was left out in the cold by us Aussies completely; he was certainly as big as the German, but his brain couldn't hack the alcohol, therefore he would either pass out cold or wreck the place. We didn't want the latter to happen, as it looked as if we could be watering in Karibib for some considerable time to come. When Nick went on the rampage it was similar to having a CAT D11 bulldozer let loose in a china shop. To placate him, Wheeler told him that the German would drink the arse off Jeff, so he got all patriotic and swore that he would be barracking for Jeff against all those Japies and Krauts.

It was a real bonzer struggle! Jeff was at his very thirstiest that night. He beat the German by half a boot before he chundered. We Aussies won four hundred bucks! The bartender got the mop out to swab up both Jeff's and the German's spew, and wasn't that pissed off with the mess considering he had sold what seemed like thirty litres of beer to the two competitors. The German, Otto Henckert, was a bit like Jeff, whereas he could carry on drinking once he had had a good puke. He soon became long-lost cobbers with the victor and they had their arms around each other's shoulders singing their lungs out; the German in German and Jeff trying to copy him. Everyone was in a good mood, for the competition had taken the farmers' minds off the drought. The other Germans started singing along with Otto and Jeff, and the Boers came out with voortrekker songs of their own; each party battling to outgun the other.

A black sheila came in with all sorts of plastic twirls and whirls hanging off her head and she was soon rubbing her arse on Ernie's crutch, making him grin like a sphinx. He was carrying on as if his balls had just dropped!

Some cops, a black one and white one, came wandering in to see what all the noise was about and they were told to have a drink or fuck off! They both had massive guns on their hips and truncheons like pick handles, but, having surveyed all before them, they gave us a sad shake of the head and beat the feet. Nick tried to do a handstand on a table, then, with me holding his legs, he tried to drink a boot of beer upside down and bloody near drowned. When I let him go glasses were smashed in all directions; still the barman was also pissed and clapped his hands with all his might. Some old white woman, who must have been the publican's wife or the owner, cut up rough, but Dave gave her half the money we had won on Jeff and she settled down with a gin and tonic. She had a really good singing voice and was soon singing a duet with Otto in German and it sounded absolutely top class. Then, to put cream on the cake, a Boer got into an argument with a German bloke over the Second World War and they started savaging each other; tipping over tables and destroying more glasses.

To make things even better, I went out into the beer garden to take a piss on a flower bed when I saw Ernie sitting at one of the outside tables with the black sheila giving him a head job. The whole exercise was most likely futile for the sheila, for she sucked away for at least half an hour before he flaked out altogether. We found out later that she had managed to lift his wallet. Losing a couple of hundred Nam' bucks wasn't too bad; although he had to make several phone calls to cancel his stolen credit cards. It was a real cracker night!

CHAPTER 28

ALBINO SCORPIONS!

Earlier preparations I had made during the day made the remainder of the night even more enjoyable! When we were setting up our camp, I noticed that the Karibib prospect was crawling with scorpions! One lived under almost every rock; some huge black bastards; some smaller and almost a kind of transparent yellow or orange colour. The latter, or from what Wilfred told me, were known as 'albino' scorpions. While the big, black bastards looked really potent with their huge tails and nippers, I was assured that the smaller albino ones packed far more of a punch. I hadn't forgiven Jeff for making a dickhead out of me at the first drill site, nor had I forgotten Nick's words about whether I would bounce or not if I went over the cliff. Using a stick and a plastic drill sample bag, I managed to capture four of the albino variety and two each went into Jeff and Nick's sleeping bags. Naturally that happened when no one was looking.

The gas lamp in Ernie's tent was the last to be turned off, and maybe twenty minutes went by before we all heard Nick's horrified yells: "Hey! What the fuck!

Shit! Fuck me – fuckin' – dead!"

The racket he made had the entire camp wide awake, and when I got our gas light going, he was nursing a dark red welt just below his right armpit. It must have been giving him a great deal of curry because he was literally shaking from the pain. Herman and Wilfred pitched up and they obviously knew what a scorpion sting looked like, and, while they assured Nick that such a sting wouldn't be fatal, he had little chance of getting too much sleep for the rest of the night.

While that was going on, Jeff was just lying back in his sleeping bag pissing himself laughing. Especially when Nick found not one, but *two scorpions* in his swag! Jeff was just lighting a smoke, but it fell out of his mouth. His hysterical words almost echoed Nick's: "Hey – shit! Oh – Christ! Fuckin' hell! What the fuck?"

He had been stung twice; once on his left hip and once on his right ankle!

That had everyone in the camp searching their bedding, and I made a special show of turning my sleeping bag inside-out. I even carried out a close inspection of my new work boots, socks and my suitcase. I worked real hard at it in order to try and stop laughing.

Nick and Jeff spent the last of the dark hours holding ice on their stings and debating on whether it was worthwhile staying on in such a 'shithouse' country or not, until I told them both to shut the fuck up because they were encroaching on my beauty sleep.

It had been quite some time since I had had so much fun in just one single night!

CHAPTER 29

THE KRAUT PROSPECTOR!

When we finally started drilling the Karibib prospect things were going pretty all right, especially when we didn't have to back up to sudden death drill sites. The ground, what with all the siliceous marble, was a fair bit harder than the schist at Klein Aub, so the rig was only going through two hundred or so metres a shift. We had the odd niggling breakdown or two, but Ernie soon had us working again. The farmer whose property we were drilling on, a Swiss joker, was a fairly decent bloke and his spouse soon had Nick having the hots for her. One day the same farmer gave us a springbok to go in our tucker-bag and Dave and I agreed to put a water borehole down on the spot of his choice.

Everything was cruising along real fine until the German prospector, Jurgen – Kurt – Seebacher, who owned the Karibib claims, turned up. A fairly short, thickset joker with a gut on him like he was nine months pregnant; he strutted around the place like the Kaiser himself. He had old fashioned sideburns that joined up with his moustache and he glared at all of us as if we were indeed *'undermensch'*. At first he started getting up Kotzé about the geology and where the drill hole markers had been placed, but we didn't mind that, as it was kind of fun watching the Japie getting pissed off. When Wheeler and I had a crack at him for putting up with all the crap, he told Dave he didn't know where Seebacher fitted into the hierarchy of things, so he was waiting for the picture to become clearer. The stupid Kraut wasn't happy to stop there, for he started whinging about the sample Wheeler was pulling from the cyclone. Not that the arrogant bastard had ever seen an RC rig before.

It was on the night shift and Dave took about five seconds of his bullshit before he shut down the rig and drove back to the camp to get Ernie, Kotzé and me out of bed. "Kotzé!" he bellowed. "Get fuckin' Adolf Hitler away from the flamin' rig, before I wrap a breakout spanner around his fuckin' head! Are you fuckin' happy with the sample we're getting?"

"Ja?" Kotzé was half-asleep. "What is the problem?"

"Adolf Eichmann here reckons we're getting too much sample. Educate the cunt, for fucksakes!"

The Boer geo' shook his head to clear his thoughts and turned to Seebacher. "The samples so far have been satisfactory."

"They are too big," Seebacher disagreed. "The holes must be caving in. We will get too much contamination and water down the gold values. This must have happened at Klein Aub, so no wonder you could not recover any good assays there."

"You a dinkum fuckwit?" Wheeler butted in. "We're drilling through solid rock!" He turned to Kotzé, "I'm not gunna argue with this spastic. Get this fuckin' squarehead off my back, or I'm not gunna drill another friggin' metre till he's thrown off the site."

"You cannot call me names," Seebacher was miffed. "I shall contact the company and it shall be *you* who is the one that has to leave. I will go to the authorities and tell them you are being insulting. I am going to call my advocate and have him sue you."

Those threats incensed Dave even more. "I don't give a fuck what you do. I hate fuckin' Krauts! You're a bunch of women and children murderers. Now, bloody piss off – squarehead – or I'll report you to the Israeli Mossad and they'll cut your balls out!"

The next day when I was running the shift, the German prospector made no secret that he was dismayed at a coloured being at the controls. As each sample was laid out in a row, he tried to weigh the bag against the last one, and then he started writing down notes and shaking his head in disgust. I caught Jeff's eye, then purposefully cut back the compressor so that the rock chips stayed down the hole and the rods jammed. Dave and Nick, who hadn't tried to get any sleep yet, had wandered onto the site. Both they and Jeff knew exactly what I was doing.

"Ah, shit – you've hit a fuckin' fault!" Nick made out that he was a real gun driller. "You're gunna need some water and foam. Here – I'll give you a hand."

The procedure was fairly straightforward. We poured about a hundred litres of water down the middle of the jammed drill rods, and then added a couple of litres of detergent. From the top of the drill head there was a hundred-millimetre-wide rubber hose that was connected to the sample cyclone some twenty odd metres away. In normal circumstances the drill cuttings were blown up through the centre of the rods with compressed air, and then up through the revolving head; through the rubber hose into the cyclone. With Nick and I taking care of the water and detergent, Jeff disconnected the hose from the cyclone and lay it down so that it was pointing at Seebacher who was leaning against the side of his little, white Toyota bakkie.

While that was going on Wheeler went up to Seebacher all friendly like. "So you've been round a drill rig or two? I saw you weighing those bags. That's the best way of judging if you're getting an accurate sample."

Seebacher visibly warmed to his change of attitude. "Agh ja, I have seen many drilling machines like this operating at the Gorob and Hope Mine and at the Haib copper project. I know how these machines work."

I stood at the controls and held my hand on the compressor lever, thus prompting Dave to go and have a piss on a thorn bush. Seebacher was still leaning against his bakkie taking more notes. Jeff told Wilfred to follow him to the support truck, so that they could fetch something, and Nick casually sauntered up to the front of the drill truck. I pulled down hard on the compressor lever and black smoke belched out of the machine's exhaust as its engine started roaring. Nothing happened for about twenty seconds, and then the rubber cyclone hose started flapping around madly; pouring a tsunami of mud, water, foam and shit all over Seebacher and his bakkie. The whole mixture was hurled out with such velocity it smashed the vehicle's windscreen and the stupid Kraut was lucky not to lose an eyeball!

What a bloody beauty! Seebacher and the bakkie were covered in mud, water and brown foam. His notebook was a sodden wad and there was crap all over the inside and outside of his vehicle. I shut back on the compressor and nearly bit through my tongue to try and stop laughing. Jeff and Nick had their arms around each other, quaking with unashamed mirth. Even Wilfred nearly wet his pants.

If there was one thing about Wheeler, he could keep a straight face under any circumstances. "Bloody hell! Sorry, mate – I thought you knew what was happening, what with you being around rigs? You should've moved your vehicle, cobber. Looks like you're gunna need a new windscreen."

Seebacher seriously wasn't very happy! Covered in shit the way he was, he jumped into his vehicle and headed for the camp, spinning the wheels half the way there. Next thing Kotzé came on the scene a very worried individual. "Agh, man, what did you do to Seebacher? He has gone into town to fetch the police. He says you tried to kill him?"

"No, mate," Jeff told him, "we just tried to blind him, the dickheaded wanker!"

The upshot of it all was that Seebacher actually went back to Windhoek and called the client company's head geologist in Vancouver, who in turn phoned the boss back in Kal', who demanded to know from Ernie what the fuck was going on? Ernie defended the situation by saying that Seebacher had no right to be so close to the rig when it was operating, and, by doing so, was lucky that he hadn't been accidentally killed; what with not wearing safety gear such as a hard hat or whatever. The boss knew exactly what had happened, but he cleared it with the client and we carried on with the contract.

BASTARDS FROM THE BUSH

Seebacher came back about two days later, and he kept a considerable distance between him and the rig. Before long it became apparent that he had a lot in common with Kotzé, for he had nothing but ridicule for the blacks. Instead of calling them kaffirs, he obviously thought he was very witty by calling them K4's. He reckoned you could be arrested and charged by the SWAPO regime for using the word 'kaffir', but K4 was simply fine. He also told us that some famous German scientist had worked out that the blacks had less brain cells per square centimetre than the whites had. Dave then told him that he must have been an albino because he certainly wasn't as intelligent as some of the abos he had met back in Aussie.

That didn't upset the chubby German all that much. In fact he came up with quite a funny jape: "What is the better one between a K4 and a dog turd? ... If you run over them with a steamroller, they both go flat, but a dog turd turns white after a time. You see – ja? The dog's turd is better, for at least it turns white?"

He also had heaps of derision for the country's president, Sam Nujoma. "Our good father Sammy, he has two Doctorates, ja? He left school at standard four to join the railways. My granddaughter has more education than him, and she is barely eight years old. If it is not bad enough having a K4 as president, we should at least have one who does not need his fingers and toes to count. Nelson Mandela trained to be a lawyer, and that is quite good for a K4. People all around the world are in love with good old Nelson, even so I wonder how long it will take for him to climb back into his tree with the other baboons like old Sammy and Robert Mugabe of Zimbabwe?"

That last comment seriously had Dave frothing at the mouth. "You fuckin' arrogant, little cunt! Who the fuck do you think you are? Nelson Mandela's shit would be hundred times better than you. You fuckin' Krauts with you're fuckin' Hitler, Himmler and Goebbels! As far as world leaders go, Nelson Mandela would be one of the greatest statesmen this shithouse continent has ever had. What have you ever achieved in life, you fuckin' idiot, to think you can even dare mention his name? ... Fuck me dead!" he turned to us Aussies who had been fairly curious onlookers, "somebody grab hold of me before I kick this fucker's head in! You've got this arsehole insulting Mandela, and I'm gunna kill the fuckin' cunt!"

Fortunately Seebacher took himself elsewhere.

"Bloody hell, Dave – what was all that about?" I asked him once the German prospector had taken off in his bakkie.

"Did you see the way the dickheaded Boers treated Mandela?"

"Yeah, they locked him up for years."

"They fuckin' got up to a lot more than that. They robbed him of the best part of his life – his marriage – his kids, but they couldn't rob him of his spirit and downright decency. And you've got that fuckin' arsehole daring to bad-mouth him? He's lucky I didn't friggin' gut him, the dirty bastard! Fuck me dead – some low life, dirty wanker insulting someone like Mandela!"

"I really thought Dave was gunna hook the prick," Nick told me once Wheeler had stormed off. "It would've been good seeing him give the Kraut a good smack in the mouth."

"Fuckin' oath!" Jeff agreed with him. "Should've kneed the wanker in the nuts, mate!"

CHAPTER 30

I BUY A MERCEDES! KARIBIB LOOKS TO BE A DUD! POMMY GEOLOGIST! DEODORANT THAT WOULD KNOCK A RHINO ON ITS ARSE!

Kotzé started receiving the assay results back from the metres we had drilled at Karibib. It was the same old story; the samples had little of economic value in them, so the rig was stood down while he desperately tried to work out what was happening. There were also a few frantic phone calls going on between Windhoek and Vancouver, then Vancouver to Kal' and Kal' back to Windhoek. To me the break in the drilling was just fine. I had bought a fairly ancient, yellow Mercedes Benz 280SE, so I didn't have to use a company vehicle to get about in when I was off the site. Jeff and Ernie went back to Kal' for a fortnight's break, whilst Nick, Dave and I decided to stay in Namibia. That most likely pleased our employer since it cut down on the cost of airfares.

Wheeler didn't take long to want a loan of my wheels, and when I questioned what he was up to, he reckoned he wanted to go to Klein Aub to visit Magda. Seebacher and Kotzé saw Dave's infatuation as being a huge, sick joke, yet the German did have some comforting words to offer: "A coloured girl will do whatever possible to break out of the miserable life she finds herself with. There is no future in Klein Aub for her, and coming from a rural *gebeid* like the Rehoboth farmlands she may find it impossible to compete with all the coloured

189

girls in the larger towns and Windhoek. To any coloured girl a white man – any white man – has to be a very valuable catch. The many years of Apartheid have stamped this into their heads. Under the Boers, no matter how useless or lazy a white person was, that person was given a special status that was accompanied by privilege, better chances of employment and a higher salary. So in most cases the whites have been able to afford reasonable housing, clothing and motorcars. Things that for years have been out of the average coloured's and K4's reach. Then, of course, any person would like to have the same status and property which is available to those more fortunate than them. If you treat her with the slightest ounce of respect and do not beat her too often, generally a coloured woman can make an excellent, loyal companion, for they are great believers in a bird in the hand. You must be careful, though, for most Baster girls are beautiful up to the age of twenty-five at the latest, then they tend to self-destruct and shrivel like prunes. What is fascinating now is that some coloured girls are making designs on the newly affluent blacks. Before the country received its independence, the coloureds considered themselves far higher up than the Ovambo, Damara and ordinary K4s on the Apartheid ladder. That must make some of your everyday coloured men very unhappy indeed."

In my opinion he was dead right, for I certainly felt that I was above the ordinary Namibian black. Somehow, having lived in Australia, I also felt that I was superior even to the white Boers I had come across in Namibia. Kotzé certainly didn't seem as competent as geologists I had met in the gold fields, and Van der Merwe came across as being as thick as fourteen planks, what with him not wearing socks under any circumstances. Also, I had come across the average Boers with their beards, fat guts and genitalia bulging out of the tiny shorts they wore, and, of course, their arrogance and guttural Afrikaans. In Krystal's instance, the thought of her being with a black African was revolting!

With nothing to do around the drill site and leaving the rig and drilling gear in the rather dubious hands of Nick, I decided to go with

Dave to Klein Aub. Wilfred and Herman asked if they could come, as they wanted to touch base with some of their mates in Rehoboth, and I was glad since I had another master plan taking shape in the back of my mind.

After dropping them off in Rehoboth, Dave and I were just within sight of the abandoned Klein Aub copper mine when we saw a strange vehicle, a Land Rover Discovery, on one of our old drill sites, so we went over to investigate. Sitting in the shade of the vehicle on a canvas stool was a joker wearing a tweed fishing hat with a variety of fishhooks and feathers sticking out of it. He wore khaki trousers and shirt and some comfortable looking, suede, lace-up boots. He had hawk-like features, brooding eyes, dark brown eyebrows that joined in the middle of his forehead; red cheeks from being a bit of grog artist, plus a tomahawk nose. All in all his clothing looked expensive and he had a gold Rolex watch on his wrist that looked as if it weighed a ton. His clean-shaven face had a look of sheer disinterest as we approached him. At his feet was an ancient Golden Labrador that wagged its tail in a friendly manner, but nothing else. The bloke had a sieve and a bucket of water, plus several clear plastic trays that had compartments that held samples of drill cuttings. He was obviously logging the drill hole, a sight I had seen on every contract back on the West Aussie gold fields.

"How you goin', mate?" Wheeler started with.

"Not too bad, mate," came the man's reply.

"You an Aussie?" Dave wanted to know.

"Thank Christ – no, mate!"

"Dave Wheeler," Dave held out his hand, and then pointed to me, "Joe Schultz."

"James Dawson-Byrne," the bloke shook both our hands boredly, without standing up.

"Doing some logging?" I wanted him to know that I knew a thing or two.

"Yeah, cobber."

"You sound like an Aussie," Dave was unconvinced.

"Only when I'm talking to Aussies, mate. I'm what you jokers call a 'Pom', not that it's any of your business... You got things to do here, mate?"

"No, we were just checking on what you were doing," Dave sounded rather disconcerted. "We're the drilling mob that put these holes down."

"Righto, you've checked. Now clear off and let me get on with things."

Wheeler and I must have looked like a couple of kicked dogs as we made our way back to my car. "The fuckin' arrogant bastard!" Dave complained as I steered the vehicle back on to the main road. "He's lucky I didn't give him a backhand."

I wasn't so certain. "I don't know about that. He was fairly fit and stocky looking. Blokes who talk like that can usually handle themselves. There were two of us and he still shat all over us. Besides, his dog probably would've bitten your leg off."

Unlike the Pommy we had just met, Magda was dead keen to see Wheeler and was even more eager to come to Rehoboth with us. Preparing to go to town for her was a rather drawn-out and pathetic affair. From what I could gather from all the activity, panties and stockings without holes in them had to be borrowed from a neighbour who was very hesitant to lose sight of them. The strap of a tattered bra had to be mended in a hurry and she had no dresses that had been ironed for some time or ever. Some aunt lent a last sliver of lipstick to her, and she rolled on a body deodorant that would have knocked a charging rhino back on its arse. All in all she brushed up not too badly, and she *was* rather pretty.

Dave was in raptures with her and he took me to one side. "I'm gunna take her into Windhoek and buy her some really decent gear. Christ, a couple of hundred bucks Aussie, and then we'll see how she shapes up."

I liked the idea of him wanting to take her into Windhoek, for it fitted in with my new plan. All I needed was the guts to front up to old Elsabeth Witbooi and ask her if I could take Krystal out. I was convinced it would be more up to her in getting Krystal out, than asking Krystal directly. Somehow I reckoned that with Wilfred going along as a kind of a chaperone, things would be made a lot easier for me. Or perhaps I could ambush Krystal at the bank she worked at, and so sidestep the old bag altogether?

When we reached Rehoboth I found Wilfred yakking on to some of his cobbers at the Total roadhouse. "Do you know where the bank is that Krystal's working at?" I asked him.

"Ja, man, it is right in the city centre on Independence Avenue. Why, boss?"

"I wouldn't mind taking her out for a meal or something. Old Elsabeth could get in the way, though. I reckon if I could meet her in town, I'd have a much better go at taking her out."

"Agh, I do not know, boss. I do not want trouble from her and Uncle Kobus. If Krystal is late arriving home, *Ouma* Witbooi could call the cops and all sorts of things. She is very protective of Krystal. There could be big trouble, boss, no one has ever taken Krystal out before."

"What if I get Krystal to phone? Hang on, there's no phone at the house. Surely there's some way of getting a message through to the old dear?"

"For ten rand," I noticed that he – like a lot of Namibians – still referred to Nam' dollars as 'rand', "I could find someone to wait here at the petrol station and he could take a message round to her, boss. That is *if* Krystal is willing to go out, which I doubt. But you must not include me, boss. I could have my throat cut by old Uncle Kobus. Aunt Sophia, too, for that matter. I do not like living dangerously, man."

"It could be as serious as all that?"

"Even worse than that, boss!"

It was a piece of piss getting some young Baster bloke to wait for messages at the Total roadhouse. Alongside the ten bucks I had to buy him two sausage rolls and a can of Fanta.

CHAPTER 31

NIGHT OUT WITH A MIRAGE!

Finding the bank that Krystal was working in was just as easy, and she looked very efficient in her teller's booth. Feeling all stupid and coy, I sent a very nervous Wilfred up to her to explain my plans. My heart sank when I saw her shake her head at the little bloke, but then she looked over at me and gave me the loveliest smile. There was a combination of more shakes and nods as they got into a real serious conversation, then Wilfred came back to me with a look of triumph but some foreboding on his face.

"How'd you go?" I was dying to know.

"We shall see, boss. Krystal will phone my Auntie Veronica here in Windhoek, and then she can phone my Uncle Manfred at his work. If all goes properly, he can go round to *Ouma* Witbooi's house, and then we shall see what happens after that. I do not know, man, Uncle Manfred may be scared that the old lady will scold him for not going to church. This could become very complicated."

"And Krystal? What did she say?"

"She is scared of upsetting the *Ouma*. She said we must wait outside for when she finishes her work."

I grabbed him by the shoulders. "You bloody – little – ripper! Come, I'm gunna buy you a drink."

He nearly shat himself when I dragged him into the Kalahari Sands Hotel/Casino. I was determined to buy him the best. We found a real flash bar that was done out in beautiful polished granite and Karibib marble. He was totally embarrassed when I selected a table amongst some German tourists who looked down their noses at us.

I hastened to reassure him: "Relax, man! You're as good as any of the people here. Look at your gear," I pointed to his flash garb that he had acquired with his new-found wealth, "you're dressed as well as anyone. Don't take any notice of these stuffed up Krauts. You've got as much right to be here as they have. What you gunna have? I'm having a beer."

A delightful coloured girl served us, though she seemed a little suspicious that a coloured such as me could afford the exorbitant prices the establishment was charging for the drinks. I put her at ease by producing a wad of one hundred dollar bills.

"Did you have a win on the poker machines?" the girl asked.

"No, I borrowed this money from my friend here," I said, pointing at Wilfred. "His father's just left him four farms near Okahandja. He's a millionaire!"

Wilfred bloody near swooned when the girl started looking him over with calculating interest, so I burst the bubble by ordering another Tafel Lager.

We met up with Dave and Magda out the front of the bank, and Krystal, who virtually bubbled with excitement when I introduced her to Wheeler and Magda, soon joined us. "I must not stay out too late," she told all of us. "Also, I shall be staying the night at *Ouma* Veronica's house. Goodness me, look at these clothes! I should have brought a change of clothing, but I had no idea that this might happen."

"Buy her a dress and some gear," Dave suggested to me. "I'm gunna buy..."

"No," Krystal butted in. "These will do fine. I shall have to be careful not to get them too creased. I can use an iron at *Ouma* Veronica's before I go to work tomorrow morning."

"Well, you can help Magda pick out something," Dave told her.

We followed Wheeler, who had previously checked out a place called the Post Street Mall that had dozens of shops of all descriptions. Dave's bucks seemed edged with gold what with the sheer undiluted joy that came over Magda. With the willing assistance of Krystal and heaps of encouragement from Wheeler, Wilfred and I, she shyly inspected all the clothing shops; amply displaying her bush-Baster origins. She was petrified of the white shop proprietors; fussy, arrogant Boer and German bitches; however she relaxed when coloured or black girls approached to serve her. At last in EDGARS, a large department store, she settled down to browse in the huge women's clothing department. She liked brightly coloured, floral dresses, so Wheeler bought her three. He didn't let her finish there; two pairs of jeans, some T shirts, two blouses, a stylish skirt and matching top. Several pairs of shoes, panties, stockings and some bras had also been purchased before they headed for the cosmetics and perfume counter.

I could easily see that Krystal was taken up by all the excitement. "Please let me buy you something?" I pleaded. "You work at a bank, so you know how much our Australian dollars are worth. Please, Krystal, I can certainly afford it?"

"All right, but nothing too expensive. Also, I will have to leave whatever you buy at Auntie Veronica's house. *Ouma* Elsabeth gets most upset if she sees such extravagance. Seriously, Josef, I simply do not know what to choose."

"Just pick out an outfit. Shoes, stockings, lingerie – the lot. You can surprise me while I go over and buy some aftershave. Don't worry about the cost because I'll be using a credit card and won't even look at the bill."

I joined Wheeler at the cosmetics and perfume counter. He had bought Magda an assortment of lipsticks and other makeup, along with some expensive perfume, skin lotions, bath soaps and *much less* lethal deodorant.

Not wanting to appear a poofter to the Boer sales lady, I let her pick out some scent, soap and things for Krystal, after I selected some aftershave. Magda was just standing there in her nifty grey suit and a lilac cotton blouse in a wide-eyed trance as she hugged a bunch of shopping bags to her breast. Old Dave was fairly loaded down also. Both shared a look of absolute contentment.

Krystal not only had exquisite looks; she clearly had excellent taste. Her selection was a simple, navy-blue dress that fitted her perfect body like a sheath. The garment was cut in such a way that only half an inch of her cleavage could be seen and the hem was barely an inch above her knees. Her black stockings and dark blue, high-heeled shoes demonstrated how perfect her long legs were. Letting my imagination run free as a ferret, I thought of her body being clad in a black suspender belt, panties and bra.

"Where we gunna go?" Dave sent my depraved thoughts hurtling in all directions. All of a sudden I wished he wasn't there. I only wanted to be somewhere private with Krystal. Preferably in some hugely expensive hotel suite. My groin was throbbing, so it appeared that my emotions might have been a mixture of lust combined with love!

"Buggered if I know," I replied. I turned to Wilfred. "You got any suggestions?"

"Ja, boss. There is another casino they call the Windhoek Country Club. I have never been in there, but some other Baster guys told me it is real cool. They have a lot of water pools and things in the garden and the food is supposed to be very good. If you get on the Rehoboth road, then turn right onto the Okahandja bypass, it should be on your right once you have gone half a kilo'."

"You coming?" Dave suggested. "You're more than welcome."

"No, boss, there are some of my friends in town that I wish to meet up with."

"Where's Herman?" I asked. "How you gunna find your way back to the drill site?"

"I am meeting with Herman later tonight. We shall be on the main road to Okahandja tomorrow morning if you come past, otherwise we can wave down an Ovambo taxi. When do you think we shall be working again?"

BASTARDS FROM THE BUSH

Wheeler shrugged. "I don't know, cobber. If you can arrange your own transport, take at least a couple of days off. Don't worry, there won't be any hassles."

Wilfred's directions turned out to be spot on, for we had no trouble in locating the Windhoek Country Club. It was all his Baster mates said it would be. There was a bar situated on an island surrounded by pools and tunnels of water in the casino gardens. It was done out in moulded concrete like some Bushman's cave, and the lawns and plastic deckchairs scattered around the water gave the place an almost Mediterranean look. The casino was done out in fairly basic, light brown, adobe squares, which – with the various palm trees and native bush – made it blend in quite nicely with the ochre coloured, parched landscape that surrounded Windhoek. A well-watered golf course adjacent to the resort complex added to the illusion of us being in some verdant oasis.

Dave and I selected a table within easy reach of the bar and Krystal and Magda's eyes were darting all over the place as if they had plans of doing a bunk. Whites of all descriptions surrounded us; mostly Germans and the omnipresent Boers accompanied by their tough wives with their shocking Afrikaans accents. I had heard Jeff telling Nick back at the camp that he had fucked men, women and children of all nations, plus most of the animal kingdom; yet if there was something he couldn't hack – it was a sheila with a Boer accent!

When I asked Krystal what she wanted to drink she insisted that she was having absolutely no alcohol. Clearly unsure of her surroundings, Magda went down the same track. Wheeler spent some time muttering with the barman and he came back with two bright red drinks with cherries, miniature umbrellas and stripey straws and things. I took a sip of Krystal's drink and it tasted similar to a strawberry daiquiri, but Dave swore there was no booze in it. That was just fine with me, for there was no way that I was about to put one over on Krystal. If I was ever going to see what she kept in her panties, it would be with her express well wishes, no matter how long or rough the road.

JOSEF SCHULTZ

I led the way into the casino complex's restaurant and a coloured joker in smart black trousers, white shirt and blue bow tie found a table for four. With a gallant flourish he lit a red candle in the centre of the table. It was obvious that he knew both Magda and Krystal, yet he didn't bother swapping any pleasantries with them. Both women were bright-eyed and nervous, for we found ourselves surrounded by whites who stared in our direction as if they had just seen unicorns. The restaurant had both a flash looking buffet and an à la carte menu. Krystal and Magda insisted on ordering from the menu as they weren't game to line up with the whites at the buffet tables, so they and I ordered fillets of springbok. Not wanting to be different Dave also ordered from the menu and asked for a gemsbok steak. I then summonsed the drinks waiter for a bottle of Kanonkop merlot and a couple of Cokes for the ladies. The wine tasted absolutely top notch, so Dave and I killed a couple more bottles.

"You must not tell *Ouma* about this," Krystal warned once she saw the prices of everything. "She really hates extravagance. What you have spent tonight would keep an ordinary Baster family in food for three months."

The arrangements for the rest of the night became fairly clear cut. Dave was sharing a room with Magda at the Casino, while I had to drop Krystal off at her aunt's place. I would also take a room at the casino after that. It was a bit like the old Cinderella story, as I had to have Krystal safely returned before the clock struck twelve, or there would be anguish to be had from her chaperones, and a posse of irate Baster from Rehoboth could come swarming after me similar to in Hendrik Witbooi's day. I delivered her to her aunt's place at couple of minutes before midnight and there was no chance of me making any hay in the car with my beautiful companion. I was given a quick hug and a kiss that ended up with her tongue in my mouth, and then she was through her aunt's front door as if she had been some wonderful mirage.

CHAPTER 32

THE POMMY GEO' TAKES OVER!
MOLESTERS OF BABOONS!

When Wheeler and I arrived back at the camp we discovered that Wilfred and Herman had long since beaten us to it. We found Ernie and Kotzé deep in conversation; frowns denting both their foreheads.

"What's wrong?" Dave inquired. "Don't tell me Nick and Van der Merwe have also driven to their deaths?"

"No, they have gone down to the farmer's house to get fresh meat," Kotzé explained solemnly.

"Another bloody geo's pitched up," Ernie told us. "A fuckin' Pommy! I tell you what – he's a friggin' arrogant cunt!"

"He wouldn't by any chance be a Pom' by the name of Dawson-Byrne?" Wheeler tried to look all knowledgeable. "He wouldn't have an old, prehistoric dog with him?"

"How did you know?" Ernie stared up at him. "He's out checking on your last drill hole."

"We saw him at Klein Aub when I went to go and pick up Magda. You're right – he's a real prickly sort of an arsehole, isn't he?"

Kotzé quickly looked round to make sure that the man in question wasn't standing right behind him. "Ja, he had no right to speak to me like that. I do not have to put up with his insults. I am the project geologist, he ..."

"The fucker really got stuck into Hermanus," Ernie interrupted.

"Ja – he did!" the Japie looked gratefully at old Ernie. His eyes had that pleading look as if he was begging for a kindred spirit.

Nick arrived holding a brown, paper parcel above his head. He then held it out to me, "Dead blackfella, cobber! The farmer shot this coloured Baster for poaching. Now we're gunna snack on one of your Rehoboth cousins."

"Whack it in the fridge," Ernie was in no mood for banter. "What the fuck you got there, anyway?"

"Oryx," Nick replied. "A kind of antelope. They've got another name for it..."

"Gemsbok," Dave really knew his wildlife. "I had some at a restaurant last night... Hey, Ernie, how come you're back so soon? I thought you still had a week's break to go back in Kal'? Where's Jeff?"

"I'm fetching him tomorrow from the airport. We had to come back early with this new geo' pitching up. Should've seen Jeff – he was as pissed off as hell!"

Dawson-Byrne drove right up to us in his Land Rover Discovery. With the Labrador at his heels he fronted Kotzé, his face looking as if he had just been handed a shit sandwich. "What university did you go to?" he demanded from the Boer.

"The University of Stellenbosch. Why do you ask?"

The Pommy looked as if he had been given another tablespoonful of shit to swallow. "I should've thought so. How did you learn your subjects – like an Af? Were you presented with a *darkie diploma* or something? What was the Boer regime doing – handing out degrees like the Russkies and Swedes were handing them out to the Afs? John Vorster, your ex-Apartheid prime minister, was chancellor of the Stellenbosch University, just like Idi Amin made himself chancellor of the Makarere University in Uganda. Believe me, the latter's post was far more credible... I've heard of keeping whites in jobs, but this's plain ridiculous. Even the actual concept of you being a competent geologist's preposterous. Of all the times I've been in this country, I've never come across *one* decent Boer professional, whether he or she be a doctor, lawyer, engineer or geologist.

You're incompetent, corrupt, unethical, lying wasters. I'd rather trust or employ an Af than have a second to do with any of your ilk. Your dishonesty and pathetic, childlike arrogance obviously comes from the genes of your voortrekker forefathers, who were also liars, thieves, cattle rustlers, and molesters of baboons. You say you've contempt for the Af, yet there's so much Af in your peoples' blood, there wouldn't be a full-blooded white person left among you. You're merely a bunch of mongrel half-chats without the slightest idea of who your Af or lower class white grandfathers might've been. The same goes for your mothers, aunts, uncles, sisters, sons and daughters."

Kotzé was all indignant: "I do not have to tolerate your insults. I am the project geologist here. My contract gives me..."

"Not any more – you're not. I've got a good mind to kick you off the prospect, you incompetent buffoon. Kindly keep your mouth firmly shut until I decide what to do with you."

"What's happened?" Dave wanted to know. 'What do you mean by 'Afs'?"

Dawson-Byrne looked him up and down with complete contempt. "Ah, it's you again. The bloke from the Aussie drilling mob. Frankly, what I discuss with this imbecile here's none of your business. If you're a driller – you'll be required to drill – if and when I decide you should. In the mean time remain on your driller's mental level and leave the more profound matters with me, where they'll be safe. As for 'Afs' – I mean the indigenes of the Dark Continent – the blacks. Surely that's obvious. " So saying, he climbed into his vehicle and parked it about fifty metres away from our cluster of tents. In no time at all he had Kotzé's labourers pitching a tent for him.

"I would've smacked him in the mouth," Nick told Wheeler. "Want me to set fire to his tent or something?"

"No, mate," Dave was staring after the Pom' with a look on his face akin to awe. "What we have here is a true-blue shitstirrer. A fuckin' aristocrat, cobber! The very best to be had. We can be educated by this great fellow, and I seriously yearn to be his disciple."

Night came, leaving us sitting round a camp table sucking down a few Tafels when Dawson-Byrne came up to us. "What food's there?"

"We've got all sorts, mate," Nick told him. "The farmer..."

"Don't call me 'mate'! I'm not your mate. You love me or something? Do I turn you on?"

That probably hurt poor Nick's feelings. "And you can get fucked, too–*mate!*"

The Pommy only shook his head. "Typical Aussie driller. Inarticulate and every second word 'fuck' or 'cunt'! Low IQ – zero education – beer guzzler. To you the most important ambition in your life is to drink as much beer as possible without vomiting. That's how you rate how macho you are... Kotzé!"

"Ja?"

"What food's there?"

"We are having gemsbok steaks, mashed potatoes, vegetables and gravy. There are also tinned peaches."

"Send some over to my tent. I want the steak properly cooked, not dripping with blood. See if you can find some fresh bread. Also, make sure you wash your hands." Following that went back to his tent.

"He's got you all worked out, Nick," Dave laughed, breaking the stunned silence. "I couldn't've described you better myself."

I also had stirring in mind. "Nick, you mentioned setting fire to his tent. Let's pour petrol over his dog and set him loose in his tent. We'll have a real Halley's Comet on our hands, then."

"Ha, ha, ha!" Kotzé thought that I was very funny. "What will you use as a fuse? When it is cooked, we can cut steaks off it and feed them to the Ovambo. I am serious – dogs are very high on the Ovambo's menu."

"Very funny, you Japie wanker," Nick wasn't amused. "You touch that dog and I'll feed your balls to the Ovambos."

The next morning there was still no drilling; therefore we went out to the rig, anyway, having left it at the last drill site. There was no maintenance to do on any of the gear, either, so we were bored shitless. We were just hanging round, yarning on, when Dawson-Byrne came along to log the last drill hole.

He had Kotzé with him and he didn't seem too happy with the Boer one bit. "What on earth were you drilling in this direction for? Look out there, man," he was pointing at a line of parallel hills in the distance. "We're on a syncline not an anticline, you damned cretin. Even if there *is* mineralisation here, you'd have no chance of intersecting it. For God's sake – look at those rocks over there. There's no trouble working out which way they're plunging."

As if working on a sixth sense his dog went up to Nick who was delighted to fuss over it. The pair cobbered-up immediately, which miffed the Pommy geologist. "Come here, Ben," he snarled. "We don't want you turning into a drunken, foul-mouthed bum, or losing your virginity to some Aussie driller."

The dog looked up sadly at Nick, and then obeyed its master. "When we gunna be drilling?" Nick wanted to know.

The Pommy geo' looked over at him with distaste. "How would I know? Thanks to our good Boer academic here," he indicated to Kotzé, "we haven't got any drill targets. It could take months, so we're gunna have to start from scratch, mate."

I saw a flash of triumph in Nick's eyes. "Don't fuckin' call me 'mate' – mate! You wanna fuck me or something?"

Strangely enough it was Ernie who got in next and he really dropped his bundle. "I've had enough of this bullshit, Dawson-Byrne! We didn't bring this fuckin' rig all the way here just to be stood down. Also, I've had a gutsful of your high and mighty, poncey attitude. We don't have to put with all this crap from you. Who the fuckin' hell do you think you are?"

If that ruffled his feathers, the Pom' didn't show it. "I can adopt any attitude I like. Unlike our good friend Kotzé here, I'm damned good at what I do. Unless I can sort out this mess, you may have to dismantle this rig and take it back to where it came from." He shifted his attention to Wheeler and he pointed at Kotzé. "This man reminds me of Ireland shortly before and after the Second World War."

"Oh yeah?" Dave was keen to see the Japie humiliated further.

Dawson-Byrne was happy to oblige. "Namibia and South Africa are in exactly the same position as Ireland was around the Second World War. Most of the energetic and intelligent whites over here have left for pastures new, and now we're left with the dregs. All the decent technicians and professionals are long gone. It was the same with Ireland – anyone with any initiative left that bog for the States or the British colonies, leaving behind all the bogtrotters. It's why Ireland's so backward. Both Northern and the Republic of Ireland. Now that the Afs have been handed government in Namibia and South Africa, all the decent whites have taken themselves elsewhere, leaving a vacuum when it comes to intellectuals or any sort of sophistication. All we're left with are cretins and morons, plus total low lives altogether... There's one fundamental difference between the Irish and the Boers, though."

"Please go on," Wheeler grinned at the Pommy.

"It's quite simple, really," Dawson-Byrne assured him, "the majority of the Irish are plain stupid, while the Boers in their entirety are both sleazy and inherently dishonest. You could trust them no further than you would an Af. They're pure and simply liars and cheats."

"Why are you not drilling?" Seebacher had arrived in his bakkie and seemed most concerned at the inactivity.

Dawson-Byrne looked down at him as if he was some kind of new species of insect. "And where do you fit in?"

"My name is Jurgen Seebacher. I own these claims till the company pays me. The claims at Klein Aub, also."

"Ah, the prospector!" the Pommy wasn't all that impressed. "The German prospector that drives such a hard deal with foreign exploration companies? I'm not supposed to tell you this until the drilling program's finished, but I shall do so with the utmost pleasure. We've found nothing of significant value so far. I can't see the company paying you any more money."

The fat, little German was instantly troubled. "There is plenty of gold here. I have taken many samples that are carrying gold. Soil samples and rock samples. All of them carrying more than seven grams per tonne."

Dawson-Byrne motioned towards the Boer. "Mr. Kotzé here hasn't found any. Are you sure it wasn't fool's gold? Plenty of people mistake it for the real thing."

Seebacher went crimson with rage. "Fool's gold! I know what real gold looks like. I have worked my own gold mine here for many years. Do you see those old shafts over there," he pointed at some old mine workings. "I got many kilos of gold from there. You cannot teach me anything about gold." He turned on Kotzé. "I told you – you were drilling in the wrong place. I have checked all the drill holes at Klein Aub, and none are anywhere near the reef."

"What reef?" Dawson-Byrne demanded. "What did you have in mind – stealing millions off the company? Looks like you're a born loser, Seebacher. I saw a copy of the option they signed with you, the pathetic idiots. A bunch of Canadian lawyers and accountants who know nothing about mining or exploration, except how to rob their shareholders. No golden retirement for you, my good fellow, you'll have to work the rest of your days. An Ovambo farmer wouldn't graze his goats on these claims, yet alone at Klein Aub. You've obviously been lying to this stupid Boer, who's just as dishonest by claiming he's a geologist... Yes, I've come across the likes of you before, so your father was most likely a toilet cleaner at some Turkish owned restaurant in Berlin." The Pom' then turned on Kotzé. "I'll tell you why we British are superior to you Boers and Germans. Take Africa for instance – the Portuguese found this place and South Africa – the Dutch and Germans developed them – the British annexed them. The same thing happened with that other German colony, Tanganyika."

The Pommy geo' went off with Kotzé, and Seebacher left the site a shattered man. "Fuckin' hell!" Dave guffawed. "That Pommy bastard's got a real chip on his shoulder. Doesn't he like anyone?"

Ernie wasn't overly chuffed. "What a bloody stuff up! Christ knows what we're gunna do if we don't start drilling ASAP. Sitting around like this's costing someone a fuckin' poultice."

"Hasn't the boss got anything else lined up?" Jeff asked him. "He reckoned there was heaps going on in this part of the world?"

The little mechanic shrugged. "He was talking about some metres in Botswana. On a platinum prospect. What with the gold price, things are fuckin' up all over."

His words didn't lie well with me. If it wasn't the Aborigines back home with their land rights bullshit, the gold price had plummeted, causing all those in gold exploration to pack the shits. Regardless of all that, the thought of leaving Namibia, and therefore Krystal, left a hollow feeling deep inside me.

I was just loafing around the camp when Wilfred took me to one side. "There is a Baster waiting at the farm gate. He wants to talk to with us, but the farmer will not let him in. It has something to do with your brother, boss."

I drove down to the main gate with him, and a white VW Jetta was parked on the side of the main road. When we pulled up behind it a coloured joker came round to Wilfred's window. I had never seen the bloke before, nor possibly had he seen me, yet he was doing a lot of pointing in my direction as he jabbered away at Wilfred in Afrikaans. When he had had his say, he climbed into the Jetta and headed back in the direction of Okahandja.

"And what was that all about?" I asked Wilfred.

"He is Willem Zes, Carl Zes' brother. Do you remember those three guys that were round at Uncle Kobus' farm?"

"Yeah. As a matter of fact I met Carl Zes at the Total roadhouse in Rehoboth. He seems to have a bit of cash about him, so what does he do for a quid?"

"A quid? What you mean, boss?"

"How does he earn his money?"

"I do not know. I think he is some kind of a businessman or something."

"So what do they want?"

"They would like to ask you a few questions..."

"Stuff 'em. I don't have to..."

"They are friends of your brother, boss. They wish you no disrespect. Talk to them, please."

"When?"

"They shall make contact with me and arrange a meeting."

I had another visit a few days later, but it was from a different Baster that time. A bloke by the name of Louis Pienaar. Like Zes's brother, he could hardly speak a word of English, so I was lucky that Herman had come along to go as a translator. Miss Elsabeth Witbooi was in the Catholic hospital and was very ill! Could I come to Rehoboth as soon as possible?

On arriving at the hospital, I found out that *Ouma* Elsabeth had had a stroke of some sort, although, in the opinion of the Cuban doctor at the Catholic hospital, the old battleaxe was getting over it very nicely. He found it quite extraordinary that such an ancient individual could be so robust, as he had seen far younger people succumb to much less.

Much to my great joy Krystal was there sitting at the old woman's bedside, and her smile of greeting lit up the rather drab hospital ward. She was stunningly beautiful as ever and I was giddy with pleasure when she hugged and kissed me. It wasn't an ordinary peck on the cheek, either!

As for Elsabeth, she certainly didn't look as if she had had a stroke or whatever and kept insisting that she would be fit enough to go to mass the next Sunday morning.

She called me over to stand beside her. "I want you to have this, Kido." She held out a silver crucifix that was suspended on a chain of the same metal. "It was your father's. Jonker has a ring of his. Come on – put it on." I fastened the chain around my neck and tucked the crucifix inside my shirt. "Wear it always, Kido. That belonged to a truly great Witbooi. If you're half the man he was, you shall make Krystal a very fine husband."

Her words went through me like electricity! I quickly looked over at Krystal, who was blushing and smiling delightfully at the same time. She didn't object to the old lady's supposition.

Zes came in and totally stuffed everything up. He had flowers for Elsabeth, plus a fairly corny 'Get Well' card with Garfield the cartoon cat on it. I cursed myself for not doing something similar.

I soon got over those troubled thoughts, and I was literally walking on air as I left the hospital. I felt slightly guilty for going behind the old woman's back when it came to asking Krystal out, for the old dear had obviously given her blessing to the possibility of me marrying the woman of my dreams!

CHAPTER 33

THE BROEDERBOND!

Though we drillers were dying of boredom, Dawson-Byrne was flat out remapping the claims. He had Kotzé and Van der Merwe in a real sweat, too, and he was all the time pouring scorn on them, "I'll be damned – you call yourselves the white elite? So you're much better than the Afs, Kotzé? You took Seebacher's word for it? Seven grams, huh? You decided to drill without taking your own samples?"

"Ja, but there are gold soil sample anomalies over this area," the Japie geo' defended himself. "There was a major mining company who had the ground before Seebacher. They did not follow these anomalies up. I was more interested in this than what Seebacher told me. Besides, how was I to know he was lying?"

Dawson-Byrne held up a map of the claims. "Look here, the soil anomalies aren't even on Seebacher's ground. They're just outside. Luckily I've applied for more ground. For the company this time – Seebacher can go to blazes. Trust a damned German? They're even lower than the Afs. The same as Boers, come to think of it."

The Pom' didn't only rail at the Japies on the job; he kept at it in the camp at night. That was when he deigned on the odd occasion to sit around our campfire. He drank whisky rather than beer.

Wheeler, being the kind of scientific shitstirrer that he was, used to subtly get him going. "I reckon Kotzé's right. The blacks over here don't seem overly bright. The average white's far more intelligent."

"You call the average white South African intelligent?" Dawson-Byrne made out that he couldn't fathom Dave's remark. "Look at the war they fought here against SWAPO. Look at the millions we saw poured into that. They had military conscription in those days and all the Boer suckers were on the front line, while the select few – the *Broederbond* – made a blind fortune. It was a total..."

"What was the *Broederbond* exactly?" Dave cut in.

"The *Broederbond* or *Afrikaner Broederbond* was – and still is – a covert organisation kicked-off by some real Japie hairy back by the name of Henning Klopper. At first he and a couple of associates started an organisation called Jong Suid-Afrika or Young South Africa. All potential members or *Broeders* are carefully screened before they can join. A member has to be a regular churchgoer, he's not allowed to divorce his wife, and his children have to attend an Afrikaans speaking school. He has to keep things so secret, even his wife isn't allowed to know he's joined. They have these peculiar initiation rites, and in the old days they had this ceremony that culminated in the threat that 'He who betrays the Bond – will be destroyed by the Bond. The Bond never forgets – its vengeance is swift and sure' ... At first the organisation was set up not only to bolster Afrikaner pride and the Afrikaans language, it was also supposed to defend the lower class Afrikaners. However, as the organisation became more elitist, making money by a few became the name of the game. Similarly with the Mafia in the States, the Bond set up trade unions to protect the white workers, but these unions, what with all the union fees and so on, soon became milch cows for a select few. Like the *Spoorbond*, a railway union... You hear people talking about the Afs being corrupt. I'm not saying they aren't, but they wouldn't hold a match to our Boer friends. Through the Bond corruption was placed on a basis far more lucrative and discreet than the Yank Mafia. Never mind the poor old Afs being exploited, the Bond had no hesitation in ripping off the common Boer. With the guise of safeguarding Afrikaner unity, they set about ripping off their own people as well. As the Bond's tentacles reached into every aspect of the common Boer's society, they also penetrated the Calvinist Dutch Reformed Church, the military, the police, the justice system and the highest positions of government and everyday politics. From lowly police constables to army and police generals, judges, church leaders, cabinet ministers and prime ministers. A total nest of corrupt swine. Take the good old Dutch Reformed Church – a church that once preached that the Af had been created by God to be a servant to the white man. It was rather pathetic the way the Boer church did a total back flip. For years they promoted Apartheid and warned their congregations about the evil of the Af. Yet, when it looked inevitable that the blacks were about to take over government, we had a total about-turn and they railed against the segregation and disunity that Apartheid had created. Overnight they told the white people that the Af must be loved, have his hand held while travelling into the future, and he was to be assisted wherever possible..."

"Ja," Kotzé butted in, "people have bent over backwards to help the kaffirs both here in Namibia and South Africa, but – tell me – is the kaffir capable of any form of gratitude? The kaffir just takes with both hands and his teeth, without even knowing that such a word as gratitude exists.

"True," Dawson-Byrne admitted, "but being a stupid, thick-headed Boer, you're missing my point. I'm pointing out the hypocrisy of the Afrikaner Church. Whilst in power the whites tried everything they could to denigrate the Afs. They wouldn't let an Af anywhere near their houses of worship, despite claiming that there was only one God who loved all individuals equally. Now they're opening their doors to all and sundry and claiming South Africa to be the 'Rainbow Nation', whereas in the days of not so long ago, the Af was to be loathed, and any white who showed him any kind of sympathy or encouragement was to be vilified by all those around him... The *Broederbond* was more than likely the party behind this change of face. Like a chameleon, the Bond's changed its colours in order to adapt to its surroundings. Apartheid's still alive and in good health, especially here in Namibia amongst the Germans, Boers and other Europeans, although in South Africa it's the poor whites who're starting to suffer. I don't mean that sympathetically – don't get me wrong – the out-of-pocket and totally unskilled whites are now at the bottom of the ladder. That's why we're seeing so many suicides amongst the lower class whites. They can't cope with Apartheid in reverse. They can't survive when jobs, previously safeguarded for them by white Apartheid, are taken away by black affirmative action."

"Affirmative action?" Seebacher had joined us and treated the words as if they resembled dog shit. "The only thing we have here in Namibia is 'affirmative shopping'. If a K4 wants something, he steals it. That is what we call 'affirmative shopping' and there is no policeman who will stop him, for the average policeman nowadays is either incompetent or an even bigger criminal."

"Who asked you to butt in?" the Pommy glared at him. "You lying, Nazi scum. I bet your father forced children into the gas chambers at Belsen with a bayonet. Your mother more than likely was in charge of pulling the Jews' gold teeth out. She must've given you some to sprinkle around here, since it's the only gold we're going to find on this piece of ground."

That made the German very huffy. He held his index finger pointed straight at his tormentor's beak like nose. "You cannot talk to me like that. Here in Namibia there are laws against such talking. I shall phone my advocate and he will issue a summons against you."

"You make me want to vomit, you pathetic, little Nazi," Dawson-Byrne sneered. "Now you want to shelter under a law that the K4 introduced? ... You people," he asked those around him," did you hear me insult this Nazi pig?"

"Not a word," Wheeler spoke for all of us. "In fact, being visitors in this country, we're getting pissed off at Seebacher calling the locals 'K4s' when he should be referring to 'em as 'comrades'."

"Exactly!" Dawson-Byrne confirmed with a smile. It was easy to see that Dave was slowly winning him over. "We can't have Nazis vilifying the local Afs, now can we? The only reason why the German government's putting so much aid money into this place and is making life slightly bearable, is because they don't want a swarm of drunken, bigoted Nazis returning home to the Fatherland. It's much cleaner and cheaper to keep them over here. By the same token, they also much prefer the Turks, Romanians, Albanians and other wogs to their ex-colonials... By Jove, but you Germans dare to be so arrogant? You're just a race of murderers. Talk about Afs going into a killing frenzy in Rwanda and Liberia? After the Holocaust in Europe you had the Germans all pointing fingers at each other – swearing their innocence and blaming everybody else – nonetheless the vast majority of Germans could hardly conceal their delight when the Nazi Brownshirts beat up old Jewish men and women and destroyed their property. When Hitler and that bunch of homosexuals – who the Germans chose to lead them – ordered the coppers to stay out of sight, the whole country was lit up by bonfires when German men, women and children went on the rampage, killing and destroying. How can a whole nation of *white* people be so depraved? During the twentieth century at that! How could they have backed such an assortment of queers and freaks – Hitler, Himmler, Goering and Goebbels? After the war they claimed they'd been taken over by force by Hitler and his perverts, but look at all the film reels that display overjoyed men and simpering woman whenever Hitler spewed his bull's droppings all over them. It simply illustrates the mentality of the average Germans – the '*Sieg Heils*!' and the '*Heil Hitlers*' to some arrogant, scrawny scrotum. Talk about the lack of intelligence of an Af?"

"Yeah, the German people really loved old Adolf," Dave backed him up.

"Precisely," The Pommy geo' nodded. "The Germans not only illustrated their mass murdering genes in Europe, they taught the Afs a remarkable lesson in genocide here in Africa. Take Namibia for instance, they weren't just happy to grab the land and tax the people into crushing poverty. Their sheer arrogance and greed was what angered the Afs the most, and, when they reacted, it wasn't simply a case of putting them down by force, but pure and simple genocide. In 1904 you had good old General Van Trotha who issued his '*Vernichtungsbeheft*' or 'extermination order' against the Herero. 'All Herero, whether armed or not – whether with cattle or not – will be shot on sight. I will not allow them to breed any more children'... Or something like that. Still, they damned near killed off the entire Herero Nation. Mowed them down with machine guns and poisoned their wells – outright, systematic genocide. Of an estimated eighty thousand Herero, only eight thousand remained. Those men, women and children they didn't kill with artillery, rifles and bayonets, they drove into the Kalahari Desert or the Omaheke desert region where a lot of them died of thirst... As a matter of fact, the slaughter of the Herero was classified as being the first genocide of the twentieth century. Trust the murdering Germans to be responsible for that? And that's not mentioning the genocide of the Jews carried out by Hitler and his Nazi swine barely forty years later. Talk about history repeating itself, during the Herero conflict you had another Doctor Mengele-type. The 'geneticist' Eugen Fischer. He used German South West Africa as a field site for developing his theories on German superiority. He was a great one for collecting the heads of Nama prisoners of war who were deliberately starved to death in the concentration camp on Shark Island near Luderitz. He forced female Herero prisoners to scrape the heads clean with shards of glass... Then again, the first battle the Germans ever fought against the Nama resulted in the massacre of mostly women and children. We have Von Francois who tried to slaughter the entire Nama Nation in his unsuccessful war against Hendrik Witbooi. All these good German officers who Seebacher here and the other Nazis hold in such high esteem."

"Do not talk for me," Seebacher insisted. "Not all Germans are proud of people like Von Trotha and Von Francois. You cannot blame us for what our grandfathers did."

"Don't talk such utter bilge!" the Pommy wasn't having that. "It depends on which company you're in. If you're with those beer-swilling Nazi pigs at the Zum Wirt or in the Ladies bar at the Hotel Thüringer Hof – out comes the sauerkraut, schnapps and *'Deutschland uber alles'*. Von Francois and Trotha are real live heroes to the likes of you, and people like Hendrik Witbooi are just murderers and cattle rustlers... What amazes me are the Herero themselves. When SWAPO took over the government there was talk of bulldozing down those statues of our German heroes in the centre of Windhoek, but the Herero wouldn't have a jot of it. They claimed it was part of their historical past and they weren't about to have the Ovambo – who they look down on with contempt – destroy it. Those statues and memorabilia may be tokens of German self-esteem, though – if you look at that obelisk in the centre of the city gardens – you may obtain a slight inkling of how treacherous a bunch of swine the German people really are. You'll see on it the names of the German war dead, then underneath the title of the word 'Bastards', you'll see how the Baster were killed in support of the Germans. At the start of World War One, when the Baster weren't sure they wanted to support the Germans, our good old Nazi friends tried to wipe them out at Sam Khubis, and they..."

"I've heard of Sam Khubis," I cut in on him. "Wilfred's uncle mentioned it."

"So you should have," he nodded. "Every Rehoboth Baster knows about Sam Khubis. It's your holiest of shrines."

"What's all that about?" Dave asked him.

"Sam Khubis?" the Pommy turned to him. "It's where the Germans tried to wipe out the Rehoboth Baster on May the eighth 1915. Apparently, at the beginning of the First World War, there was a British or Boer flying column invading the colony from the south. Unsure as to whether the Baster would side with them or not, the Germans decided to kill them all. Men, women and children. The Baster got word of this, so they fled to a mountainous area of granite called Sam Khubis. You actually pass it on the left as you're coming into Klein Aub. The Germans had them penned up in a valley and their

Schutztruppe blocked off all the escape routes and managed to kill a fair few of their former allies. The general plan was to starve the Baster to death, but, as luck would have it, the surviving Baster managed to escape in the dark of night. I haven't seen it, but there's supposed to be a burial ground at Sam Khubis where the Baster congregate every year on May the eighth. I'm going to look it up some time."

CHAPTER 34

HEROES DAY! CIVIL WAR!

One Saturday Dawson-Byrne announced he was having the day off and was heading to Okahandja. He invited Wheeler along, for the Herero were celebrating their annual 'Heroes Day' in that town. Not to be left out, I grabbed Nick and Wilfred and we decided to go in my car to see what was going on. That prompted Kotzé, Van der Merwe and Seebacher to go along in Kotzé's vehicle. Ernie and Jeff had gone to Windhoek to see if Nick and Jeff's new passports had arrived to replace the ones that had been incinerated in the tent fire.

What a delightful fanfare there was as the Herero celebrated their most important day of the year. Especially with the Herero women! All clad in near identical, red dresses with puffed out skirts reaching to the ground; their upper parts clad in intricately embroidered, black bodices; they glided along in columns, their upside-down, red tri-corn hats bobbing ever so gently. A picture of absolute regal dignity as they practically floated past. The Pommy mentioned something about the Okahandja locals needing to keep an eye on their sheep and goats, as a Herero woman's billowing skirts was an excellent place to hide an animal or two.

Unlike the women, the men looked a pretty uncoordinated lot, both in their marching and in their dress, though they made up for it with the expressions of sheer, warlike pride they had on their faces. There were squads of youths; some in khaki and berets; those without footwear and no headgear at all; others wore polished belts, plus there were those who wore military-style badges. They marched briskly; their eyes staring straight ahead as each outfit followed a standard bearer.

Older men followed them, also on foot, in some kind of order. Their military-style uniforms were more sophisticated; khaki and grey uniform jackets; leather leggings or brown and green bandage-style puttees; peaked caps and felt hats folded up on one side Aussie digger-fashion. Some had carefully polished boots; others had polished Sam Browne belts with a cross shoulder strap. One bloke had bright red braces and a Sam Browne get out as well. All looked terribly bad to tamper with.

Then came the cavalry on an assortment of horses; the animals all pricks and ribs. Their colours varied from light grey, dun to claret; most looked as if they could urgently do with a feed of hay. The uniforms of the riders were just as varied; shiny peaks on caps, some of which had a red band around them; military badges and old campaign medals. There were buttoned to the neck uniforms; those with waistcoats; mostly of German military fashion. The riders sat bolt upright in their saddles; some of professional manufacture, others homemade. Besides a collection of ancient swords or whatever, there were no other weapons to go with all the military gear.

I raised the topic of weapons with Dawson-Byrne and his reply was fairly ominous. "No, there aren't any firearms on display here. The government prohibits it in case a few hotheads decide to get carried away with themselves. But you can bet your life every Herero can put his hands on a firearm of some sort. It isn't like the old days where the Herero had to fight with spears against German Gatling guns, Mauser Model 88 rifles and artillery. This county's awash with rifles and handguns of every description and calibre, and one day people could be dodging bullets coming from all directions."

"Why's that?" I asked.

"Civil war – that's why. When do-gooders like you Aussies, the New Zealanders and the Swedes or whoever started championing the Af's cause over here in Africa... Hang on – of course – you're a Baster with an Aussie accent. Anyway, when the Australian government and the rest of the do-gooders insisted on having their way, *who* actually bothered to study the implications of handing over independence to the noble savage? You even had a United Nations peacekeeping force over here in Namibia for some considerable time, but who stopped to think of the ongoing ramifications? The boundaries and borders of most African countries where designed back in the old days when there was a scramble for Africa. Territories had been marked out by the British, French, Belgians and Germans, though these were mainly worked out geographically along rivers and mountain ranges and so on. Very rarely was there any consideration given to human or tribal ethnicity. So what do we have here in Namibia? We have a dehydrated piece of the African Continent that encompasses a myriad of vastly different peoples or tribes – the Ovambo, the Herero, the Nama and the Damara – to name the main ones. The Ovambo are in the majority, so we find them governing the place under the white man's rules of democracy. But who asked the Herero? Who asked the Nama? Never mind the Damara, the Herero and Nama have been kicking their backsides ever since long before the whites came along... Okay, so who sat down and talked about democracy with the Herero? As far as they are concerned they used to control most of northern Namibia, and the Ovambo only came from the far northern reaches of the country, what with most having come down from Angola. So the Herero have swapped masters for the third time. First the Germans – then the Boers – now the Ovambo. The blacks may dislike being ruled by the whites intensely, but their hatred for other blacks and their tribalism goes far deeper than that. If there's one remarkable feature about the Herero, it's their pride. Also their intelligence that totally outstrips that of the Ovambo. Then, judging by the run they gave the Germans, they certainly know how to take part in a jolly good fracas... So what's to make them so overjoyed with an Ovambo government? Especially now that SWAPO's taking a firmer grip on the country and is stealing or squandering most of the country's funds? Look at old Sammy Nujoma with his luxury jets and his plans for a new presidential palace. The old Government House isn't grand enough for our Sammy. Then again, we have rampant inflation that creates massive unemployment which in turn's created the appalling crime-rate that's now plaguing Namibia. Besides the odd white run school over here, the education system's in total disarray and the Afs are finding that their children had a better chance of being more properly educated under the old Boer regime. They're handing out matriculation and school leaver's certificates to the black students like so much confetti, so we now have students at the University of Namibia who don't even know how to spell their own name, yet they're given degrees and diplomas having graduated none the wiser. We also have a huge, overstaffed public service riddled with nepotism, and then we see an arrogance that falls hardly a hair behind that of the Boers and the Germans. You'll find with Af leaders – the more useless, stupid and uneducated they are – the more arrogant buffoons they become. Look at Robber Mugarbage of Zimbabwe, Kenneth Kaunda of Zambia, and good old Sammy Nujoma over here."

"These Hereros here seem a fairly cheerful bunch?" I pointed out to him.

"For the time being perhaps, but as things start to disintegrate like they've done in most African countries, and as Namibia's balance of payments dive farther into the red, pressure will be piling up on all these people, regardless of skin colour or tribe. The donor nations in Europe and North America are getting fed up with all this, and they've enough problems of their own with all the terrorism going on around the world. The extraordinary idea of the 'noble savage' is long dead, and the donor nations have long since grown weary of empty-headed, despotic African leaders plundering their countries. The open chequebooks of the sixties, seventies and eighties have been put back in the bottom drawer, so as poverty and hunger start taking hold – crime, tribal hatred, violence, and then civil war becomes inevitable... You can see by what happened in Rwanda and what's going on in the Sudan that the whites are becoming hesitant about sticking their noses in, regardless of the carnage and starvation. The French like making noises about preventing genocide and tribal war, but they – like the Yanks in South America,

Iran and Iraq – are always backing the wrong guys and are more interested in selling weaponry to all comers. The Swedes, what with the way they like subsidising everything, end up further complicating matters, or taking back twice as much as they give. It's the same with the foreign aid workers and advisers that are sent to Africa by the British, French, Dutch, Germans, Belgians or whoever. They're generally useless individuals who can't find work in their own countries, neither in the government nor private sectors. I suppose it's a handy way of getting them out of the way. They've got exactly nothing to give to the Af, who's always got both hands out looking for something for nothing... I digress. We started off with civil war, an activity always found in great quantities in sunny Africa. Tribalism won't go away, or the despotic baboons who grab power. Regardless of what the asinine do-gooders want to believe, democracy in Africa's a total pipe dream. In fact the chances of bloodshed and general mayhem are even more in abundance than when the early settlers saw the blacks trotting around with spears and loincloths. These African countries can never show a profit with the people breeding the way they are. With our white man's medicines and what have you, we've turned the entire continent's ecology upside-down. There'll be wars fought over water resources, yet alone tribal strife, food and territory. They say AIDS is doing a wonderful job, still it's hardly working fast enough. Like the Brazilians and Indonesians, the African farmers are destroying the vegetation with their slash and burn agriculture. Twenty years ago Namibia had a population of five hundred thousand. There's probably three times that amount now, or they've lost count altogether. The way they're going they'll even double that in the next few years. To top it all off, some of the SWAPO leaders over here are claiming that AIDS was a scare tactic invented by the white regime that once ran Pretoria. I suppose that might be a good thing, as it'll help to kill a few more off because you'll never come across a black leader using the prohibited words '*birth control*'."

"So you reckon these Hereros might have a go at the Ovambos one day?"

He nodded. "Civil war's coming to Namibia, as surely as it shall in South Africa. Most probably more sooner than later. The Herero could just become one of the factions. So far they haven't been really tested, but there'll come the time when the Ovambo push them too far. The Botswana government aren't overly enamoured with the Ovambo or SWAPO, so they'll most probably give support and arms to the Herero, what with some of their people being blood kin. Then, with the Ovambo and Herero killing and massacring each other, the Nama won't want to be left out of things, so they'll grab their innumerable hidden weapons and also start flaying away. The Damara will probably receive a thumping from all sides."

"And what about the whites and coloureds?"

"Them? Unlike Zimbabwe, Kenya and places elsewhere, the whites have been allowed to hang on to their private arsenals. Though I dislike them intensely, you place five hundred average Boers into an army or commando of some sort, and those hairy backs could whip the pants off any Af rabble. As far as most coloureds in the south go, it's difficult trying to differentiate a 'coloured' from a 'Nama'. I doubt that the coloureds – who don't fit into that category – would like to be left out of things, either, but they're bound to stick with the whites. In turn the whites can stay on the sidelines and hammer any faction that looks like harming them. Some of those whites fought against SWAPO during the war and they're well trained when it comes to murder and mayhem."

We dropped the subject of civil war to follow the Herero march. The object of their journey was the cemetery, where they filed passed the graves of past leaders: Maharero or Maharero Tjamuaha, Samuel Maharero and Hosea Kutako being amongst them. Ignoring their array of fantastic military garb, I sized them up as being fighting men, and they certainly did look a formidable bunch.

CHAPTER 35

NICK GETS ONTO SOME HERERO SNATCH!
THE WAR IN IRAQ! BOERS WITH LOVERS BALLS!

Nick had managed to get onto a piece of Herero pussy and was determined to discover what she was hiding under her layers of petticoats, so I leant him my Mercedes and hitched a ride with the Pommy geo' and Dave. Wilfred had disappeared after assuring me he would be back in camp by the following morning, and there was no sign of Kotzé, Van der Merwe or Seebacher.

As we headed in the direction of Karibib, Wheeler drew Dawson-Byrne's and my attention to Namibia's parched landscape. "The whole flamin' place's turning into a desert!"

"That's all this country needs," the Pom' agreed with him. "It won't be long now before Uncle Sammy starts screaming out for more aid. It won't stop him buying luxury jets and building himself mansions, all the same."

"And the aid people'll let him get away with it?" Dave was unconvinced. "What about the international media?"

That seemed to amuse Dawson-Byrne. "Since when has the Af ever bothered about what the rest of the world thinks? A while back I was in central and eastern Africa for a Danish exploration company, and I was using Kenya as a base. Now there's a country coming apart at the seams. Naturally you kick things off very nicely by installing a dictator like Daniel Arap Moi. He can only be a dictator by spending most of the country's GDP on the military who're keeping him in power. Yet that's not enough since his paranoia behoves him to build a multimillion dollar international airport just outside his principal headquarters at Eldoret. No international airlines land there, only his personal intercontinental jet. It's his fast horse out of town if he can't pay the military enough to protect him. Every black leader has his getaway jet. Dos Santos in Angola, Sammy Nujoma in Namibia, Obasanjo in Nigeria, Mbeki in South Africa – you name it... Then, of course, the vast majority of Kenya's military, police, and government ministers are rotten and corrupt to the core and they're filling their pockets to overflowing and bankrupting the country. The coppers are literally bandits and make a living out of setting up roadblocks on Kenya's highways, so's they can extort bribes from anyone who comes past. As a matter of fact, when they finally got rid of Moi, the major highlight for the locals was when the cops were ordered back to their barracks. The place was much safer without them harassing the public with their daylight robbery, thuggery and extortion... Kenya was once regarded as one of the tourist Meccas of the world, as it's only one hop-skip-and-jump from Europe. They still have to this day – despite the poaching and corruption in the Ministry of Wildlife – one of the vastest arrays of Africa's wild animals, but the roads in the interior are impassable through sheer lack of funds being available for maintenance. All the money's been stolen. On the coast they have some of the most beautiful beaches in the world and hundreds of thousands of tourists from all over Europe and the States used to flock to the myriad hotels and resorts that can be found there. But now the water supply to Mombasa and its suburbs has totally broken down, so the people on Mombasa Island have reopened the old Swahili wells and only water contaminated by sewerage is available to the local residents. Typhus and cholera then becomes the order of the day. The electricity supply doesn't function for days on end, and you can be without a telephone for weeks. So the tourists hear of all this and they stay away. That in turn starts whole hotel chains and groups going into liquidation, and, as a logical result, thousands are put out of work. The Kenyan government's totally lost control of law and order in the coastal region, but why should the politicians back in Nairobi be bothered? The people on the coast are a different tribe to them, so any chaos in that region's good for the government thugs in the capital both politically and security-wise. Tourism was always Kenya's greatest asset – far more important than agriculture, manufacturing or any other industry. The country's over endowed with natural assets, yet the Kenyan Afs have managed to destroy almost everything."

"It can't be as bad as all that," I argued.

"It's worse! You'll find that in most African countries it's a core of expatriates or possibly ex-colonials who keep most of the depleted infrastructure running. The whites in the mines in Zambia. The Germans here in Namibia. The French in certain countries of West Africa. When Jomo Kenyatta was the first president of independent Kenya in 1963, the country had more than fifty thousand white farmers, businessmen and quite a few in the public service. Now there are barely three thousand left because the place's unliveable by any kind of world standards, and since incompetent, black affirmative action's taken over the running of the country. You see quite a few whites there, but they're non-resident technicians, aid workers and advisers that wouldn't be able to get employment in their own countries. The majority get around in the latest Mercedes Benzes, BMWs and expensive four-wheel drives, and they dine in the best restaurants and spend most of their time at cocktail parties or having drinks beside the swimming pools in the most expensive hotels. That's when some of them aren't sodomising little black boys or raping little black girls. Millions in aid are being blown annually by these parasites, and then after what funds are siphoned off by the by the various Af governments, only a fraction of the aid's making its way to the really needy. No wonder there's bound to be a civil war one day in Kenya. Any day now the starving hordes might come bursting out of their slums and they'll slaughter every damned thieving and corrupt Kenyan politician. The exact same thing can happen in Zimbabwe and countless more Afs could be slaughtered. The sooner the better, I say."

"And I take it that's why there was a civil war in Angola?" Dave asked him.

"Not exactly. The rivalries started among the various factions fighting the Portuguese for independence. Still, that doesn't mean to say that the country hasn't turned into a cesspool. All possible infrastructures such as electricity, water, road maintenance, hospitals and education have totally disintegrated, though – admittedly – that was speeded up on account of the civil war. Same as in Mozambique, but you don't necessarily have to have civil war to have total disintegration in an independent African country. Zambia, Malawi and Tanzania didn't require civil unrest to become an absolute shambles. Take Zambia for instance. They have one of the richest mineralised belts in the world, but most of the mines and treatment plants have been shut down on account of them sacking the white miners and supervisors and replacing them with black incompetents. The health system in that country's the biggest killer of all. In order to find sufficient blood supplies for the various hospital blood banks, it's compulsory for the Zambian coppers and military personnel to give blood. Both the police and military are riddled with AIDS. The average black's life expectancy in Zambia's barely thirty-seven years. Far too long, though, I must say."

"There must be some basic, underlying problems that are causing all this?" Dave suggested.

The Pommy smiled at that. "Of course there are. Take this country for instance. The whites here have had to hand over the country to their black brothers and sisters, and most of the whites you meet here – the Boers that is – will tell you that the blacks are no better than baboons and that it's their entire fault that the country's on the skids. This condemnation of the blacks in general just illustrates how pathetic the Boers are. In America, Britain and other white-governed countries they've proved beyond all doubt that some blacks are possibly as intelligent as whites. If given a level playing field – peace, security and the proper education – there are some damned fine blacks out there. In Africa there's never been a level playing field for the Afs, as independence was handed over when they were totally unprepared. Despotism, nepotism and corruption are rife because of the incompetence and thieving ways of the various countries' regimes. With that comes civil unrest and the universities and their academics are the first to be targeted since the people who generally grab power *are* baboons, and they're paranoid about whoever may be brighter than them. How on earth, with all these anomalies, can the average African country prosper? Overseas investment isn't available to them – their professionals have long since gone on to greener and safer pastures – their law and order machinery's totally broken down. As a result of that any form of progress is impossible, so the average Af's far worse off."

The topic changed immediately once we had listened to a news bulletin on the car radio. The same old thing was going on in Iraq; there was blood and guts everywhere and even more American soldiers being killed.

"So now you know, chaps, why our Yankee friends look like getting their backsides kicked in the Middle East," Dawson-Byrne announced.

"How come?" I asked.

He spoke to Dave instead. "Seeing as we're talking about the Middle East, let's go back to Biblical times, as that's where most of the countries mentioned in the news are nowadays? Also where all the bother's coming from besides Afghanistan. Why were the Romans and Persians so successful militarily? For starters, they had no television journalists and bleeding-heart do-gooders. No cowardly creatures sitting back in their lounge chairs at home being appalled about how they conducted their military campaigns. Seriously, the ancient Romans and Persians fought their wars *to win*. You take when the Romans invaded a country. If they received any resistance or any form of guerrilla warfare, they flattened the place. They slaughtered anyone who got in the way, and they left no building standing or a stone unturned until their victory was complete. If the Muslims want a war, they should be given one, and the Yanks and their allies should give them everything they've got, even if it means using nuclear weapons. There's no other way to go about things... What I've just said would cause an uproar in the politically correct West. There'd be all manner of howls and yelps from the do-gooders. The Yanks are having their troops killed left right and centre, but their hands are tied behind their backs by world opinion. Exactly the same happened to the Rhodesian and South African security forces... The most pathetic thing about the Yanks' situation is that the world wants *them* to step in whenever there's any trouble about the place. They want them to put up all the money and their young men and women's lives on the line, yet every time the Yanks or Brits – and even your Aussie soldiers – try and stick up for themselves militarily, the world screams blue murder!"

"Yeah, well," Dave shrugged, "but it's like I mentioned to Joe back in Kalgoorlie – with the Romans and the Greeks – their empires and civilisations collapsed when they all resorted to homosexuality and queerdom. Now you've got the friggin' Yanks with their same-sex marriages and all those poofters and lesbians on their TV programs. The Aussies are following in their footsteps."

"Yes, what a pathetic business," Dawson-Byrne agreed with him. "Nonetheless, I feel sorry for the American people themselves. They may have the world's largest economy, still that doesn't necessarily mean that they owe anybody anything. It's through sheer hard work by reasonably decent American people that built such a successful country, and now you've got everyone making out that America has some kind of debt to pay. The Yanks may've entered both World Wars rather late, but why should they have gotten involved in the first place? Both wars were European affairs and had nothing to do with them, as they had been rightfully going about minding their own business. You couldn't really blame them for wanting to keep their noses out of Europe's affairs, but *thank God* they did step up and lend a hand. Never mind that, you look when there's any catastrophe around the world – civil war, famine and AIDS. Everyone's demanding that something should be done about it, and naturally it's always the Yanks who *do* actually do something. Also, have you noticed when aid's distributed to the poorer countries around the world? You'll discover that it's always the Yanks who have to dig deepest – food aid, medicines, emergency funding and so on. Whenever you see a refugee camp, how often do you see USAID being offloaded by the ton? How often do you see American soldiers first to reach the front line? The Yanks, through their extraordinary aptitude for picking the most moronic leadership nowadays, may have bungled things on occasion, but their hearts have always been in the right place. We have so much to be grateful to them for, David, and you can't judge all the American people by the actions of a few, and this planet would be much worse off without them... Can you imagine what would've happened if the Russians had won the Cold War and ended up as the world's only superpower? It's just too terrible to contemplate."

"So what do you think about those same-sex marriages that're going on in the States?" I queried the Pommy. "That has to be a load of crap – fuckin' blokes marrying blokes and sheilas marrying sheilas. They're even talking about adopting kids. What kind of chance would any kid have being brought up by a couple of bloody queers?"

He frowned at that. "Yes, it's a damned shame, Josef. That whole rotten business started in the Netherlands and Scandinavia. If the Russians and the Cold War couldn't bring down the Yanks, this kind of behaviour will because it'll undermine any culture or race of people. Generally the blacks in Africa look upon homosexuality with abhorrence, though I see this gay liberalisation's sweeping through Cape Town and a great many people are looking the other way. They're even having those gay marches like you have in Australia. If South Africa hasn't got enough on its plate already, social decadence is something we certainly don't need imported from the West."

"I notice that the French and the Germans are keeping their noses out of things when it comes to Iraq," Dave told him. "Smart bastards, if you ask me,"

The Pommy geo' slowed the vehicle down as we approached some cattle herders on the side of the road, and he looked over at Wheeler. "Can't see what they need the Frogs and the Huns for. The Frogs as a nation are slowly dissolving – their language's being spoken less and less around the world because English is taking over, and their religion's falling apart at the seams."

"What gives with their religion?" Dave asked him.

"It seems they're running out of priests. The average priest in France is over sixty. The situation's becoming so tenuous they're actually bringing in priests from the Dark Continent. Fancy that – having to import Afs in order that they can follow the right path to the Almighty? Some of those murdering Hutu priests from Rwanda should make excellent shepherds... As for the Huns, we don't want them going on some genocidal rampage where they try to slaughter everybody – man, woman and child – like they did under Hitler. We can't have them mustering women and children into concentration camps, and turning them into ash and fertiliser in their crematoriums. Rather uncouth, wouldn't you say? Unfortunately their gene pool hasn't yet been sufficiently improved by the Turks, Rumanians and Bulgarians who've suddenly taken a liking for sauerkraut and bratwurst."

Wheeler thought that was quite amusing, although his demeanour soon changed. "Then there's the Israelis murdering Palestinian women and children with their tanks, fighter jets and helicopter gunships, and the poor fuckin' Palestinians have got fuck all to defend themselves with. Without them we wouldn't be having all this bullshit in the Middle East."

"I'd be careful there, if I were you," Dawson-Byrne cautioned, "or you'll have Mossad, Shin Bet and the CIA hunting you down in no time. Plucky fellows the Israelis are, and what you need to realise, David, is that they're on our side of the coin. The West's – that is. They're the last of the world's true warriors. I would sincerely hesitate when it came to causing them any annoyance, and with all these Muslims calling for a Jihad against the West, the Israelis make very useful allies indeed. Like the ancient Romans and Persians, they know how to fight a war properly, and the Yanks and the Brits could sure take a leaf out of their book. You've got the nuclear non-proliferation people in a sweat about Iran's nuclear ambitions. They should pay the Israelis to blow up all of Iran's nuclear facilities, like they did with that nuclear power station old Saddam was building in Iraq. One-stop solution that, for what can the Iranians do about it? The same as the Iraqis, they wouldn't have the stomach to take the Israelis to task for it, even so you'd have the world's do-gooders wetting their pants with shock and horror. Seriously, they should give the Israelis the job to tackle, and while they're about it they should do something about the despots that we have in Africa. Kill the dictators and all their corrupt henchmen, and then the average Af would be far better off – more food on his table – more security for his wife and kids. When you come to think about it, he's almost come full circle."

"What do you mean by full circle?" Wheeler demanded.

"It's quite straightforward. When the whites first arrived they found the blacks busy raping, plundering and slaughtering each other. Village against village – tribe against tribe. Back in those days they had absolutely no security over their families, food supplies or property. The colonials came and stopped it temporarily, and now we've got the Afs back to their unashamed murdering, torturing, corruption and banditry. What we've seen is a perfect, full circle."

"Yeah, but the whites only plundered the blacks when they colonised the place," Dave argued. "They just took everything for themselves."

"Of course, they did," Dawson-Byrne nodded. "There was nothing unusual about that. The strong taking from the weak – the more intelligent species dominating the less intelligent species. They took over with their superior intelligence and their more advanced technology such as rifles and artillery, plus they used an adequate amount of discipline and determination."

Dave removed the cap from a bottle of beer. "What fucks me is how the Boers around here think they're so superior to the blacks. After what I've seen of 'em, they're no better than the average blackfella around here. Take Kotzé for instance."

That amused the Pommy geo' no end. "Believe me, Kotzé's rather bright compared to some Boers I've come across. You go just south of the border in South Africa – into Namaqualand. Down there you'll meet some really impoverished, inbred Boers." He burst out laughing.

"What's the joke?" Dave asked him.

"The Apartheid regime's Immorality Act."

"Immorality Act? What was that all about?"

"An example of Afrikaner stupidity. The white men were forbidden from fornicating with the black or coloured women, and the blacks most certainly were barred from ever touching a white woman. It was made the absolute law of the land and you could be chucked into prison if you were caught. Now that the Immorality Act's been repealed, you've got quite a few Boer farmers down in Namaqualand and around these parts walking around with swollen testicles. You've seen how the majority of the Afrikaner women are fat-arsed and have the most meagre of charms... So, with their hard faced and overweight wives to contend with, some of these old Boer farmers are lusting for the odd coloured maiden or two. In the old days they could've gone to jail or their friends could've put them in complete purgatory if they were caught sleeping with a coloured, but now they can if they want to. You've seen quite a few of the coloured girls on your travels in Namibia and some are really quite attractive. Not only that, the whites around here firmly believe that coloured women are more promiscuous, so they're all the more tempting. Where you had these old Boers drooling over all this forbidden fruit in the past, their frustration must be far worse now that the Immorality Act's gone."

"Who the hell would've had the power to introduce such an act?" I asked.

He chuckled. "Why, the good old National Party, of course. It was another way of tightening up their Apartheid system. They didn't want their white blood being contaminated, even though most of the Boers have a touch of the tar brush in them. It was similar to the Krauts with their ambition to create the perfect Aryan race. Now things are really becoming unravelled around the place."

"Why's that?" Dave rejoined the conversation.

"Because the Afs have taken over lock-stock-and-barrel. All of a sudden they're equal to their white oppressors. Now they want the same pay as the whites for a day's work, and who can blame them? They had to fight for years to get equal rights and now they've got legal unions demanding that they be paid a whole lot more. In the old days, if a black worker tried to organise a union, he or she got a bullet in the back of the head for their trouble. The South African Bureau of State Security people, or BOSS, were no different to the Russian KGB or the German Gestapo. Just as willing and adept when it came to administering a little torture and murder. Things can't work quite the same now that you've got legitimate black unions... As you pointed out quite correctly before, David, plenty of South Africa's whites made a fortune from not having to pay anywhere near a decent salary to their black labour forces, and a great deal of South Africa's industry and progress wouldn't have been possible without the sweat of underpaid black workers. A lot of these farms around here wouldn't have been developed if it hadn't been for ridiculously cheap, coloured labour. No government in South Africa or Namibia from now on – ANC, SWAPO or otherwise – can ever be able to enjoy that situation again. Unless, of course, these countries sink into a quagmire like Angola, Mozambique, Zambia and Zimbabwe. Which they surely will."

"You aren't making sense," Wheeler told him.

"Let me explain, then?" Dawson-Byrne suggested. "Whether we like to admit it or not, every successful country owes its accomplishments to good governance and an efficient public service. Both Namibia and South Africa are running out of both. Soon the money has to dry up and their economies will wither on the vine. In South Africa we see municipalities and entire provinces that've been placed in the care of baboons. Money's being stolen, budgets are being blown out, and funds for maintenance and infrastructure have totally disappeared or been squandered on posh motorcars and mansions for the provincial premiers, the mayors and their favourites. The Namibian economy's already in a shambles. The higher salaries that the Afs are demanding will also dry up altogether because employment shall cease to be on offer to the majority. That's where in a couple of decades you'll see the majority of the blacks working for a pittance, but there won't be any more public infrastructure being created without overseas aid, and all government services and development projects should disappear... We might be seeing some justice here, now that we have the opposite to the Boers' Apartheid laws. Take for instance down in Namaqualand where the Boer sheep farmers have bred just as prolifically as the Afs, if not even more so. Now you have untold amounts of illiterate, dim-witted Boer progeny who're falling through the cracks caused by this black affirmative action. Apartheid isn't around to guarantee them work anymore, and we're seeing a class of whites suffering as much as the blacks and coloureds did under their old regime... Yes, perhaps there *is* some justice on this continent after all?"

CHAPTER 36

OX-DRAWN AMBULANCES!
NICK NEARLY GETS HIS BALLS CUT OUT!

When we finally reached our camp we found that Jeff, Ernie, Kotzé and Seebacher had also returned. By all appearances Namibian beer brought unity amongst mankind since the Aussies seemed to be getting on quite contentedly with the Boer and the German as they sat around the mess table with perhaps a couple of dozen empty beer bottles before them.

Seebacher was particularly jovial when he called Dave's attention to an article he had found in a *JOHANNESBURG STAR* newspaper. "So what do you think of our good K4s now?" he asked Wheeler.

I leant over Dave's shoulder to see what was in the newspaper. According to an article Zimbabwe's Minister of Health was very excited about how UNICEF had donated nine ambulances to his department. *Ox-drawn* ambulances!

"Our Zimbabwean K4s are returning to the Stone Age!" the German crowed.

In the newspaper article a member of Zimbabwe's opposition party echoed Seebacher's assertion, though some health official claimed that ox-drawn ambulances were appropriate technology and a luxury to Zimbabwe's rural community where most of their hospital clinics had Panadol as the only available drug.

Dawson-Byrne, who I noticed had been swigging from quite a large hip flask all day, was also in agreement with the German prospector: "Now do you see what I mean about the Afs going full circle? In Zimbabwe the hospitals are in a total mess. There's a total lack of clean bandages, swabs, syringes and protective gloves, plus there's an AIDS epidemic on. The laundry infrastructure in most hospitals has completely broken down and bloodstained linen and second-hand bandages from AIDS patients have to be washed by hand. Never mind the people the virus's killing, there's a similar number of deaths due to the lack of essential supplies. In Zimbabwe you've a baboon leader whose cabinet ministers are grabbing land supposedly intended for the peasants, and who're taking huge bribes every time a government contract's given out. You also have a leader whose wife's spending millions on houses in the most expensive suburbs in the Zimbabwean capital and on shopping sprees all over the world. You have a despot who's trebled the amount of budget funds on defence spending. A good deal of those funds end up in the pockets of the generals in order to keep them on side. While this's going on you literally have people in their thousands dying through famine and sheer neglect. Couldn't that be judged as crimes against humanity? Where's true, global, community justice gone to?"

"Ja, what you are saying is very true," Seebacher was plainly delighted that the Pommy had agreed with him. "We have thousands of K4s dying all over Africa as a result of the corruption and incompetence of their leaders and government. Nonetheless, we should not worry too much about this – there are plenty more where they came from and there are far too many already on the way."

Dawson-Byrne studiously ignored him, and then a further item in another South African newspaper brightened him up rather considerably. It was a full-page article with photos of some rebel blokes who had taken over a place called Bukavu in the Democratic Republic of Congo. Pictures of hundreds of blacks looting shops, houses and the town's hospital; all appearing to be having a reasonable time of things. It was hard to work out who was doing most of the looting, the victorious rebels, the retreating government forces, or the local civilians? While that was going on there were shots of bodies and blacks being beaten up; triumphant civilians waving branches, and whole truckloads of captured weaponry. The newspaper story calculated that several hundred people had been killed during all the fun.

"Typical!" the Pommy burst out. "Here's Africa for the tourists. Never mind the lions, elephants and giraffes – let's see the noble savage at play? Let's see the bloodshed, pillaging and destruction? Who gives a hoot about another couple of hundred innocent people being massacred?"

Another news item grabbed his attention; three Kenyans had been taken hostage by insurgents in Iraq. "Has the world gone totally insane?" his words were filled with mock shock and horror. "Why on earth have the Yanks let the Kenyans in fouling up Iraq? How many subspecies *have* they let in? First we have the Filipinos, Nicaraguans and Hondurans making a bolt for it, and now we've got chimpanzees getting in the way. I know the Yanks are trying to keep on the right side of world opinion, but *this's* downright preposterous!"

Some time later Nick arrived on the scene a much shaken man! "Fuck me dead!" he looked all aghast. "Bloody near got my dick cut off! Hey, Joe, you know that Herero sheila I was try'n to get on to?"

"Yeah, what the fuck happened?" I asked him.

"I was just getting her into your car, and all these black cunts waving fuckin' swords surrounded me. Apparently she was some kind of Herero princess and you had a mob of blokes wanting to cut my fuckin' balls out!"

"Man, but you are lucky!" Seebacher assured him. "You must never play around with Herero women, as their men will not tolerate it. When we had the United Nations' UNTAG peacekeeping soldiers here, several of them had their testicles cut out when they were caught interfering with Herero women!"

CHAPTER 37

LADIES BARS! RAT SHIT YANK TV! IRISH CATHOLIC PRIESTS COME FROM PEAT BOGS!

Despite Dawson-Byrne's best efforts there was still no target to drill on the Karabib claims. The situation was exactly the same as with the Klein Aub prospect. The inactivity was starting to wear thin, especially with Ernie since it was his job to communicate with our employer, who in turn was becoming more and more abusive with every phone call.

It was also hard to tell who owned the Englishman's dog; he or Nick, for it spent equal time with both men. Although the Pommy geo' was trying to keep the ancient Labrador's weight down, Nick was busy spoiling it with pieces of gemsbok, kudu, springbok and the very best of German snaggers.

Dawson-Byrne had to take his vehicle into Windhoek for servicing, so I went with him on the off chance of seeing Krystal on her lunch break. When I fronted one of the other tellers at the bank and asked after her, I was rather surprised to discover that she was taking a week's holiday. That really pissed me right off since I could have gone down to Rehoboth to visit her, what with the rig being idle.

I wasn't in that jolly a mood when I joined the Pommy in the Ladies Bar at the Hotel Thüringer Hof. For some reason or other they called cocktail bars 'Ladies Bars' in Namibia. I was served a Tafel Lager by a delightful coloured sheila by the name of Leslie, and Konnie the

German ex-wireless operator, whom I had met on my first night in Namibia, soon joined me. He reckoned Leslie was his favourite bar manageress and that she had been working at the hotel for as long as he could remember.

Dawson-Byrne had had quite a few whiskies by then and he was silently studying a group of local German and Swiss blokes pouring ridicule over Leslie's Ovambo offsider. They kept calling him 'Savimbi' – after some Jonas Savimbi character in Angola – as they ordered him around, and they thought it was all quite hilarious. In fact they kept on and on humiliating him till in the end it was even giving Leslie the shits. "Leave him alone, or you can go and drink in the Wurlitzer Bar," she told them.

"Yes, go and drink somewhere else, you blasted Nazis and Swiss cowards!" the Pommy geo' added his bit, making the Ovambo's tormentors' mouths drop.

I was fairly stuffed by that as well. He was taking on half a dozen jokers all at one go, so, if I needed to give him a hand, it would be a three to one blue!

"Do you know this man?" Konnie whispered in my ear.

"Yeah," I said back just as quietly. "Don't take any notice of him. He hates everybody – Boers, Germans, Australians – you name it. You're too nice a bloke, Konnie, so don't get involved."

"Do not worry. I certainly shall not."

The Pommy swallowed another double whisky in one swallow and turned his attention to the jokers who had been having a go at the black barkeeper. They had sort of fallen into an uneasy silence. "I told you to go and drink somewhere else, you damned Nazis," he reminded them. "Either that, or apologise to the bartender."

The Germans and Swiss ignored him. One of their number got up and left.

Dawson-Byrne still wasn't fulfilled. "I bet those Germans among you are related to a war criminal. And as for you cowardly, neutral Swiss – your banks are full of gold that was stolen by the Nazis from

Jewish Holocaust victims. Gold taken out of women and men's teeth. What's more, if it wasn't for your Swiss bankers, the war would've ended years earlier... Thank God we beat you Germans in both World Wars. It was simply a case of good overcoming evil. You swine with your '*Gott mit Uns*' – fancy thinking God was on your side? He soon proved you wrong when we thrashed you on land, sea and in the air. We British are the 'Master Race' – not you. All you Germans could beat were Nama women and children, plus the Herero who only had spears and clubs to defend themselves with. You Germans couldn't fight your way out of a wet paper bag. SWAPO's PLAN liberation fighters with their AK-47s could muster people more courageous than you lot. I ought to know because I was up against them."

The bloke who had left the group came back with a manager of some sort in tow. The manager was also German and appeared to know Dawson-Byrne quite well, for he smiled at him. "Ah, Jim..."

"Don't call me 'Jim'! My parents wouldn't have otherwise bothered to christen me 'James'."

"Ja – if you wish – James. But we do not need the First and Second World Wars fought all over again, ja? Surely there has been enough blood wasted already? We new-generation Germans are far more friendly." He turned to the scowling Germans and Swiss. "Let bygones be bygones, gentlemen. Unless you wish a duel with an ex-*Koevoet*."

That had the Germans and Swiss looking hurriedly away. "What's this koo-foot," I quizzed Konnie.

"Very bad news! The *Koevoet* were an elite fighting unit during the war against SWAPO. They are professional killers who can use anything as a weapon. Especially with their hands. People called them bounty hunters, for they were paid by the number of people they killed. Terrible people!"

Leslie's patrons seemed keen to be elsewhere; leaving Dawson-Byrne and I the sole occupants. Having switched on a TV at the end of the bar, she too, disappeared after topping up our drinks. The Pommy lit up a Cuban cigar and its marvellous fragrance filled the premises. An American cop show started on the TV and in the first five minutes three police detectives were gunned down on some crappy hotel's staircase. There was blood and guts all over the place! Up the walls, all over the carpets – everywhere! The cops had all been wearing supposedly bulletproof jackets, but the villain had used Teflon bullets that had gone straight through them.

"Lovely stuff!" my companion was all scorn. "Excellent, educational material for the local Afs. So what do we have here – two cops and one policewoman being blown away – the bad guy's used only the most correct ammunition – the cops don't know where to start looking for the gunman! Teflon, or 'cop killer' bullets are readily available here in Namibia and South Africa. You can buy them off the corrupt coppers. So what *has* the average Af crim' learned here? It's quite simple, really – if the cops come on the scene – shoot them! Also, use ammunition that really does a proper job. What excellent advice for the local teenagers who've just purchased or stolen some of the thousands of handguns available on the black market? If the cops show up – shoot them with 'cop killer' bullets! Nothing hard about that. It's what this continent truly needs, imported American violence on the television. With the average black we're not dealing with a very sophisticated individual at all. We're talking about a person who's genetically half a hair away from a baboon. A chimpanzee has a higher IQ than him. He's somebody who's only recently climbed down from a tree and learned to stand upright. What can possibly go on in his mind when he watches American television? His brain's so minute, he can't determine the difference between televised fiction and reality. When he sees coppers being shot and women being raped on American television, he sees white people being involved, so naturally his tiny brain tells him that he should copy them. There've been several debates on whether television violence has an effect on people, but – in the Af's case – it just *has to be* downright lethal."

"Dave Wheeler gets seriously pissed off about Yank television," I informed him.

"Yes, I've heard him mention it a couple of times. He also has a total dislike of the Catholic Church. You'd have to look askance at anyone who tells the world he or she won't be having sex for the rest of his or her life. If that's the case, you may as well castrate them right away. The men, that is. Any chappie who makes that kind of decision has to be sinister. It's totally unnatural. Or is it that the Catholic clergy are a super organised gang of pederasts and paedophiles? Look at the Christian Brothers in Western Australia where so many young boys were sodomised by those heavenly brethren? I hear the Catholic Church in Australia's loath to pay any compensation to the victims of their priests and brothers. Instead they're handing out brochures to tell you what to do if you fall foul of one them... Ten things what to do – or not to do – if you are buggered by the Catholic clergy in Australia. First, hold your cheeks apart as wide as possible. Last, don't look at a Catholic priest sideways, or he'll be after your backside in no time. That's why they had the Spanish Inquisition – you had every chance of being burned at the stake if you refused to hand over your bum to the visiting abbots, cardinals or monsignors."

"You're – you're really weird," his incredible imaginings had me doubled over laughing.

"Have you noticed that a good number of Catholic priests are Irish?" he continued.

That touched a nerve I had nurtured since my childhood. "So?"

"It's simple. Ireland's been a classic breeding ground for the Catholic Church. Most of those bogtrotters have come off farms where they've mostly grown up having sex with sheep and whatever, so no wonder the Catholic brethren don't have any trouble abstaining from human womenfolk? There must be some species of malignant spore that can only be found deep in the peat bogs of Ireland that surfaces whenever it's raining – which's always in the Emerald Isle – and that's where the farmers harvest all the Catholic priests, nuns and brothers. Have you noticed how most of the sex offenders are McKinneys, O'Doughertys, O'Riellys, O'Shaugnessys, O'Connors, O'Briens and Murphys? No wonder the Irish have chips on their shoulders and are so annoyed with the British? The reason why the Irish got stomped on so often by us Brits is because they spend ninety percent of their time stabbing each other in the back. They're perpetually jealous of each other and there's nothing they won't do to bring each other down. Never mind the Protestants versus the Catholics, it's just the Irish versus the Irish. Nowhere else will you ever come across such treacherous low lives. They're a bunch of genetic throwbacks, or the Celtic equivalent of Africa's Pan troglodyte."

"What's that?"

"The African chimpanzee."

"What have the Irish ever done to you?" I demanded. "I heard you telling Dave Wheeler that your family comes from Northern Ireland."

"Yes, though from original British aristocracy. My great-great grandfather was given estates in Northern Ireland, for he must've slaughtered a good many of the bogtrotters at the Battle of the Boyne. The Protestants and the Brits have been celebrating that battle every year since. It's good to let the Irish know who their betters are... But, let's return to the Catholic Church. With all that celibacy nonsense, the Catholics have set up a situation ideal for perverts, pederasts and paedophiles. How anyone lets children anywhere near such a diabolical institution's totally beyond me. It simply doesn't make sense. When a priest or brother claims he's abstaining from having anything to do with a woman for the rest for his life, you just have to know that something really perverted's going on. The whole Catholic Church must be like a magnet to queers and depraved individuals, as they can get stuck into one another sexually in the monasteries, and then there's an excellent chance of laying their filthy hands on children in the various Catholic schools and orphanages. Paedophilia and homosexual perversion organised on a *grand* scale. The founding members of the Catholic Church must've been a collection of homosexuals, perverts and pederasts in order to think up such an equation. Perhaps that explains why the Aussies and Kiwis are always accusing each other of being sheep molesters?"

"What the bloody hell has that gotta do with the Irish?" I demanded.

"Anything and everything. Have you considered the possibility that the majority of those who annoy sheep in both countries come from good Irish stock? There are a great many Aussies and Kiwis that proudly claim Irish ancestry. I can't say much about the Kiwis, but it's good, British, convict blood which's put the backbone in all your bronzed Anzacs."

"Crap!" I told him.

CHAPTER 38

STUFFED LOOKING BEGGARS! GREEDY & CORRUPT BASTARDS HANGING OUT TOGETHER! SAM NUJOMA'S MOTORCADE!

With the *Koevoet* business having been mentioned, I regarded the Pommy in a new light as we wended our way down Independence Avenue in the direction of the garage that had serviced his vehicle. I noticed that he stopped to drop a dollar coin in all the beggars' bowls, cups or hats as we went past them. I started doing likewise when he turned to me, practically swaying on his feet. "I never give money to children who're begging. Handouts give them the wrong outlook on life. Also, I only give money to beggars with genuine physical disabilities."

All the beggars we saw along the way certainly fitted in with that criterion, considering most were fairly stuffed looking. I also noticed that Independence Avenue was festooned with the portrait of Namibia's President, Sam Nujoma, on placards attached to every second lamp post, and on every other lamp post there was a picture of some other black bloke beaming down at everybody. "What's going on?" I asked my companion. "How come the president's photo's everywhere? Also, who's the other black joker?"

"His Excellency the King of Swaziland's come to visit. Whenever you see some Af or supposed dignitary pitching up, the whole of Windhoek's polluted with posters of that idiot Nujoma grinning at you like a gorilla on marijuana. I can't see what everybody's got to be so joyful about, as our good King Mswati III's presiding over a bankrupt piece of dirt in the middle of South Africa where half his subjects are dying of AIDS. That's when he isn't kidnapping young women and forcing them to marry him against their will. What we're seeing here is a flashback to the Dark Age, nevertheless I hear he has a fondness of private jets. Most of the donor agencies have pulled out of Swaziland as a result of him spending millions to buy himself a luxury, private jet, and I now hear that over half a million of his people are starving. In addition to that he's about to marry his twelfth wife and shall want to build a palace for her, despite the fact that his so-called kingdom's broke and you have people dying like flies from AIDS and lack of food. The lucky lass was picked out of twenty thousand bare-breasted virgins. Where on earth would they find twenty thousand virgins on the entire Continent of Africa, yet alone the Kingdom of Swaziland? ... No, you'll only find despots visiting Namibia, or Africa in general – Gaddafi, Castro, Chinese and North Korean government officials. It's not so much a case of birds of a feather, but scum rubbing up against scum. That's why the African governments get on so swimmingly with the likes of Cuba, North Korea and Libya – corrupt, murdering trash enjoy the company of other corrupt, murdering trash. Countries with atrocious human rights records make comfortable bedfellows"

We had to cross a large car park in order to take a shortcut to our destination, and we were halfway through it when two kids intercepted our path. No more than toddlers. One of them, a tiny girl, was dressed in what had to be her very best Sunday dress and shoes, while the other kid, a little bloke, was obviously in his best shorts and shirt. He had no shoes, though. They hesitantly spoke to us in some language that Dawson-Byrne seemed to understand perfectly and a regular conversation was struck up. Finally he handed both a five dollar coin and we went on our way again.

"And I thought you never gave money to kids?" I queried.

"Unlike you, I'm human and make the odd exception. Did you see the way they were all kitted out? Their mother must've gone to a great deal of trouble."

"What language was that you were talking in?"

"Oshivambo."

"You know the blacks' languages?"

"It's obvious, isn't it?"

We picked up his vehicle, and though he was fairly pissed, he insisted on driving. As we headed south down Robert Mugabe Avenue I noticed cops at every intersection; at the traffic lights and the 'Stop' and 'Give Way' signs. All decked out in bright orange plastic jackets with the label POLICE stuck on them in luminous letters.

Suddenly there was a cacophony of sirens coming up behind us and Dawson-Byrne quickly stopped the vehicle on the side of the road. Next thing a procession of motor bikes, dark blue BMWs and black Mercedes Benzes raced past at top speed; sirens wailing and blue lights flashing!

"What the fuck was that?" I asked the Pommy.

"That'd be our good old Uncle Sammy Nujoma on his way to Eros Airport. He keeps his private jet there."

"Why all the cops and sirens?"

"Typical Af for you."

"But look at all the cops. There must be hundreds of 'em! It must cost a bloody fortune every time he wants to go anywhere?"

"It most likely does, but the Af leader doesn't bother about the economics of anything. Like Robber Mugarbage in Zimbabwe and most other African leaders elsewhere, our good Father Sammy's been watching the Yanks on the telly, what with their presidential motorcades and so on. He probably thinks he's just as important as George Bush, regardless of the money it costs the taxpayers. Here in Namibia we have fifty percent unemployment and about seventy-percent living below the poverty line. In fact there are three hundred thousand people who're literally starving. Still, our good Sammy *must* have his motorcades and intercontinental presidential jet. Namibia's nearly bankrupt and imports nearly ninety-five percent of its consumables from South Africa, but SWAPO are spending or grabbing any money that might be left lying about and they don't give a damn about the ordinary man in the street. Old Sammy, and probably every leader in Africa needs such security, what with the double-crossing, the killing and the bastardry that they employed to steal power. He's probably dead frightened that his ex-PLAN fighters might bump him off."

"I heard you mention PLAN liberation fighters at Leslie's bar. What were they all about?"

"PLAN means Peoples' Liberation Army of Namibia. SWAPO's freedom fighters – or terrorists more like it. It was the PLAN fighters who were slathered by the South African security forces, whilst our good war hero Sammy was resting up in some five-star hotel. He and his cronies promised the PLAN fighters the world – good jobs, houses, motorcars, whisky and women – as long as they kept fighting and dying for the SWAPO cause. When independence comes along, a select few grab all the goods and the remainder of the PLAN fighters receive less than nothing. A couple of hundred have been put in the country's police force, so maybe you'll get an idea of what the average Namibian bobby's all about... Yes, old Sammy' has a fair bit of looking over his shoulder to be doing because all along he's been rather a treacherous fellow. During the war he and his good friends Kenneth Kaunda of Zambia and Julius Nyerere of Tanzania managed to kill off countless PLAN people who objected to Sammy's and the other SWAPO leaders' excesses. There were death camps in Angola where they murdered hundreds of them. If not thousands!"

CHAPTER 39

THE REVEREND CANAAN BANANA!
PAEDOPHILES AND
PEDERASTS IN THE AID AGENCIES!

When we got back to camp I caught up with Kotzé and Seebacher whom I found in a very dismal mood. They brightened up a bit when I quizzed them about the *Koevoet*.

"They were a highly trained, counter-terrorist unit that was created during the Border War," the German prospector explained. "Most of them were South West African policemen, but some of them were ordinary farmers and conscripted people. On occasions they used Special Forces from the South African Defence Force, plus they had mercenaries from ex-elite units of the old Rhodesian Army, such as the Selous Scouts. Each individual had expertise in different fields, such as in tracking and in mines and explosives. Also in communications, in marksmanship, in intelligence and interrogation. Most of all in terrorising and killing. There is a story that they were only paid by the number of terrorists that they killed, but I am not sure if this is true or not. Just let it be said that they were very dangerous. I know some *Koevoet* and they are not like ordinary people. There were those that cut off the ears of the PLAN fighters that they killed and they wore them on pieces of string around their necks. Some even removed their victims' penises and used them as penholders."

"Bullshit!" I thought the Kraut was talking crap as usual.

"Nah, what he is saying is true. Who told you about *Koevoet*?" Kotzé wanted to know.

"I was at the Hotel Thüringer Hof. One of the managers reckoned Dawson-Byrne was an ex-*Koevoet*."

The Boer was all derision. "I very much doubt that. We have a war and everybody emerges as a war hero, whether they have fired a shot in anger or not. Our Mr Dawson-Byrne is English, so I doubt whether they would have had him in *Koevoet*. Why would they now? Look at their Royal Family – they are carrying on with the same morals as the kaffirs. Look at the queen's children and not one has had a successful marriage so far. That Princess Anne prefers horses to men and her ex-husband has supposedly sired some bastard in Australia or New Zealand. Good Prince Charlie, the future king of England, wishes he was a tampon, and one day he might be head of the Anglican Church. You hear all sorts of people criticising the Dutch Reformed Church, even so you do not see our church leaders behaving like that. Then what about that other princess who enjoys having her toes sucked by her lovers and she is advertising cool drinks on the television. No wonder Australia is talking about becoming a republic, for who would give allegiance to the likes of people such as that?"

"Were you in the war?" I asked him.

"Me? Agh, we all had to do our call-up in Namibia and South Africa. I was given some training, although it was mostly marching up and down like an idiot just outside of Pretoria. It was the good fortune of everyone that they never put a gun in my hand for mortal combat."

"In Namibia everybody was involved in the war in some way or another," Seebacher informed me. "Though they hardly ever got farther south than Grootfontein or Tsumeb, we never knew where the terrorists would strike next. When out on the highways we were told to ignore the speed signs and to drive as fast as our motorcars could go. A few farmers up north got murdered in their farmhouses, but the war did not generally effect the civilian populations in the southern or central parts of the country. SWAPO killed many more of their own Ovambo civilians than they did whites. Also, many more PLAN fighters were killed by their leaders than by the security forces."

In fact it was Herman and Wilfred who confirmed that Dawson-Byrne had indeed been in *Koevoet*. "How do you know?" I asked.

"I have a cousin who worked with *Koevoet*," Herman explained. "He was not *Koevoet* himself, but was involved in one of their fights with PLAN. Now he works at the Navachab gold mine near Karabib and he saw you and the other Australians with *Meneer* Dawson-Byrne. The *Meneer* is a very dangerous man, boss."

I went to find Wheeler and I came across him and Dawson-Byrne having a drink under the Pommy's tent awning. The Englishman was recalling some chapter of his life's history and he invited me to join them.

"As I was saying," he continued, "the Rhodesian whites were also duped by the Smith Regime. The Rhodesian Front government introduced all kinds of currency controls, making it impossible for some whites to leave the country, as they couldn't take their money with them. All the politicians and government ministers didn't have such a problem. They'd well and truly got their corrupt and stolen funds out when independence was handed over, leaving the other white suckers to cope with the new black government. It was blatant and they took their fellow whites for a ride."

"Yeah, but weren't you saying you'd been in the Rhodesian armed forces?" Dave asked him. "How'd you get involved in all that?"

"I'd just graduated from Oxford and there was a bit of a mining recession going on around the world. The Nickel Boom had recently petered out in Australia and the gold price was worth nothing. The only geological job on offer was at a place called Gwelo in Rhodesia, which's now called Gweru. I met a woman there, so I decided to settle down and marry her. Rhodesia was fighting a war, therefore, like most of the white male civilians, I was called up to do my National Service. Though I was a geologist and was earning a fairly reasonable salary, the glamour of the army seemed to have far more appeal. I was a good deal younger then, and the wife's brother was an army officer who was forever at me to enlist at the officers' training set up. Next thing I know, after a couple of years I'm a first lieutenant in the Rhodesian Light Infantry and I bump into this Colonel Reid-Daly who's setting up this unit called the 'Selous Scouts'. I joined that new unit and it was just as though I hadn't received any kind of training before that. They taught me every trick in the book when it came to counter-terrorism. Needless to say, destroying the opposition was our main priority, their soldiers, civilians, their women and kids. We had to learn not to have a conscience whatsoever, as quite often cock-ups occurred and the wrong people found themselves killed. After a time I found my particular role becoming more and more blurred at the edges and it was becoming increasingly difficult to determine who were the good guys or bad. All along it was obvious to anyone with a speck of intelligence that the whites couldn't win, what with world opposition and sanctions, nevertheless to some of us it became a kind of addictive, real life Dungeons and Dragons game, where our wits became our best weapons... We certainly didn't spend all our time wearing uniforms. Then again, our targets weren't necessarily militants in the sense that they had anything to do with carrying arms. In many cases taking care of the financial interests of certain high-ranking military personnel, politicians and people in the private sector was our highest priority. All kinds of people were winding up in the mortuary for a host of different reasons. Both black and white, but mostly black. There were those who were so immersed in this game, we were virtually freakish zombies, so consequently divorces and losing our families became par for the course... Then came the inevitable and the blacks took power. Prime Minister Robber Mugarbage took over with his capable cohort, the very Reverent Canaan Banana."

"You're kidding?" I scoffed.

"Kidding about what?"

"This bloke – Canaan Banana."

"I jest with you not," he crossed his heart. "Zimbabwe's first president's surname was indeed Banana – Canaan – Sodindo – Banana. It was always quite amusing seeing visitors arrive at the Harare airport. While waiting to clear with the immigration people, they'd all be studying their surroundings. First they'd discover old Robber Mugarbage scowling down at all and sundry with that demented gorilla's grimace of his, and then there was a portrait of the Rev' Banana. I never saw a person who didn't laugh. It was a darned good advertisement for what the country had become... No, seriously, Zimbabwe's first president wasn't only named Banana, he was notorious for his penchant for hanging around the backsides of young soccer players, so his middle name 'Sodindo' is appropriate. He's retired and has been replaced by Mugarbage himself, and I hear he's been given the right to stay in the country's State House for the rest of his life and he's on a full salary till he dies. There's word travelling around that his aide de camp – Mr Jefta Dube – shot someone dead because he was accused of being Banana's wife, and there's all sorts of bother going on."

The Pommy took time out to recharge his drink, and then continued: "Never mind that, the war in Rhodesia was a total, tragic, uncalled for disaster. The whites had their chance long before the blacks eventually took up arms. Just before the Smith regime took power the previous government was edging towards giving the blacks minimal autonomy and an elite few the vote. When I say 'elite', I mean the various tribal chiefs and some of the blacks who'd shown capabilities in business. There was a lot of room for that idea. By giving the chiefs decent positions in Rhodesian society, they in turn would've kept their own people in line. Then, of course, the black entrepreneurs would've supported the chiefs as it would've meant stability. You can't make both profits and war at the same time, unless you're in government or a government favourite. Give the chiefs a posh government motor car with all the trimmings. Allow them reasonable housing in a white suburb, then – most of all – give them the respect that their position warrants. Even more so, give them a seat in parliament. Not too many seats, mind you, simply enough to reflect a slight modicum of democracy. If that had come about the issue of independence in Rhodesia probably wouldn't have been raised for years to come. But no, the whites wouldn't even consider that. There was no way that even the lowliest white was prepared to have a dirty kaffir above him. It's why Smith and his cronies were so popular, as they promised the lower class whites that under no circumstance whatsoever would they ever have a kaffir elevated above them... So what had to happen then? Even the most moderate chiefs had to give way to the more radical individuals in their tribes. What could've been a peaceful transfer of partial power was replaced by terrorism. Instead of getting moderate black politicians, who could've been selected on account of their tribal lineage and business acumen, they ended up with terrorists who only climbed to power in their own ranks through their sheer brutality and ability to crush those in opposition to them. So what are the consequences of that? Thugs and morons in power – zero compromise – and the black man in the street's far worse off."

"So what happened to you once the blacks got independence?" Wheeler asked him.

"After all the activities I'd been involved in, I couldn't quite settle down to civilian life. Neither my wife nor her family wanted anything to do with me, what with my drinking and foul moods. Thank God we never had children! I went back to the UK to see my parents and they were also quite anxious to see me gone. I did some geologising for various companies in South America, Australia and Canada, but I was still fairly restless in those days. Through an associate of my father's I managed to get a position with an aid agency, and that was where I first acquired my abhorrence of international aid agencies in general. It was a Yank and Canadian outfit. Fotheringay's North American Aid for Children, or FNAAC. It was started off by some horribly rich old biddy who donated nearly half a billion US dollars... My first post was in Kenya. I met my station head at the Nairobi Hilton, and the chap was a downright pederast. He was a Canadian and supposedly a nephew of the founder. His first instructions to me were never to trust the blacks – not to waste my time with them as they were hopeless – to always use a condom. Even with the five year old black girls. According to him, even at that age there was a hundred percent chance that they had AIDS or terminal syphilis. I soon found out that I'd virtually joined a paedophile ring. There were people from the other aid organisations involved, plus diplomats from the various consulates and embassies. Almost all the men in our Nairobi office were up to their necks in it, and it wasn't only with the little black girls, either... And the pay and the perks were very good. A hundred and thirty thousand US a year – tax-free. Brand-new Range Rover to call my own – excellent hotel accommodation – best restaurants to feast in – all my expenses to be picked up by FNAAC. Those involved the best wines shipped in from France, lobster and Beluga caviar brought in via Belgium, twenty-four hours a day sex with the locals if one was that way inclined. I wasn't. The same lifestyle was on offer to most of the aid agencies I came in contact with. Sheer bliss, excellent food and drink, excellent everything, and not that much to do when it came to any kind of real work... My first job was to familiarise myself with the country. Using my trusty Range Rover I visited the Masai Mara and saw all the animals – the elephants, the lions, the giraffes, wildebeest and zebras and so on. I saw the pink flamingos at Lake Nakuru and the countless bird life at Lake Naivasha. At the latter lake I spent a fortnight drinking booze and fishing for black bass. I went up to Lake Victoria and fished for Nile perch and Tilapia. I caught a blue marlin at Malindi – I fell in love with the Nyali Beach at Mombasa. All the very best hotels. I was living the life of a millionaire, just like most of the aid people. I didn't like the hotels on the Mombasa coast, though, as the electricity and water supply had gone to pot. Even in the best hotels we only had a couple of hours of electricity. The lifts kept getting stuck and the food for the guests was rotting in the refrigerators. Having no reliable refrigeration was a terrible hindrance, as sometimes there was a scarcity of ice for the myriad of cocktail parties the various aid agencies used to invite one another to. What a catastrophe – we had people starving and dying of AIDS all around us – and there was hardly enough ice to put in the cocktail shakers!"

"So you reckon all the aid people had these perks," I asked him.

"Not all, but the vast majority that I came across... Yes, there I was in an outfit where most of the male employees had a penchant for having sex with children, and I was just sitting around enjoying the finest things that Kenya had to offer. Finally I pestered the station head enough to give me something useful to do. He took me out to this huge cashew warehouse that was practically stacked from floor to ceiling with condoms and contraception devices such as loops, diaphragms and the pill. Our organisation had originally set out to encourage the Kenyan locals to use family planning. An AIDS screening gadget, or something or other, had also been donated by FNAAC, however President Moi personally outlawed it. Apparently he claimed that using the device would be tantamount to admitting that there was such a thing as AIDS in his beloved country. In his opinion there was no such thing as AIDS in Kenya, therefore the gadget was banned. Now let's face it – in everyone's book – the man simply had to be a moron. No other way to describe him... Nonetheless, undeterred by the total idiocy of the country's president, I still go about my way doing my utmost to save the various peoples of sunny Kenya. I visited the Masai in the Athi Plains, the Pokot and the Turkana in the north of the country, the Kikuyu in the Central Highlands and the Wakamba in Machakos. I visited the Luo around Lake Victoria and the Taita in the coastal and Tsavo areas. Without exception they thought family planning was either taboo or an absolute joke, though they were fairly polite when it came to verbally doubting my sanity."

He stopped to light a cigar. "I discovered several things about independent Africa on my travels. Firstly, the interior of Kenya was rapidly being turned into a desert and there was catastrophic overpopulation. Secondly, the people living outside the cities and towns – the farmers and tribes people – were far better off than their urban counterparts in the slums. The rural types still had a tribal or family system that provided for all. They still had an entity to be proud of and you could find parts of their rich culture preserved. In the towns and cities it was a different story altogether. Poverty, homelessness, drugs, prostitution and violent crime. I went into the slums, a nether world out of some horror movie. The stink of garbage and open sewers, the despair, the poverty and the child prostitution. In the slums there was a new embryo tribe being born, united by their hopelessness and abject poverty. Also, unlike their rural counterparts, life wasn't worth a Kenyan shilling. Here we had the nobody people who literally preyed on each other. An individual would have no hesitation in killing for a shilling, and the slum people's mob justice would have no hesitation in killing that individual for stealing that shilling... Then, of course, I came across the AIDS victims. Out in the Kenyan villages I saw the rows of graves and I saw the people dying in their mud huts by the score. You don't see the stricken dying in the streets, they're at home and hidden from the television cameras. Their illness brings further poverty and hardship for their families. They keep talking about coming up with special drug mixes that give some chance against the virus, but how can the average Af afford those?"

"So what happened with your job in Kenya?" Dave asked him.

"I got the sack, but it wasn't for anything I did. There was a scandal caused by some newspaper that had been investigating all the paedophilia. The entire Nairobi office was dismissed, and I was booted out simply for being there."

I took the tops of a couple of bottles of beer and passed one to Wheeler. I turned back to the Pommy geo', "So what did you do after that?"

"I went back to Zimbabwe for a spell and I met another Selous Scout who was about to join the South African Defence Force. Next thing he and I joined *Koevoet*."

"Where does the name '*Koevoet*' come from?" I asked him.

"It means 'Crowbar or Cow Foot'. The latter's the way the Bushmen described the unit. We had several Bushmen trackers working in with us, and without their help a huge number of terrorists would've got away."

"And this *Koevoet*," Dave wanted to know, "they were the same as the Selous Scouts?"

"In some ways – yes, then in others – no. We spent more time at the front line, be it in Angola, the Caprivi Strip, or anywhere on the border. Similar to the Selous Scouts, our main job was counter-terrorism, although we were also used to boost the confidence of the ordinary rank and file. The South African military used mostly civilian call-up troops, and the regular army and air force did their bit here and there. With *Koevoet* dashing around like the cavalry, blowing up and shooting every terrorist on sight and openly displaying our body counts, it was a huge morale boost for the ordinary troops. It also frightened the stuffing out of the PLAN fighters... Yes, if there was any terrorising to do on our side, the job was given to our group and we became fairly good at it. The PLAN fighters weren't really scoring any points by blowing up their fellow Af civilians with mines, so some of us decided to capitalise on that. It wasn't only terrorist land mines causing such havoc, for we decided to plant a few of our own. It was rather like setting traps for foxes or rabbits back in the UK. We used to position the mines the night or week before, then the following day or week we'd go back and check on the results. Now and then a cow or goat would be blown to bits, or perhaps some wild animal. Then we had times when you'd blow up an Ovambo herd boy, or a vehicle carrying black civilian passengers. The mines just carried out their job by blowing up, and naturally they weren't designed to discriminate. An excellent weapon for counter-terrorism."

"Is it true about the *Koevoet* going around cutting of the blacks ears and wearing them as necklaces?" I poked at him. "Also, I heard that they cut off the PLAN fighters' cocks and used 'em as penholders or whatever."

"Oh yes, there was a great deal of that going on," the Pommy agreed. "We were out to cause shock and horror, and – as I said – PLAN was petrified of us."

"But you still lost," Wheeler poked at him.

"Indeed we did. Same as during the Rhodesian war, we shortly began to realise that we were going to lose. It was the same old story. The world was against the South Africans and the sanctions started crippling the South African economy. Being an unconventional war we had no defined forces that our army could come up against face-to-face, otherwise we could've beaten them... Even the people back in Pretoria knew, for even they must've realised that South Africa itself was next to go under the chopping block of world and do-gooder opinion. They were only playing for time, so they could suck out every last cent possible. Back in those days the war was costing South Africa a fortune – ten million rand a day – and that was when the rand was level pegging with the US dollar. But where was most of the money going? Creating the infrastructure for war can be an incredibly lucrative business for some. Weapons, aircraft, ammunition, uniforms, armoured vehicles, transport and rations for the troops. Someone was making real big money and they conned the South African whites the same as they did the whites in Rhodesia with patriotic slogans and bull's droppings. They never let on to the white population and they used everything in their power to drag things out. Now, of course, South Africa's in a total mess. Soon one faction will be lining up against another, and then the rest shall join in when it suits them. Just like what's bound to happen here in Namibia."

"I can see your point," Dave agreed. "If you don't have all out war among the ANC and the Zulu Inkatha Freedom people, crime'll soon do the job, anyway."

"True," Dawson-Byrne nodded, "that's if AIDS doesn't wipe out the Zulu Nation first. There's always been a problem with crime in South Africa and Namibia, but now that both countries have received independence, it's totally out of control. During the days of the Apartheid regime, if you had some white, brainless slob who was good for absolutely nothing, the only vocations on offer to him were either the police force, the army or the South African railways. In the army or railways you probably needed some grey matter, so most of the absolute dim-witted good-for-nothings joined the police. Equally demented low lives probably spawned these types, therefore they made excellent upholders of Afrikaner law. As well as being brutal, their animal cunning soon latched onto the fact that the blacks were out there to be robbed and exploited. Corruption became their main source of income, while their families openly supported their brutality when it came to keeping the Afs in place. Beating and torturing black prisoners in cells became a nationwide, accepted police practice, condoned by even the police generals. When it came to moving the black squatters out of the cities and the other so-called forbidden areas to blacks, the coppers were encouraged to bash a few heads in, rape a few women, kick a few babies in the teeth, and then cause as much damage to the Afs' property as possible."

"But now there's mostly black cops," I pointed out.

"There most certainly are. Here in Namibia you have two different types of crime committed by people with totally different circumstances. You take for instance the simple, bush Af. He leaves his village or kraal to live in the bright lights of the city. He's convinced those dazzling lights auger limitless opportunities, as he's looked in all the shop windows in Windhoek and all the fine goods he sees there make him both ambitious and materialistically-minded. Back in the bush there's nothing like that to tempt him. No motorcars, no television, no posh clothes, no nightclubs – no nothing. If he's eighteen or older he's probably got a wife and more than one child whom he takes to the big smoke with him. He tries to find a job, but without contacts or experience he can't get one. What's more, you've got fifty percent unemployment over here. If he's lucky, he'll receive help from friends or family who've already set themselves up. Then again, if he hasn't got family or friends, he either has to go back to his home village or he has to do something drastic fast. There's no dole in Namibia worth speaking of, and the hopeless Af red tape could mean months before he can get a red cent. Being from the bush he mostly probably hasn't received any official ID documentation, and filling out the multitude of forms – that are carefully designed to deny people welfare benefits – is an impossibility to him. Then, if he does manage to fill out the forms, there's the compulsory bribe required in order to ensure that those forms aren't tossed in the waste paper basket or become 'lost' in the system. The typical filing apparatus favoured by the Af civil servants is the first waste paper basket to hand which's not already overflowing, or the ubiquitous briefcase that you see every black civil servant carrying. If his swanky case isn't for carrying his lunch in, it's used for taking his 'work' home so that he can burn it in the cooking hearth. Much more efficient than a shredder, as it helps cook the evening meal... So, if the bush Af has a family with him, any food or money he has quickly runs out. His wife and children are starving, so he has to steal anything he can in order to survive. He's left the bush to better himself, and he's probably sold everything he had back home in order to make the move. There's probably less there to go back to, unless his relatives have sufficient resources to carry him until he gets back on his feet. All in all he has to resort to crime just in order to feed his family. God help him if he can't share accommodations with someone... That kind of criminal one can possibly sympathise with."

He studied both Dave and me for a couple of seconds. "The reason why one can sympathise with this particular individual is because he's desperate – his family's hungry – his stomach's empty. Who knows how we here would react under such circumstances, especially if we or our family are starving? ... Generally, though, you give the average Af around here any sort of an opportunity and he'll work hard and give you his best if you give him his due respect and a fair day's pay. Look at the blacks and Baster you people have brought with you from Rehoboth, they're as good as any team of workers you'd find back in Australia. They're really going to be devastated if we don't find any economic mineralisation around here, for the work you've given them's most likely the only worthwhile opportunity that'll *ever* come their way...

No, you give the Af his own property and he'll look after it – give him a house and he'll keep it tidy and maintain it. Make water available to him, and he'll keep himself clean. You hear the Boers calling them lazy, still I wouldn't take any notice of such garbage. Furthermore, the notion that the average black's more dishonest than the whites is a mythical one. Who can blame a man who has nothing – no future and no possibility of improving himself – for doing *anything* to better his lot?"

"And the other kind of criminals?" I asked him.

"In most cases the other kind of African criminal you'll come across is in the government or public service, and no sympathy should be wasted on him or her. The Boers certainly weren't better than the Afs, even so they were far more restrained and there was always a certain amount of taxpayers' money left over for government infrastructure and services. The Africans in general have no way of controlling their excesses, as they're far less sophisticated and totally devoid of any such thing as a conscience. The Boers also totally lacked a conscience with their treatment of the blacks, nevertheless the Af can watch his own people starve to death with total, hollow-eyed detachment. They simply can't keep their noses out of the trough, similar to our ex-Boer politicians. Different pigs, but the same trough. Uncle Sammy's only been in power since 1990, so how did he come by the millions of US dollars he's got stashed in various overseas bank accounts? Soon all pretence of accountability goes out the window. Take Robber Mugarbage and his thugs in Zimbabwe, the cabinet ministers in Kenya, and the governments in Angola and Equatorial Guinea. In all these countries we see countless people literally dying of starvation and disease while those in government have thousands of millions in foreign bank accounts. What have the do-gooders and the champions of the noble savage got to say about that? Mind you, the Boers' judges, police, politicians and army generals may have plundered merrily away, yet the average Af was better off in a lot of ways under the old regime."

"You're beginning to sound like Seebacher and Kotzé," Dave warned.

"Never! On the other hand, they're partly right in some cases. Take the do-gooders you've got in Australia and New Zealand, plus – God forbid – the UK. The average civil rights activist has this vision of making every person equal. He or she sees the noble savage being far better off under the government of his own choice or race. The deserving Afs are now free, so his or her work's been done. All their excellent efforts have come to fruition, and now it isn't politically correct to suggest that more than a few African politicians are a bunch of downright crooks. It's not fashionable to say that African leaders, in most cases, won't hesitate to have an opponent jailed on trumped-up charges, or even bumped off. Like with you Australians and New Zealanders, who appear to be the doyen of political correctness, you're always telling other countries how to run their ethnic affairs, so how do you react when someone calls an Asian a slopehead or an Aborigine a boong? I'm not talking about people such as yourselves – Australian drillers are amongst the most foul-mouthed bigots I've ever come across – but what about your collection of do-gooders? The champions of the queers, the blow-ins from Asia and the Aboriginals? They've got you ordinary Australians by the testicles. What was that woman's name – the one that doesn't want Asians swamping the place?"

"Pauline Hanson," I reminded him.

"That's right – Pauline Hanson! She's the only one who had the nerve to stand up and actually voice the opinions of the majority of Australians. I was over there a couple of years back. I saw all the rallies in Brisbane and Adelaide and wherever, where all these people banded together for national unity. Even your Prime Minister Howard claimed that Australia was 'a magnet for multiculturalism'. But who got the most votes for being the most popular Australian? Pauline Hanson – that's who."

"You're dead, bloody right!" Wheeler agreed with him wholeheartedly because the Pom' had touched on one of his favourite themes. "About people championing the queers. Australia's going through a really queer time itself at the moment. And when I say 'queer', I mean queer in the sexual sense. We're undergoing a kind of Sodom and Gomorra phase. If we haven't got fuckin' Supreme Court judges committing suicide for being caught giving blokes blowjobs in public shithouses, we've got friggin' judges saying it must be enjoyable for twelve year old girls being molested by their stepfathers..."

"Which judge was that?" I interjected. "The one giving blokes blowjobs?"

"A judge by the name of Clarke. I can't remember if he was in West Aussie or not. It's fuckin' dinkum – I swear... As I was saying, we're going through this really queer period. The old Anzacs'll be really spewing in their graves... Take the fuckin' ABC TV. Are they chock-full of gays and Lesbians, or aren't they? If it isn't bad enough having poofter parades marching through Sydney and Perth, why does the fuckin' ABC have to force it down our throats on the television? Is it so that the other poofters can sit at home and wank themselves? ... Then you're having lesbians suing doctors for sexual discrimination when the doctors won't have a bar of artificially fertilising them. The Australian Labour Party must be crammed full of bloody queers, too, 'cause it was them who started all this poofter-loving crap."

"The white Aussies are as lazy as they say the Aboriginals are," Dawson-Byrne told him. "The do-gooders, lesbians and queers at least make the effort to push their point across. The majority of Australians generally dislike homosexuality and know it to be against all the basic fundamentals of logic and nature, but they won't climb off their backsides to protect their children from it. It's the same when it comes to the Asians swamping the place, though at least the average Australian in the street can have some say in political matters. Here in Africa, even under the old white regimes, one could be thrown in jail or have a bullet between the eyes for speaking out."

"Yeah, true, but under the Keating Labour government it was getting that way that our freedom of speech was being taken from us completely," Dave argued. "It's the same with the Howard government today. If you're heard in pubs talking about abos or Muslims, you can be arrested under the racial vilification laws, but racism's something you're born with. White people are born being suspicious of people of a different colour, or people who're different to 'em. Take the Asians with their slit eyes. Then, of course, the blacks and the Asians are suspicious of whites because of our pink skins and different coloured eyes. Mind you, that's not to mention the fact that every time our ancestors saw a different race or people with a different skin colour, they tried their best to kill 'em... No, racial prejudices go back to the beginning of Biblical times. What about the Tower of Babel? Why was God so determined to segregate people by giving 'em different colours and languages?"

Nick was listening in by then since I had called over to him to fetch more beer. He just had to put his two bobs' worth in: "Dave's right. That's why we can't get on with the fuckin' slopeheads back in Aussie. None of the bastards speak English. Have you heard when their women sing on the SBS Channel? They sound like a bunch of cats fuckin'!"

"My God – who pushed this creature's button?" Dawson-Byrne wasn't happy to see the man.

Nick's pride wasn't hurt that easily, and he had further words for the Pommy geo' to ponder on, "You reckon us Aussies are lazy about poofters? What about that fuckin' cop TV show you got – the 'Bill'? It's making out that half the Pommy cops are either poofters or lesbians, and then you've got some joker fuckin' his mother. If that's not fuckin' bullshit enough, there's two fuckin' blacks to every white bloke or sheila, so it means your cop shops are run by bloody poofs, lezzies and blackfellas."

Wheeler only agreed with him on very rare occasions, "Yeah, I used to enjoy watching that show until – like Nick said – it started being overrun with poofters and lesbians. We've got an Aussie cop show called 'Stingers' and the show's writers must be copying the 'The Bill' word for word. You've got this cop inspector who wants to fuck his daughter, and the daughter tries to fuck all the other cops in her old man's squad – both men and women. What has western society come to when – in order to keep its ratings up – a family cop show has to go in for queers and fuckin' incest? I've got a teenage son and two teenage daughters, and with all the shit we're seeing on the TV, they're growing up starting to think that queers and fuckin' lesbians are acceptable... Still, that flamin' Pommy cop show's far worse than anything the Aussies can come up with."

Dawson-Byrne was equal to their jibes. "I don't watch the telly all that much. Mostly the news and current affairs programs."

"I thought you might be a big fan of that Coronation Street you Pommies have as a sitcom?" Dave suggested. "What a fuckin' load of crap that is!"

"I can only agree with you there," the Pom quickly admitted. "I have indeed watched a couple of episodes of Coronation Street out of sheer, masochistic, morbid fascination. They should call it 'Cockroach Street'. What an insipid, mouldy, blackmailing, backstabbing, putrefied, double-crossing collection of toilet bowl stains ever assembled in one street? You have white British women kissing and fornicating with creatures with the most questionable of genetic backgrounds. All these surrounded by homosexuals, plus all manner of species of bacteria that you'd find under a baboon's fingernail once it's scratched its backside. We have low life women totally disregarding their bastard children that have been sired by these genetic unmentionables, and the males come across as a collection of amoebas and other lowly swamp life. Like with you Aussies, the local pub is their temple, but – unlike you – they haven't ventured further than the end of the street. They're just spineless, pathetic, characterless..."

"Hang on a sec' – it's only a TV show!" Dave busted in.

"I know that, David, but one would assume that it's a portrayal of your average, urban Brit. A picture put together by a British television company. An attempt by a British media organisation to create a facsimile of the day-to-day lives of a collection of cockroaches, body lice or sewer rats. If that's the way the British want to be displayed to the world, no wonder there are all sorts plotting and scheming to blow up London. Then again, if Coronation Street *does* in fact give an accurate representation of the average Brit, then I can only assume that the British – as a nation of people – have sunk as low as the French, Belgians and Dutch. Or – perhaps even lower than that? They might've descended to the level of the Spaniards, Italians or the Portuguese? The Latino chimpanzees? ... No, it's true what you say – we're being inundated with total garbage on the telly nowadays. It simply shows you what happens when one's country has been overrun by people from the rest of the world – Arabs, Pakis, Indians and Nigerians. I suppose it proves that Enoch Powell really knew what he was talking about."

"What, with his 'River Tiber running with blood'?" Dave asked him.

"Exactly! Powell's proved to be a prophet far more accurate than Nostradamus in every sense of the word, when you consider that every third person you see in the UK appears to have a varied genetic profile. When it comes to his 'Rivers of Blood' speech, those three thousand plus souls killed at the World Trade Centre could be described as a 'River of Blood'."

"But that happened in the States," Wheeler reminded him.

"Very true, David, nevertheless I see our top copper in Blighty, Sir John Stevens, is claiming that there are up to two hundred Al Quaeda terrorists operating in the UK, and the threat of terrorist attacks is very real. So where can our terrorists be found in the UK? Sheltering amongst the countless Arabs, Pakis and the multitude of religious fanatics that've invaded the place. There are certainly plenty of places to hide – it'd be like trying to find a needle in a haystack – and there's plenty of swamp vermin only too willing to assist. You look at all the people who've filtered in from India, Pakistan, Bangladesh and all over Africa – I doubt if they're in the UK strictly for Queen, country and the Union Jack. They're there for the dole, the National

Health Service, and in most cases they're loathe to even associate with the true Brits. Like Powell said, 'How could I say such horrible things?', but am I speaking the truth or not? Is the truth supposed to be inconsequential when it comes to political correctness? ... All the same, I see that the British government's having all kinds of bother passing new anti-terrorist legislation. Is this the result of the excellent work being carried out by our human rights activists and do-gooders? The progeny of those who're depicted in Coronation Street, who didn't have the stomach to go out into the world when good men fought and conquered all those before them to put the 'Great' in Great Britain? Do the watered-down, never-leave-your-armchair types have control of Blighty nowadays? People who haven't the nerve to go further than the end of their streets?

"Yeah, but I read somewhere that it's members of the House of Lords that are blocking the legislation," Dave pointed out. "Your Peers of the Realm."

The Pommy sat back in his chair and grinned, "It's quite extraordinary to encounter an Aussie driller who has a higher IQ than the vast majority that can only gaze at photographs in pornographic magazines. The Peers of the Realm – you say? Just the pathetic results of totally immoral interbreeding. Weak people whose grandfathers set them up, and who've since done nothing worthwhile for themselves or their country... They should revert back to the days of good Queen Liz the First. A time when Englishmen were men. If they caught anyone up to mischief in those days it was called 'treason'. They had an excellent cure for terrorists during her rule. Hang, draw and quarter them, then impale their heads on a pole in a public place. That should teach anyone to think twice before they go about committing acts of terrorism."

CHAPTER 40

AFRICA IS SERIOUSLY STUFFED!

I moved onto another subject by asking him, "What did you do after leaving the South African army?"

"I stayed on here in Namibia for a while. A lot of the professionals had moved down to South Africa, or they were trying to find positions in overseas countries. I was asked by a friend of mine in the UN to remain behind and help hand over the various government offices to the incoming SWAPO appointees. I'm a geologist, so I helped with the Mines Department, and what a total, utter farce that turned out to be. I loathe saying this, but Kotzé and Seebacher *do* have a point. First off, the country's handed over to an individual like Sammy Nujoma, who's had less education than a ten year old white child. Then the Ministry of Mines was handed over to a really wonderful old gentleman by the name of Andimba Toivo ya Toivo. When I say wonderful, I mean precisely that. The old chap was imprisoned on Robben Island with Nelson Mandela round about 1967 and he was released in '84. He was one of the original nationalists and was also responsible for forming the OPO, or the Ovamboland People's Organisation. At least old Andimba used to pay you the courtesy of listening to you for a while before falling asleep, whereas the other ministers had lesser attention spans than a goldfish. Andimba was ten times more intelligent than Sam Nujoma and he had a hundred times more courage than him. He suffered first-hand the bastardry of the Boers with their beatings, imprisonment and torturing. Sammy was a total coward and kept right in the background out of harm's way... Nevertheless, while there wasn't too much damage done in handing over the ministerial portfolios to inexperienced big wheels in SWAPO, handing over the public service posts to such idiots was catastrophic, and we're seeing the results of that today. Naturally the deputy minister posts were also taken up by SWAPO favourites, but that's where it should've stopped. But no, posts such as permanent secretary were also handed over to SWAPO buddies, so that meant giving top public service positions to totally incompetent buffoons. With the Mines Department it was even worse. Under the SWAPO permanent secretary we had some Boer and British civil servants such as the Mines Commissioner, Senior Mines inspector, Chief Surveyor and so on. An absolutely useless bunch that would've had no chance in finding a position in the private sector. By that time all the decent public servants had long gone to alternative pastures... So what did we have – ministers and deputy ministers that didn't know what time of day it was – equally useless permanent secretaries, and a totally useless bunch of incompetents below them."

"They can't *all* have been useless?" Wheeler didn't believe him.

"Useless is not the word for them – pitiable is more appropriate," Dawson-Byrne disagreed. "Then the nepotism came in. Most of the white Mines Department secretaries had been sacked and replaced with black women who couldn't even spell their own name, or switch on an electric typewriter or computer. Those secretaries, of course, were nieces, sisters, mothers and cousins of the various newly introduced government officials. Then they brought in so-called black assistants to go with every public service post. Assistant commissioner, assistant mines inspector, assistant mines engineer and so on. All totally incompetent, and all some relation or other of a political favourite. If they weren't relations or particular favourites of SWAPO, kickbacks had to be given to the kind souls who gave them the job. Naturally they were put there to eventually take over from any white that had remained in the public service. Worse than that, Afs with 'darkie diplomas' immediately became department heads, and, having been given their training and diplomas in places like Russia, Hungary, Finland and other Scandinavian countries, we find another collection of morons. Then, to exacerbate everything, we had visiting quasi-experts introduced from Sweden, Denmark, Europe and Canada, who came over to *train* everyone. Like the Boer and British public servants that had remained from the old regime, these supposed 'experts' had also been completely disregarded by the private sectors of their own countries. You had the blind leading the blind, cretins advising cretins, and any decent, working public services that remained were conclusively thrown into disarray. That happened in every ministry. Training workshops were set up in the best hotels in Swakopmund and Windhoek, all paid for with overseas aid money plus taxpayers' funds, and all the Af officials went flocking to them. They either fell asleep during the lectures or didn't bother attending at all, but when it came to the specially prepared luncheons and banquets, they attended those in their entirety – gorging themselves on the food – drinking themselves into a stupor. Best food – best alcohol – best accommodation. When all these junkets were going on nobody was there to do the work. Absenteeism was rife amongst the public service, as it is today, nonetheless who could sack the deputy minister's brother, or the permanent secretary's niece, or the assistant commissioner's sister? To add to that, who would be bold enough to dock these people's pay on account of all the days off? ... What I noticed most was that the more incompetent an Af official was, the bigger the ego he had. Take Sammy Nujoma for instance – he'd have a brain the size of a gnat's. Then, as the public service became bloated with black assistants and assistants' assistants, government cars had to be allocated to all these valuable people. Not ordinary, run-of-the-mill, everyday cars – Mercedes Benzes, BMWs and Audis. The very best and most expensive German technology, with the exclusion of a Ford Mustang that was given to one of the permanent secretaries for mines. He killed himself by trying to drive it up a tree. Possibly he was trying to visit his mother? I can't say for certain, but these idiots were probably given their driver's licences with the job, for which humble Af copper would dare fail their driving tests? Within weeks of independence we saw Mercedes Benzes, BMWs and a whole variety of government vehicles being written-off by the score. If they weren't being smashed, no proper maintenance was carried out on them, so you had engines seizing from lack of oil, and Afs driving around with flat tyres and so on. Even the Namibian army was no better, as the various ex-South African military bases soon became crammed with broken-down Kasspirs, personnel carriers and troop trucks. In the various government vehicle yards you've got hundreds of vehicles of all descriptions, either smashed or out of order from negligence... So who has to pay for this, but the taxpayer and overseas aid donors? Then, of course, with independence being handed to the righteous, only certain people have to pay their taxes, electricity and water bills. About nine percent of the population and mostly whites."

"The bloke next door to our company house in Windhoek had his electricity and water cut off," I told him. "Kotzé reckoned he's a fairly high-up cop and is black."

"Possibly so," the Pommy acknowledged, "but in life we always have some anomalies. Especially in Africa. It was probably because your good policeman was living in Klein Windhoek. Take the inhabitants of the Township of Katutura. They're ninety percent Afs and about two percent – if that – pay their electricity and water bills. The economy of this country's being nurtured by about nine percent of the population – who're mostly white – and their tax dollar's being squandered on presidential jets, luxury vehicles for government officials, and a public service five times overstaffed with baboons... Here in Africa there's nothing unusual about that whatsoever. The same thing's transpired in about every other black independent country. South Africa's heading in the same direction, so in no time they'll be screaming out for economic aid. Here we find another total farce in itself, as you've still got ninety percent of the aid money being stolen. That's the money that actually escapes the fees and commissions filched by the various aid bureaucracies. With black government officials there are three kinds of attention span periods, whether the official's a minister, a permanent secretary, or a lowly clerk behind some public counter. A – he or she's keen to see you just in case there's a profit or a backhand to be had by that particular individual. B – absolute interest in your case, if there truly *is* an opportunity for personal gain. C – when it comes to that individual making a decision – and there's no profit to be made – the eyelids and shutters come down in an instant and fingers start making their way up nostrils. You study any Af who has to make a decision, and the finger up the nose is a sure fire method of relieving mental dilemmas."

"You're full of bullshit!" Wheeler sat back in his chair laughing.

"I am not!" the Pommy geo' was deadly earnest. "I'm being absolutely serious now. Take the committees they put together when it comes to the granting of mining permits. They bring people in from the Mines Department, the Tax Department, the Ministry of Finance and the Ministry of Conservation and so on. You end up with about twelve members in the committee who're supposed to meet every month to decide who should or who shouldn't be issued with a mining tenement. If a bribe isn't paid to someone, or you don't have a sleeping partner in SWAPO, you're really carting uphill. If one of those members of the committee doesn't deign to attend, which's bound to happen on account of the very high absenteeism in the whole of government, then any decision's postponed because that member's absent. They'll do practically anything to avoid making a decision, so having a mining claim granted can take years. Namibia could miss out totally on this latest gold boom, as the gold price's really on the skids now."

"What about the ground you've just been on?" I asked him. "You only applied for it in the last couple of weeks or so. Have the Mines Department people put things forward for you?"

"No, they wouldn't know how to," he grimaced. "I thought it was worth taking the risk, what with there being no decent results on any of Seebacher's ground. When I went to lodge the application I was given a perfect example of everything I've just told you. The Mines Department's in total chaos, as applications have piled up in their hundreds or have gone missing altogether... It's the whites in the department that really get my goat. The blacks are absolutely useless and I've known that all along, but you should see the whites that have managed to cling on to their jobs. What a pompous bunch of apes! Similar to those white bureaucrats you find in New Zealand. They wouldn't find work sweeping streets back in Blighty or in any decent white-governed country, yet alone posts in the public service. They're worse than the Afs... Still, returning to black incompetence and corruption, the entire continent's rife with it. At long last those useless cretins in the World Bank – who're almost identical to the expats I've described over here – have woken up to the fact that Africa's being strangled by deliberately imposed red tape and daylight robbery. Suddenly they've discovered that four-fifths of the hardest countries in the world in which to do business are in Africa. You take Canada – in two days you can set up a company. In Mozambique it takes a hundred and fifty-three, and in Angola it takes three years before any form of contract can be enforced. When it comes to setting up a company you'll only find three necessary procedures in a place like Finland, whereas twenty-one procedural requirements are compulsory in Nigeria and nineteen in places such as Chad. In countries such as Kenya and Zimbabwe it can be more complicated than that, depending on how much in bribe money you're prepared to pay. This red tape's deliberately set in place by some African governments so that every opportunity can be taken to milk or rob you along the way. No wonder it's almost impossible for businesses to survive in Africa and there are almost zero chances of employment? Nevertheless, who gives a damn about the unemployed Afs, anyway? The next civil war might keep their numbers down a fraction... Still – never mind Africa – the worst white run country I've ever come across has to be New Zealand."

"How do you mean?" I asked him.

BASTARDS FROM THE BUSH

"Like the Afs in Africa, the New Zealanders have a bureaucracy that far exceeds the worst I've seen in any white-governed country. A bureaucracy that's designed to block you and milk you for every last cent possible. The entire country's populated by civil servants whose main charter is to tax you – penalise you – and ensure that every barrier possible is put up to delay you. Any progress any individual might make is totally abhorrent to New Zealanders. Any advertisements encouraging people to invest or do business in New Zealand are almost tantamount to fraud. On several occasions I've been sent to New Zealand by mining and exploration clients, all hoping to develop or explore for mines. Also, similar to any Af country, in New Zealand it's extremely useful having someone in government on your side, or some ex-public servant to oil the wheels, and naturally that'll cost you a fortune. Even with having one of the most corrupt systems in the western world to assist you, it can take too long for you to be able to get something worthwhile going, therefore you stand to forfeit any investments you've outlaid. No matter what you try and do in that country – you'll find a whole mountain of opposition designed to stop you. So no wonder New Zealand is the first white run country to fall into recession whenever there's a downturn in the world economy. As I said – they're no better than the Afs."

I nodded at Jeff. "Where the fuck have we heard this before?"

He nodded back at me. "Sounds like Andrew wasn't bullshitting after all."

"What's happened to the fuckin' gold price?" Dave drifted away from Africa's and New Zealand's shortcomings. "Has it really fallen through the floor?"

I was also very interested in Dawson-Byrne's answer. Being drillers, Wheeler and I had seen what a crash in the gold price could do to our particular industry. A knot was slowly tightening in my stomach.

He had no comfort to offer either of us: "The price fell over twenty dollars US last Friday. It's picked to fall to three-fifty, if not much lower. Apparently most of the European Community countries have sold off most of their gold reserves in order to conform to some new financial treaty or whatever. No, chaps, gold's fast losing its shine."

"Christ, I don't know where that'll leave us," Dave was obviously sharing my unease. "If that friggin' Mabo wank back in Aussie isn't enough to send our mob down the tubes, the flamin' gold price will. There'll be rigs parked all over the fuckin' place back in WA. The trouble with this bloody game – there's too much fuckin' boom and bust!"

"I couldn't give a fuck if it means getting out of this shit hole," Jeff informed us. "Who the fuck could live in this craphouse country? They reckon Africa's a great place for tourists, what with its lions, elephants, giraffes and so on. Namibia's just fuckin' thorn trees, blacks with their arses hanging out of their daks, and fuckin' AIDS! Like I told Joe here on the plane – it's the bloody arse-end of the world!"

"The sheilas and piss aren't that bad," Nick tried to stick up for the place.

Jeff wasn't persuaded. "That's if you don't mind rooting blacks and coloureds. Give me a white woman any day. The only white blokes you get fuckin' blacks are the ones who can't get onto a white woman."

Dawson-Byrne looked in my direction; however there was no way I was about to let Jeff get under my skin. The thought of being without a job as a result of the collapsing gold price was far more worrying.

"Well, it looks like Namibia's going to lose out altogether because of the typical, useless, African bureaucracy," the Pommy told Wheeler. "You look at all the mining lease applications that have been held up for the past few years. There could've been millions of dollars spent on exploration here. Some projects may have been interesting enough to weather the unstable gold price, but it's much too late now. So the ever climbing unemployment rate keeps going up, accompanied by runaway inflation, poverty, crime and unfettered corruption in government."

CHAPTER 41

THE POMMY'S DOG IS KILLED!

The following morning greeted us with a tragedy. Some bastard had killed Dawson-Byrne's old dog during the night! In addition to that the animal had been expertly skinned; its body was left in such a manner that it could have still been alive the way the head rested on the front paws. The pelt was put over the driver's seat of the Englishman's vehicle like a special seat cover.

After burying the dog's remains its owner drove out on to the claims alone, and Nick announced to all and sundry, "Don't worry – I'm gunna mangle the fuckin' bastards who done this! The Pom' hands out a lotta shit, but whoever killed his dog didn't have the guts to front him face-to-face, so *whoever you are*, your fathers fucked your mothers up the arse to get you. And your mothers had the clap and pox dripping out of their noses. Did you hear that – you gutless cunts? Bloody have the guts to deny it! Stand up for your fuckin' poxy parents!"

I knew that I hadn't done it and also Dave wasn't that kind of a bloke. In addition to that, he really seemed to admire the Pommy geo'. Nick *definitely* hadn't done it, and it was an expert skinner who had carried out the job on the dog. I doubted if Ernie had such skills, though I had seen Jeff skin a kangaroo or two for dog tucker back in the gold fields. He might have done it, or Ernie could have had an accomplice. Still there were Seebacher, Kotzé, Van der Merwe and the labourers; not forgetting Wilfred or Herman.

It helped to break the monotony, as we all became detectives. "By

Christ, I feel almost sorry for the bastards who done it," Dave assured me. "If Nick and Dawson-Byrne catch 'em, there's gunna be blood 'n guts all over the fuckin' place!"

"Who do you reckon might've done it?" I asked him.

"It wasn't Ernie. He wouldn't have it in him, the useless, old fart. Dawson-Byrne never gave Jeff too much curry. Strangely enough – he leaves the ugly, fat bastard alone. I reckon it's either Kotzé, Van der Merwe or Seebacher."

"It could've been the labourers. You saw the expert job they did on skinning that ostrich."

"Herman, you mean?" he reminded me. "He was doing all the skinning when it came to that ostrich."

"He wouldn't dare. He knows that Dawson-Byrne was in that *Koevoet* business. His cousin told him."

Nick came up to us. "You better not've done it, Joe. You darkies are all the same. Friggin' savages!"

That truly bugged the crap out of me! "No, I didn't, but I paid someone fifty bucks to do it. I told him to make sure the dog was still alive when it was being skinned. It must've died just before the Pommy found it."

His eyes nearly fell out of their sockets with rage, as I lined up a smack to his mouth.

"Put your fuckin' eyes back in!" I snarled at him, "Before I kick the fuckers out! Come on – Nick! I'm seriously in the mood – you fuckin' dickhead!"

"Nick! Joe! Don't be so fuckin' stupid!" Wheeler got in between us. "Nick, what reason would Joe have?"

Nick wasn't entirely satisfied with that. "Then who do *you* reckon done it?"

"Seebacher! But you'd better find some proof first before you nail the cunt, otherwise he'll run to the cops. Stick at it and you'll soon get the evidence you need."

"You reckon it was Seebacher?" I asked Dave when Nick had gone stomping off. "What makes you reckon it was his him? How do you know it wasn't Kotzé? Dawson-Byrne's been making his life hell lately."

"Kotzé hasn't got the guts. You look at him sideways and he craps his pants. The bloke's a fuckin' coward."

"That's just it," I argued. "Kotzé's a sleazy, conniving bastard. He's the type who'd pay a labourer big money to do it. Big money's a hundred bucks over here for some people."

"No, it's that dickhead, Seebacher," Dave was adamant. "He thought he was gunna make millions out of these claims. Dawson-Byrne told him that he was gunna recommend that the company should pull out of the option deal, and the bloody Kraut's hopes and dreams have been shattered. He desperately wants to believe there's a gold mine here or at Klein Aub. He isn't young anymore and doesn't fancy having to work for the rest of his life. I swear – when the Pom' scorned his claims – Seebacher looked as if he was fuckin' gunna kill him!"

When Dawson-Byrne returned to the camp in the late afternoon, Wheeler and I joined him for a sundowner outside his tent. He reckoned he may have had a target for us to drill; though didn't promise too many metres. If the assay results stacked up, things could expand from there. If they didn't, that was it and *no more* drilling. The target, if it was indeed a target, would be ready in about a week's time.

Unable to contain myself, I asked him about his dog. "Who do you reckon killed your dog, Jim?"

"Don't call me 'Jim!' My name's James. I'm not like you common folk – David being called Dave – you, Josef, being called Joe – Nick – Jeff – Ernie. It annoys the damned hell out of me!"

"Okay – okay," Wheeler tried to calm him down. "James it is. But, tell me – who do you reckon done that to your dog?"

"I don't reckon. I know for damned certain!"

"How's that?" I asked.

"Take my word for it. I'll make them pay in my own good time, so forget it ever happened."

"You say 'them'?" Dave pointed out.

"You heard what I said."

CHAPTER 42

GREAT MEN, CITIZENS AND ALL THAT CRAP!

Wilfred got word that Carl Zes and his mates wanted to have a chat with me. The venue for the meeting was the Oanob Dam; not at the resort, but in some rowing boats. In no time at all I found myself out in the middle of the dam; Zes and I in one boat; Petrus Klaase and Fritz Manasse shared another. I felt rather nervous, for, if they had wanted to do me in, there was nothing like a drowning accident.

I examined those around me as we bobbed up and down on the water. Zes, who looked to be in his late twenties or early thirties, was tall and heavyset in a muscular sort of a way and had dark skin like an Indonesian. His hair was jet black, straight and was cut fairly short. He had handsome, clear-cut features also like an Asian and his eyes were a dark green turning to black. His pearly white, perfectly shaped teeth had a lot of gold in them that glinted in the hot Namibian sun. He wore a gold chain around his neck, a gold bracelet and watch, and he had several gold rings on his fingers. He wore his good clothes in a casual, comfortable way and it was easy to see by his manner that he was a man superbly confident in himself. His movements resembled that of a cat ready to pounce. Klaase and Manasse came across as slobs in comparison to him. In many ways they themselves could have been twins. The two of them skinny; Manasse a fair bit taller than Klaase, and they both wore denim cowboy like shirts that had white sweat stains at the armpits. Both had dusty looking denim jeans and elastic-sided, leather riding boots on. Klaase was the lighter skinned of the two, about equal coffee to milk, and his short hair was also straight. Although he was in his late thirties his moustache was like that of a sixteen-year-old. His face held a perpetual, happy grin.

I found out later that Manasse was almost black because he had a fair bit of his grandfather's Nama blood in him. His hair was also short, though it was crinkled in tight balls that clung closely to his skull. He was roughly the same age as Klaase; yet there was a fair bit of white in his hair. His closely shaven beard was also slightly frosted. He, too, smiled at everything, and both his two bottom front teeth were missing. The two skinnier blokes had a casual – who-gives-a-shit – manner about them. All three men smoked.

"How long will your people be working in Namibia?" Zes wanted to know.

I shrugged. "The way things are going, we'll be heading back to Australia at any moment."

"Why is that?"

"We can't find any gold or anything. The drilling rig's been idle for weeks now, and it must be sending somebody broke."

"You can find gold in Namibia?" Klaase seemed interested in the possibility. "How do you look for gold?"

"It's a bit complicated," I told him. "Let's just say there was none where we were looking."

Zes shook his head glumly. "That is too bad. It is a pity you did not discover any at Klein Aub. When the copper was being mined the wages our people received had a huge benefit to offer the Rehoboth community. Now all we have is farming, but the drought has all but wiped that out. Even if we receive very good rains and the pasture returns to the way it was when the Baster first trekked here, there is no stock left to graze on it. It is the same in Damaraland. They have some good veld pasture up there, but the stock is long dead and gone."

"Do you like Krystal?" Fritz Manasse steered us onto a totally different course.

I looked him up and down, then around at the others. "It's none of your bloody business. Look, I've gone along with all this to find out about my brother, not to spend the time talking bullshit. Either tell me about him or take me back to the shore. I've had enough of this crap from you, Jakobus Van Wyk, and old Elsabeth Witbooi for that matter. If my brother's alive and close by, let's get on with it?"

"Okay," Zes agreed. "But, if your brother was in trouble with the police, would you betray him?"

"Why? Has he murdered someone? Did he rob a bank or something?"

He smiled. "Not exactly. His problem is political. Namibia, just like every African country, has conflicting political matters. Your brother has been involved in some very unpopular politics as far as the government is concerned, so he is wanted for questioning and we wish to avoid that. Nothing more."

"So you're convinced now that he's my brother?"

"Ja, we have no doubt about that," Klaase joined in. "*Ouma* Witbooi says she is sure that you are Jonker's brother."

"I see," I told him. "She's fairly fired-up politically. What's she and Jakobus gotta do with my brother?"

"She brought Jonker up," Zes told me. "The same as Krystal. With the help of some of the great men she has groomed him for what he is doing now."

"Great men?" I asked.

He shook a cigarette out of its packet and turned to the others inquiringly. On receiving shrugs of approval, he lit the cigarette before explaining, "In the old days our people where ruled under what they call a 'commando'. This system mainly fell away under the Germans and the Boers, but now that we have this new Ovambo regime, a number of people have formed a new commando to protect our people's interests from both the new Namibian and South African governments. Somewhere in the equation we have been left out totally. Normally, back in the old days, a commando came from a single community. Gibeon, Berseba, Rehoboth, Windhoek, Warmbad, and other communities such as them all had their own commandos, but this new organisation is made up from all the Baster and Nama communities. We even have members in South Africa – Upington, Steinkopf, Khobus, Kamaggas – nearly all over Little Namaqualand and Griqualand. Similar to the old days, a kaptein and a *raad* run this commando. Normally the kapteincy was hereditary, however the links from the past have been well and truly severed by both the Germans and the Boers. The kaptein is now selected by the *raad* which consists of ten great men. Jakobus is one of these great men. You have seen that new Datsun bakkie of his?"

"Yeah?"

"He was given the bakkie by the commando to help him with his work as great man."

"Ja," Klaase agreed, "that is why it was very disrespectful when you swore at him."

I was taken aback immediately. "I didn't swear at him – only in front of him."

"That may be so," Zes nodded, "but our great men have the highest respect from all of our people. We are divided in two ranks – citizens and *bywoners*. In the past citizens could only be male persons who owned a gun, at least five cows, or fifty sheep or goats. A *bywoner* was also male, but did not have the required wealth, even though he was a free man and had some movable possessions. There were also servants, but we do not have these anymore... Anyhow, nowadays a citizen is determined by his income, education and intelligence. Bywoners are recruits who show that they have talent that can be built upon. Similar to the old days, no women play any sort of role, except for possibly *Ouma* Witbooi who is a kind of Matriarch to the Rehoboth section of the commando. Her incredible historical knowledge of our people is required as a foundation or a corner stone, if you like. We have a great past that needs to be protected. Krystal shall take over when she dies."

"And where do you and my brother feature in all this?" I inquired. I decided to take a jab at them, "I suppose you three are great men?"

"Agh – no way – man!" Manasse laughed. "Old Kobus Van Wyk would have a heart attack if he heard you say that."

"Who's the kaptein?" I asked.

"We cannot disclose that to strangers," Zes said. "We have a kaptein of Rehoboth, but our overall kaptein's identity is a secret."

"And my brother?"

"He is somewhere in between a great man and a citizen. He is more or less an organiser like your father was."

"So are you returning to Australia when you have finished working here?" Klaase wanted to know. "Have you ever thought of living in Namibia? This is where you come from."

I shook my head. "I've got too much going for me back in Australia. Besides, it's my home. I've got a house and everything over there."

"What about Krystal?" Manasse demanded.

"Leave her out of it," Zes intervened. "Like Kido said – his feelings for her are none of our concern."

"Very true," I agreed. "But what about my brother? Why do we keep drifting away from the story about him?"

He leaned forward and looked at me gravely. "Ja, I know. Nevertheless, regardless of what he may have done, or what he might do – would you betray him?"

I shrugged. "He's lived his life and I've lived mine. What he's done is of no concern to me. I just want to see him, that's all. Who am I to judge?"

"Very well, then," he nodded. "We can arrange things very soon. You will not be leaving permanently in the next week or two?"

"I very much doubt it. Even if we stop drilling altogether, it'll take some time to pack things up and whatever. There's a chance that some work may come up in Botswana."

"I think you should stay," Klaase insisted and the others smilingly agreed. "This is your home and the only place for a Baster to be. One day soon we shall have our own country."

CHAPTER 43

DICKHEADS IN THE AID AGENCIES!
SERBS AND CROATS BACK IN OZ!

Back in the camp I found Dave and Dawson-Byrne yarning on as usual. The Pommy geo' was further proving that he liked just about nobody: "The lowest lives on earth are the expatriates and aid people that come over here to Africa. Nearly half the funds budgeted as 'aid' are blown away on salaries and perks for these so-called advisers. The Swedes, the Finns, the Danes – most of these creatures come from Scandinavia. From France, England, Canada and the USA, too, for that matter. There's anything between eight and eighty thousand over here at any one time. All living in the most luxurious accommodation – all with expensive cars, huge salaries, the best education for their kids, and trips backwards and forwards to their home countries. The average one earns between one hundred to one hundred and fifty thousand US dollars a year tax-free, and I'm being conservative. Most of the aid money goes on funding their bureaucracies and damned little of it makes its way down to the people who really need it... I'm not joking, these expats' are a bunch of self-serving, useless parasites who can't find employment in their own countries, so their governments – not wanting such a pitiful bunch hanging around on the dole – send them as 'advisers' over here. They're a bunch of quasi-do-gooder, loser mutations, who'd have no chance of finding employment in private business. A pious lot they are, too, who have – in a fit of petty jealousy

– gone out of their way to suck potential local entrepreneurs into non-productive farces."

"They can't all be like that?" Wheeler argued.

"Most of the ones that I've come across are," the Pommy assured him. "On my own bat and expense I travelled around Africa and saw some of these multinational aid projects, and, without fail, every one was a disaster – or was about to become one – and none were appropriate to the lives of the people they'd been designed to assist. Like I said, the Scandinavians are the lowest of all. I was in north-eastern Tanzania near the Usambara Mountains some years ago, looking at some copper deposits, and I saw how damned useless the Finns can be. The forests of the Usambaras are literally crammed-full of biological diversity. They've thousands of plant species, hundreds of which don't occur anywhere else in the world. All the same the good Finnish aid organisation, Finida, decided it would be a spiffing idea to log these forests. Income for the local Afs and an excellent source of hardwoods for the Finns themselves to resell at a very tidy profit. Their 'experts', who'd come over as advisers, decided that the best way of reaching the mature trees in the centre of the forest was by bulldozing in haul roads. For nearly five years they wiped out thousands of hectares of trees – millions of rare species – as they selected one tree at a time. It should've been a scandal, but it was helping the needy blacks – wasn't it? ... Next thing the country has record rains and the bulldozed roads are washed away, causing mud slides that wipe out villages, thus causing the deaths of hundreds of Afs. It cost the Finnish government at the time a fortune to try and make things right... No, I tell you, this 'aid' business is just an elaborate scam."

"But the aid people have helped in quite a few instances," Dave stuck to his guns. "Food-wise, I mean. Look what happened in Ethiopia with that Band-Aid and so on. What about the Rwandan refugee camps in Tanzania and Zaire? Also, what about the agricultural projects some aid outfits are involved in?"

"As I said – mostly disasters," Dawson-Byrne shook his head. "I'll answer both your questions with examples. Take Zambia as a case in point. In 1992 the country was hit with one of its worst ever famines on record and their maize crop was almost non-existent. All the donor nations bandied together and eventually, after about a year, grain relief was pouring into Zambia, though by then the rains had returned and the next crop was a bonanza. The grain kept flooding in from overseas because the various aid bureaucracies simply *could not* stop it. Grain had been collected for the Zambians and they would receive it whether they needed it or not. So naturally the price of local maize falls through the floor and the local farmers are left with a ninety thousand tonne surplus since the National Milling Company – typical Afs – was buying the cheaper donated grain via the black market... Then we have the UN Food and Agriculture Organisation, or the FAO. This shower's 'experts' decided that the Egyptians should take up fish farming. They set up dams and whatever have you, but neglected to do a simple soil sample analysis where these dams were located, considering the soil was like blotting paper and all the water was totally absorbed. So the fish died in no time... The same kind of 'expertise' was used by USAID in Mali. Their fish farm relied on a nearby irrigation canal that only carried water for about four months of the year, so when that ran out they then had to go to the huge expense of installing a diesel pump. For the remainder of the year they had to pump water from a well two kilometres away, and the final cost of the fish was around five thousand dollars US a kilogram... Look, I'll give you an absolute fact. In the '80s about seventy-five percent of the World Bank's agricultural projects failed in sub-Saharan Africa! Nonetheless, what the hell do they do with these aid 'experts' who get all the stupendous salaries, posh housing and perks? They just put them on the next *brilliant* scheme... Take my word for it, David, the international aid bureaucracy's deeply dangerous to the people it claims to help. It's legitimised brutal despots here in Africa and has an organisation of self-serving hypocrites. Aid's a waste of time and money. It's now become a multi-billion-dollar, self-perpetuating industry with a massively bloated, useless, often corrupt bureaucracy that in the main causes more disasters than it averts."

"But not necessarily in places like Rwanda and Dafur," Dave insisted. "Apparently they're saving countless thousands of lives up there."

"And for what?" Dawson-Byrne was unimpressed. "They've only been upsetting the local ecology. Like the Serbs, Croats and Bosnians – the Hutu, Tutsi and Sudanese have been slaughtering each other for centuries. It's good for the environment, as it helps keep the population in sensible and manageable numbers."

"Those fuckin' Serbs and Croats are bunch of murdering dickheads," I felt it necessary to partly agree him.

That perked him up. "They're no better than the Afs are. Like the Germans, they love their little bit of genocide. Women, children – all the better. Bunch of sick cowards, the whole damned lot of them. Children against children, neighbour against neighbour – the bunch of them sadistic, perverted cowards, rapists and murderers."

Wheeler, who generally wasn't into cultural bigotry and mostly tried to discourage it, also had shit to pour all over those people from the Balkans. "Yeah, I read in the paper that the fuckin' Serbs and Croats are up to their fuckin' bullshit back in Aussie, the friggin' queer bastards."

"How so?' I asked him.

"They're getting stuck into one another at soccer matches over in Sydney – burning cars and shooting at each others' clubhouses. They're scaring the fuck out of the Sydney cops."

"Yes, just what Australia needs," the Pommy agreed with him. "Imported ethnic hatred amongst the Serbs and the Croats fouling up your country. Really decent imports you have there. I wonder how long it'll take for them to start mowing each other down with machine guns and hand grenades? Soon you'll be getting innocent Aussie women and children being caught in the crossfire, and there'll be blood all over Sydney's streets. As I said, they're no better than the blacks over here... Nevertheless, returning to Rwanda, I was there shortly after the genocide. Came in from Uganda. A friend of mine who's a doctor volunteered to help out in one of the refugee clinics in Zaire. Talk about the noble savage. Half the medical and food aid was siphoned off by the Zairian government people, which they in turn sold back to the aid agencies for five times the price. Relief planes couldn't land without paying exorbitant fees to local officials who were running little empires of their own. Zaire – or the Democratic Republic of Congo as it's known now – can no longer be classified as a country with borders and cohesive administration. It's one massive free-for-all. Old Mobutu drained the innards out of the country decades ago and now the current gangsters are mopping up what little's left. The Af doesn't give a damn about his fellow black, aside from what he can loot, plunder and steal off him. The refugee situation's been a godsend to some of the local thieving entrepreneurs. Who gives a damn about how many innocents are chopped up? The '*innocents*' – if given the opportunity – would gladly change places and introduce their own particular brand of mayhem. I mean it – there are no innocents in all this. Each group takes turns in annihilating the other. The Hutu woke up one morning and decided to wipe out the Tutsi. As a matter of fact the French government and the South Africans trained the killers and supplied all the weapons. There were over thirty thousand trained, and their orders came from the highest Hutu authorities. There was a list drawn up of all the names and addresses of the Tutsi in the various neighbourhoods. It was the same as with the Germans – it was very organised genocide. The leading Rwandan radio station was calling out to the Hutu to kill every Tutsi they could find. The damned Frogs made a big show of saving Tutsi lives once the massacre was on, but it was only to save some kind of face. As usual – like the Yanks always do – they'd backed the wrong side. Now it's the Tutsi's turn to get their own back on the Hutu, and *they shall* as sure as night follows day." He topped up his whisky and looked off into the distance. "I saw the Hutu refugees marching back to Rwanda. All along the way their *own* people ambushed and pillaged them, plus the Zairian rebel Tutsi and the so-called Zairian Army. I saw how a Hutu woman had been hacked to death because another Hutu wanted her sack full of fire kindling. I watched another woman trudging along, leading two toddlers by the hand. Her older daughter was carrying an infant on her back. When the mother wasn't looking, the girl let the baby drop on the track and kept on walking. It was dead by nightfall. When the mother found out, she said nothing. It was similar to taking a puppy or kitten off its mother – nothing was said – there even seemed less signs of regret... Tragic victims, you could say? What a load of codswallop! Those Hutu, or at least ninety-eight percent of them, all thought massacring the Tutsi was a terrific idea. Hutu professionals – doctors and even nuns – all gladly took part in the killings. Then, when the refugees had been herded into the camps, the Hutu militias murdered and terrorised *their own* people... And all us so-called civilised Brits, Aussies and whoever else are shocked and horrified, are we? Don't worry, in a couple of years' time it'll start all over again in both Rwanda and Burundi."

CHAPTER 44

THE RAIN COMES! NICK GETS HIS FERRET OUT! KOTZÉ GETS DONE! VAN DER MERWE DEAD!

Half a dozen test drill sites had been set out on the ground adjacent to Seebacher's claims. We were half way through the job when it started pissing down with rain, which made moving the rig bloody awkward. For drilling purposes the rain was a total pain-in-the-arse; the samples couldn't be split and there was mud and shit everywhere. To the local Namibians, on the other hand, the torrential showers brought enormous joy! The pubs and watering holes in Karibib soon became venues of much celebration amongst the German and Boer farmers. We drillers decided to give the Hotel Ströblehof a rest for a while and we ventured on to the Hotel Kaiserblick. It was night and things had progressed very nicely when all of a sudden some German sheila decided to kick everybody out! It wasn't that late, so naturally we considered her actions totally up to shit, and at first we decided to ignore her 'last drinks' commands.

She kept on at us and insisted that we should leave, so she was really starting to bug all and sundry. Especially Nick, who was as pissed as a ferret. For some reason best known to himself, he reckoned he had a more than even chance of invading her pants. It was hard to work out why he was so chuffed, for she wasn't unlike a racing goanna or a Queensland cane toad as far as looks went. He tried saying all the right things in order to achieve his evil ambitions, yet was met with the absolute cold-shoulder. In the end, possibly in sheer desperation, he got his donger out and pointed it at her. It wasn't a pretty sight; all erect and throbbing; purple veins sticking out all over the place; foreskin pulled back to reveal a plum-like head. That didn't make her soften one bit and she had the cops over in seconds flat!

A fairly decent dispute cropped up when three black cops arrived. Us drillers, the farmers, the locals; all to a man denied that Nick could have been so ungentlemanly. The sheila then started blubbing and ordered the cops at the top of her voice that we should be thrown out. An argument ensued about the proper closing time, but – possibly as a result of the good rains we were having – all agreed to vacate the premises forthwith. That made the cops so happy they actually recommended that we should soldier on at a bar-cum-nightclub that was situated in the main street of Karibib. In no time at all we were surrounded by local black and coloured women, plus eardrum-splitting music, so it looked as if Nick wasn't about to waste his hard-on after all. The black sheila that ripped Ernie off was also there; although she soon made herself scarce. Those local Karabibian punters certainly liked their music at full-bore. So much so, some of the town's elite – mostly whites – actually objected to all the noise. Their whinging and carrying on was hopelessly in vain, for the black cops, who were fairly pissed themselves, had knocked off for the night and they also really liked their music flat out.

Jeff won a couple of hundred bucks in a beer guzzling competition with his former adversary, Otto. The dopey Kraut just couldn't take a lesson. When it was time to head back to the camp Jeff then decided to shit in his daks. We didn't know if he had done it on purpose or not; even so it was sheer bloody murder sitting next to him as we headed home. Ernie and I tried to make him sit on the tray of our Land Cruiser, but he became belligerent and we were too pissed to force the issue.

When we reached our tents, we – once again – came across all kinds of confusion! Kotzé had had seven kinds of crap kicked out of him!

There was no other way to describe it. He was a real hospital case and the labourers were all milling around in a panic. In our drunken stupor we didn't know what to do, and Dawson-Byrne was nowhere to be found. The Japie geo' was in such a bad way that we weren't game to move him. Whoever had laid into him certainly knew their business, for his face was pulped and his beard was like a bloated sponge full of blood. Dave lifted his shirt up and his guts was a mass of bruised swellings. The Japie geo' was moaning and carrying on; however his mouth was too full of blood from the teeth that had been knocked out. Ernie bombarded him with questions, but the Boer was totally incoherent.

At long last an ambulance from Okahandja carted him off and when the sun came up the following day we had quite a few mysteries to dwell on. "It was that Pommy bastard," Wheeler told me adamantly when we were alone together. "I bet it's 'cause of what happened to his dog."

"Van der Merwe was with Kotzé last night," I reminded him. "Where the fuck's he got to?"

"Fuck knows. Kotzé's vehicle's still here."

When Ernie asked the labourers what had happened, they told him that a white or beige Land Rover had pulled up just outside the lighted area of the camp. Kotzé and Van der Merwe had approached the vehicle and there was a fair palaver carried out in Afrikaans, followed by a great deal of shouting and swearing and so on. Since the altercation was obviously between whites, the labourers had decided to keep their distance and mind their own business. Kotzé had only just managed to reach the tents before passing out, and there had been no sign since of Van der Merwe's whereabouts. The skinny, sockless Boer had simply vanished altogether!

Naturally the cops became involved and some top brass came all the way from Windhoek. They had taken matters to heart since the Boer geo' had lost an eye and had severe haemorrhaging from where his crutch had been kicked to scrambled eggs. Us jokers, who had been in town, certainly had had nothing to do with it and neither did Seebacher who had gone back to Klein Aub in a desperate bid to salvage the reputation of his claims. Van der Merwe was nowhere to be found, so that left Dawson-Byrne.

Herman was also missing and I questioned Wilfred about that. The two could seldom be found apart; therefore Herman's absence was mystifying.

"I do not know, man," Wilfred looked equally confused. "When he saw you and the others driving off to town, he went down to the main road and started hitchhiking. He said he would be back this morning."

"Where was he going?"

"Karibib, boss. He has some friends in the black location."

"So he could be back at any moment?"

"Ja, man, especially now that we are working."

The cops organised a search party for Van der Merwe, and the farmer whose property we were on and some of his mates joined in. They even found a little Bushman joker in Usakos who was supposed to be a gun tracker.

During the time all that was going on Dawson-Byrne pitched up and demanded from Dave and I why we weren't drilling? It started raining cats and dogs again, making things even more awkward. Wheeler and I looked him up and down rather warily and told him what had happened.

"Don't look at me like that," he objected. "I was in Windhoek chasing up sample results. How on earth could people just come up to the camp – beat the living daylights out of Kotzé – abduct Van der Merwe – then simply drive off? I know you disliked the Boer, but isn't that taking things a bit far? Besides, did the stupid cretin have any other enemies?"

"We were in Karabib," Dave pointed out. "Kotzé was a bit of a dickhead, still whoever thumped him was playing for flamin' keeps. We found him more dead than alive."

"Let's carry on with the drilling, shall we?" the Pommy seemed bored with the subject. "I can't promise you too many more metres because it looks as if we've really got some barren ground on our hands."

I went to go find Nick and Jeff, and then there was quite a bit of shouting and carrying on taking place at Seebacher's old mine workings. The end result of it all was that the Bushman had led the searchers to an old underlay shaft, and at the bottom of it was Van der Merwe. Dead as a mullet!

"This is reelie seerious!" a white cop inspector kept saying over and over. "We have a murder investigation on our hands now. This man was bashed before he went down the hole. The fall is not what killed him, he has bled to death. This is reelie seerious!"

"By Jesus!" Dave whispered in my ear, careful that the Pommy was nowhere near. "This has to be Dawson-Byrne's doing. He was trained to do stuff like this."

"But they reckon there was two of 'em," I pointed out to him. "We'll soon see, as he'll need to have an alibi if he really was in Windhoek. Christ, if Kotzé and Van der Merwe were the bastards who killed his dog, a bloody good thumping should've done the trick. Chucking jokers down mine shafts is jumping off the deep end a bit."

"Fuckin' oath – it is! " Wheeler was in full agreement. "It was Dawson-Byrne, I bloody tell you! You saw his face when he reckoned he knew who'd killed his dog. He had an accomplice or something... The whole thing is, the labourers never saw anyone going over to the mine workings. There was a fair bit of a moon last night."

"Yeah, but it was raining off and on. The clouds could've blocked it out when they dumped Van der Merwe."

The cops really got stuck into things after that. The little Bushman bloke was convinced that two people, carrying a light to medium load, had approached the mine workings. By the way the blood trail indicated, Van der Merwe was still alive when he was being carted to the shaft. Though the rain had washed away most of the evidence, the two people concerned had then returned to the white Land Rover, and once the vehicle had reached the main road it was pointed west towards Swakopmund.

We all had to give statements to the white cop, who kept telling everyone to slow down so that he could take notes. His writing was like a four year old kid's and his spelling was pathetic. He was obviously from the old regime; uneducated; overbearing; a dickhead in general. He must have thought he was back in the old Apartheid era when it came to interviewing me: "Where were you given this passport?"

"Kalgoorlie – Western Australia."

"Are you sure it is yours?"

"It says so on the front page. That's a photograph of me, isn't it – so what's the fuckin' problem?"

"You might have a problem if you keep swearing and give me any more of your lip. Where did you get this passport?"

"I told you."

Wheeler had come along by then. "What the fuck's happening, Joe?"

"Kindly stay away when I am interrogating this man," the cop told him.

"He doesn't believe that this's my passport," I explained. "Have I changed that much since I've been here?"

Dave was a little displeased with the cop's behaviour. "For fucksakes! Nick – Jeff – get your arses over here! Is this Joe's passport, or is it fuckin' not?"

Nick didn't help one scrap! "Nah, officer, I've never seen this joker until yesterday. He doesn't look like an Aussie to me. More like one of your Baster blokes. He's probably stolen the passport."

That had the dickheaded cop calling for reinforcements; nevertheless sanity prevailed once Nick admitted he was only bullshitting and he and the others swore blind that they had known me back in Australia for years. The inspector wasn't overly enchanted and muttered something under his breath about Australians being arrogant and me having a doppelganger and being too smart a '*Hotnot*' by far. I was still fairly pissed off with Nick, and was plotting to give him a whack around the ear with a shifting spanner, just like Jeff had done back in

West Aussie. A dent in the other side of his head would balance him out a bit.

Much to Dave's and my interest, Dawson-Byrne reckoned he had booked into the Windhoek Country Club and the security people there could vouch that his vehicle had gone nowhere during the night. He even claimed that he had watched the CNN news most of the time in his room, and there had been some opinion poll amongst the Yanks whether same-sex marriages should be allowed or not. Of all the Yanks interviewed; sixty-two percent appeared happy with poofters and lesbians marrying one another. That really charmed Wheeler no end, and he carried on about his Greek and Roman civilisation theory.

Nick had the most perfect alibi of all, as how could the German sheila at the Hotel Kaiserblick *ever* forget him brandishing his pork sword at her?"

CHAPTER 45

HERMAN'S BODY FOUND!

The mystery of Herman's disappearance was cleared up about a week later. Some blacks, who had been grazing a German farmer's cattle on the side of the Karibib-Okahandja road, had noticed a swarm of flies buzzing around a culvert. After looking to see what was attracting the insects, they had found Herman's body which was seriously starting to stink! We drillers got to hear about it while we were having a few beers at the Hotel Ströblehof. A coloured had been found under a culvert just east of Karabib with his head bashed in! No identification had been found on the body.

"I bet it's fuckin' Herman," I told Nick and Dave.

"It could be," Wheeler agreed. "How long's he been missing?"

"Must be nearly a week," Nick was certain.

"Let's go over to the cop shop," I suggested, "so's we can find out for sure. Fuckin' hell – I hope it's not him."

The Karibib cops reckoned the body had been carted to Windhoek, so Dave, Nick and I decided to go there. Jeff and Ernie didn't want a bar of dead bodies.

We first went to the Windhoek cop shop that was across from the Hotel Thüringer Hof. When the cops at the front desk found out the purpose of our mission they called the Japie inspector who had interrogated us at the drill site. He saw me and didn't bother hiding his suspicion. "What do you know about this?" he demanded from me.

"We've got a coloured drill offsider who's gone missing," Wheeler stepped in. "We heard about a body being found on the Karabib road. It could be him?"

"And why do you think it is him?" the white cop wanted to know.

That upset Dave. "It's bloody obvious, isn't it? A coloured joker goes missing from our outfit and a coloured's been found in a culvert not far from where we're drilling. If you don't want our help, you can go and fuck your boot! Come on, you blokes," he told Nick and me, "let's get the fuck out of here!"

That humbled the dickheaded cop. "The body is in the morgue at the Katutura hospital. If it is your worker, we need you to identify the corpse."

"Much fuckin' better!" Dave pointed out to him.

The drive to the Katutura hospital was terrific! We went in an unmarked, white Toyota Camry police car and the black driver, an Ovambo, drove as if he was after bank robbers. We had no flashing lights or anything like that, but under the bonnet of the vehicle there was a siren that made all sorts of horrendous noises. We reached speeds of up to one hundred and seventy! In and out of the traffic we flew; through red lights and all, and the Ovambo nearly lost everything on one corner! He assured us that everything was okay, as he often drove in President Sam Nujoma's motorcade. I noticed that the white cop had used his own transport.

Herman was lying there on a morgue drawer like a beached mullet. Some disinfectant or whatever had been poured over him; even so it did nothing to stop the stench. A hospital orderly lifted his head to show the gash in the top of his head. Someone had hit him so hard that pieces of his skull had sliced through his brain! He had been found with his pockets empty; hence the cops had put his misfortune down to a fatal mugging.

"Would he have been carrying much money?" the Japie cop asked Wheeler.

"Wouldn't have a clue."

"He was on pretty good money," I told the cop. "He was always flashing it around in Rehoboth. He had this ostrich skin wallet and he never carried less than five hundred or so in it."

"It must have been robbery, then," the Japie was convinced.

"So what you gunna do about it?" Wheeler asked him.

"The Karibib police are investigating. We have our hands full with what happened out at your campsite. We have one murder to investigate already, plus a brutal assault."

Dave wasn't reassured by that. "So you're spending all your time checking out a white's murder? So that's your priority, is it? Coloured jokers – don't they fuckin' count?"

"Come on, Dave," I grabbed his arm. "Herman's dead and you carrying on isn't gunna help anybody."

The ride back into the city centre was even quicker, and I was positive the Ovambo driver was trying to break his record over the same distance. Even better, we got him to drop us off right in front of the Wurlitzer Bar; his siren wailing. That harvested quite a few queer looks from the other punters. "We've just robbed a bank," Nick told all and sundry, "and that was our getaway driver dropping us off!"

CHAPTER 46

WE GO TO A FUNERAL! A HUNDRED AND SIXTY PROOF RUM! JEFF TRIES TO GET INTO A BLUE WITH SOME GERMAN FARMERS! THE CORPSE FARTS IN THE COFFIN!

Not long after that Wilfred asked for a couple of days leave, for he wanted to go to Herman's funeral that was being held down at Kalkrand. "Let's go to the funeral?" I suggested to the other Aussies. "He was one of our crew, so let's show him some respect? The Baster people would probably appreciate it?"

"Fuck that!" Jeff was dead against it. "I've never been to a funeral and ain't ever gunna go to one. The only funeral I'm gunna go to is my own."

"And who's gunna carry your flamin' coffin?" Dave fired at him. "You might go to your own funeral, but no fucker's gunna go with you!"

"Yeah, let's go!" Nick was all for it. "It'll give us something to do. Beats the fuck out of hanging around here. We can always get on the piss after."

"Yeah, we can," I assured him.

"You take your own fuckin' transport, if you're gunna do that," Ernie told me. "Remember what happened to Bob and Steve."

"Who's going then?" I asked all of them. "We can take my bus, but there's only room for five at the most."

"We're *all* fuckin' going!" Wheeler declared. "If Bob and Steve had been buried over here, we would've all gone to their funerals. Let's show the people around here we've got *some* bloody culture, huh?"

"You're only looking for an excuse to get on the piss, you fuckin' alky," Jeff wasn't persuaded. "Nick, you want to go because you might get to fuck a Baster sheila... Hey, Joe," he turned to me, "I wouldn't go letting this white trash get in amongst your women. He'll give all your people the pox."

Jeff's last remark pressed home the change in attitude amongst my workmates. It seemed that in Namibia they no longer regarded me as an Aussie but a Baster. Although it had been subtle, I didn't quite know how to take that change of outlook. I asked myself which would I prefer being looked upon as – a Baster or an Aussie? Krystal was a Baster and the most beautiful human on God's earth; however the other Baster I had come across hadn't really impressed me all that much. Old Jakobus and *Ouma* Elsabeth and the other coloureds I had seen around Rehoboth. Besides their Afrikaner accents and way of talking English, they smelled different. They used soap and deodorants just like my Aussie associates did; still my nose didn't react to them in the same way. Would I prefer to live among the Baster in Rehoboth rather than the whites back in Kalgoorlie? Absolutely no way, as I was totally unlike them other than my skin colour. To have Krystal living with me in my old house in Lamington – who could give a damn if I was an Aussie, Baster or even an abo or Asian?

"You can stay behind and look after the gear?" Dave suggested to Jeff.

Jeff liked that alternative even less, so on the day of the funeral the five of us stuffed ourselves into my groaning Mercedes. Being the driver, I made the others draw straws to see who would be sitting in the front with me. As luck would have it, Dave won, and it was hilarious watching the others squeezing into the back seat. Jeff and Nick, both big men, had the skinny, little mechanic wedged between them.

"Fucksakes, get your elbow out of my balls, Ernie!" Jeff complained. "Just keep still, ya fuckin' mutant!"

"Hey, Ernie, cop a whiff of this," Nick forced the mechanic's face under his sodden armpit and the little prick almost gagged. So much for him being Nick's boss!

We weren't actually going to go to the funeral service, but would be attending the graveside ceremony. There was no possibility that Dave, Nick or Jeff had any intention of entering a church under any circumstances, and there was absolutely no chance of me going anywhere near some poxy Catholic set up. They had some really queer times for doing things, nonetheless, since the Catholic Church service was only going to be held at three in the afternoon in Rehoboth, and the coffin was only expected to be lowered into the ground in Kalkrand between five and six. We arrived at the Aris Hotel about lunchtime.

"Pull up!" Dave instructed me. "You never fuckin' know when dehydration's gunna set in. We've only gotta be in Kalkrand around five, so there's plenty of friggin' time to kill."

We started off with Tafel Lager. Shortly after, for some idiotic reason, Nick suggested we should toast our lost comrade, Herman. Beer alone wasn't good enough for that – no way – consequently we ordered Stürtebecker schnapps. Toast after toast was called; *fiege* or fig schnapps chased down with Tafel; *pflaume* or plum schnapps chased down with Tafel; *apfel* or apple schnapps chased down with Tafel; *pumpelmuse* or grapefruit schnapps chased down with Tafel; *waldbeere* or wildberry schnapps, and so on. If that wasn't enough, we then got stuck into the Stroh '80' rum, an Austrian spirit that was eighty percent alcohol or a hundred and sixty proof!

The bar in the Aris hotel was festooned with game trophies; the heads of springbok, kudu, impala, oryx and wart hogs were on every wall, and that nearly started a punch-up! In pride of place, hanging over the middle of the bar, was a huge wart hog head. The head's glass eyes bulged out in all directions; its tusks threatened all below, and it had a really pissed off look on its face! While we were happily guzzling Stroh rum and Tafel, two German farmers had come in and they got into a fairly deep conversation in German with the hotel owner, who was obviously of the same nationality. Nick captured their attention by slamming a Tafel bottle down on the bar. He pointed up at the wart hog head, and then suggested to the Germans: "He is your Kaiser – yaarrr? Kaiser Von Schwein – yaarrr?"

The Germans totally ignored him and that troubled Jeff. He got up from his barstool and stood before the glaring wart hog. Then, after clicking his heels sharply together, he threw out a Nazi salute: "Heil Hitler!"

One of the Germans, who was roughly the same size as Nick, advanced on Jeff with his fists up. Dave, being the fucking killjoy that he was, quickly jumped between the two of them, waving his arms like a windmill and apologising as fast as he could go. The upshot of it all was that the owner wouldn't sell us any more grog and he was prepared to call the cops if we didn't leave his hostelry forthwith, so we bought two more bottles of *pflaume* schnapps from the bottle store beside the hotel, plus a crate of Tafel.

After stopping off in Rehoboth for some smokes and biltong, we pulled up at a rest stop about six miles north of Kalkrand in order that we could take a slash. We were all as rat-arsed as stung mullets! Wheeler was almost incoherent, "We can't pitch up pissed like this. We'll – we'll just make fuckin' dickheads out of ourselves. Wassa fuckin' time?"

Jeff was that soused he could hardly read his watch. "S'only three – time for one more."

"Fuckin' bullshit!" I told him. "We've gotta try'n sober up."

"One more beer," Wheeler insisted.

"Fuck you, Dave!" I was adamant. "Like you said – we'll only make arseholes out of ourselves."

We camped at the rest stop and tried to overcome the effects of the grog. At about four-thirty a blue bakkie went past with a coffin on the back and we counted at least fifty cars and bakkies full of coloureds following it. "Fuck me dead, the world and his flamin' wife are gunna be there!" Dave was positive.

BASTARDS FROM THE BUSH

The Kalkrand cemetery was in an open space of ground not far from the N7 Highway to South Africa and it was crammed with Baster of all descriptions. There was a cloudless sky and the place was sweltering despite it being fairly late in the afternoon. Desperately trying to disguise our inebriated state, we snuck in and stood coyly just inside the gate. Every coloured in that cemetery was staring at me; also busy pointing in my direction and whispering to each other. Dave noticed what was going on and he, too, whispered in my ear. "What's happening? Why they all staring at you?"

"Fucked if I know," I whispered back. "What makes you think they're only staring at me? They're probably surprised we're here."

Then Wilfred came up to me and took me to one side. He also spoke in hushed tones: "Your brother could not be here, boss, so could you take his place and be a pallbearer?"

His request both sobered and frightened the crap out of me. "No – way! I can't do that. I've had a fair bit to drink. I'm too drunk. I can't! Find someone else."

"Everyone has been drinking, boss. Except for the women, most of the people here are a little drunk. Please, boss, it would make *Ouma* Elsabeth and Uncle Kobus very happy. Krystal – too."

"Elsabeth and Krystal are here?"

"Ja, man," he pointed to the other side of the cemetery. True enough, there was Elsabeth and Krystal in the company of Kobus and Sophia van Wyk, plus some other ancient woman.

Krystal waved a white handkerchief in my direction and that sobered me even further. I turned to Dave. "They want me to help carry the coffin!"

He was a really big help: "Don't drop the cunt!"

Like some condemned man being led to the gallows, I followed Wilfred over to the blue bakkie. There was a fair bit of stuffing around when it came to lining us pallbearers up in pairs because the priest wanted the coffin as level as possible. As it turned out I was paired off with Herman's uncle, whose breath stank like a dog's turd. Then, just as we approached the open grave, farting noises and belching started coming from inside the coffin and the six of us nearly dropped everything! Herman's uncle's eyes stuck out on stalks and the joker in front of me was shaking like a leaf and also farting with fear. Then there was a stuff up with the lowering ropes and we nearly somersaulted the casket into the hole!

I was drenched in sweat by the time I got back to Wheeler and the others. "You sure Herman was bloody dead when we saw him?" I whispered in Dave's ear.

"Fuckin' oath, he was! Why?"

"There were farting noises coming from the coffin! True as God – we fuckin' near dropped it!"

Dave knew all about that sort of thing. "It's the bloody heat. Those would've been body gases escaping. Herman's folks probably wouldn't've been able to afford proper embalming. Look at that bakkie – they obviously couldn't afford a proper hearse, either, so the coffin must've been baking in the sun. You get a fright?"

"Fuckin' near scared the living shit out of me!"

As the crowd broke up and we headed out of the cemetery, Wilfred grabbed my sleeve. "Please wait for *Ouma* Elsabeth and Krystal. They want to thank you for being a pallbearer and for the rest of you for coming to Herman's funeral."

I ended up introducing Elsabeth and Krystal to my Aussie associates. The old woman who was with them was a niece of Elsabeth's. After that, out of nowhere, Dawson-Byrne suddenly appeared. He was with Kobus van Wyk and Kobus' brother, Manfred. I was introduced to a whole lot more coloureds after that and they all looked at me as if they had seen a ghost.

"Who was that sheila, Krystal?" Nick wanted to know as we headed back in the direction of Windhoek.

My hackles rose. "She's a cousin of Wilfred's. Why?"

"What a fuckin' little ripper!" Nick was adamant.

"Bloody oath!" Jeff agreed. "What a little honey!"

I was instantly proud. "A Baster woman for you."

"What the fuck was Dawson-Byrne doing there?" Dave changed the subject. "The dickheaded snob – he fuckin' ignored us."

"What the fuck would he want to talk to you for?" Nick challenged. "Even though he's a Pom', he's got *some* fuckin' pride."

"Why don't you get fucked, you cretinous moron?" Wheeler suggested.

"Hey, don't use big words like that, Dave," Jeff butted in. "Nick might think you're paying him a compliment."

"True, Dave," Nick agreed. "If you love me – just say it." After so saying, he dropped a fart that flooded the car.

"Hey! Joe! Stop the car!" Ernie yelled. "I'm gunna fuckin' chunder! Stop the friggin' car!"

We had desperate bodies going in all directions once I pulled the vehicle up. Ernie was crouched over spewing his guts up, and Jeff was chasing Nick down the road: "I'll fuckin' kill you – you bastard – I'll fuckin' kill you!" Talk about déjà vu!

A white Opel sedan pulled up behind the Mercedes. Kobus Van Wyk was driving and he had Wilfred, his brother Manfred, plus Krystal and Elsabeth with him. "What is happening?" Kobus wanted to know.

That was the last thing I needed, what with Ernie chundering and Jeff wanting to kill Nick. "One of our people's sick," I offered stupidly.

Kobus obviously wasn't satisfied. "Why is that fellow chasing the other? Why is he shouting?"

"They're only having a bit of fun. They've had a fair bit to drink. I think the funeral might've upset 'em."

"Come round and visit, Kido," Elsabeth instructed, and then Kobus drove off.

I was pissed off as hell. "You fuckin' animal, Ernie!" I berated him. Jeff and Nick had come back to the car by then, so I ploughed into them also, "Grow up, ya dickheaded arseholes!"

"What the fuck gives with him?" Nick asked no one in particular.

CHAPTER 47

SMART-ARSED HUNGARIAN GEOPHYSICIST!

As a last resort Dawson-Byrne called in a geophysics mob to try and locate further drilling targets. According to the Pommy geo' there may have been a shear zone running diagonally across the new piece of ground that he had applied for, and that it had possibly been the source of what little gold there was on Seebacher's claims. The geophysicist in charge of the geophysics crew was an expat Hungarian who the Pommy introduced as being a Doctor Andreas Onda.

While killing a few beers outside Dawson-Byrne's tent, Wheeler was crapping on about something the Boers had done wrong in Namibia. Actually Dave had shit on his liver when it came to the whites in both Namibia and South Africa.

"I have recently returned from Australia and New Zealand," Onda informed him. "When I am not in the field I lecture at the Rhodes University in South Africa. I was asked to speak to the students at the University of Western Australia, then at the Otago University in the south island of New Zealand. The topic was the possibility of economic ore bodies to be found in the Proterozoic. I was over there for about six weeks. You Australians certainly do not have all that much to be proud of."

"Oh Yeah?" Jeff immediately started to bristle.

Onda grinned. "You paint yourselves as 'tanned Anzacs' or something like that. You are supposed to worship your sportsmen and women.

BASTARDS FROM THE BUSH

I recently saw on the television that some of your Olympic athletes have complained about other countries whose athletes are taking steroids, and they are accusing everyone of cheating. When it comes to cheating, what about that kind of football that is your national game?"

"Aussie Rules, you mean?" Nick asked.

"Ja, that is the one! Every week you have players going on to the field deliberately setting out to cheat. Sporting violence is supposed to be forbidden in your country, yet it is the favourite past time of the players, and the crowds and commentators simply love it. Every week there are tribunals where players are accused of punching, kicking, eye-gouging, spitting, pinching and biting. Throughout the country countless players are called up because of violence on the field. You even have people buying videos of all the violence, as if they cannot see enough of it during the games... Talk about the hypocrisy!"

Jeff became all repugnant, "Yeah, but you wogs wouldn't have the guts to play Aussie Rules football." That was so typical of his rather blunt approach! We hadn't known the Hungarian for more than a couple of hours, and there was Jeff calling him a 'wog'!

Nevertheless, that just seemed to bounce off the geophysicist. "Ah, so it is necessary to be brave to play such a game? You are from Western Australia and I understand you have two favourite teams – the Eagles and some other one? I cannot remember its name?"

"The mighty Fremantle Dockers!" Nick held his fists in the air.

"Fuck the Dockers!" Jeff scorned him. "They have to sit down when they take a piss."

"So, you are an Eagles supporter?" Onda asked him.

"My oath!" Jeff was adamant. "The fuckin' Dockers are a bunch of sheilas."

"Is that true?" Onda seemed pleased. "Then perhaps you can explain this ritual that the Eagles players have at the end of the football season?"

"What do you mean?"

The Hungarian shook his head in mock amazement. "You say that only brave men can play this game? Then why do the Eagles players like to dress up in their wives and girlfriends' clothing – evening dresses, high-heels, lipstick and earrings? Apparently it is a passion with them at the end of the season?"

That had Jeff completely stumped, but he wasn't going to give up without a fight: "We've only got a population of twenty million and look how many sports we're world champions in. Cricket, Swimming, women's netball, rugby league, rugby..."

"Ah yes, rugby league!" Onda burst out laughing. "The world has heard about your rugby league teams and how they go to motels to bond with one another. Where they drink too much alcohol then pack rape women with absolute impunity as a result of their clubs and the police gathering together to discredit their victims. When are the rape victims' stories ever believed by the courts, police or the press? If there is one thing about your Australian Rules footballers and rugby league players – they certainly appear to have a low regard for your Australian women. Surely you agree there may be something rather odd about that? Not only do your nation's sportsmen treat women like so much garbage, you see contempt for women everywhere. In Europe, and even amongst the blacks here in Africa, we come across titles and labels of endearment for women, but amongst your young men in Australia you hear the terms 'sluts', 'molls', 'slags', 'bitches', 'town bikes' and 'bush pigs' used in many cases. Do these young men and boys use this terminology because they resent their own inadequacies, or is it the result of the total lack of a civilised upbringing? Australian men seem to have an obsession about a woman's morality, yet they take huge pride in their own immorality. Everywhere I went... "

"Have you found us any more drill holes, Andreas?" Dave quickly tried to move the conversation onto other matters, for Jeff had that look on his face that meant the Hungarian was fast becoming overdue for a smack in the mouth! Nick and I rather fancied the sight of Jeff exploding, as the geophysicist bastard was just an outside contractor, so – if Jeff thumped him – there was no chance of him getting the tramp.

"Unfortunately not," Onda also appeared to have sensed the danger. "The shear that James thought might be to the west of here is only a band of iron-rich schist. It comes to the surface on the north-eastern border of the claims. Such schist belts are common here in the Erongo region and they are generally barren."

CHAPTER 48

DICKHEADED AFRICAN LEADERS AND SAVAGES! ALOE VERA IN SHIT PAPER!

The conversation drifted over to Africa's shortcomings and it became obvious that Onda and the Pommy were both up to date with the continent's affairs. "I notice that all of – or most of Africa's – current leaders have assembled around Mwalimu's grave?" Dawson-Byrne turned to Onda.

"Ja, I saw that," the Hungarian nodded. "I see the old man has died at long last. At least there is some good news to be had out of Africa nowadays."

"And who's this Mwalimu?" I broke in.

The Pommy searched around for a cigar, and then took his time unravelling the cellophane wrapper. "Now for those of you who don't know who Mwalimu is – he's our dearly departed Julius – Kambarage – Nyerere, or 'Teacher'. He used to be the president of Tanzania and the Afs are claiming that he's Africa's 'father'. We're having all this sorrow over a man who condemned his country to unadulterated poverty and strife through his idiotic social reforms. The cretin's finally fallen off this mortal coil and all of Africa's leaders are supposedly totally grief-stricken... Are these people really brainless, or do they totally lack self-respect, moral fibre or human dignity? The Afs seem to revere the long line of thugs and dictators Africa produces. Leaders that plunder their countries into a coma, then hold out the begging bowl to white run nations while at the same time openly insulting them. The defenders of the noble savage would be appalled at me running down poor, old Julius, but when will they wake up to the fact that under black leadership Africa is – to ninety percent of its citizens – a continent of corruption, poverty, pestilence, disease, war, deprivation, famine and outright fear? While the same do-gooders look on with rapt detachment at the succession of demagogues, thieves and murderers – who barely manage to stay one step ahead of their incompetence, excesses and murderous ways – what about the average Af in the street? I, for one, can't think of any black leader of modern, post-colonial times who could stand on the world stage and deservedly and substantially qualify for any modicum of greatness. When it comes..."

"What about Nelson Mandela?" Dave pushed in.

"I was just about to refer to him as being one incredible exception," Dawson-Byrne nodded. "Nonetheless, in the do-gooders' search for such icons, they've been rewarded with poverty, pestilence, fear and mass murder. In fact, under the patronage of the civil libertarians and lovers of Afs, these strutting and posing murderers and buffoons are letting the entire continent slide totally and inexorably to its doom. No wonder that eighteen out of the World's twenty poorest nations are African? Seriously, when you consider the history of Africa over the last forty years, what can the defenders of the noble savage be so chuffed about? While not mentioning Robber Mugarbage and his generals in Zimbabwe – what about Uganda under Idi Amin and Milton Obote? Then there's the current situation in the Sudan, also Somalia after the glorious rule of Siad Barre, and that's not bringing to your attention Liberia under Charles Taylor and when Ethiopia was under the rule of Mariam Mengistu. All the aforementioned countries, plus Angola, Sierra Leone, Mozambique, Rwanda and Burundi, plus the Democratic Republic of Congo have seemingly held a competition in atrocity where millions of people have been programmed to endure indiscriminate slaughter, torture, amputations, starvation and fear.

Parents have been murdered by their children, sisters raped by their brothers, and neighbour has murdered and pillaged neighbour. Most of Africa's now become a place where even good, old-fashioned, wholesome violence has become debauched."

"What James says is true," Onda was all agreement. "You take what happened in Sierra Leone's civil war for example. Each side thought they could beat each other psychologically by inflicting the most appalling atrocities on civilians. You see, it was not only a case of trying to vanquish your enemy militarily – it was a matter of seeing if you could frighten your enemy by your sheer brutality against helpless women and children. It worked very nicely, for look at what happened there. There was nothing like pouring molten plastic into children's eyes to capture the right effect. Foday Sankoh and his friends in the RUF had become past masters at that... Even so, it is not necessarily only an African idea. The Serb and Croat militias and police forces used the same methods by murdering and torturing civilians, and they also used the mass raping of women and children as a method of ethnic cleansing."

"Yeah, but there are world courts looking into that," Dave pointed out. "Also, I see they've got something going in Tanzania in order to sort out that Tutsi massacre in Rwanda. Do you reckon they'll ever do anything about Mugabe and what he's doing in Zimbabwe? Hundreds up there are being killed, raped and tortured every day."

"Ja, the situation in Zimbabwe can only be described as catastrophic," Onda concurred with him. "I understand that some US lobby group is claiming that Mugabe and his crooked government are deliberately preventing aid agencies from helping hundreds of thousands that have been left homeless by Mugabe's so-called land reforms. Reforms touted by the Mugabe government as being a tool to eliminate poverty. Perhaps they are deliberately starving these people to death? I wonder if the world community could even be bothered?"

Dawson-Byrne sat forward in his camp chair. "I very much doubt it, Andreas. The slaughter of a few hundred civilians here and there on this continent won't raise too many eyebrows around the world nowadays. It's happening every day and most people are growing bored of atrocity stories coming out of Africa. As far as this continent goes, you could probably kill up to ten thousand innocent people and still avoid any serious repercussions. Once you start getting into the hundreds of thousands it could be a different matter, but they aren't doing too much in places such as the Dafur region in the Sudan. After what's happened in Africa over just this last decade, how many dead Afs amount to a lot? Would ten thousand be too many? Would a hundred thousand? Is a million adequate enough? It'll be interesting to see what happens about the slaughter we have going on in Dafur, especially after what happened in Rwanda... I suppose there must be some magical number involved? I mean – how many people do a party have to kill on this continent in order for the world community to really take things seriously? Furthermore, why didn't the West interfere militarily in order to stop the Hutu from slaughtering the Tutsi? Far too busy trying to save white lives in the Balkans. Total low life white lives, I agree, still the Bosnians were given a much higher priority than the victims in Rwanda. Africa holds no priorities in people's lounge rooms anymore. There's more tears and sympathy to be obtained from news items covering cats stuck in trees, fox hunting, whale harpooning or clubbing seal cubs to death. The bloodshed and mayhem going on in Africa almost every day of the week's become tiresome. The countless lines of refugees, the snot and the flies on the faces of starving children, and the endless tales of the Afs' woes aren't registering anymore because the same, old, sorry tale's been told year after year and decade after decade."

"You're right there," I agreed with him. "When we were back in Aussie – when we did get to see some TV – just about every news program had a story about strife going on in Africa."

"And it'll be the same for decades to come," he was certain. "Especially when you consider that corruption's costing this continent over two hundred billion dollars US a year. Places such as Asia and

South America are slowly pulling their act together, but you aren't seeing that here. In fact, to the average Af's way of thinking, if you're not corrupt – you're damned stupid. Why do you think there's so much murder, mayhem and misery over here? When the whites handed back countries to the Afs as a going concern, with all the infrastructure, mining and agricultural development, there was plenty for the blacks in government and the public service to steal. Then, when everything supposedly belonging to the public sector's either been filched or left to disintegrate, the Afs in power then expropriate the private sector's assets, so there's unemployment followed by famine and starvation. Taking Zimbabwe as a case in point, where there's hardly anything left to extort, expropriate and plunder, Robber Mugarbage's desperate hold on power's becoming more and more violent. As a result of that you're seeing more and more unemployment, impoverishment and possibly genocide... Furthermore, as I have pointed out to David here before – the more useless the Af leader – the bigger the ego he has. Also, in most cases, the bigger the ego – the greater his greed. I challenge any simpering lover of the noble savage to prove me wrong."

"It was not so much the case with Julius Nyerere in Tanzania," Onda disagreed with him. "Our dearly departed Mwalimu never actually stole so much for himself. He was only an idiot with the IQ of a monkey. Even though the rest of the world had seen the economic failure of collectivisation in communist countries such as Russia and China, our idiotic Mwalimu – for sheer egotistical reasons – decided to press on with his supposed reforms. He forcibly removed millions of peasants from their land and herded everybody into collectivised villages, thus he thrust upon them famine, starvation and hopelessness. Despite all the misery he caused, he managed to stay in power for a quarter of a century... But you are right, James, in most other cases. The international media are pulling out of Africa since the overseas public are fast becoming bored with being inundated with the scenes of bloodshed and misery. The tragedy in the Sudan amply illustrates the fact that people are becoming inured to Africa's problems. People are far more interested in what is happening in Iraq and Afghanistan because the Americans and the British are involved there. Everybody has observed the severed heads lying on tables and on the roads in Liberia. They have witnessed the massacre of thousands of Hutu refugees in camps in the DRC. They have seen the people stoned or shot to death in Sierra Leone, and, most of all, they have been given more than adequate television coverage in regard to the terrified, starving African children. Pictures of starving women and black children have become so commonplace over the years, people would rather donate their money to endangered wildlife such as whales, polar bears and rhinoceroses. A Rwandan gorilla has more appeal than twenty Tutsi or Hutu children. As the Americans say – they get more bang for their donor buck by supporting wildlife agencies. The African's plight is now way down the ladder when it comes to worldwide sympathy. That in itself is the greatest tragedy, gentlemen. People have forgotten that Africa's victims are mostly innocent. The people who have to put up with all this misery and who have to watch their children starve to death, or succumb to diseases that are unheard of in your countries, are mostly blameless... To summarise, gentlemen, I think we can put it this way – while you hear of white people insisting that Aloe Vera should be put in toilet paper to soothe their backsides – you have black women and children starving and dying of disease over here due to the greed and total lack of conscience of their leaders."

"A rather unusual analogy, Andreas," Dawson-Byrne nodded, "but fitting for a continent such as Africa. But, as you said, we can't lay *all* the blame at the Af's doorstep. A good many of those enlightened ones amongst our own white culture are doing just as much damage as the noble savage. What about the cretins running the universities in Scandinavia, the States, Europe and the UK? Some of them are handing out honorary doctorates, degrees, and knighthoods to despots and murderers in places such as Africa and south-east Asia. You take those idiots in the good old US of A for instance. The University of Ohio has given our good Sammy Nujoma an honorary doctorate in legal science. He's been made an honorary citizen of Atlanta and has received decorations from San Francisco, Chicago and New York. Not to be outdone, he's also received an honorary doctorate in technology from the Federal University of Technology in Nigeria, although that's an institution obviously run by Afs. Why on earth have the management of supposedly upright institutions prostrated themselves at the feet of a murderer and a coward? His doctorate in Legal Science was probably awarded to him because the bodies of the SWAPO dissenters he murdered in Angola still lie in unmarked graves where no one has bothered to look for them? Was he given the degree in technology because he managed to serve a cup of tea to a railway passenger without spilling a drop? Or did he get the doctorates and accolades from all those fine and upstanding Yank cities for stealing millions of dollars? Firstly, the contributions given by do-gooder countries to SWAPO's war efforts, and – secondly – the tax dollars that are going missing as we speak? If I'm right, he's well and truly earned them. You, Andreas, earned a Doctorate in geophysics and I an MSc in geology, as we proved to the Dons and our peers that we had the appropriate expertise. Who are the more pathetic – the Afs – or those who shower doctorates or honorary degrees on so many African despots, murderers and baboons? What on earth could they be trying to achieve by insulting the competence and integrity of those people who *have* earned such qualifications? Are these people representative of the rot we're finding in our own society?"

CHAPTER 49

WAY TO STUFF CANE TOADS!
DOGS' DICKS FOR TUCKER!

Although the immediate future looked bloody uncertain, it was pleasant sitting round the fire, and the grog was going down a real treat. Onda didn't seem content with that, and he took another jab at us Aussies. "I cannot say I really envy you people in Australia.'

"Oh yeah – how's that?" Jeff was still in a prickly mood.

"I mean no offence," the Hungarian quickly assured him. "It is your immigration laws. You once had a 'keep Australia white policy'?"

"Yeah, until that fuckin' wanker Gough Whitlam changed everything," Jeff agreed with him.

"It was also that dickhead, Malcolm Fraser," Nick reminded him. "He let in heaps of Vietnamese boat people, and now Aussie's saturated with 'em."

"Exactly!" Onda nodded. "Your various governments have let radical Muslims come into you country by the plane load, and I hear that certain Muslim leaders are preaching violence and hatred against ordinary Australian citizens. Africa may be overrun with corrupt dictators, but you would not see that kind of behaviour being allowed here. It cannot be comforting to know that your government has allowed people in that wish to blow you and your families up? That has to be insane?"

"Fuckin' oath!" Nick concurred. "Fancy letting bastards in that want to cause friggin' shit? Look at those suburbs in Sydney which are bloody crawling with fuckin' all sorts. Who the fuck let 'em in – in the first place?"

"Now that's what you could call pollution on a grand scale," Dawson-Byrne grinned. "Never mind that you Aussies are wrecking the planet with your total disregard for the environment – what with your scrub clearing and coal-fired power stations – you've allowed yourselves to be inundated with hordes of dusky foreigners."

"And what about flamin' Pommyland?" Dave pointed out. "You're always complaining about how the place is chock-full with Pakis, Indians and allsorts from Africa."

"True," the Pommy put his hand up. "You'll recall our chat about Enoch Powell the other night. As far as the UK's concerned, there's no point in trying to lock the stable door, as the horse has well and truly bolted. It's most likely the same in Australia, but your various governments have achieved the same status quo in record time. In Blighty it took almost sixty years, but you people have achieved the same in a couple of decades."

"But that's the Labour governments – those fuckin' wankers, Whitlam and Keating," Wheeler agreed with him. "If there's one thing I can say for Howard – at least he's try'n to put a lid on things. Still, as you said, the horse has most likely fuckin' bolted."

"Who knows?" the Pommy shrugged. "Mind you, I don't think I've come across anyone who's more of a patriot than your average Aussie. In fact, the way you carry on, it's almost a pain in the backside. But bravo – nevertheless! If there was ever a time Australia needed your true-blue patriotism, it's right now. The same with Great Britain. We used to have patriots back in Blighty, but they've been well and truly watered-down by now. Too many Indian curries, I suppose, as curry has become our national dish... That reminds me – I read somewhere that Indians make up the third largest migrant group coming into Australia. If that's the case, you're well and truly doomed."

"Why's that?" I asked him.

"I can see what James is attempting to say," Onda answered for the Pom'. "You take Natal in South Africa – especially Durban. More than a century ago the British introduced Indian indentured labourers to cut the sugarcane. They were supposed to have a strict policy whereas once an Indian labourer had completed his contract, he was to be shipped back to India. It was made a very strict law that *not one* Indian was allowed to stay. Apparently some of them must have slipped through the net because now Natal is teeming with Indians. The whole of South Africa for that matter."

"Yeah," the same thing happened in Fiji," Wheeler cut in. "They brought in the Indians to cut the sugarcane over there, and now they've got an Indian prime minister. No wonder the native Fijians are pissed off as all fuck?" That caused the Pommy to burst out laughing. "What's so fuckin' funny?" Dave wanted to know. "You bloody Poms caused all this shit."

"Indians – sugarcane – cane toads?" Dawson-Byrne guffawed. "What do they have in common, gentlemen?"

"What you on about?" Dave demanded.

"Don't you see?" the Pommy seemed mystified by Wheeler's query. "In their wisdom the Queensland farmers introduced cane toads to poison or devour anything that looked like harming their sugar cane. Now I hear that these beastly toads are now advancing on Western Australia, poisoning everything in their path – the local fauna – domestic cats and dogs – you name it. There's a cane toad plague that's threatening to take over the whole of Australia... So what's the difference when you're letting in the Indians as the third largest migrant group? It's like in Natal and Fiji – the Indians have multiplied more than everyone else twentyfold. They've even been able to outbreed the Afs in South Africa! Never mind the cane toads – soon your country will have an Indian prime minister, so maybe you Aussies will have to move on to Antarctica? The Indians won't want you hanging around... Then again, I suppose you Aussies could all convert to Islam and the Lebanese, Afghan and Iraqi migrants you've invited in might help you blow them all up – both the Indians and the cane toads... Or, by the same token, I see your various governments and private sector haven't really bothered about training your kids in regard to trade skills and whatever have you for several decades now. There's been no thought of investing in Australia's future or youth for way too many years. So – to rectify that – they're bringing in Chinese tradesmen in order to try and make up the shortfall. It's well known that the Chinese have a penchant for eating scorpions, snakes, beetles, dogs' penises and testicles, plus certain varieties of maggots and cockroaches, so perhaps – if you bring enough of them over – they can eat all the cane toads? None of those Chinese will want to return to their motherland, and I doubt if your government will force them to... So you'll have a breeding competition between them and the Indians. If I was to put my money up, I'd back the Indians.

"Yes, but getting back to the radical Muslims in Australia," Onda returned to his original topic. "How can your government allow people to preach ethnic and religious hatred? Not only against ordinary Australian people, but also against your culture and society?"

"Yeah, it's also got me fucked," Dave admitted. "You've got Howard and them almost begging the fuckin' Muslims to pull their heads in, but the Muslim leaders are screaming religious intolerance and are more or less telling everyone to get fucked. Fuck me dead – their own countries weren't good enough for 'em to live in, and now they're try'n to cause all types of shit in Aussie... What do you reckon the Aussie government should do, Andreas?"

The Hungarian drained his bottle of Tafel Lager and reached out for another. "What you have is similar to what is happening in Britain where there are groups of people who are intent on enforcing their ideology on your whole population. They are dissatisfied that the majority of you and the British are Christians. They openly despise you for it, and loudly voice these opinions in their mosques. Some of them are even teaching the Muslim youth that a war should be waged against your people, and most likely sooner or later some of those youths are going to do something terrible. Despite the fact that your country has given these radicals a sanctuary where they can live in freedom and enjoy democracy, they wish to destroy your very way of life... There is only one word that can describe that kind of behaviour. Treason! In the old days in most countries there was only one penalty for treason against one's government and fellow citizens – the death penalty. If people come to your country and wish to destroy you – or encourage others to do likewise – they should be put to death... But, before that, all potential terrorists such as radical Muslims should be barred from entering your country in the *first place*. Those that are already there – those that even look like breaking your laws or threatening your people – they should be instantly deported."

"Fuckin' oath!" Jeff felt obliged to say.

The Pommy was also in total agreement. "Oh – absolutely! It's all very civilised the Australian government's approach to radical Islam, but this pussyfooting around with political correctness will – like you said, Andreas – cost Australian lives more sooner than later. Let's not forget Bali? There are Muslim factions in Australia that are just treating the government with contempt. So these people are prepared to use violence or terrorism to achieve their aims – are they? If violence and terrorism is not used to counteract violence and terrorism, then normal, law-abiding Australians in the street will have no protection whatsoever... I just wonder if the average Aussie realises that there actually *is* a war being fought out there, and these are *very* dangerous times? Never mind the fact that they've got troops in Afghanistan and Iraq, do they realise that the same war has to be fought at their front door? If they have neighbours who are conspiring against them, those neighbours have to be confronted forthwith. The only safeguard a country can have is total unity amongst its citizens. If things are pushed far enough, you'll have a civil war amongst your own people – between the ordinary Aussie and the politically correct do-gooder. Never mind the Muslims, they'll just mop up what's left. You take that opposition leader you Aussies have got over there. Instead of trying to back the Howard government in regards to your national security, he's doing his damnedest to get political mileage out of splitting the country down the middle. So he'll withdraw your troops from of Afghanistan and Iraq – will he? He'll let the Yanks and the Brits or the Canadians fight your battles for you? If Australia adopts that kind of attitude, you'll hardly..."

"That, friggin' wanker, Beazley, you mean?" Jeff came charging in. "He's got fuckin' Buckley's chance of ever being Australia's prime minister!"

Incredibly enough, the Pommy agreed with Jeff a second time. "I certainly hope so, Jeffry. Trying to obtain political mileage in such a very real crisis is only undermining *everyone* in Australia. Just like the British and American governments, Australia's leaders have to have an iron resolve if they want to protect their people from terrorism. They have to be united and fight fire with fire. There's no other option."

"You reckon the Chinese like eating dogs' balls?" Nick asked the Pom'.

"Indeed – they do!" Dawson-Byrne assured him. "They have entire emporiums that deal exclusively in animal penises and testicles. Those of dogs, donkeys, snakes – you name it. Apparently snakes are very popular because they have two penises... Seriously now, you take the Guolizhuang Restaurant in Beijing. Claims to be the leading purveyor of such delicacies. It appears that Chinese men believe animal penises are good for virility... Ye gods, that's all the planet needs – virile Chinamen! Never mind greenhouse gases and carbon dioxide pollution – what could be worse than hordes of lusty Chinamen?"

"And did you go into that Guolizhuang Restaurant and sample some dogs' dicks?" Dave asked him.

"Certainly not!" the Pommy quickly shook his head. "As a matter of fact, I hurried past the place. Nothing worse than being accosted by some randy oriental. They may be generally small in stature, but how do you fend one off that has made up his mind that he just *has to have* his way with you?"

"You're talking shit," I told him.

"I can assure you, Josef, I am not," he looked a picture of sincerity.

"They even had the menu on the pavement. There was Russian dog penis hotpot, or you could have it cold and raw like sushi. It was the favourite venue of businessmen where they invited corrupt government bureaucrats along who could do them favours. Apparently the menu was thought up by a certain Mr. Guo who travelled the world researching the benefits that animal appendages had to offer mankind. Not only does a dog's penis have a low cholesterol content, it increases one's sex drive and is a panacea for just about every kind of ailment... Furthermore, gentlemen, if Indians are your third largest migrant group, there is another reason why – like us Brits and the Afs in Natal – you're doomed."

"Why?" Jeff pressed him.

The Pommy removed a piece of folded paper from his back pocket. "I saw this on the internet while I was staying at the Windhoek Country Club. I couldn't resist printing it out for you."

A survey of more than 1,000 men in India has concluded that condoms made according to international sizes are too large for a majority of Indian men.

The study found that more than half of the men measured had penises that were shorter than international standards for condoms.

It has led to a call for condoms of mixed sizes to be made more widely available in India.

The two-year study was carried out by the Indian Council of Medical Research.

Over 1,200 volunteers from the length and breadth of the country had their penises measured precisely, down to the last millimetre.

The scientists even checked their sample was representative of India as a whole in terms of class, religion and urban and rural dwellers. The conclusion of all this scientific endeavour is that about 60% of Indian men have penises which are between three and five centimetres shorter than international standards used in condom manufacture.

Doctor Chander Puri, a specialist in reproductive health at the Indian Council of Medical Research, told the BBC there was an obvious need in

India for custom-made condoms, as most of those currently on sale are too large.

The issue is serious because about one in every five times a condom is used in India it either falls off or tears, an extremely high failure rate.

And the country already has the highest number of HIV infections of any nation.

'Not a problem'

Mr Puri said that since Indians would be embarrassed about going to a chemist to ask for smaller condoms there should be vending machines dispensing different sizes all around the country.

"Smaller condoms are on sale in India. But there is a lack of awareness that different sizes are available. There is anxiety talking about the issue. And normally one feels shy to go to a chemist's shop and ask for a smaller size condom."

But Indian men need not be concerned about measuring up internationally according to Sunil Mehra, the former editor of the Indian version of the men's magazine Maxim.

"It's not size, it's what you do with it that matters," he said.

"From our population, the evidence is Indians are doing pretty well.

"With apologies to the poet Alexander Pope, you could say, for inches and centimetres, let fools contend."

"Doing well?" the Pommy guffawed. "I'd say they're doing well! Besides the meagre size of their willies, they'll outbreed you Aussies fifty to one, and you can mark my words on that one!"

CHAPTER 50

NO MORE DRILLING!

The drilling packed up altogether after that, as there was nothing economically viable on the Karibib claims, except for a few skinny quartz veins that did carry some gold. Naturally Seebacher insisted that Dawson-Byrne didn't have a clue about finding gold, then eventually the Pommy geo' had had a gutsful of him: "Listen, I've got some excellent advice for you, Seebacher."

"I do not need advice from you," the chubby German assured him. "I shall find another company who has geologists who know what they are doing. There is plenty of gold on these claims, so I am thinking of mining these claims again myself."

"No, don't do that," Dawson-Byrne shook his head. "Tell me – do you own a firearm?" "I own several firearms. Why?"

"What kind of firearms?"

Seebacher shrugged. "A .303 rifle – a .22 – a .38 revolver. Why?"

"Why don't you take the .38 – go behind a bush – and use it to blow your brains out? It's really the most intelligent thing to do."

The prospector was somewhat annoyed with that. "I do not have time to listen to your nonsense. I must be going."

"No, wait," the Pommy stopped him. "What else *can* you do? Even if there's enough ore here to mine in a small way, you'll need a treatment plant and capital to develop it. Once I've lodged my report with the Mines Department, *nobody* will touch this place with a long stick. You won't even be able to con an idiot like Kotzé. There's no point in going back to Germany, since no one wants you there. You wouldn't know how to do a decent day's work, anyway. Besides, you're too old for anyone to employ you anywhere and the K4s have got all the jobs over here because of their affirmative action... There's no point in applying for a pension back in the Fatherland. The German government won't give you one, as they're too busy supporting all the Turks and Bulgarians who're taking over the place. The Namibian pension's only a hundred and sixty Nam' dollars a month, so that won't even pay for your petrol. It looks like you're about to live out the rest of your days in abject poverty, so why don't you just blow your brains out? It won't hurt – simply put the barrel in your right ear and pull the trigger slowly... You may have to shoot your wife first, as it would be a shame to leave her behind at the mercy of all the K4s. Don't you realise that you're a complete loser, Seebacher, and worse than an Af, so why don't you put an end to all your misery?"

"A bloody fond farewell," Dave grinned as Seebacher went off in his bakkie. "Tell me, James old chap, are you in the habit of taking nasty pills? Old Seebacher's probably gunna blow both his and his missus' brains out. You could've pushed him over the edge?"

"One can only live in hope," Dawson-Byrne agreed with him.

We certainly had fond; though sad farewells to issue when we paid off our labourers. Also, true to the Pommy geo's prediction, some were truly devastated, as the work we had given them was the first they had come across in years, and most likely the only employment they would find for some years to come. Poor old Wilfred was nearly in tears. For us Aussies it was also fairly traumatic, for there was no immediate further contract to go to. Unlike in Western Australia, where there was always a chance of getting at least *some* work, we found ourselves stuck in Namibia where absolutely nothing was going on.

The uncertainty made us all edgy. "Your fuckin' job as big boss cocky didn't last long," Jeff poked at Ernie. "You were really up yourself when the boss put you in charge of us."

The little mechanic also had shit in his spleen, "Yeah, but at least I'll find a job when I get back to Kal'. I'm a fully qualified mechanic and diesel fitter, so I can get a job anywhere. With all that poxy Wik and Mabo crap and the low gold price, you'll be flat out getting any drilling. Dave and Josef'll be all right 'cause the boss'll keep 'em on. You'll be tramped right away, so I don't know how you're gunna support that wife and tribe of kids of yours. You're gunna have to cut down on the smokes and the piss, and stop bloody breeding."

Whilst Nick and I hoped that Jeff would slather the little arsehole, Wheeler had a far better idea, "Let's go down to the fuckin' pub? All this's depressing me something chronic."

We required no second bidding and headed for Karibib. Nick insisted that we should go to the Hotel Kaiserblick, for he still reckoned he could get into the pants of the German sheila who had kicked us out. The rest of our number decided to go along with him since watching his efforts might lift our spirits.

Jeff raised certain imponderables such as which method would be best employed to shag her; up the fanny or the arse? Nick, who was really starting to believe that he could succeed, was adamant that he would be adopting the conventional path. There was no way, he assured us, that his Italian sausage was going to be head-butting any German sausage that may be lurking in the sheila's darkest regions.

There was no sign of his intended prey at first, though the hotel's bar was nearly full of locals absolutely ecstatic as the result of the fabulous rains that looked as if they would never go away. Otto Henckert was there and he greeted Jeff like a long-lost mate. We had plenty of questions fired at us about Kotzé, Van der Merwe and Herman; had the cops arrested anyone and so on? For a bunch of foreigners who had spent such a short time in the area, we sure had been surrounded by murder, mayhem and mystery!

Naturally too much grog was taken aboard by all. Nick and a German character by the name of Freidrich Hegner decided to have a sword fight with two ancient *Schutztruppen* sabres they found hanging behind the bar. It was a bloody dangerous affair, considering the sabres were the absolute real McCoy, so the rest of us drinkers got right out of the way. The two combatants slashed at one another, calling each other 'swine' and 'pig dogs', and the ringing of the steel blades was almost deafening. They leapt on to tables that collapsed under their weight, sending glasses and bottles flying in all directions, and the floor was virtually carpeted with glass. There was yahooing! and hurrahs! as the crowd barracked for their favourites, then suddenly a shotgun went off, causing a shower of plaster to come raining down from the ceiling!

It was the German sheila and she was fit to be tied! Nick clicking his heels broke the dead silence that followed, and then he kissed the blade of his sabre and bowed to her . That must have tickled her funny bone, for she burst out laughing, then glass scrunched under our heels as we went to the bar for fresh drinks. We passed the hat round to pay for the damage. About half an hour after that Nick was sitting on a stool propped against the bar and the German sheila was perched on his knee sipping a Jägermeister. It was a miracle, or so the locals swore, for never had they seen that particular lady show any compassion to any man whatsoever. Perhaps it was the rain?

"Christ, I wish Magda was here," Dave told me.

"You really serious about marrying her?" I asked him.

"Fuckin' oath, I am! The sooner we get out of this mess, the fuckin' better. I'm taking her back to Aussie with me."

"She'll need a passport and visa," I cautioned. "That could take weeks over here."

"I hadn't thought of that," he admitted. "As soon as the flamin' rig's back in Windhoek, I'll start on it first thing."

"You're just being a fuckin' mug," Jeff assured him.

Wheeler looked him up and down, "Look – Jeff – why don't you go and fuck your hand?"

When we got back to the camp it started pissing down rain again. While every farmer, their wives, children plus their dogs in Namibia were delighted, there was only one joker who didn't seem so happy. The Pommy! "Those poor wretches in the squatter camps," he told Dave.

"What about 'em?" Wheeler asked him.

"You saw the squatter camp in Rehoboth."

"Yeah?"

"There are thousands of poor blighters living in squatter camps throughout this country. Not only Rehoboth – Keetmanshoop, Gobabis Windhoek – you name it. The majority live under bits of plastic and cardboard, or whatever they can find. When it rains they're washed out and drenched. What little belongings they have – the kids, babies – everything. First the wind will flatten any shelter they've got, so it has to be totally unbearable for the poor sods. We see the farmers on the one hand rejoicing, and on the other the poor swine in the shanty towns in sheer, out-and-out misery. It's starting to get damned cold, so that means children and the old and infirm shall start dying in no time because most of the people in the squatter camps don't have nearly enough to eat. When you have malnutrition, cold and wet conditions become killers. Believe me, David, there are people dying in the Rehoboth slums as I speak. Unless the Rehobothers give them shelter. I doubt if they will, though."

"Why wouldn't they?"

"Why should they? The Baster certainly don't owe the Ovambo any favours. They didn't ask to be invaded and have their kaptein humiliated. Old Sammy's nice and warm tucked up in Government House. Just shows you the total farce that comes with black independence on this continent. Uncle Sammy spends millions on private intercontinental jets, Mercedes Benzes and BMWs for his motorcades, and he's got children dying of cold, malnutrition and disease in the squatter camps. I wonder what the champions of the noble savage think about that one? In most black African countries you've got an elite few stealing everything and living in the lap of the gods, and then thousands, if not millions, living in abject poverty. So much for the Af and his do-gooder admirers."

CHAPTER 51

NICK STUFFS THE SHITHOUSE!
JEFF GETS THE SCREAMING SHITS!

We moved the drill rig and all the gear back into Windhoek and it was only then that we learned that the mansion in Klein Windhoek was no longer available to us. Ernie had booked us into a fairly cheap, crappy pension that was run by an ugly, alcoholic German woman who had obviously come out of Noah's Ark. With booze being outlawed by the old bitch, and stray women being forbidden; naturally we were pretty pissed off.

"Fuck all this!" was all Dave had to say.

"Yeah, look at the bloody place, we've been in better fuckin' dumps in the outback," Jeff agreed. "Do you reckon the boss's gone broke?"

"This whole caper must've cost him a fuckin' poultice," Wheeler shrugged. "Ernie reckons the boss's gunna sue the client for breaking the contract, though with us being here in Namibia and the client being in Canada, I don't fancy his chances."

"Hey, Jeff?" Nick jumped in.

"What?"

"Why don't you give the old bitch a fuck? Maybe then she might let us have a few beers in our rooms?"

"Fuck her yourself!" Jeff was against the idea. "She's more your type. Make sure you spit on her fanny first, or you'll grind your dick away."

All in all things became fairly depressing. All the romance of travelling to Africa had been completely sucked dry. There had been high points for me what with meeting Krystal; still all the hopeless inactivity had left us all feeling very insecure. Back in Aussie being flat out was the norm; going from one contract to another; we certainly weren't used to that sort of carry on. Nick and Jeff discussed snatching their rent with the boss, but Ernie reckoned they should hang on a while, as the drilling in Botswana might go ahead. The rock-bottom gold prices didn't help, either.

I took stock of my own particular situation. I definitely was head-over-heels in love with Krystal. There was no way I would be able to talk her into leaving Namibia, yet the idea of turning my back on Australia was unthinkable. Drilling was all that I knew and I could always find work in Australia, even if it was only part-time. I had enough savings to carry me for a couple of years, and by then another mining boom would more than likely come along. No drilling opportunities whatsoever could be found in Namibia; consequently the thought of doing something else in that country was impossible.

Dave was really pissed off with the Australian government. "Those typical wanker politicians and government bastards of ours," he told me.

"What've they done now?"

"They've gone and sold just about all of Australia's gold reserves. So what kind of friggin' confidence is that gunna give to the Australian gold mining industry? If that isn't fuckin' enough, they must've sold our gold at the lowest prices."

"Where'd you find this out?"

"It was on the bastarding news! Even the South Africans can't work out why Australia's dumped its gold. The industry's employing thousands of Aussies and I bet there'll be mines closing down by the dozen. It's like I told you back in Kal' – the fuckin' government doesn't give a fuck about the people in the outback. There are too many city wankers' votes."

Nick spent his time literally sabotaging the workings of the pension, and some of his schemes turned out to be quite hilarious. One of the best was when he decided to put the main shithouse for the guests out of action. On the rig we had chemicals for various troubles that came our way in drill holes. When we had a hollow piece of ground around the drill hole collar, we had two chemicals that, when mixed together, swelled up and made a tough seal. Two litre-tins of that stuff could virtually take up the space of a decent-sized furniture van, and, when it solidified, it would take a hammer and chisel, hacksaw or a blowtorch to get the stuff out. Two tins went down the shithouse bowl and into the sceptic tank pipes. When he called Jeff and me to see his handiwork we were confronted by a huge, spongy looking mass that had grown out of the bowl like some obscene, gigantic mushroom! The foamy but solid mound almost reached the ceiling! The old landlady nearly had a stroke when she saw it and needed almost half a bottle of a hundred and sixty-proof Stroh rum to calm her nerves. The cops, like the plumber she had called, hadn't been around drilling rigs, so they couldn't point the finger at us. One particularly dense white copper reckoned it was some kind of exotic, septic tank algae and he wanted to call in scientists from South Africa and Germany.

Nick didn't cease his activities at that particular juncture. He used quick-drying drill cement to completely block the shower taps and drains, plus those of the hand basins and the baths. That further mystified the plumber and we went for a couple of days unable to wash ourselves. Such an embargo proved a particular handicap for Jeff one morning. Having had far too much to drink the evening before, he was snoring, slobbering and moaning away when Nick snuck into his room in the middle of the night. The fact that something untoward had happened was heralded by, "You fuckin' cunts! You wait till I get the fuckin' mutant who done this! I'll break his fuckin' neck!"

He came bursting into the guests' kitchen with what appeared to be two massive black eyes! Nick had smeared black boot polish over the back of Jeff's thumbs and forefingers in such a way that when he rubbed his eyes on waking, the polish had surrounded them. Nick's devilish cunning didn't finish there, either, for he had crept up on Ernie who was also in an alcohol-induced coma, and dabbed polish on the end of his fingers, thus making Jeff want to kill the little mechanic. The absolute beauty of it all was that Ernie hadn't a clue of how he had got to bed, and he had such an arse-splitting hangover he was in no fit condition to deny anything with any credibility.

There was another similar incident that didn't particularly brighten Jeff's demeanour all that much. We had all found out from fairly bitter experience that eating out in Windhoek could sometimes be a dicey business, for on several occasions one of us had come back with a crook guts. Jeff had had a mixed grill at some place called O'Hagans, and it wasn't long before he was dashing around as if his arse was on fire! For a couple of days there he serenaded those around him with grunts, groans and long, spluttering, gurgling explosions as he sandblasted the guests' shithouse bowl. Not the one that Nick had sabotaged. After trying in vain to heal himself with various pills and potions he had purchased from the chemists, Jeff tried to kill the bug with a bottle of overproof Dutch gin that he had smuggled into the pension. The fiery liquor must have given him some relief, for he was quite able to sit down and eat a superb platter of shepherd's pie that Nick had prepared in the pension's kitchen. Then, after drinking the remainder of the gin, he crashed out on his bed.

It was a short while later when Nick struck, and his evil intentions must have been given a great amount of forethought! So much so that he had knocked off a couple of shackles out of the support truck, plus a length of thin, stainless steel cable. With those he managed to wire Jeff's ankle to the corner of his bed.

It was probably after an hour, perhaps a little longer, when the rest of us – who had no knowledge of Nick's activities – got to hear and see the results. First of all there was the crash from something very heavy falling onto the wooden floor boards! Such an impact that the entire pension shuddered! Then there was: "What the fuck?" as loud as Jeff could muster. Next we heard a banging and scraping noise as a bed was being dragged violently across the room. "You fuckin' cunts!" Almost half a minute of silence. "I swear to God, I'll fuckin' kill the fuckin' mutant who done this!" There was another crash when the bed was driven into a wall. "Come on, you bastards, I'm seriously busting for a shit!" his voice began pleading.

Dave got to him first and managed to switch on his light. I was just behind him with Ernie and Nick peering over my shoulders seconds after. There was Jeff lying on the floor, clad only in his underdaks; his ankle still firmly attached to the corner of his bed. There was an overpowering stink wafting over us, as he had well and truly shit himself!

Our main dilemma was the weird glare in his eyes, for he left us with no doubt that the uppermost thought on his mind was to grab anyone who went near and tear him limb from limb! He looked bloody scary! Most fortuitously Nick had tightened the shackle pins with a Phillips screwdriver, so it was impossible for Jeff to unfasten them with his bare fingers; regardless of the rage he was in.

Dave had stepped well back from the door and his focus was on Ernie. "You're the fuckin' boss, so you can get him free. I don't know who done this, but I'm not bloody going anywhere near him."

Ernie was only too happy to display his chicken liver, "Fuckin' Joe – Nick – whichever of you bastards done it – you can fuckin' let him go!"

Knowing I was totally innocent, I got stuck into the little mechanic, "And you can get fucked, Ernie! I had fuck all to do with it... Hey, Nick, was this *your* friggin' idea?"

"Don't look at me, you black cunt!" Nick tried his best to look wounded.

More bubbly, farting sounds could be heard as Jeff squirted more liquid into his underdaks. That enraged him further, "As true as Christ, I'll fuckin' kill the lot of you, if one of you don't bloody let me go!"

I had always suspected that Nick had a streak of insanity in him, but I was totally buggered by what he came out with next: "You get that old German bitch who's running the place to fuckin' let you go. Were you and her into bondage sessions, you sick, fat prick?"

That started Jeff kicking at the bed with his free leg, and it in turn was crashing against the wall. By that time Wheeler was worried that some serious damage would be done to the room or that the bloke might injure himself, so he called over to Jeff: "Listen, mate, I swear I had fuck all to do with it. If I let you go, you pick on some other bastard. Is that fuckin' clear?"

Dave hunted around in the kitchen cupboards and eventually found some pliers with which he undid the shackle pins. By that time Jeff was desperate to take a shower, and he then spent most of the remainder of the night sitting in the shithouse. It was doubtful that anyone got too much sleep after that, for we weren't sure *on whom* he would take his revenge. Thankfully it was Nick. A couple of days later he discovered that Jeff had emptied his bowels into his brand-new suitcase; his old one having been destroyed by the tent fire. Where such retaliation was all the more effective; Nick had kept his suitcase packed just in case the platinum drilling job did come up in Botswana.

Once we got to know her better, the old German biddy, Mrs Kruger, turned out to be a fairly good scout. When at last we broke the ice with her and could bring grog onto the premises, we discovered that she was a desperately lonely soul who dearly missed her deceased husband. Like Elsabeth Witbooi, she truly was ancient, for she could remember her days in Karabib as a little girl when the Boers and British chased the German *Schutztruppen* all the way to the Angolan border before they surrendered. She reckoned the British treated her politely and that she and quite a few Germans had been dismayed when the South West came under the Boer mandate.

Nick was warned off his sabotage stunts, and being the kind of bloke he was, he was soon in the garden repairing flowerbeds and painting the fence or whatever. Mrs Kruger had a one-eyed cat that was most likely as ancient as its owner in cat years, and both it and Nick became lifelong mates in no time; even though it was incontinent and sometimes shat in his room.

Disaster struck when it also targeted the end of Jeff's bed on one occasion and that precipitated quite a decent blue between him and Nick. For starters, Jeff caught the runny-arsed feline in action. Grabbing it by the scruff of the neck, he then drop kicked it into Nick's room, causing the animal's back legs to collapse. Nick came out throwing punches like an electric fan and Jeff was almost done like a dinner before he could pull himself together. Fortunately old Mrs Kruger had gone to see the doctor about her arthritis and there was no way that Ernie, Dave or I wished to intervene. It was also most fortunate that the fight ended up in the back yard, as only one hallway table and a glass vase had been wrecked.

Jeff, because he was literally fighting for is life – also as Nick had gone completely troppo – managed to gain the upper hand and he was soon sitting on top of his opponent, raining punches on his head and shoulders. I found the shovel that Nick had been using to do the garden up with and knocked Jeff cold with the back of it. I let Nick kick him a couple of times in the guts, and then things settled down after that. They both had magnificent shiners and could hardly talk through their swollen lips. As things turned out it was all pretty harmless fun; however, when Nick went down to the Wurlitzer Bar to lick his wounds, Dave had to put the cat out of its misery by belting it over the head with the same shovel. I disposed of the body by swinging it by its tail into the neighbour's back yard, where a couple of red setters yelped with joy. There wasn't much left of it after they had fought over it for a couple of hours.

CHAPTER 52

I FINALLY GET TO MEET MY BROTHER!
GONORRHOEA IN THE PEA SOUP!

The news from Rehoboth, as usual, came via the agency of Wilfred. My brother Jonker was in that town and was waiting to see me!

I met him in Elsabeth Witbooi's house and it was like two tomcats fronting each other for the first time in a back alleyway. It was also like looking into a mirror! He was the exact same height and weight as me; still the scar on his neck was totally different altogether, although it was roughly in the same place. His emerald green eyes looked identical to mine; however his straight, pitch black hair was similar but more speckled with white hairs and he wore it much shorter. Also, unlike me, he sported a nifty, neatly trimmed moustache. His skin was the same colour; his ears the same shape; we were very nearly identical twins!

After shaking hands we sort of circled each other, neither with anything to say. Old Elsabeth was giggling like a teenager; Jakobus Van Wyk, Carl Zes, Manasse and Klaase were all grinning like Cheshire cats. I was glad for the first time that Krystal wasn't around, as I felt so dopey in front of my brother.

"Do you take alcohol?" he inquired.

"Sometimes."

"Then we have something in common."

"I won't have drunkenness in this house!" the old lady Witbooi scolded. "Jonker, you know my rules."

341

"Come now, Elsabeth," Jakobus interjected worriedly. "This is one of the greatest reunions we are ever likely to come across. There is so much to celebrate. Please – just this once?"

"What do you mean 'just this once', Kobus Van Wyk? How many times have people had to siphon you out of my house? I don't know how Sophia puts up with it... Oh, go on then, only this once."

"There are some refreshments in my car," Carl Zes was quite the gent. He brought in two bottles of brandy and some large plastic bottles of Coke.

Not being used to spirits and scarcely wanting to make a dickhead out of myself in front of my brother, I sipped very slowly at my drink that was about ten parts brandy to one of Coke. I found it totally impossible to say anything useful.

Jonker, perhaps because he was amongst friends, guzzled away quite freely and he was all chatty with the others in Afrikaans.

"Don't be so rude!" Elsabeth berated him. "Speak English – Josef doesn't know a word of Afrikaans."

"I am sorry. I always thought your name was Kido?" he turned to me. "Our father gave you the name Kido, so I insist on using that name in his memory... So what is Australia like?"

"Not bad," was all I could offer.

"And our mother? I heard what happened to her. Did you know her well?"

"She left when I was very young."

His mouth curled up in disgust. "Ja, and I was even younger when Herr Schultz took her away. Did you know that our father was totally unaware that she was being unfaithful with that German pig? All the time..."

"Enough of that!" Elsabeth butted in, winning a nod of agreement from Kobus Van Wyk. "You were both too young to have anything to do with what happened. How could either of..."

"I would simply like to remind everyone," Jonker interrupted her back, "that it was the good Herr Schultz who tore our family apart. I have nothing against Kido here. Of course he could not do anything, but I am just making my feelings clear. I do not want to hear Herr Schultz's name mentioned again."

I felt a challenge coming on, "He was good to both me and our mother. Like our father, he never recovered when our mother left to go with some useless punk. He *died* of a broken heart. Perhaps it's our mother we should be talking about? She was behind all the heartache."

At first he looked as if he was about to go crook at me, then he relaxed. "Perhaps you are right. All these years I have tried to keep our mother on a golden pedestal. It is evident that she was rather flighty. Never mind that, the past is the past and it is very good to see you. I hope we can spend a lot more time together. I am very busy and I hear your visit to Namibia could be terminated at any time?"

"How are things going with your work?" Kobus wanted to know. "Is there any chance that Wilfred can get more work with you? He tells me you spend more time getting into trouble than you do working? He also says that you Australians are always rude to each other and call each other terrible names? You also love fighting each other?" "Too right!" I agreed. "Our whole trip over here's been a total disaster. We've had two road deaths, a murder, a fatal mugging and a geologist nearly beaten to death. To every day of work, we've had ten doing nothing. There's supposed to be some work coming up here or in Botswana, but God knows when we'll start on that."

"A murder and a fatal mugging?" my brother was all interested. "What happened?"

I told him about the Van der Merwe and Kotzé saga and what had happened to Herman; however didn't volunteer any suspicions.

"I hear the cops are baffled?" Carl Zes queried. "They say in the newspapers that professionals were involved in the murder of the geologist? South Africans?"

"They are always saying that the South Africans are behind all the serious crime here," Jonker laughed. He then turned back to me, "I hear you have an ex-*Koevoet* working with you?"

I nodded, thinking that his reference to Dawson-Byrne was really uncanny. "Supposedly. Do you reckon he might've had something to do with it?"

"No – no, I was not saying that at all. This *Koevoet* is fairly well known by some of the Baster. He is supposed to be good man."

That made me laugh. "A good man? That bloke hates even his own shadow. He wouldn't have a kind bone in his body."

"The Border War did some shocking things to some," Elsabeth sighed sagely. "This man led some of the Baster up at the border. Some Bushmen, too. He was reputed to be a very fair officer, which is quite unusual for white military men."

"Ja, he was very popular with the coloureds," Kobus agreed.

"He's British," I pointed out.

"We know," they said almost in unison.

"Hang on a sec'," I remembered, "he was with you people at Herman's funeral. I was wondering what was going on there."

Krystal arrived from Windhoek and the hairs on the back of my neck fairly stood up when she and my brother embraced. I felt only slightly better when I was given the same treatment, and then I watched both like a hawk from that second on. Though they carried on like brother and sister, I was sick with jealousy.

As events turned out my twin brother and I found ourselves alone at Carl Zes' house. The rigmarole of keeping his presence out of the notice of the other Rehobothers all seemed fairly corny; still I felt it wasn't really my place to make any scornful comments. It was dark when we left Miss Elsabeth Witbooi's abode, yet Petrus Klaase and Fritz Manasse went in both directions of the street out front to make sure there were no unannounced observers, and old Kobus Van Wyk checked the back of the house. All being clear, we climbed into the back of Zes' BMW; Jonker wearing a broad brimmed, felt hat and dark glasses, despite it being night time. What made everything all the more ludicrous was that I was identical to my brother, therefore would surely attract any unwanted attention if it existed.

BASTARDS FROM THE BUSH

Zes' house was one of the best dwellings in Rehoboth; situated on the right hand side of the highway as it headed south to Kalkrand. Everything about the place was fairly affluent by what I had seen of Namibian standards; the furniture, the window dressings, the wall paper and so on. Zes not only had a BMW, but a brand-new Mercedes Benz C240 and a shiny, blue Isuzu bakkie. He wasn't married, so it seemed a bit extravagant him having three cars.

"And where do you live?" I asked Jonker.

"Here and there. My work keeps me on the move a lot. Do you own a posh house in Australia? I hear from Wilfred that you are earning a great deal of money? He was being paid a huge amount for an unskilled Baster?"

"Yeah, I've got a house, though it isn't as flash as this one by any means." I decided to cut the small talk bullshit. "When I first came to Rehoboth, on the very first evening people have been very cagey when it comes to mentioning your name and you being my brother. Zes and them carried on like the Mafia. What're you – some kind of bank robber or something?"

That made him laugh. "No, nothing as exciting as that. I am in politics. A kind of organiser – messenger – odd job man – jack-of-all-trades. It is just that some of the things I do are very unpopular with certain people."

"Such as?"

"Many – many things. I am supposed to have all kinds of special talents."

That was all crap to me. "Then why are people so mistrustful of me? How could I do you any harm?"

"I suppose, if you really wanted to, you could. There is a huge undercurrent both here and in South Africa. There are a lot of disaffected people and I have been chosen as one of their agents. I am a small part of a vast network that chooses to remain anonymous. I have been seen in too many of the wrong places at the wrong time, that is why it is preferable to keep a low profile. I possibly know too much – who knows?"

"And all this's worthwhile?"

"Very worthwhile! *Ouma* Witbooi and some of the Rehoboth community tried their best to help me after our father was murdered by the Boers, but I have no real qualifications such as university diplomas or degrees. I am totally unqualified academically and have no trade of any sort. Like many other Baster, I do not possess the skills of our forefathers because I spent most of my youth under the Boer regime with their 'Bantu' education system. I saw Apartheid in real action and it was far more rigid in some cases in the South West than it was down in South Africa. We – the coloureds and the blacks – the Baster, Nama, Herero and the Ovambo were all thrown into the same pot. Even the Boers' church claimed that we had been placed on this earth to serve the whites. Their Bible insists that God created us to be hewers of wood and drawers of water... That is why I have a positive dislike for Herr Schultz's memory. He was privileged – he was white – our father had absolutely no chance of competing with that German, even though he was at least thirty years older than our mother was. Just like any Baster girl, our mother took the opportunity to escape the poverty and deprivation... I must admit one thing all the same, the German risked everything he had when he married her openly under the Boers. At least ..."

"Enough about them," I cut him off. "I'm more interested in what you've been up to and why I've been given such a run around."

"Ja, okay, I shall come to that, but let me give you some background first... Having a total lack of recognised skills, this work I am doing is the most satisfactory available to me. Independence certainly has not given the Baster any novel opportunities. We may have most of the white-collar jobs in the banks and suchlike, yet we are no better off overall. Independence has brought even more pressure on our people and we are, in fact, a great deal worse off. Similar to the coloureds in South Africa, the rest of the world's people are totally ignorant of us. We once had our own *gebeid* here in Rehoboth, and now it is slowly being taken from us. Our leaders have been humiliated by the barrel of a gun. Our people have taken this issue to the world's highest courts, but we are too insignificant to attract any notice. We are only a collection of non-existent people going nowhere, and most of our youth are unemployed drunkards and dope addicts. Probably more liquor is consumed in Rehoboth per capita than anywhere else in Namibia, so there are drunken Baster everywhere. Hopeless people who have lost all ambition. If something is not done, we – as a race or nation of sorts – can only disappear into nothingness. During the old regime we were not white enough – now we are not black enough. That goes for the Nama, the Rehobothers, the Cape coloureds and the Griqua. Never mind the Bushmen, they may be popular for the tourists, but they are being treated as if they do not exist at all."

"So what can you do about it?"

"Do? We can unite those people who have clung to their pride. We have been conquerors before and we can do it again. I suppose *Ouma* Elsabeth has given you her spiel?"

"About our illustrious ancestor?"

"Ja, old Hendrik himself."

"My word, she has! She gets quite worked up when she talks about Namibian history. How old is she?"

"I know she does," he agreed. "But you have no idea of the important task she is carrying out. We have to have something to cling on to. Though in a small way by world standards, we have a noble past. Our ancestors certainly were not the drunken fools you see surrounding us today. They took it upon themselves to throw off the shackles of the whites. They trekked – they conquered – now we are back to where we started. Homeless in a national sense. We are being pushed to the brink again... As for her age, even she does not know. I have heard old Kobus calculate it to be at least one hundred and five. Her mother was one of the few survivors at Hoornkrans when the Germans attacked it in 1893."

"So what's your political organisation try'n to achieve?"

"Not all that much," Jonker shrugged. "We want our own nation – a stretch of territory straddling the Orange River – part of Namaland

and part of Griqualand. Let us say from Rehoboth in the north and Upington in the south. A portion from both Namibia and South Africa. We are not after the Namibian diamond mines, or any especially valuable land belonging to the South Africans. We only want a territory that we can govern ourselves. Our people have many talents in farming, building and several white-collar services, so we can export them to our neighbours in Namibia, Botswana and South Africa. We have selected some of the harshest, wildest country on the continent and that is why we need water from the Orange River for irrigation. We are not asking Namibia and South Africa for much, therefore surely the world cannot begrudge the Baster and Nama a homeland of their own? We the Baster, the Nama, the Griqua and Koranna have no tribal or cultural affinity with the Ovambo or any of the Bantu Nations, so how can anyone refuse such a simple request?"

I pointed around at our plush surroundings. "So how did Zes get all this, plus the three flash cars?"

"He is a very astute businessman. He has dealings here and both in South Africa and Angola. He also represents our organisation in most of those business affairs. Let us say that it is his task to arrange some of the funding for our activities. No one asks any questions, therefore he does not have to tell too many lies... Tell me – how well do you know this *Meneer* Dawson-Byrne?"

I was quite surprised that the Pommy geologist's name kept cropping up. "All I know about him is that he's one of the most unfriendly bastards I've ever come across."

He smiled. "You and I are both bastards, Kido. In the real sense of the word. James and I have been friends for many years, and he can be far more different if he so chooses. It is hard to describe it, but he has been like an elder brother, or perhaps an uncle to me for a long time..."

"You're kidding!"

"No! As a matter of fact I have stayed at his home in England. His castle, more like it. Were you aware that he is very, very wealthy?"

"No."

"He comes from the English aristocracy who have their roots in Northern Ireland. He has an estate, servants, plus a Rolls Royce and Bentley. I am telling you the truth," he quickly assured me after my incredulous shake of the head. "I have stayed with him on several occasions. He finds life in England boring, so he goes off to places like Australia and Africa. Mostly Africa. He has been in just about every country on this continent, and I first met him when he was with *Koevoet* up on the Angolan border. Carl Zes and I used to help him and others lay mines up in Ovamboland. That dog of his that was killed at your camp near Karibib?"

"Yeah?"

"James had it up north during the war. It must have been about sixteen years old when it was killed. It saved his life on more than one occasion. Many of our unit's, too. Its aptitude for detecting danger was incredible... Anyhow, James' skill at winning the confidence of the coloured troopies and Bushmen was also extraordinary. He was quite often vilified behind his back by the Boers."

"How come you ended up staying with him in England?"

"It was shortly after the war, when the UNTAG people from the UN oversaw the ceasefire between SWAPO and the South African defence forces. James and I found ourselves at a totally loose end and both he and I began to realise that the new plans for the country did not involve the Baster. It was the same in South Africa. Power in both countries was heading from one end of the spectrum to the other – white to black – there was going to be nothing special for those in between. Then, of course, we had heard about our neighbouring countries and what had happened in Zimbabwe, Zambia and Malawi. That is not to mention Mozambique and Angola... Our organisation, or commando as the Namibian people like to call it, originated long before SWAPO took government. It was first set up as a defence mechanism against the Boers, then, when the Baster saw SWAPO rule was inevitable, the cause just directed its actions against this new enemy. The same situation exists in South Africa. For the past couple of decades defence mechanisms such as ours have come into being all over southern Africa. Take for instance the Muslims in Cape Town. They could see that black rule was inevitable, but who could they trust? The blacks, whom they think are inferior, or the good democratic wishes of the overseas people who are unaware they even exist? Now, when you come across political changes in Africa, there are no subtleties or grey areas. Like I said before – power has gone from one extreme to the other – positive pole to negative pole – white to black. The Muslims believed that they would be left out in the cold, so they set up their own organisation and defence mechanisms, and they are now a clandestine and powerful force to be reckoned with. The cops in Cape Town are petrified of them, so they are a law unto themselves. Organisations such as theirs have been set up all over the place – Joburg, Durban, East London, Port Elizabeth – even in the smaller and medium-sized towns. All these various factions are based along racial or religious lines – coloureds, Muslims, Indians, Cape Malays – all having a common enemy in the blacks. Independence has had nothing to offer them, neither are they likely to ever benefit from it. All they can see is law and order breaking down around them, and hospitals, schools and other services – once taken for granted under the Boers – falling into an abyss, while the only defence left now is their unity... Kobus Van Wyk and others could see our position deteriorating. The position of the Baster under the new government was heading in a far worse direction. Since independence we have had the influx of the Ovambo. They are not only taking over Rehoboth and the town lands, but also Windhoek, Luderitz and several places in Namaland such as Mariental and Keetmanshoop. Even uninhabitable places such as Kalkrand and Karasburg. They are coming down from the north in their hundreds of thousands, all being given special privileges by the new regime. You can see the plan – the more Ovambo in the other tribal areas – the more votes for SWAPO in those areas, until there is a one hundred percent SWAPO parliament.

If that happens our people, the Nama and whoever else, would have no say in government whatsoever. As I said earlier, many years ago we Baster had been given our own *gebeid* under the control of a kaptein. The current Rehoboth leader is Kaptein Diergaardt. Not long after independence the Namibian army surrounded his house with all kinds of weaponry and he was humiliated in front of everybody. There was very nearly bloodshed. Old Kobus and ..."

"Yeah, Wilfred told me about that," I butted in.

"Did he? Ja, there was very nearly blood spilt, though it is a pity, really, that people were not killed. More and more Ovambo have moved in, and so far all our appeals to the world courts have fallen on deaf ears. Perhaps if there had been a bloody incident, more people might have taken more notice? Kobus and several others rallied around the kaptein, but their ancient old rifles would have been useless against AK-47s, rocket-propelled grenades, heavy machine-guns and Kasspir armoured personnel carriers. The very same Kasspirs that the Boers used during the war and for keeping civil order in the black locations such as Katutura... So, in desperation, people like Kobus, his brother Manfred and other respected elders decided to set up a new Baster and Nama commando as an effort to ensure some kind of survival. People have been selected from some of the oldest, most esteemed families – the Klaase family, the Zes family, the Manasse family, the Detlinger family, the Swartbois, the Lamberts and the Goliath's – not only the Witbois. We have cells in Gibeon, Berseba, Tses, Bethanie, Mariental, Keetmanshoop, Warmbad, and that is not taking into consideration major centres such as Windhoek, Rehoboth and Luderitz. Every centre, or at least nearly every centre, has supplied a great man to the *raad,* plus citizens such as Carl, Petrus and Fritz. All these families and centres fought each other in the past, but now we are united."

"And you reckon South Africa's going the same way?"

"Ja, there has been a breakdown in law and order right throughout the country. In different ways and in different places. In Joburg the cops' efficiency is totally shattered. There are certain areas in the city that they simply avoid altogether, for the criminals have taken over. Some of the suburbs have become armed camps of terrified citizens, and the city centre itself has become the domain of Nigerian gangsters where drug dealers and prostitutes thrive unchallenged. Places where bribery and corruption are rampant, and where a person can disappear without there being any chance of the cops even bothering to investigate. Cape Town has always been regarded as a peaceful haven in comparison to Joburg, but over the last decade – since the country got its independence – gangsters and drug peddlers have become the overlords. Especially in the poorer suburbs in the Cape Flats, the Mitchell Plains area and other coloured and black locations. Nowadays we have a minor civil war going on amongst the criminals and people who are sick of having their children and themselves constantly exposed to violence and drugs. The whites, the wealthy ones that is, have battened down with their sophisticated security systems and white armed security guards, whilst the poorer whites live in a no man's land. The so-called affirmative action has taken their jobs and they have to compete against coloureds and blacks who are masters at surviving on nothing. No one wants these whites. They are refugees in their own country and no overseas country will take them in. In Cape Town you see white beggars in the streets and white families sleeping in parks and under bridges, so perhaps there might be a God after all?"

His last words sounded so bitter, I felt I was forced to comment, "All whites can't be that bad. I've met some pretty good whites over the years. It's a pity you haven't met some of the Aussie drillers I work with 'cause they're some of the best people I'm ever likely to meet."

He shook his head and shrugged. "You may be right, but you will find no lower kind of life than the poor, uneducated white South African. The Afrikaner Boer. Under the old regime they were the scum of the white social order, nonetheless the Apartheid segregation laws put any white way above blacks and coloureds who had ten times more intelligence and sophistication than them. The poor white men and women had to be the cruellest, most degrading people of all, for – in their jealousy and misery – they always had some black or coloured to vent their spleen on. Someone to kick like a dog, or someone to enhance their non-existent stature... Believe me, I would not dare to ask for better times. All this confusion opens huge doors of opportunity, albeit mostly criminal opportunities. Ten years ago we had no chance of making a ripple on the surface of the pond of opportunity, now everything is there for the taking."

He stood up. "Would you like a drink?"

"Bloody oath, but a beer not brandy. I don't really go in for spirits."

"Most un-Baster-like," he smiled. "I'll see what Carl has got in the refrigerator. I think I will have a beer myself." He found a six-pack of Windhoek Lager and opened two stubbies.

"So what was Apartheid like?" I queried him.

"Apartheid? You are lucky you missed out on that, Kido. Under Apartheid the coloureds and blacks had to carry pass cards twenty-four hours a day. If you wanted a job with someone, you had to produce your pass card. My card warned any prospective employers that they should contact either the municipal council or the cops before employing me. That was because I was Christian Witbooi's son. A political agitator. I was barred from the council, the railways, or any government or civil departments. I could either work for a Boer or German farmer for three rand a month or possibly as a garden boy in Windhoek for roughly the same. That card meant that anybody, who chose to employ me, was taking a risk. And taking that risk meant that I was very lucky to be employed by the risk-takers, therefore they were not obliged to pay me very much. You see whites with dark birthmarks on their faces, well the information that was put in my pass card was exactly like having a white mark splashed across my forehead. Like the arrows on a convict's clothes. When I was seventeen I worked for some of the Baster farmers in the Rehoboth *Gebeid*, but they paid virtually nothing. My pass documents forbade me leaving the *gebeid*. In those days a bit of mielie-pap and goat's meat, some tobacco and maybe one rand every two months was all I got. Despite being the son of a revered Baster nationalist, I had to sleep out in the open with one blanket amongst the goats and sheep, and may all the angels in Heaven help me if a lynx or jackal took an animal. I had to work sixteen hours a day, seven days a week... When I turned eighteen the Rehoboth Baster had been given more autonomy by the Boers and we had coloured cops taking care of law and order and travel documents. I had my pass card altered so that I could look for work in Windhoek, although my potential employers still needed to be warned and had to contact the authorities. After searching through every white suburb in Windhoek I found work as a garden boy for three rand a month, but I still had to commute the ninety or so kilometres between Rehoboth and Windhoek. Luckily Manfred Van Wyk gave me lifts back and forth in his boss' bakkie. Manfred is a top building contractor nowadays... Anyway, I got a job with this big, fat Boer. His wife was just as fat and growing a beard, and his kids were lazy, sadistic slobs. The Boer gave me the nickname 'black arse' and his kids thought that was terrific. 'Do this, you fockin' black arse – do that, you fockin' black arse!' The Boer's son was the worst. 'Who focked your mother to get you – you fockin', stinking black arse? Some focking, dirty *soutpeil*?"

"What's a *soutpeil*?" I asked.

"It is what the Boers call the English. They say that the English have one foot in England and one foot in Africa, and that their pricks dangle in the sea. Thus the salt-prick. They had all sorts of names for us coloureds – goffels, skollies, half-kaffirs... Once the Boer's son shot me in the back with an air rifle. The pellet went through my skin and hit a rib, and I was positive I was about to die. When I went to his mother for help, she made me walk all the way to the Katutura clinic and she told her son that the air rifle was for shooting birds not skollies. She never scolded him. In fact she never said anything to him. Shooting me was a non-event and I could do nothing. There was no point in going to the cops or complaining to anybody, as I would have instantly lost my job. That could have put a further black mark in my pass card, for I would have needed a reference from the people who had sacked me. When I got back from the clinic the Boer's son shot me again in the backside. I had to have the pellet removed when I got back to Rehoboth that evening. His mother still did nothing."

"Dirty bitch!" I tried to commiserate with him.

"Ja – she was worse – I can assure you. Not only that, the Boer's daughter had a corgi dog that used to go berserk every time I arrived for work. Talk about humans being racists, you should see how dogs behave. You send any coloured or black near a white's dog and see what happens. On one occasion the Boer's son sicced the dog on me and I was quite badly bitten. When I told Manfred about it, the next morning he gave me a ball of sheep's fat that looked very similar to wax, and he told me to feed it to the dog when no one was looking. I carried out his instructions for about a week – feeding it balls of fat – and it did not take long for the dog to go downhill. The vet checked it for various illnesses and could find nothing. He even checked it for poison, but still nothing. It took about ten days for the dog to die. Towards the end it was just lying in its basket with blood coming out of its mouth and nose. When I asked Manfred about it, he told me he had mixed ground glass into the fat... The dog not only died rather slowly, another small benefit came my way."

"And what was that?"

"It is customary for an employer in Namibia to supply at least one meal a day to domestic workers. The cheapest meal was either some stale bread crusts or perhaps a dollop of mielie-pap porridge. I used to prefer the mielie-pap, however it was served to me on the dog's plate, as the Boer's wife was afraid that some goffel's germs might contaminate her good crockery. They never replaced the dog, so at least I had my own plate from then on... Ja, Kido, various methods of retaliating against those Boer pigs could be put into practice. When the housemaid or cook had their eyes elsewhere, I thought up plenty of ways of getting revenge in the kitchen. A blob of phlegm in the yoghurt, a bit of excrement rubbed on the meat, a drop or two of urine in the orange juice. I became a master at concocting various potions for my employer and his family. I had a friend in Rehoboth, Frikkie Albrecht, and he had managed to get himself a chronic dose of gonorrhoea. He had all this green pus coming out of his prick and he was too scared to tell his father. I also spoke to Manfred about that and he got some pills from the Katutura clinic. I swapped the pills with Frikkie for an ENO bottle with about a tablespoon of pus in it. In my naivety I thought the Boer and his family would also go down with gonorrhoea, though it managed to make the Boer's daughter very sick instead. You see, I mixed the pus in some leftover pea soup, and she was the only one who had any of it."

"Bloody hell – you've gotta be kidding?"

That gave him huge amusement. "I swear, I am not. I had no other way of defending my pride. That is what had me amazed at the Boers. They used to take every opportunity to abuse or debase their servants, yet they insisted that their food should be cooked and served by the same people. I often wonder how much contamination must have gone on in the various Boer households? Seriously, Kido, under Apartheid, if you did not happen to be a white, you had no rights whatsoever. If you caused any trouble, you could be thrown into jail. You could be accused of theft, or assault and have no way of defending yourself, as it was a matter of your word against that of a white. White women were the most dangerous, for they could falsely accuse you of indecently touching them or making improper remarks. For a coloured or black to touch a white woman – that was the most cardinal of sins. You had to take abuse from the white kids and it was nothing for your white employer to punch, kick or humiliate you. Under Apartheid you shared the same status with animals."

"And how long did you work for those Boers?"

"About a year and a half. I was not sacked by them. I actually got into trouble in Rehoboth, so I had to hide out on Kobus Van Wyk's farm."

"What happened?"

"It is not important."

"Go on – what happened?" I prodded him.

"It was over Krystal. As you know, the *Ouma* brought us up together like brother and sister. I was at a shebeen and there was this Baster talking about Krystal."

"What's a shebeen?"

"A shebeen nowadays is a bar with possibly a dance floor and music. You find such places in the coloured or black locations. In the old days it was an illegal bar where illegally procured or illegally brewed alcohol was available. I was at this illegal one when this Baster was talking about Krystal."

"What was he saying?"

"He called her names. Like so many Baster men who came from Rehoboth, he had fallen in love with her, but she rejected him under *Ouma* Witbooi's orders. That's what makes you one in a million, Kido. The old lady approves of you. You are also one of Christian Witbooi's sons."

"So what did you do?"

"I stabbed him in the stomach and groin."

"And he died?"

"No, but the cops soon got wind of it, so I had to hide out on old Kobus Van Wyk's farm, as that was the only place I could think of running to. That was almost like jumping from the frying pan into the fire because his whining and scolding made it compulsory to get well away from him as soon as possible. He had me working from daylight till dusk on that farm of his without paying me a cent. Not long after I managed to hitch a ride to Keetmanshoop, and that was when I started going around with Petrus Klaase and Fritz Manasse. They were also wanted by the police, so we decided to embark on a life of crime together. Our first adventure in crime was to steal a car. An old Ford bakkie. We used that to raid a German farm on the Luderitz-Keetmanshoop road. Another Baster who was working on the farm told Fritz that the farmer and his wife would be in Windhoek, so we raided it just on dark. There was no money worth mentioning, but we did manage to steal the farmer's wife's jewellery, three handguns, a rifle and hundreds of rounds of ammunition. With the guns we became much more daring. We robbed several dozen farmers at gunpoint all over Namaland and became quite a scourge. We held up the Standard Bank in Karasburg, then the Barclays bank in Mariental. We tried the same thing with the Standard Bank in Keetmanshoop, but walked straight into a police ambush. Fritz was hit immediately, and it was a miracle that Klaasie and I managed to get him away. What saved us was that we had a four-wheel drive Toyota. It was not as fast as the cop cars, but it could certainly handle rough terrain that they could not. As soon as we reached the outskirts of Keetmanshoop – in the direction of Grunau – we smashed our way over a farm fence, which left the cop cars stranded. Then, keeping off the roads by travelling through the veld, we circled back north in the direction of Mariental. By then Fritz was in a very bad way, so we took him to the Haib Rhenish mission where there was a fully trained Baster clinic sister. She was a cousin of Carl Zes'. A couple of days later the three of us had to hide out with old Kobus again and he nearly drove us mad with his scolding and lecturing."

"And what happened after that?"

"There was an amnesty put out on wanted criminals, on condition they went to fight up at the border. I reluctantly joined the South West African security forces, and that is how I met James."

"And what gave that scar on your neck?"

"An irate Baster tried to kill me."

"Over a woman – a jealous husband?"

"No!" he chuckled. "It was much more mundane than that. It happened in a little Baster/Nama centre called Tses. On the main highway to South Africa, between Mariental and Keetmanshoop, there are two settlements called Berseba and Tses that are just about opposite each other on each side of the B1 highway about thirty or so kilometres apart. Nevertheless the south, being as incredibly dry as it is, has always had problems with water and the people of Tses got into a feud with the people of Berseba over water rights. I was down there for political reasons at the time and managed to find myself in the middle of a fight. It was a fairly close thing. Another inch to the left and my carotid artery would have been severed... What happened to you?"

A feeling of revulsion came over me as I thought back to my early youth. "Believe me, your scar's far more honourable. A Catholic brother came in the middle of the night to molest me. In order to escape, I jumped out of a window, but forgot to open it first. I tell you..."

There was a knock on the back door. Jonker looked at me, then put a finger to his lips, indicating I should be silent. Much to my amazement he pulled out a snub-nosed revolver from under his leather jacket. He called out something in Afrikaans.

"It's me, Jonker." I could recognise that voice anywhere; it was Dawson-Byrne! "Ah, so the twins meet at last!"

When I queried the clandestine entry via the back door, Jonker explained: "We cannot be too careful. If SWAPO's secret police had come visiting, I might have had to use this," he put the revolver back in his belt."

"It's still a bit corny," I hinted to the Pommy. "Just about everybody in Rehoboth has seen me around. I was at Herman's funeral and helped carry the coffin – remember?"

He nodded his head. "True, but as Jonker said, he can't be too careful. SWAPO can't abide any sort of political activity against them, and seldom do their secret police take any prisoners."

There was a further knock on the door, and the Pommy opened it for Carl Zes and Fritz Manasse. Zes had brought a bottle of brandy with him, and he filled up a tumbler with the light brown liquid. He drank the brandy down in one hit, topped up the glass and poured a slug out for Manasse. He then turned to Dawson-Byrne. "It was just as we envisaged – he is out on bail. Klaasie picked him up at the court.

You should see the commotion at that new court building – talk about it being a huge white elephant – nobody knew what was going on. It took about half an hour to find our way out of the place."

"Where is he now?" Jonker wanted to know.

"Klaasie has taken him down to Schlip, as was arranged. He is safe there for the time being, but not for long if the people at Schlip discover that he is there."

"What's happening?" I asked my brother.

He studied the faces of Zes and Dawson-Byrne before replying, "Rehoboth has been the home of many notorious people, both men and woman. One such woman we used to call 'the ghost'. Her real name was Marian and she once used to be regarded as one of the most beautiful women in Rehoboth and Namaland. She would not have been more than thirty at most, yet looked about seventy. She married fairly early – about eighteen I think – because every Baster man from here to South Africa was after her hand in marriage. At last it was Willie Beukes who captured her heart, and for the life of every red-blooded male in Rehoboth we could not fathom what he had that no one else had... Never mind that, Willie was killed up at the border when the Ratel armoured car he was fighting in received a direct hit from a Cuban anti-tank gun. On the news of Willie's death many suitors lined up to take his place, but Marian's heart had been exploded like that Ratel. She started drinking and neglecting herself. When she ran out of the few savings she and Willie had, she sold Willie's little Datsun bakkie. Some time later she received compensation from the South African military, although that quickly ran out. Next she sold the furniture, the house, everything. She received the nickname 'ghost' for she literally haunted all the liquor outlets and *drankwinkels*. Gradually her hair, clothes and body became covered in grime. People tried to take her into their houses, but she reacted like some trapped animal. Behind the Shell garage in Rehoboth there is an abandoned car that became her refuge. A Toyota station wagon, I think. The cops tried to evict her, but she and some of us made such a fuss, they agreed to leave her in peace. Many have tried to help her

– the Rehoboth Women's Committee, the Catholic priest, plus nursing sisters from the hospital – all were so rejected by her, they had no choice but to let her be. People on occasion used to leave food leftovers outside the car and they always gave the odd fifty cent piece or dollar coin to her when she begged outside the *drankwinkels*. No one had seen her sober for years and gradually she became a toothless skeleton. Her harassing and begging became a great annoyance to everyone, nevertheless no one objected that much that they would do her any harm."

"That was until about two months ago," Zes added.

"Ja, not till recently," Jonker agreed. He paused to help himself to some of Zes' brandy. "Give me your opinion on something here, Kido? What should happen to an individual – a man – who lures such a person as Marian to a place where he tortures her to near death? He does not rape her, but mutilates her genitals. He burns almost her entire body with cigarettes, and then eventually tries to stab her to death. This went on for hours and hours."

"What's he on about?" I asked Dawson-Byrne.

He lit a cigar before replying, "This fellow bought a couple of bottles of wine and invited the ghost out for a little drink or two. They ended up out at the abandoned Swartmodder copper mine, and after a few drinks he started abusing her. First off, he punched her around for a while, and then he started cutting her up with a knife. The knife was pushed up her fanny and then he started burning her breasts with cigarettes. God knows what she must've gone through... If that wasn't enough, he stabbed her in the neck and chest about a dozen times or so and left her for dead."

"Not quite, though," Zes followed up. "By some incredible miracle the ghost recovered enough to walk back to that bridge south of town that straddles the Rehoboth River. It is on the main road to Kalkrand. One of the workers out at the dairy farm found her hanging on to the bridge railings and took her to the hospital. She lived long enough to tell constable Alby Klein what had happened and the guy was arrested shortly after."

"Who was this bloke?" I turned to Dawson-Byrne once more.

"A horrible little Baster chappie by the name of Koot Basson."

"Ja," Jonker's expression looked sour. "After trying to kill Marian, he was very busy establishing an alibi with his cousin Izaak Basson. As you can imagine the cops were very uptight, so they held on to Koot, regardless of what stories he and his cousin came up with. Koot had come to their attention before as a result of his beating up several women."

"That is correct, he had a penchant for beating women," Zes affirmed. "Once the police transported Koot up to Windhoek to the lock-up there, Klaasie and I did a bit of interrogating of our own. We took Zakkie Basson for a little ride out to Sam Khubis, to the Baster cemetery. It was night time and the moon gave the graves the required effect we wanted. We told him to pick a spot for his own grave, as he would be having his throat cut after he had said his prayers. We only needed a short while to get him admitting that he had covered up for Koot. It also took very little to convince him that every Baster – male or female – in the Rehoboth *Gebied* would gladly disembowel him if he tried to alter the course of justice on behalf of his cousin."

"Every Baster in the Rehoboth *Gebied* went to Marian's funeral," Fritz Manasse added. "People came from all over – Keetmanshoop, Warmbad, Gibeon, Bethanie, Tses and Berseba. There was very nearly a riot as people screamed for Koot Basson's blood. Nobody really paid any attention to the ghost when she was alive, but her death sure had a uniting effect on the Baster."

"Now he's out on bail," Dawson-Byrne shrugged his shoulders at no one in particular. "The Africans, black ones that is, have an incredibly forgiving nature. As soon as SWAPO took over the government, the first thing they insisted on was banning the death sentence. Just shows you what..."

"It was the country's new constitution that banned the death penalty," Zes cut in.

"True," the Pommy admitted, "but SWAPO were most adamant about that when it came to drawing up the new constitution. It's the same in South Africa – capital punishment's outlawed over there – the ANC can be held responsible or blamed for that... Nevertheless, Basson's out on bail, and, even if he's convicted, he'll be out in three or four years. The country's prisons are overcrowded."

"We now have our hands on Basson," Jonker told me, "so that we can ensure that justice is carried out. We have been instructed to do so by the *raad.*"

CHAPTER 53

THE DARK SIDE OF THE POMMY!

Zes, Jonker and Manasse had some meeting to go to, thus leaving the Pommy geo' and me alone together. It started flogging down rain and I noticed that despite the house's opulence, the roof leaked in certain places.

"It's going to be a record year for rain," Dawson-Byrne declared, as he placed plastic buckets in strategic positions in order to catch the drops of water. "The trouble is the Von Bach Dam at Okahandja isn't receiving too much. It's the main storage dam for Windhoek and it's only about forty percent full. Should keep the place running for another couple of years, still, with all the rural Afs moving into the squatter camps, the city's population's growing way too fast."

I changed the subject altogether, "How come you're involved with Jonker? Why's my brother so special to you?"

He poured out some of Zes' brandy. "There are several reasons why I don't mind giving Jonker a helping hand now and then. To start with, let's go back to the Border War. People like him, Zes, Manasse and Klaase joined up to fight on the South Africans' side because they preferred the whites to the blacks, regardless of the bloody-mindedness of the Boers. If the whites can be prejudiced, the blacks can be tenfold, and you can't really blame them. When it came to the Boers' bastardry, the average black was treated far worse than the everyday coloured, and the blacks regard the coloureds as being half white not half black. They're also jealous of the coloureds' superior mentality... Look, I'm not being bigoted here, if someone was to run an IQ test between the coloureds and the blacks, the coloureds would come up trumps every time. It's the same as your Australian Aborigines – it's the half-caste ones who're at the centre of all the land claims they're having over there. Them and the money-grubbing, white lawyers. The full bloods, if there are any left, wouldn't have a clue of what day it was... Nonetheless, it doesn't take a Mensa student to realise that the coloureds are being given a rotten deal. If not now, things can only get worse for them. As your brother's most probably told you, the Ovambo are migrating down from the north in their thousands. God knows, there's scarcely enough work in the south – Mariental, Keetmanshoop, Gibeon, Luderitz – the Ovambo are taking over everything. When…"

"But you're a bloody geo'," I butted in. "What're you doing hanging around with Jonker, who's obviously in the shit with the authorities?"

"Very true, but I fought with these people up in Angola, and when you've got your life in other peoples' hands, you learn as much about them as you can and fast. People like Zes, Manasse, Klaase and your brother came across absolutely one hundred percent. They never hesitated when it came to putting their lives on the line for you, and all they expected in return was just the slightest token of respect. The low life Boers couldn't even muster that."

"So what'll happen with this Koot Basson bloke?"

"Can you keep this to yourself?"

"Yeah, I reckon so."

"Good man! As you know, some of the Baster have set up an organisation in order to get some independence of their own. They're not asking for all that much, really, just some homeland that they can govern themselves. The way they've gone about it, there's a fairly good chance they might succeed."

"I can't see how," I disagreed. "They're talking about taking over land both in Namibia and South Africa. If South Africa's ANC and SWAPO object to it, they'll have no chance. Like you told Dave

Wheeler and I before, the do-gooders seem perfectly happy with SWAPO and the ANC being in charge. Not only that, the world's governments are probably satisfied that Namibia and South Africa have got democratically elected governments, so they certainly won't go out of their way to help Jonker and his mob... Never mind that, what's all this gotta do with Koot Basson?"

"Everything. Amongst other things, Jonker's job in the organisation is recruiting and keeping people in line. Every now and then he has to do something fairly drastic in order to demonstrate to the ordinary people that this organisation's a force to be reckoned with. The Baster are appalled at the cruelty and suffering that that Baster woman had to go through, regardless of how hopeless she was. They see all Namibian courts as being SWAPO courts and they want good, old-fashioned justice."

"Such as?"

"They're going to bump him off."

"You can't be serious!" I was incredulous. "You mean they're actually gunna kill him?"

"That's exactly what I mean. You going to the coppers or something?"

"No."

"Why should you, anyway? Tell me – what would you do with Basson, if you knew you could get away with it?"

"I'd do exactly the same to the bastard as he did to the woman. I wouldn't hesitate."

"I couldn't agree with you more! An eye for an eye and a tooth for a tooth. Moses had the right handle on things. There's no room for the New Testament nowadays, as turning the other cheek's certainly not applicable here in Africa. Like I've always said – they should hand over all those who rape, kill and abuse women to the fathers of the victims, and then you'd see some logical justice."

CHAPTER 54

CEMETERY AT SAM KHUBIS!

It was still dark when I awoke the next morning. The Pommy geo' was gone and my twin was in the kitchen brewing coffee and making some kind of a porridge out of mielie-pap that he served up with sour milk and honey.

"Where's Zes and the others?" I queried.

"They have gone down to Schlip. We shall be joining up with them this afternoon."

"Dawson-Byrne said you were gunna kill Koot Basson. He was kidding, of course, wasn't he?"

He stirred away at his porridge as if he was making cement, then he looked over my shoulder, totally avoiding eye contact. "A good many of our Nama and Baster people know an organisation such as ours exists. We are deliberately trying to remain a mystery to them, so that they feel some benevolent shadow is taking care of their interests in these troubled times. Under the old regime the Boers would have allowed a Baster court to try Basson. Perhaps he would not have been sentenced to death, but at least the people could have seen appropriate justice carried out by Baster hands. While we make out in one direction that we are benevolent, we also have to amply display that we are a very dangerous organisation when it comes to betrayal. We have to..."

"Like a kind of Mafia?" I interrupted him. "You take care of the big family, but God help anyone who rocks your boat, or looks like betraying you?"

"You are as intelligent as I am," he smiled. "You have it in a walnut shell."

"A nutshell?"

"Ja, in a nutshell. We are here to protect the peoples' interests – uphold their values and history – to maintain strict loyalty and unity. By dealing with Basson we can achieve all three... Tell me, have you ever been stopped by the authorities over here? Being my exact double, I would be most surprised if someone has not pulled you up for questioning."

I thought back to the immigration official at the Windhoek International Airport, then the cop who had questioned me outside the mansion in Klein Windhoek. Also, of course, there was the white inspector who was investigating the demise of Van der Merwe at Karibib. "I've been asked strange questions by a couple of cops, but I always had the other drillers to vouch for me. Naturally your unsavoury reputation's gone before me?"

"Most probably. You will find my photograph in every police station and at every border post... Nevertheless, we must leave here, as there is something important I want to show you."

He and I climbed into Zes' Isuzu bakkie and we headed west down the Klein Aub road just on noon. The rain had fairly stuffed the road up, and we passed two red graders bravely battling to make something out of the gravel, mud and slush. As we passed Kobos I noticed that the shell of the wrecked Toyota was still there and I felt a pang of regret when I thought of Steve and Bob. As the tiny village of Klein Aub was coming into view on the horizon, Jonker turned on to a track that headed north, and then stopped to allow me to open a gate. After that we headed towards a range of granite mountains and the track deteriorated considerably as we wended our way through them. We travelled through a series of natural amphitheatres; huge boulders of granite and other kinds of rock piled on top of one another, then all of a sudden we drove through a large archway that had a massive sign reading: 'SAM KHUBIS'.

He pulled the Isuzu up close to the concrete wall of a graveyard. All in all the cemetery wasn't very big. Perhaps forty metres by thirty. It was surrounded by a three or maybe four foot wall. Some of the graves had concrete covers and the odd headstone with faded or illegible names on it; others were barely discernible in the sandy soil. There was mostly stark, brown-grey concrete in equally rough and barren surroundings. My brother pointed to the granite walls that encircled us. "Try and imagine what it was like. Our people had come to this place for refuge, and the German *Schutztruppen* tried to kill all of them with rifles from the mountains around us." He pointed to the graves within the confines of the cemetery. "Do you see that big one over there?"

"Yeah?"

"That is a mass grave. I think there are nine or ten buried there – no one knows for sure. This is the most holy shrine of the Baster."

"I met an old man at Klein Aub who reckoned he was here at the time," I told him. "He had an old medal he wanted to show me."

"Ja, that would be old *Meneer* Elias Bloedoog. He is ancient, but remembers everything quite clearly. He has a son who is a great man in our political organisation."

"So there was a slaughter here?"

"Ja! As *Ouma* Elsabeth would have told you, the Baster fought on the German side on several occasions. Then, at the commencement of the First Great War, when the Germans needed their help the most, the Baster were uncertain as to whether they wanted to fight other white armies such as the British from overseas, or the Boers to the south. History has it that the Baster assured the Germans of their neutrality, however the Germans did not want to take any chances and resorted to their age-old solution for problems by trying to wipe out the Baster altogether. When word arrived in Rehoboth that the Germans were coming to destroy them, the Baster fled to this place, hoping that they could hide in these mountains. The *Schutztruppen* cavalry quickly caught up and they and had them surrounded here. As you can see by the graves, they achieved part of their objective... Then word must have arrived from the south that an enemy column had either just crossed the Orange River or had landed at Walvis Bay. A guard picket of a handful of *Schutztruppen* were left to guard the Baster, while the remainder headed south or wherever to see what was going on. Nobody is exactly sure of what happened after that, but in the dead of night the surviving Baster somehow managed to sneak past the German pickets. Word has it that they managed to cut a few German throats when doing so, though there are no German graves here. There are stories I have heard of people finding rusted, old German bayonets, plus cartridges and even an old Mauser rifle in the mountains surrounding us."

"So this's like some kind of a shrine to the Baster?"

"Our most sacred place! Once a year on May 8th we hold a church service out here and the people have a kind of wake afterwards. Alcohol is supposed to be banned, but nearly every male carries a quarter-jack or two of brandy in a hip pocket. *Ouma* Elsabeth has attended just about every gathering that has ever taken place here, and she really comes down on anyone who she finds with liquor on their breath. Krystal, too, for that matter... Are you sure she is the one for you, as she and Elsabeth have come from the same mould?"

I decided to be perfectly frank with him. "Never in my life have I met anyone like Krystal. Never in my life have I ever been in love before. I must love her because every time I think of her or her name, it really makes me feel good. If you or God wanted to tell me that I could spend the rest of my life with her, I'd be the happiest man on this earth."

He nodded. "Tell me – do you believe in God?" He pointed to the sky. "Do you actually think there is a God up there watching over us?"

"In my own way I do."

"I do not know so much. The predikants or priests tell us that God loves all men equally, regardless of the colour of their skin. How come some are so lucky, and then others are so unlucky? I am not actually talking about race or colour in particular, simply how some individuals are so fortunate, while others suffer misery and misfortune? Why does God seem to discriminate so much between one individual or another? If God loves all his children equally, then why has He created beautiful people and ugly people? We used to often ask the predikants that. Take for instance the film stars in America or elsewhere. In most cases film stars are chosen on account of their good looks, and then after that they are worshipped by their fans and make millions of dollars. It is the same with those female pop stars – not only do they sing magnificently, most are beautiful as well. You hear of film stars refusing as much as twenty million US dollars because they did not fancy a particular part in a film... Then what about the sportsmen and women who are also paid millions of US dollars? How come God created them, whilst he also created those who are condemned to spend their lives in pain, mediocrity or a wheelchair? What is the name of that man who has that big computer company in America? He is supposed to be the world's richest man?"

"Bill Gates, you mean?"

"Ja – Gates is his name. He is supposed to be worth over fifty thousand million US dollars. Can you imagine that? ... No, the predikants lied and religion is a fraud. Someone told me that we possibly live more than one life, and, if we are good in a previous life, we enjoy the next life even more. If you are poor in one life, you are rich in the next one. I have never seen that written in the Scriptures."

"You've read the Scriptures?"

"Our father knew the Bible almost by heart. I was brought up by *Ouma* Elsabeth, so what do you expect? Personally, I think the Scriptures, the churches and the whole way of religion is a total racket. Turning the other cheek – loving your fellow man – total rubbish! There are plenty of people who rob, lie, murder and cheat, yet the world to such people is all milk and honey. Look at the way the Boers exploited the blacks and coloureds here in Namibia and in South Africa, and how they grew rich by doing so? The Bible says that it is easier for a camel to pass through the eye of a needle, than it is for a rich man to enter the Kingdom of Heaven, nonetheless give me the cash any day. With the cash you get freedom, privilege and respect. Most importantly – freedom. Without the cash you are nothing and a slave to others. My philosophy is that I am prepared to do absolutely anything in order to get my hands on the cash."

"Too true," I agreed. "It's the same back in Aussie. Over there money's everything. You're judged by how much money you've got. If you've got none, people want to kick your arse, but, if you've got heaps, people want to crawl up your arse. It's the Aussie way... Talking about money, are you making anything out of this political business?"

"Ssh!" he said, pointing at the graves. "We might have people listening to our conversation. Ja, I am being amply compensated for what I am doing. I do not go along with the Scriptures. I believe we are given one life and we have to make the most of it by fair means or foul. If life, luck, brains, skin colour or privilege do not give you the means, take them with both hands in any way that becomes available. The richer you are, the more powerful you are. Only a fool fails to realise that. Power is the most wholesome commodity on offer as far as I am concerned. To get that I need money – lots of it – and I could not care how I get it. This hardly makes me so bad. God has smiled on many who have used any method available to enrich themselves. There are vast possibilities in the..."

He fell silent as we heard a vehicle approaching in the distance. It was almost five o' clock in the afternoon and Sam Khubis had been extraordinarily quiet; neither the wind nor the sound of a bird had penetrated the silence. I looked about me once more; the cemetery, the granite mountains and the azure sky had an awesome effect, and the sound of the approaching vehicle seemed to bring an ominous message with it as it came nearer and nearer.

"Sounds like a vehicle's coming this way," I stated the obvious.

"They have brought Basson," Jonker touched my arm. "Come, let us meet up with them."

"Basson?" I couldn't fathom what he was getting at. "What's going on?"

He turned his back on me and headed for the cemetery gate. "You shall soon see."

Zes, Manasse and Petrus Klaase drove up in a Toyota Hilux dualcab, and they had a very nervous looking coloured individual with them. Basson looked to be about thirty-five or so, and he was a skinny, sloppy specimen; his brown, curly hair was matted; he was unshaven and his white shirt and grey trousers looked as if he had slept in them for months. He had odd socks on, one lime green and one navy blue; his black shoes were coming adrift from their soles and were dusty and scuffed from the lack of any care. His face had a puffy, emaciated look about it and he had an ochre coloured skin. He had almost Oriental eyes. My brother shook his hand in a perfectly friendly manner, then introduced him to me, "Koot – my brother, Kido – Kido – Koot Basson." I could smell brandy on the bloke's breath when I shook his hand.

Zes produced another two of his omnipresent bottles of Brandy. He, Manasse, Klaase, Jonker and I sipped out of one, and Basson was given one for himself. We surrounded Basson in silence as nobody seemed to have anything in particular to say.

Finally it was Basson who broke the silence: "It has been ages since I last saw you, Jonker. No one told me you had a brother – he looks just like you." When he was given no reply, he went on a different tack, "Thanks for picking me up at the court house. It was a good idea to go to Schlip. Some of the Rehoboth Baster still think I was the one who hurt the ghost. There were a lot of those people out to get me."

Zes pointed right at him. "But you *did* do those things to the ghost. You beat her with your fists – cut her with a knife – mutilated her vagina – burned her with cigarettes – stabbed her many times."

Basson's eyes flew wide with fright and he started shaking uncontrollably. He quickly tried to look at all those surrounding him at once, and then he held the bottle of brandy to his chest with one hand, while trying to shield his face with the other. "Agh – no, man!" he wailed. "Please – I am innocent! You can ask my cousin, Zakkie. I was with him the whole time at his house. I was helping him fix his bakkie."

"We have already had Zakkie out here," Klaase assured him. "He told us you came nowhere near him on that day and that he was covering for you... Here, look at this." He removed a fairly tatty brown envelope with a window in it from his inside jacket pocket. From the envelope he took out a folded piece of paper that he opened up. "For Kido, who does not understand Afrikaans too much, I will read this out in English. Here we go – 'I, Izaak Basson, do hereby swear that my cousin Koot came to me in order to make a plan to cover for him. At the time Marian Beukes was attacked, my cousin was nowhere near me or my house, but he asked me to say that he was. I swear this on my mother's and father's graves'."

Basson started blubbing then. "He is telling lies in that letter, I swear it. He has never liked me. He has always tried to cause me trouble. If you want, you can take me back to the cops and they can arrest me again."

"Have some more brandy," Manasse encouraged.

Basson welcomed those friendly words from Fritz like a starving dog and he took a huge swallow of brandy that nearly made him cough his lungs out. When he recovered from the fit, Zes handed him a lighted cigarette, then pointed to those around him who had Basson penned in. "We are representing all Rehobothers. We – the police – the community know that you murdered Marion Beukes. It was scarcely the first time you abused a woman. You cut Rosie Boois' face. You kicked Rena Cloete in the stomach after you knocked her down. She was pregnant and nearly lost her baby. She could not prove it, but it was you who beat up Sara Lebe... You dearly love abusing women."

"Please!" Basson sobbed. "Please take me to the cops. I will confess to everything. I am very sorry. Please, I shall ask to be locked up for the rest of my life."

"Drink your brandy!" Fritz ordered, his voice much harsher that time.

Basson took another swig of the fortified wine, and most of it slobbered down his chin. His grey trousers turned a charcoal colour as he pissed in them.

I looked over at Jonker, but his eyes avoided mine. It was hard to work out what was going to happen next. Perhaps they were going to give Basson a good hiding, then turn him over to the cops?

"You are wasting my good brandy," Zes snarled. "Drink the bottle. I will give you more when you have finished it. Come on – drink!"

I took a quick sip from the other bottle; though my guts didn't take to it very kindly, what with all the tension that surrounded us. Ignoring my guts, I took a much bigger mouthful to calm my nerves. The spirit seemed to have raced to my brain, as it felt as if I was walking on a huge sponge. I seemed to have difficulty placing one foot in front of the other, and the colours around me seemed to be changing hue and shape every few seconds. I fought down the impulse of giggling, as I was determined that the others wouldn't think I couldn't handle the grog.

Under Zes' menacing glare, Basson swallowed more and more of the spirit, as if his life depended on it. Tears, snot and some of the liquor dribbled down his face. He stank from where he had shit his daks.

"We are going to kill you, Koot," Zes told him matter-of-factly, "so I think it is time that you made your peace with God. Come, kneel down, so we can pray with you."

"No, please," Basson pleaded. "Take me to the cops. Please, I will..."

"Kneel down!" Jonker pulled him down on his knees.

We all knelt around Basson. Zes, Klaase and Manasse held their hands in front of their chins, their eyes firmly shut. I snuck a glance at my brother; he held his hands in the same position, and he was busy avoiding my attention. Basson was just sobbing his eyes out.

"We are but specks of dust in comparison to Your Magnificence, oh Lord," Zes began, "but we spend each day doing our utmost to serve You in all ways. We beg Your forgiveness for Koot Basson." From there he started droning on in Afrikaans, and then he uttered some sort of incantations that were copied by the others except Basson. It was all pretty weird; still I was amazed at how four tough males could be so gentle and fluent when it came to their religion. After about ten minutes of prayers we stood up.

Leaving Fritz to guard Basson, my brother called the rest of us to one side. "Okay, what is next?" he anxiously whispered to Zes. He also looked fairly pissed because his eyes rolled in all directions and his voice was becoming slurred. There was saliva drooling down from the corner of his mouth. Klaase and Manasse looked equally rat-arsed, although Zes seemed to have his wits about him.

He looked deep in thought for a while, and then he nodded. "We do as planned. We do to him what he did to the ghost. We will..."

"Surely you're not gunna kill him?" I couldn't believe what I was hearing. "What about the bloody cops?"

"Let us make him very drunk first?" Petrus Klaase made out that he hadn't heard me.

Zes nodded. "What do you think I am doing? We had better have a bit more brandy ourselves. Here, Kido, finish this bottle."

Two more bottles appeared. Basson was ordered to drain his first one and was given another, a couple of minutes after we opened the other one and passed it round. The sun had sunk below the granite mountains to the west and there was quite a racket as a swarm of birds argued over roosting opportunities in a nearby camel thorn tree. My head was spinning like a top and I still had the urge to burst out laughing. I was that pissed, I could hardly light a smoke properly. Finally I managed to grab Jonker's arm. "So what you gunna do? Now that you've got proof that he hasn't got an alibi, are you gunna hand him over to the cops? You're kidding about killing him – right?"

"No, Kido, the cops have already had their chance. The SWAPO cops, that is. Now it is time that some real justice is served."

CHAPTER 55

THE MURDER!

As if in some nightmare I watched Fritz Manasse start the ball rolling by punching Basson in the face. The skinny coloured was knocked sprawling, then Klaase kicked him in the groin, making him puke all over the granite sand. Zes pulled him up by the scruff of the neck and dragged him over to the cemetery wall so that he could see all the beckoning outlines of the graves. It was getting quite dark by then. "See there," he pointed at the graves with one hand, while holding Basson's neck with the other. "These are the resting places of our heroes. Who knows if a Heaven or a Hell truly exists, but you will be meeting up with them very shortly. I wonder what kind of reception you shall find?"

It required quite a lot more brandy to manage with what happened after that. Jonker produced a knife, a kind of Bowie knife, and cut Basson straight down the side of his face from his eyebrow to his chin. It wasn't a deep cut or anything, yet it had Basson screaming. Zes then sliced the bloke's nose wide open, and passed the knife to Fritz. With brandy and bile stinging my throat, I watched Fritz cut Basson's left cheek sideways. The knife was very sharp, for the gentle pressure he used had the blade scraping against his teeth. Basson was screaming, crying, jabbering and trying to escape all at once, but the others held him firmly. Klaase had a go next, although Bassoon was well and truly out to it by then; his face having been cut to ribbons.

I tried to shout at them to stop, but couldn't get a word out. Instead I lost my balance and fell sideways onto the ground. It seemed to take an eternity to get to my feet once more.

"Should we still burn him with cigarettes?" Fritz asked Jonker, as we all took more brandy on board. "I think we should."

"No, let us just kill him and be done with it," Zes argued. "There is no need to..."

"Hang on a sec'," I tried to intervene. "Haven't you done enough already? You kill him, and you'll be up for murder. Fair go, he's had enough..."

Totally ignoring me, my brother stabbed Basson first, thumping the blade into the man's stomach, causing his body to jack-knife. With all kinds of rainbows and coloured dots flashing before my eyes, I saw Petrus send the knife gouging into Basson's throat. He stabbed him twice more, and after that Fritz and Zes stabbed him about a half-dozen times each.

"Is he dead?" I demanded almost hysterically as we stepped back to survey the blood-soaked body. "Fuckin' hell – what've you done?" I felt I was about to chunder at any time and could barely stand upright.

"Make sure he is," Jonker instructed Fritz.

Fritz cut Basson's throat, and did such a good job the head was almost severed from the body! Blood came spurting out, but didn't travel too far on account of the sandy soil.

Klaase spewed out a mixture of brandy and green slime, which for some extraordinary reason made me feel a whole lot better, then Zes made a crack about wasting good liquor and we all started pissing ourselves laughing.

Zes shook my hand. "Although you took no part in the murder, you are one of us now. We may depart in death, yet here we have come together in death." I thought that was rather melodramatic; still I didn't want to ruin the moment for him.

The others shook my hand and I could see that my twin was tickled pink by all that had happened. It didn't take a wise individual to realise that they had me over a barrel if ever there came a time when I might betray them. While I had had nothing to do with the killing, it would be their combined testimony against that of mine. Somehow that didn't seem to matter too much, for the brandy brought about an inexplicable euphoria within me.

"What you gunna do with the body – you just gunna leave it here?" I asked Zes.

He pointed to the base of one of the mountains. "No, help us move it up there into those boulders, and we shall blow it up."

"Blow it up? How you gunna do that? Why blow it up?"

"So the forensic people have nothing to use if the body is found," my brother explained. "It is an old trick we learned during the Border War when it came to certain embarrassment with prisoners of war. James was a very good teacher."

It was quite a chore carting Basson's body up into a collection of boulders, for we were all fairly rat shit from the brandy. My hands and feet had gone numb and I was seeing three versions of everything around me. I had never felt pissed like that before, so put it down to not being used to brandy. Zes had opened a fifth bottle! I was almost in a trance as I watched him and Petrus bind about a dozen light grey, plastic sticks around the corpse with lengths of broad, brown, plastic tape. "Won't people for miles around hear it when it goes off?" I asked Jonker. "You seem to have enough there to blow up a train?"

He and the others thought that was outrageously funny. "The more explosive the better," he replied after he managed to stop laughing. "We will vaporise the body. Stop worrying, we shall be miles from here when it explodes. Carl is using a very slow-burning sump fuse. About half an hour, Carl?"

"Maybe a little longer."

We didn't go back to the Klein Aub road; instead headed farther north up a bush track, each of us leaving in the same vehicle we had arrived in. After about a kilometre or so my brother and I reached a fairly good road, and then he stopped the car.

"Why are we stopping?" I asked.

"We had better wait and check that the explosives go off. Klaasie and Zes are experts with explosives, nevertheless we want to make certain before we leave altogether."

"Where are they?"

"They have taken another route. We shall meet up back in Rehoboth. It is better that we split up."

After almost an eternity we heard a dull thud in the distance and a white plume of smoke headed skywards. The drive back to Rehoboth wasn't a pleasant one, considering I had to have a chunder twice on the way. It was hard to tell if it was from too much brandy, for the influence of the liquor had left my brain and the enormity of what I had seen really came back to hammer me! I was revolted by what they had done. At any second I expected the Namibian cops to pitch up either in front or behind us. I was convinced that there would be a police roadblock waiting for us just around the corner. By some circuitous route we ended up on the Oanob Dam road that emptied out on the main Windhoek-Rehoboth road just slightly north of Rehoboth. We reached Zes' house without being arrested, and there was no sign of him and the others.

In order to take my mind off things, I asked Jonker, "This war on the border you all keep talking about? Were you forced to go, or was it voluntary?"

"As I told you last night, Klaasie, Fritz and I had to join in order not to go to jail. Carl volunteered. It was in 1980 when conscription was introduced in the South West. Zes joined first, then Klaasie. Fritz and I fronted up at the same time about three months later. The pay was good and the food was very good."

"Not all that much incentive to risk your lives?"

"True," he agreed, "but we were camped very close to Zes. He was with the Quartermasters' Corps and devised a multitude of ways when it came to robbing the South African military blind. All the Cuca shops up north were overflowing with brandy, wine and beer. Courtesy of our Mr Zes."

"What's a Cuca shop?"

"It is the name they have for liquor shops or *drankwinkels* up north. Cuca comes from the name of some Angolan brand of beer. Carl siphoned off truckloads of the South Africans' alcohol and made a small fortune by doing so. He hardly stopped there – food, clothing, vehicle parts, furniture and canvas of all descriptions. If he had been caught, the Boers would have put him in front of a firing squad."

"And how come you and Dawson-Byrne met up?"

"It was mainly through the Bushman trackers. There was segregation in all the camps – whites, coloureds, blacks – so they billeted us with the Bushmen, and James was in charge of a platoon of those people. Klaasie, Fritz and I were with the sappers and it was our job to clear the roads of mines. We used to collect the odd mine or two for James and he and some other *Koevoet* used to use such devices against the PLAN fighters. Somehow our unit merged with his unit and he became our commanding officer. We were prepared to follow that man to the very ends of the earth after that."

"Did you get to kill any PLAN fighters?"

He shrugged. "It is hard to say how many, really. Nothing was actually that cut and dried. Some I killed because I aimed my R4 at them and pulled the trigger – watching them drop. In most contacts in heavy bush you simply fired as fast as you could in the direction you thought the enemy were. Most of the time you kept your head as close to the ground as possible and did not shoot at all. We travelled a lot in helicopters and fired from them, but we seldom saw the enemy when we were doing that. It was very frightening at times, but we were quite safe with good officers and NCOs. Our side's kill ratio was at least seventeen times that of the enemy... I quite enjoyed myself in the army."

Zes and the others arrived at last and they had a goat carcass that they wanted to cook on a spit; however the rain forbade it, so we had to eat inside. The others were in such a hale and hearty mood, it was impossible to believe that they had just murdered another human being that afternoon, whilst I drank beer after beer in order to chase away my memory of the event.

CHAPTER 56

ZES TRIES TO BLACKMAIL ME!

The next day I not only had a ball-tearing hangover, I was petrified with fear as well. Especially since I had been left alone with Zes, who was busy making phone calls to all and sundry in Afrikaans on a mobile phone. Finally, after having a gutsful, I decided to get the hell away from Rehoboth.

"Where are you going?" he asked me.

"Back to Windhoek. My Australian mates'll be wondering where I've got to."

"And what are you going to tell them? If you tell them about what happened to Basson, you might be implicated or be seen as an accessory. We made need your help some time in the future and I shall let you know how and when."

As crook as I was from the grog, I sized him up and down and reckoned I had more than an even chance of giving him a bloody good thumping. I prodded him hard in the chest and saw a flicker of fear in his eyes. "Implicated? An Accessory? You fuckin' try'n to blackmail me or something?"

He quickly shook his head. "Not necessarily, but like I said – we may depart in death, but we were brought together with Basson's death.'"

"Fuckin' bullshit!" I prodded him again. "I had fuck all to do with what you bastards done to Basson. I've got a good mind to fuckin'..."

Jonker and Klaase walked in, and I immediately felt I was gone a million! There was no way I would be able to cope with the three of them, and then I remembered the revolver that Jonker kept under his jacket.

"What is going on?" my brother asked.

I decided to go further on the offensive and pointed to Zes. "This fuckin' arsehole here! I reckon he's try'n to blackmail me. Listen, Jonker, I had fuck all to do with what you cunts did to Basson."

"True, Kido, I am sure..."

"Don't bloody call me Kido. My name's fuckin' Josef!"

"Ja, all right," Jonker put his hand up to placate me. "What has Carl said?"

I pointed at Zes again. "He reckoned I could be seen as an accessory to what you did to Basson. I didn't have a clue as to what was going on. If you were gunna fuckin' kill him, why the fuck did you have to drag me along?"

"No – no, Kido, I am sure..."

"Stop calling me fuckin' Kido!"

"Ja, okay – okay." My brother took me by the arm and led me into the house's lounge room. "Calm down, Josef. I just wanted you to see what my organisation has to deal with, and why I need to stay out of the sight of the cops. It was up to us take care of Basson, otherwise there would have been no justice. We Baster are seeing very little justice nowadays."

"Yeah, but Zes reckoned I could also be in the shit. How come you involved me in all this bullshit, Jonker? Is it so that you could fuckin' blackmail me?"

"Do not worry, I shall have a talk with Carl. You are right – you are totally innocent of what happened... Look, I tell you what, there is someone you should meet before you go back to Windhoek. Perhaps then you shall see that our cause is an honourable one?"

CHAPTER 57

JESUS HAWALA THE BUTCHER OF LUBANGO!

Not far north of Rehoboth we called in on a farmhouse, and there I met one of the most extraordinary Baster I was ever likely to come across!

"Kido, meet Rassie Van Zyl," Jonker introduced me to him, while an elderly Baster woman poured out coffee. "Major Van Zyl of the Namibian Defence Force."

My hand was nearly crushed by a short, but wide and muscley coloured joker with a handlebar moustache and the most charming smile. He had a deep voice and his laugh accompanied just about everything he or anyone said.

We all talked about this and that until my brother prompted Rassie: "Tell Kido about Jesus."

The major's merry smile disappeared. "I should tell him?" he asked Jonker.

My brother nodded vehemently. "He is my brother and I want him to know the truth about SWAPO."

"You have brandy?" Rassie asked him. "Zes always has a bottle of brandy behind the front seat of his bakkie."

It appeared that Zes *indeed* always had a bottle of the stuff hidden in his vehicle, and we all had glassfuls of it in front of us to go with our coffees when Rassie began to talk. "I fled the South West in 1979. I originally came from Keetmanshoop, where a Boer farmer whipped my father to death with a *sjambok*. The authorities did absolutely nothing since my father was known to be a political agitator and they claimed that he had attacked the farmer first. I tried to protest against that injustice, so I was imprisoned in a concentration camp at a place called Keikanachab, which is situated approximately ten or twelve kilometres north-west of Mariental. That is a town not too far south of here. It was right in the badlands where the temperature in our zinc cells reached sixty degrees Celsius. The Boers were not satisfied with just beating me and hanging me suspended by my feet – they gave me electric shocks – to the sides of my face, my nipples and my testicles. It got that way that I prayed that I would die... Eventually, after six months or so, they released me, and I and two other Baster made our way first east to Botswana, then north to Zambia. We had joined the SWAPO movement and had been encouraged to go into exile in order to become freedom fighters, or terrorists as the Boers called us. At that time thousands of Namibians were fleeing the white South African regime, so it made it quite difficult for the Boers to police every inch of the various borders. My friends and I arrived at a place called the Old Farm near Lusaka, and that was the first ever Namibian refugee centre started up in that country. We soon discovered certain disagreements and tensions amongst the various leaders of SWAPO. The old guard versus the newer and younger guard. My associates, being young themselves, decided to follow the leadership of the new guard, however I – having learned a bit about human nature under the Boer wardens at Keikanachab – decided to have good look around first before choosing sides. Also my friends were determined to get military training as soon as possible, so that they could start taking their revenge on the Boers. From my months in detention at Keikanachab I had seen the military might available to the whites and knew that defeating them was going to be no easy matter, therefore I was in no great hurry to go to the frontline. Especially when it was easy to see that the whole SWAPO movement was a complete shambles. SWAPO had training camps in Angola, Zambia and Tanzania, nonetheless –

after the training was completed – there was no worthwhile ordinance to be given to us, anyway. In fact, in the early days, those on the frontline had been sent with very little food or equipment, and most nearly starved to death."

"Ja," Jonker agreed with him, "most of the PLAN people *were* starving by the time they reached the Namibian border."

Rassie nodded. "It was things like this that brought the new guard against the old. The old guard – Sam Nujoma and his band of thugs – had more of an interest in living in luxury in Lusaka and had no intention of venturing anywhere near the front. Some even owned nightclubs, bars and brothels and money was pouring into their pockets. In most cases the money to buy these enterprises came from donations given to SWAPO by overseas sympathisers such as Sweden and other Scandinavian countries. They were bought with stolen aid money... Words like incompetence, waste, ineptitude, lack of responsibility, dictatorial style of leadership, bribery and loose morals could soon be found on the new guard's lips, till in the end they accused the old guard of being totally corrupt. Which was absolutely true in all instances. If it had not been for the newcomers, most likely Sam and his friends would still be up in Zambia running their nightclubs, brothels and casinos. Then, of course, there were all the donor funds to be pocketed. When I started..."

"Talking of brothels," my brother interrupted him, "women recruits from Namibia were forced to work in these brothels by some of the corrupt SWAPO leaders. Namibian women were very popular amongst the Zambian armed forces, as they were from different tribes, and thus more exotic. They considered Namibian women 'cleaner' than local Zambian prostitutes, so Sammy and his friends made a fortune out of them."

"Ja, he is right!" Rassie agreed enthusiastically. "The truthful allegations being made by the newcomers about SWAPO started to rankle the old guard, and they decided to do something about them permanently. The main ace the old guard had up their sleeve was the fact that they had the Zambian and Tanzanian governments on their side. Perhaps those governments might have been benefiting from all the corruption – who knows? I cannot say for certain, but it is more than likely. None the matter – a good many of the new guard started to disappear. There was nothing surprising about that, for back in '76 a thousand SWAPO people under the leadership of people such as Andreas Shipanga left the organisation in protest against the corruption, and they were sent to the Mboroma death camp that was hidden in a mountainous area on Zambia's Copperbelt. They were either tortured to death or shot, and most disappeared off the face of this earth. Not only that, our dearly departed Mwalimu – Julius Nyerere of Tanzania – threw open his death cells for Sammy to use and hundreds of the SWAPO dissidents suffered indescribable misery in that country... I decided to back the old guard. I made this quite clear and it was fairly simple convincing them that I was prepared to lay down my life for them. That totally false loyalty earned me a quick trip to Moscow where I ended up in the Lubyanka. There the KGB taught me all there is to know about espionage, terrorism and torture. I even spent a time at the Patrice Lumumba Friendship University where I was taught all the Marxist-Leninist ideologies and jargon. It was when I was in Moscow that I met a certain Solomon Hawala. The KGB had also trained him in torture and terrorism, however he was taught more in the subjects of security and interrogation. We met again back in Zambia in 1982 and he wanted me to join a special new SWAPO security service. I and about two hundred and fifty others joined him and our headquarters had been set up in Angola at a place called Lubango. Hawala was by then the deputy commander of the liberation army and he rather fancied the code name 'Jesus'. He was by far one of the most powerful men in SWAPO. Even the members of the SWAPO leadership feared him. He was answerable only to Sammy Nujoma and his job was to sniff out so-called 'spies and South African agents'. For some reason or other, probably because we had become friends in Moscow, I became Hawala's chief confidant.

He could hardly make me his second-in-charge considering I was a Baster, for that kind of rank could only be given to another Ovambo... You see, tribalism was fairly entrenched in SWAPO. Although they professed that all freedom fighters were equal, regardless of tribe or sex, the Ovambo slowly but surely took over all the senior positions, or positions that held the greatest political power. What is more, most of the people who were incarcerated, tortured and murdered came from central and southern Namibia and were not Ovambo... This is excellent brandy. Please may I have some more?"

Jonker topped-up the major's mug and no coffee was added to it. "So what happened then?" I prodded Rassie.

"As it turned out we could not find many, if any at all, spies or South African agents, therefore we had to manufacture some of our own. Thousands of them, in fact. Sam Nujoma and most of the other members of SWAPO's leadership had a paranoia about intellectuals, or those with superior education. Also, as I said, the Herero and other southerners had to be given special attention. The procedure was fairly straightforward – we selected a member of the aforementioned – tortured him or her, and then obtained confessions to all sorts of crimes that they had committed against the 'cause'. In typical KGB style we also forced them to point their fingers at other 'accomplices', so we soon gathered in quite a harvest. The torture procedure was also quite straightforward, such as beating, hanging by the wrists, electricity, starvation, threats against their family and children. Even if some of our victims could not come up with credible confessions, we would invent a whole range of stories for him or her. There was no end to the methods we employed. We did such a good job that 'Jesus' Hawala soon became known as the 'Butcher of Lubango'... It was bit like the Nazis and the Jews. Our main hunting ground was in Zambia where we at first used to send our prisoners to Lubango by truck, but our organisation became so busy we had to fly our so-called 'spies' into Angola in convoys of military transport planes. Hundreds each week and thousands each month. An estimate of fourteen thousand people went missing without a trace whilst serving SWAPO, though I am sure there was far more than that. The average non-Ovambo SWAPO individuals were in a state of terror, as no one knew when he or she would be next. We made videos of our prisoners' confessions and in these videos they named people who we had not yet arrested, so they in turn were victimised – if not brutalised – by other SWAPO supporters, and so on and on it went. Lubango shortly became five times its original size in order to accommodate our organisation and its victims. As we always had South African spotter planes flying overhead, the old guard leadership became petrified that the South African Defence Force intelligence and propaganda people would discover what was happening, so we kept most of the prisoners under the ground. Their first stop was the Karl Marx Reception Centre that consisted of underground accommodation for the guards. There the detainees were interrogated and searched thoroughly. All their money and valuables were taken from them, and then they had to eat their toothpaste, body lotions and deodorants, on the grounds that perhaps they might be poisonous and meant to kill SWAPO leaders with. The underground torture rooms we kept elsewhere. The cells, or dungeons as we called them, were a vast network of pitch-dark, underground caves of different sizes. Because of the volume of people that we processed, they were always hopelessly overcrowded and little or no sanitation was provided. I used to hate going in to fetch out people for interrogation, for the air was so foul you would need a sharp knife to cut through it. Every morning I had step over the corpses of those who had suffocated during the night. If our torturing and beating was not sufficient to kill the prisoners, the conditions and the food certainly took care of a lot of them. Hundreds died every month, and their bodies were thrown into a deep mountain crevasse... We detained not only men at Lubango. Thousands of women passed through our hands, so naturally rapes and ensuing pregnancies became rampant. In a way, in the women's cases, it was not much different to the female freedom fighters on the frontline. Despite Sam Nujoma claiming all the fighters to be equal – men and women – the male SWAPO soldiers had a habit of raping and sexually abusing their female counterparts, so there were quite a number of bastards born near the battle zone."

"You're kidding?" I found it hard to believe him.

"I swear that I am not. All the time Hawala was becoming stranger and stranger. True, he had been amply trained by the Russian KGB, but the enjoyment he obtained from all the death and misery was terrifying. He had a totally unbridled mandate from the president of SWAPO, Sam Nujoma, to indulge in any brutal excesses that took his fancy, and he exercised that authorisation to the full. No one felt safe being anywhere near him, and even some of his closest associates ended up in sometimes worse straits than the average detainees. All that power obviously drove him insane. After the war I heard a journalist liken him to Idi Amin or the Emperor Bokassa of the Central African Republic, however, unlike them, he was condoned and egged on by his master, our president of Namibia and others of the SWAPO leadership who are in government today. Thousands died from the torture and impossible conditions they were subjected to, yet who was the most to blame – Sam Nujoma or 'Jesus' Hawala? Who was the most evil? You could say that I should also carry part of the blame, but, like the Nazis at Nuremburg, I would tell you that I carried out my duties in order to survive. But Hitler and his henchmen had either been killed, committed suicide, escaped into exile or were hanged. The people I am talking about are now ruling the country."

"So – you see," Jonker cut in, "Nujoma and other SWAPO leaders most likely murdered more Namibians than the Boers did."

"That is true!" Rassie agreed with him. "Do you hear how they have war criminal courts in Bosnia? Countries in Europe and the Americans are trying to catch Serbian and Croat war criminals, and they are putting them on trial. Why are they not doing that here? Firstly, they should hunt down the murdering Boers with their interrogation squads and torturers. Then SWAPO. Sam Nujoma was involved in the killing of Namibians right up to his neck. I remember one of his

390

speeches that he made word for word, since I know the man who wrote it for him. Sammy was always considered a rather inarticulate dunce and he was always embarrassing the SWAPO leadership whenever he opened his big mouth. I remember the exact date that he made the speech. It was on April the twenty-first 1986. It went something like this: 'I greet you in the name of our great forefathers and all the great leaders who gave their lives in the cause of freedom. I do not know why you love money so much and why you have put your hearts on beautiful things such as motorcars, money and the white man's houses and farms. Your fathers sired, and your mothers gave birth to spies and traitors of the Namibian peoples' cause. You will be kept in my underground dungeons until we get freedom, then you will be paraded in front of the free Namibian people and your throats will be cut by the Namibian people as a punishment for being traitors.'"

"Can you see the hypocrisy?" my brother insisted. "Back in 1986 you had Sammy accusing innocent people of being traitors, spies and being greedy. Look at him with his jets, motorcades, farms and millions of dollars in overseas accounts? Tell me – do the Europeans and Americans have two sets of standards? Do they really care about the murderers and war criminals that came out of SWAPO? Do they care about the war criminals that represented the Boers, or do they not care about the innocent African war victims at all? Are they sick and tired of Africa's problems altogether?"

"So what happened to this Hawala?" I asked Rassie.

"What happened to him? He is – as we are sitting here – chief of the Namibian Defence Force. He is very much alive, very wealthy and in very good health. When the war ended I was given this position in the Namibian army, although I receive a lot more than a major's pay. It was the SWAPO leadership's way of keeping my mouth shut. Just before the hostilities came to an end with South Africa, an attempt was made on my life because I had witnessed all the atrocities, so I escaped from Angola and hid with friends of mine in Luderitz. In 1989, when some of the detainees managed to make their way back to Namibia and the stories got out, I came out of hiding and decided to blackmail some of the SWAPO leaders into guaranteeing my safety. By then the entire organisation had to do a whitewash on what happened at Lubango, and they had to keep their noses clean, for the elections were coming up. Since then I have been excellently trained as an officer, which…"

"Ja!" Jonker butted in, "And he is part of our organisation."

"True," Rassie grinned broadly, "but I would still like to question the people overseas who claim to have assisted the people in taking the country from the Boers. Are they satisfied with people such as Moses Garoseb, Solomon Hawala and Sam Nujoma ruling Namibia with so much treacherous blood on their hands? Will the good people overseas demand to know what happened to the countless victims of SWAPO? They say that in a civilised country a person can be hunted down, tried in court, and then jailed for life for a single murder. Like Jonker says – are there double standards – one for African leaders – others for white leaders? Sammy and SWAPO did not murder these people as an act of war on the Boers, they murdered them to ensure their own comfort and to accommodate their sheer greed and lust for power. Shall anyone try to determine what really happened? I was there and saw the bloodshed, raping and suffering. I saw the unmarked mass graves and the bodies thrown into a crevasse. The bones of thousands of Namibians are lying lost in Angolan soil, far away from their homes. Could it ever be written into our history books, so that our children can learn the real truth? Has the world turned their backs on those people, and will SWAPO ever be called to task? … There are a great many parents throughout Namibia who still believe that their sons and daughters shall return one day. Every year we have a public holiday called 'Heroes Day'. There are marches and bands that go down Independence Avenue and the people are encouraged to be very patriotic and proud. There are a good many people who have every right to be proud, nevertheless everything is fraudulent when you consider the ultimate outcome. You now have people in power who were indisputably more evil than our enemies the Boers were."

CHAPTER 58

HUMAN SKINS FOR SALE! BULLET PROOF NIGERIAN HEALER GETS HIS HEAD BLOWN OFF! HEADLESS BURLESQUE DANCER! WE'RE OFF TO SOUTH AFRICA!

The journey to Windhoek was an anxious one, for at all times I expected to be arrested for murder. I met up with Dave and Nick at the Zum Wirt, and they told me that the drilling rig's hydraulic power pack was about to shit itself.

"Where the fuck you been?" Dave asked. "You been on the nest and couldn't get off?"

"You get fucked!" I told him. "The fuckin' boss must be really charmed with the friggin' rig being idle."

"Fuck the boss!" was all Nick had to say.

It was bloody good to be back with them, especially after what had transpired over the last forty-eight hours. I couldn't think of anything to say to them, and their Aussie accents and way of speaking gave me a great deal of comfort. It seemed as if I hadn't seen them for months.

Dave could see right through me. "What the fuck you been up to? You look as if you've just robbed a bank. You shit yourself or something?"

"Nah, I've fuckin' got one helluva hangover. The old Rehoboth Baster blokes sure know how to knock back the grog."

"I've made up my mind that I'm gunna marry Magda," Dave

changed the subject. "Some time ago I faxed my lawyer in Kal' and told him to start on things. As for my missus – the fucking bitch – some other arsehole's fuckin' her. A dirty fuckin' Kiwi, would you believe? She's going along with a divorce, so I wonder how much I'm gunna have to pay her out? I tell you what, you blokes, I let you all down flamin' sadly. While she was fuckin' every other bloke in the gold fields, I should've organised a fuck or two for you jokers as well."

I noticed that his distress at his wife leaving him had been swapped for anger. Her title had been changed from the 'the missus' to 'that fat slag', 'the slack-arsed bitch' and 'mangy, scabby, bow-legged whore'! He still seemed to harbour kind thoughts for his kids all the same.

"Where've you been, ya fuckin' boong?" Jeff made an entrance.

"You get fucked, ya fat slut!" I instructed him.

"We're thinking of snatching our rent," Dave informed me. "We've had a gutsful of this Africa caper. Ernie's back in Kal' already. The boss called him home for some reason or other. Possibly about that drilling that could be coming up in Botswana. Even if we get some drilling, it looks like the hydraulic motor's gunna fuck up at any second and we can't find anyone here in Windhoek to fix the cunt. Parts are coming in from Aussie, but I'm fucked if I know when. Stand-downs and fuckin' breakdowns – that's all we've had in this godforsaken place. We've made fuck all in drilling bonuses, so what's the flamin' point in carrying on?"

"How's the gold price affecting things?" I asked him. "If it was tough for drilling with the Mabo caper, how's the gold price gunna affect us getting another job?"

"It's still way down to buggery," he shrugged. "The copper price's okay, same as most base metals. The market and share punters have changed over to those. Most of the wake-up gold producing companies have most likely forward sold a lot of their gold, so they should be hedged for the next eighteen months or so. There should be plenty of grade and pit sampling drilling, but that's if you don't mind going onto a smaller rig."

"Bloody hell!" his last words did nothing to comfort me. "Has Dawson-Byrne got any ideas? Even if we pull out now, it's gunna take weeks to get the Schramm back to Aussie?"

"Fuck the Schramm!" he was unconcerned. "The boss kept threatening Ernie that he was gunna sell it to some government water boring outfit over here. So – let him fuckin' sell it. The problems we've had over here weren't Ernie's fault, but the boss keeps on saying he's gunna tramp him."

"Fuck Ernie!" Nick was unsympathetic. "He's spent half his life up to his boots in the boss' arse, the crawling, brown-nosing, little prick... Hey, Jeff, let's fuck off back to Kal'?"

"Follow me – I'm right behind you," Jeff agreed.

Dawson-Byrne came marching along the bar and joined us. After ordering a double whisky, he unfolded a South African newspaper and held it out to Dave after pointing out an article written by some Dutch professor expert on religious and ritual killings in Africa. Apparently the professor had recently returned from Nigeria's Anambra Province where thirty people had been arrested for cult or ritual killings, and their victims had been treated rather horribly. He went on to add that the removal of human lips, testicles, hands and intestines was becoming commonplace in countries such as Nigeria, Uganda, Tanzania and South Africa. In fact the latest craze was human skins; some fetching as much as ten thousand US dollars a pop! The consumption of human skin, genitalia and various other vital organs was considered excellent for business success or obtaining romance. Also, according to the prof', the incidence of witchcraft had increased fiftyfold throughout Africa in the last couple of decades since AIDS had arrived on the scene, and he was dismayed at the regular practice of raping infants and the ingestion of various kids' body parts as a cure for the virus. He went on to cast considerable doubt on the effectiveness of witchcraft altogether, as he had personally witnessed a Nigerian traditional healer come horribly unstuck. In his wisdom the healer had mixed up a potion that would make him immune to bullets, and when he had arranged for one of his patients to shoot him, the stupid dickhead had his brains blown out! His patient was arrested shortly after for taking part in all the fun.

Dawson-Byrne wasn't satisfied with the humour the professor had inadvertently supplied him. "I see even the bogs of Ireland are being corrupted by our Af brethren, David. Now – we all know that the Afs have a habit of losing their heads over certain issues, but it seems some Malawian lass has got herself carried away altogether."

"What the fuck you on about?" Dave hadn't seen the humorous side of things.

"It appears that a certain Ms Paiche-Unyolo-Onyemaechi has mislaid her head and officers of the local Kilkenny Garda are having a devil of a job trying to help her locate it. It's been suggested that it was removed during some Nigerian *muti* or ritual killing. Her decomposing body was found by a stream in the shadow of the scenic Comeragh Mountains. She was Malawi's Justice Minister, Leonard Unyolo's daughter, and was married to some Nigerian fellow who's also gone missing and has probably done a bunk back to Nigeria. By all accounts Ms Onyemaechi first arrived in Europe in the late 1990s in order to study business administration in London, though the bogtrotters in Dublin and Limerick much preferred her nightclub dancing talents. You'd expect a perverted, low life Irishman to come up with something like that – a headless burlesque dancer. I suppose it's one way of getting the men to crawl out of their bogs and hollows. I wonder. . ?"

"Stop talking bullshit," Wheeler told him.

"Upon my soul, David," the Pommy tried his hardest to look genuine. "I dare jest with you not, as I heard it on the BBC. The Garda Siochana's searching all over the place for her missing noggin, and the whole situation has supposedly sent a shudder though the significant Irish-African population... What in damnation is the Republic of Ireland doing with a significant African population? Mind you, I suppose it has to be beneficial when it comes to raising the national I.Q in Southern Ireland."

"You're a bitter and twisted, pathetic, little man," Dave informed him.

"I wouldn't say that," Dawson-Byrne disagreed. "It seems I've found you some drilling in South Africa. A diamond pipe not far from Kimberley that actually contains diamonds. I found the thing myself. You'll like South Africa. Not so many thorn trees, deserts and so on. Should be able to keep you going for at least a year."

The atmosphere in the bar changed instantly as the doom and gloom evaporated! The rig was going to South Africa, thus a new adventure was in the offing!

CHAPTER 59

HAUNTED BY THE MURDER!

I managed to get the Pommy geo' alone. "Listen, James, that whole Basson business has frightened the crap out of me. He got what he deserved, but I reckon I could've stopped the others if I hadn't had so much brandy. I don't want a bar of that sort of caper. Now I'm absolutely shit-scared that the cops are gunna arrest me at any second, and my nerves can't hack it... I'm thinking of asking Krystal to go back to Australia with me. Are you fair dinkum about this work in South Africa? If not, I need to start making plans about her getting a passport and so on."

He arched his eyebrows at that. "Are you sure Krystal's the one for you?"

"Why, is there something wrong with her?"

He frowned. "You'll need to talk to your brother about that one. Look, I tell you what, let's go down to Rehoboth tomorrow and you can wish Jonker adieu. First I'll call him, so we can make sure he'll be there... Listen, I know how you must feel. Carl, your brother and the others have witnessed violence and death too many times. It must've been very traumatic for you. The cops will never find out what actually happened. I have a contact in the Windhoek CID, and the detectives there aren't really bothered about Basson being missing. They know that every Baster or Nama south of Windhoek would gladly do him in, so they won't give him a second thought. The coppers have got a lot more useful things to do with their time. Besides, they haven't got the resources – can only handle open and shut cases. It's the same all over independent Africa. If you were in the UK or Australia you'd have every reason to pee your pants, but this place's totally different. It seems that as soon as the Afs take over government in Africa, things immediately start deteriorating in every instance. It's a fact that even the most asinine do-gooder and admirer of the noble savage would have to agree with. You take Zimbabwe, Zambia, Kenya and even South Africa, thousands of murders are left unsolved because their police forces have neither the funding nor the inclination to do anything about them. It's every man or woman for his or herself. It's a bit like the toilets you come across in African airports. The urinals stink since there's no money for deodorant blocks, or there are no seats on the toilets because no one's even bothered to think about such trivialities. It's like the painted lines you have in the middle of bitumen highways and street signs. African governments don't see them as important anymore, as they've stolen all the necessary funds, anyway. That's why the tourists who come here spend days being tortured by dysentery since the health authorities no longer check for food hygiene. In most cases such authorities don't even exist on this continent any longer. You don't dare go into an African hospital, for there's an excellent chance you'll come out worse off than when you went in. If you don't catch AIDS first... Seriously, that's the only instance where you can find black-ruled Africa reliable under any circumstance – the Afs take over – everything goes down the plughole. You don't have to be a high priest or dragon of the Ku Klux Klan, or an Afrikaner member of the *Broederbond* to work that one out. The Af has absolutely no way of coping with normal, modern society. He's better off back with his witch doctors and mud huts... Take South Africa for instance. The country's only had independence for scarcely a decade now. The coppers down there are stranded, as most of their vehicles have been written-off and there's no money for petrol to put in the vehicles that *are* still on the road. Despite the chaos here, you've got sufficient whites in the private sector, so Namibia's held up more than most. Even so, whenever it rains whole suburbs like Klein Windhoek have to go without telephones for months on end, or, if it isn't that, overseas calls are jammed for hours. Mail simply disappears between one post office and the next, or public services totally break down because most of the supervisors are both black and incompetent... So the chances of the cops ever following up on Basson's disappearance are a million to one. Justice has been served, so forget about it. There's no need to worry."

"What about Jonker and them? I'm going to South Africa with Dave and the others. Dave's talking about marrying Magda, and I'm hoping to do the same with Krystal. I just want to get the fuck out of Namibia."

"Can't say I blame you," he nodded. "I'll have a chat with Jonker and Carl and tell them you're leaving. Naturally – what occurred at Sam Khubis – never happened?"

"Bloody oath, James, but do you reckon they'll come after me if they hear I'm leaving Namibia?"

"Leave it to me. I'll make sure that the matter of your departure doesn't become an issue with your brother and the others."

He opened up another newspaper. It didn't take him long to find another item of news to ponder on. "I see our good Boers are struggling with the idea of a 'new' South Africa. Damned good show, I say!"

"You dislike the Boers?" I suggested.

"Hadn't you guessed? It's not them exactly, but their total, inane hypocrisy." He held up the *CITIZEN* newspaper. "The Boers are complaining about receiving shabby treatment. This Afrikaner ethnologist from the Rand Afrikaans University was telling some conference on cultural, religious and language rights in Pretoria that he believes that the gulf between the Afrikaners and the state's deepening, as they're being pressed to apologise for their very existence. He says here that almost everything that's remotely unedifying in the country has been laid at the door of either the Afrikaner or his Apartheid regime. He's going on about how Afrikaners are under pressure to admit guilt and atone for a variety of sins. In his capacity as a people, he – the Afrikaner – must acknowledge the fact that his character's been sullied, that his burden of sins is heavy, and that he's been deformed by sin upon sin. If that isn't enough, the good professor's gabbling on about how the ANC government's so-called non-racist policies are in fact disguised discrimination on the basis of race and colour – especially when it applies to appointments in the public sector. White efficiency's being spurned in favour of black inefficiency and the same pattern's taking shape in the private sector. Should anyone dare to complain about or protest against black-favouring or reverse discrimination, he or she's soon branded as a rogue and a racist. All this's likely to cause a new consolidation in the Afrikaner ranks... Although I agree wholeheartedly with his allegations of black incompetence, who the hell do the Afrikaners think they are? What on earth do they expect? For decades, if not centuries, they totally denied the very *existence* of the blacks. They denied the Afs freedom of movement, land ownership, self-respect, or any rights at all, and they damned well made sure that absolutely no training was given out in order to overcome their incompetence... So the Boers are feeling sorry for themselves, are they? Every Afrikaner, man, woman and child were totally comfortable with their Apartheid regime treating the blacks as if they were less than dirt. They found comfort with the fact that their Afrikaner regime would hammer or vilify anyone who opposed Apartheid. They kicked the blacks from pillar to post – restricted their freedom of movement – tortured and abused them in their police cells. White children reigned supreme over adult black men and insulted them in front of their own children, yet all this was condoned by the system... I tell you what, when it comes to forgiving and Christian virtues, the Boers couldn't hold a candle to the blacks. Why shouldn't the blacks look after themselves, especially after the years of insults, suppression and murder?"

"I suppose so," I shrugged, "but apparently this SWAPO government's a pretty murderous bunch in their own right. I heard they killed thousands of their own innocent people?"

"Jonker's obviously introduced you to the redoubtable Major Rassie Van Zyl. You're right there, all the same. That's why I told you the other day that old Sammy Nujoma had some looking over his shoulder to do... The most pathetic thing about it was the churches."

That had me rather mystified. "How's that?"

"The most nauseating thing about do-gooders and the churches is that they can be just as ruthless, conniving and as greasy a people as the Boers. Take the various German churches for example – the Lutheran World Federation – the Evangelical Lutheran Church of Namibia – the World Council of Churches, for that matter. They all knew for certain that Sammy and his gangsters had been murdering their own people hand over fist, just because the victims objected to all the SWAPO corruption that was going on. Word got out about the torturing and killing in Angola and Tanzania, but the churches did their damnedest to cover it up. Who could give a toss about the thousands who virtually disappeared? What are a few thousand innocent souls when it comes to the churches satisfying themselves that SWAPO was best to govern Namibia? They can sleep peacefully at night, knowing that a pack of murderers are now running the country? They claim to be a civilising influence on the noble savage and that they themselves are from enlightened countries and establishments or whatever have you. What's the murder and torture of a few thousand nameless victims to anyone?"

"So that Rassie bloke wasn't bullshitting? Christ, when you think about it, this bloody place's soaked in blood compared to Aussie."

"Rassie was telling the absolute truth," he assured me. "One of the first missions I was given when I joined *Koevoet* was to investigate the rumours of death camps, underground dungeons and torture chambers that the SADF intelligence people had got wind of. With my British accent I was given the cover as an Anglican priest and I saw first-hand what was transpiring in Zambia. In Lusaka I soon learned that the rumours were unadulterated fact. The SWAPO refugees were absolutely petrified. They simply didn't know who or what to trust, regardless of their loyalty to the SWAPO cause. People were either disappearing altogether or were being carted off to Angola or Tanzania by the planeload. Some begged me to help them flee the country since good old Kenneth Kaunda and the Zambian army backed Sammy to the hilt and got a real kick out of rounding up and abusing the so-called South African 'spies' and 'agents'. If they thought of coming to me as an Anglican priest, you can bet your life they must've been running to the Lutheran clergy, what with the Lutheran Church being so entrenched in Namibia. When I told Pretoria what was going on, the churches in both Namibia and Zambia were informed, yet they claimed that it was only South African propaganda. The Swedish and other Scandinavian churches also knew what was happening, still they denied it with all the lies and bull's droppings they could muster. Quite rightly they wanted the Boer regime overthrown, but they were more than content to let another pack of rabid killers take their place. I doubt if there's many people around the world who know what went on during the '80s, since the churches did such a wonderful job of covering things up. Sammy and his thugs had a habit of killing or imprisoning anyone who questioned their inept and thieving ways, and they were obviously given the full blessing of the do-gooders and the churches... Ye gods, the good old Lutheran Church really have a heck of a lot to be proud of! No wonder old Martin Luther was constipated!"

"What?"

"I'm telling you, old Martin Luther was permanently bunged up. Couldn't move his bowels neither for faith – love of God – nor money. He most likely had some influence on the church that took his name, for as far as morals are concerned, they're also permanently bunged up. Great ones for converting the noble savage the Lutherans are. I wonder what happened to these good people when Hitler and his cronies took over Germany? There's positively no difference between the old SWAPO guard and the Nazis, what with their concentration camps and torturers. Was there a whisper of complaint from the

Lutheran Church when they saw the Jews being slaughtered in their millions in Europe? Even before the War when the Brownshirts went around beating up old men and women and destroying their homes and businesses? Did we hear a peep out of the German churches then? Did the Rhenish and Finnish missionaries complain at all when the German colonists and their Imperial Army tried to wipe the Herero off the face of the earth? Take old Hugo Hahn the German missionary who first set up shop amongst the Herero. He loved to organise a bit of bloodshed and mayhem between the *Oorlams* and the Herero. I know old Elsabeth Witbooi gave you a rough background of your people's history, but were you aware that the *Oorlams* had totally banned capital punishment, yet the various missionaries that attended them harboured no such qualms? In most cases German missionaries... No, when it comes to the Germans and their missionaries and churches, I don't much like their rotten, murdering, hypocritical ways."

"Do you like anyone?"

"Nope!"

CHAPTER 60

THE TRUTH ABOUT KRYSTAL! HEAD FOUND IN COURTHOUSE BUILDING!

The following day I found out that taking my old Mercedes to South Africa would eventually cause me more hassles than it was worth, what with licensing the vehicle and eventual customs duties, so I decided to give it to my brother. If he didn't want it, maybe he could give it to Wilfred or old Kobus Van Wyk? The Pommy reckoned that was a bonzer idea, and that he could pick me at Carl Zes' place, for that was where Jonker could be found.

I had to go through the routine of parking in Zes' back yard and making sure there were no prying eyes before I knocked on the back door. My brother was alone and didn't beat around the bush. "So you are going to South Africa with James?"

"Yeah, but one of my drilling mates is taking a Baster girl home with him, and I'm hoping that Krystal will do the same."

"I see. Perhaps there is something you should know about Krystal?"

I had a sudden sinking feeling in my guts. "What, is she married or something?"

He got up from a kitchen chair, filled a glass with brandy, and then held it out to me. "Here, take this."

"No thanks, a beer'll do me. I can't hack brandy."

"No, please take it. Take at least half in one swallow. Please, Kido, you shall thank me afterwards."

405

His eyes were pleading with me, so I did as I was told. It was twelve year old brandy, but the liquor still burned my throat and made my eyes water. "Well?"

He filled another glass with brandy and took a slug out of it before answering, "There is something you should know about Krystal. I was hoping to tell you before, but I could never pick an appropriate time. I just could not find the right words... Krystal's surname is not Diergaardt, it is Van Wyk. She is Kobus' and Manfred's great niece. Her grandfather was having sex regularly with her mother and she was the tragic result of that relationship. Krystal cannot have children. Much worse than that, she was born without nipples and she has no womb. She is a beautiful, loving, kind woman, but now you know why no one goes near her. Most of the Baster men know about it."

His words literally blocked my throat! I could scarcely breathe! I felt I wanted to shout, cry and puke at the same time! Dropping the glass of brandy, I lurched to the back door of the house and wrenched it open. The hot Rehoboth wind was there to greet me and a pair of pied crows took off in a real pissed off fashion. Despair, anger and hatred took turns at swamping my mind as I walked up and down in the back yard. Hatred soon took over everything. Hatred for the Baster – Jonker, *Ouma* Elsabeth, Wilfred, Kobus – all the Baster I had met in Rehoboth. Most of all I hated old Elsabeth Witbooi, as the stinking, incontinent, conniving, old slut had egged me on. Next I hated people like Fritz Manasse, Petrus Klaase and Carl Zes, for they knew the feelings I had had for Krystal. Wilfred, the slimy, little cunt; not to mention old Kobus Van Wyk. The fucking sleazy, conniving Baster!

My brother came up behind me. "I would rather that you came inside. How can you stop loving Krystal, for she has done absolutely nothing wrong? She is still human and she needs love like any of us. You insisted that she should love you in return, no one else. With most of the Baster men knowing of her affliction, she has lived a very lonely life, Kido. She has longed for the love and companionship of a man, and you came along and swept her off her feet. Krystal is not all that extraordinary, as there are thousands of women who cannot have children."

"Yeah, but not for the same reason that Krystal can't. There's nothing like a Baster to fuck his own daughter. Where's the grandfather now? I'd like to cut his fuckin' balls out."

"You are too late by years. Manfred and Kobus ran him over with a lorry. The cops could not find too much left when they finished with him."

"You still could've told me. Every fuckin' Baster I've met knew about it. Carl, Fritz, Klaasie – Kobus Van Wyk. Even bloody Wilfred! I bent over backwards to get him good money. He could've fuckin' told me? Further still, that fucking old bitch, Elsabeth, how come she kept leading me on? I was just played for a dickhead!"

"No, you are very wrong there. You were Wilfred's hero and he would have done anything to spare you any embarrassment. It would have been *Ouma* Witbooi who told him to keep his mouth shut. Believe me, old Kobus and Manfred were delighted that you had come back. Like the old woman, they saw it as some celestial sign – a sign from God, even. Yes, *Ouma* Elsabeth was the most delighted of all. The stupid old bitch was only deluding herself about you and Krystal. Our father was also her hero – a true Witbooi... I swear no one meant you any harm. It was simply too embarrassing for them. Most of all it is unfair to condemn Krystal. She could not help falling in love with you. She is human, too, you know, and she has feelings like everyone else. She could hardly have asked to be born under those circumstances. If you despise her, you are worse than any Baster I can think of. You are worse than any Boer. She is not some hideous freak, but a very beautiful, gentle woman with love and feelings of her own. You said you loved her more than any woman you had ever come across, so does she mean nothing to you now?"

That left me in a total dilemma; still I went on the offensive, "There isn't another Baster who'll touch her. Don't you think there's something unusual about that? Why's that, Jonker, is it because she hasn't got nipples and a proper womb? Are they scared that the other Baster'll think they're a freak of some sort as well? Don't they want to be involved with a kid from a father-daughter relationship? Are they scared of what everybody'll think?"

"Answer those questions to yourself," he challenged. "Your feelings ride on quite a pendulum – on one side you love a person with all your heart – then it takes one swing and you are filled with loathing, contempt and disgust! ... Anyhow," he held his hand out, "that sounds like James' vehicle has arrived. Farewell, Kido, I hope to be in South Africa myself very shortly. Perhaps we can meet down there? What about Krystal, *Ouma* Elsabeth and old Kobus? Will you be seeing them before you go?"

"No, I don't think so. It's best that I just disappear, Jonker. People always make false promises when saying goodbye to others." I shook his hand. "It would be great to see you again away from Namibia. Good luck with your political movement and so on. Please say good bye to the others for me. Take good care of yourself, Jonker. I guess I'd better be going."

He gave me a hug then led the way to the back door. Just as I was about to open it, he grabbed my arm. "I shall be keeping in touch with you via James. Perhaps one day we will be able to spend much more time with each other?" There was the sound of a car's horn outside. "Here, you had better not keep James waiting. Good luck, Kido – good luck!"

The Pommy geo' was parked out in the backyard and his tomahawk nose, as usual, was buried in a newspaper. Once I had climbed into his Land Rover and had buckled up my seat belt, he held out the newspaper. "Take a look at this, Josef."

"*HEAD FOUND IN NEW COURTHOUSE BUILDING!*," the paper's headlines screamed. I read on to find that the horribly mutilated head belonged to a Mr Koot Basson, who was out on bail for murder!

Feeling quite faint, I sat back in my seat and closed my eyes. A few seconds later I looked over at the Pommy in horror. "What the fuck's going on?"

He only grinned. "Makes quite a nice touch – doesn't it? It should stop people from going around torturing and stabbing defenceless women. Have a look on page two."

What I saw nearly made me puke with fright. There was a photograph of Koot Basson's head on a stainless steel mortuary table. In the background was the white cop inspector who had shown so much interest in me at the Karibib prospect.

"Oh, shit!" was all I could say.

"Don't worry," he reassured me. "They haven't a clue about what happened. Like I said – when it comes to suspects – they've got the whole Baster and Nama Nations to sort through... Cheer up, Josef, the drill has a substantial amount of work to go to, and South Africa's one of the most beautiful countries in the world."

"The sooner we get there, the bloody better."

"Did Jonker enlighten you in regards to Krystal?"

"Yeah, he did."

He nodded. "Well then, enough said. "Let's find the others and start making preparations to go south."

HERE ENDS THE SECOND CHRONICLE!